D0342107

TREEHAVEN

TREEHAVEN

By
Kathleen Norris

THE BLAKISTON COMPANY
Philadelphia

Triangle Books Edition Published June, 1946
by arrangement with DOUBLEDAY & COMPANY, INC.

TRIANGLE BOOKS is a series published by
The Blakiston Company, 1012 Walnut St., Philadelphia 5, Pa.

PRINTED IN THE U.S.A.

TO

GERRY AND BILLY

Some love begins with duty,
Some answers call of blood,
Some is the claim of beauty,
    Or youth, or need, or mood,
But some abandons highways
And laws and rules, to prove
One of the happy byways,
    The luxuries, of love.

CHAPTER ONE

CYNTHIA TREZAVANT never could remember a time when she did not mean to get married, and get married young.

Even as a baby she had chattered confidently of "my husbin" and "my children"; had selected favorite names and characteristics for them all.

And if, in the early teens, the high school years, she had been a little less articulate on the subject of men and marriage, it was only because a delicate admixture of pride and shame and fear had kept her silent as a young woman, where as a child she had felt no hesitations. Of course she and Gray and Leslie and Lucia would marry; but it seemed that it all depended on the men, and it was rather nicer not to talk about it. If they asked you, you married; if they didn't, you were—well, out of luck.

Secretly this was regarded by Cynthia as manifestly unfair. Why should the boys have all the say? Why, she would reason in her own mind at fourteen, as she and Leslie and Lucia and Gray rattled up and down the muddy old road that lay between the California ranch house and the village school—why should girls want something like marriage, which boys either could give them or refuse them? Suppose boys for some reason or other didn't like one, and "ganged" against one in this matter of marriage?

"Gray," she might inquire, lying on the hearthrug reading about the Would-be-goods in the long winter evenings, "what do you do if you want to get married and nobody asks you?"

Gray, the oldest sister, composed and motherly at sixteen, as indeed poor little Gray Trezavant had had to be, would look up smiling from her French grammar.

"Don't worry, Cynthia. Somebody'll ask you!"

"But, Gray, suppose nobody does?"

"Somebody will, darling."

"I wouldn't care if nobody ever asked me, because I'm not ever going to get married," Leslie, twelve years old, always stated firmly. Lucia would look from face to face, with her blue-gray eyes, but she had little to say. When Gray had been sixteen, Cynthia fourteen, and Leslie twelve, Lucia had been but an infant of nine, after all.

"Because—listen," Cynthia might begin to argue. "If one girl throws a boy down, at least he can ask another. And he can go on asking until he finds one."

"One?" Gray liked conversation to be exact; she had some of her father's qualities, even at sixteen.

"One wife. But the girl," Cynthia would continue her protest—"the girl just has to wait. And if she waits too long, why—she's an old maid!"

"Well, that doesn't kill her!" Gray would say, laughing.

"No, but——" And Cynthia would put her head—the only dark head in the group—in the air and purse her lips. She was proud; all the Trezavants were proud. And she hated to think that she must either take his admiration from a boy as a favor, or do without what she knew was the fullness and sweetness of life—for her at least. Long before she was grown she knew that she wanted popularity, admiration, love-making, marriage.

At seventeen she had thought much of these things, waiting for life to come to her, waiting for love. Nothing had happened. And so at eighteen—nineteen—twenty. Sometimes Cynthia wondered if her three sisters were thinking the reckless and terrible thoughts that came to her.

They talked of everything, the four Trezavant girls. But perhaps the other three stopped short of complete frankness on this question of marriage, as Cynthia did. She suspected that they did, anyway.

The years went by, and they were good years. Gray went to college, coming and going every day in the car. During her four college years she took Cynthia and Leslie and finally Lucia too to high school. It was an eighteen-mile run each way, but the girls were chattering French or history or gossiping idly or memorizing "The Highwayman" and Coventry Patmore as they drove, and they liked the trip.

They had lunch at their respective schools; Gray, in Stanford University, lunched at the "Union" or at any one of a score of hospitable sorority houses or at one of the restaurants in the neighboring town of Palo Alto. The girls always arranged, before they parted in the morning, for their hour of meeting, and fitted study hours and dressmakers' appointments in the town into spare time. At half-past four they were usually spinning down the highway again, past Mountain View and Sunnyvale, over the track at Azule, through the village and up the hill. The trip took less than an hour; they were always home in time to wander about the garden before supper, dressed and brushed and freshened, and they could have a comfortable breakfast at half-past seven in the morning.

Cynthia had wanted to go to college too, but she had not passed her entrance tests. It had been a bitter blow in her eighteenth year; she had even dared, in her disappointment, to ask Papa if she might try for the State Agricultural College at Davis. Her father had said mildly, "What complete insanity is this? Do you think I could permit you to live away from home at eighteen?"

No, of course not. So Cynthia had stayed at home, and

in two years Gray had graduated and joined her, and they had been very happy, fussing about the house together and managing everything—their father included, he complained —reading, and doing everything Hing and Mack would not do.

Leslie had had two years of college, and then the Dean of Women had swooped down on Leslie, innocently staying to have supper with Professor Scoville one stormy night. Professor Scoville, nearly forty, and with a daughter almost as old as Les! Gray and Cynthia and Lucia had been indignant about it, and Leslie, who was the simplest of the four, had been frankly bewildered. Leslie was a fine student, but the ways of the world were blind trails to her, and she had assured the Dean, with hurt dignity, that she had not intended to return to college anyway, next fall.

But this had cut poor Lucia out of her college work too, for Papa had flatly refused to have any one girl make the trip alone. So now they were all at home: Gray twenty-four, Cynthia twenty-two, Leslie twenty, Lucia almost eighteen.

During school years boys had figured somewhat in their lives. Papa had despised the idea of boys, holding to the good old solid ground that fine men would come after his daughters "when the time came," but Papa had not been with them in school hours, and without Papa's ever suspecting it many an ice cream sundae had been paid for in "Sticky's," and many an undergraduate friend had buzzed about their car when the four blooming Trezavants were ready to start for home. Sometimes Gray had stayed with Frances Baker and had gone, properly chaperoned, to a dance, and now and then boys had even percolated up as far as the ranch for shy luncheons and swims in the pool. Not suitors exactly, but friends, anyway.

But of late years, with the ending of school days, even this ineffectual fluttering had somewhat died away. Cynthia watched it like a barometer. She saw it go down, and hope went down with it.

Even in the books she read, Cynthia had never been quite happy until the heroine married. No other solution of life's problem would do. Cynthia loved Miss Yonge's stories of large families, all of whom married. Whether happily or not was unimportant; what Cynthia wanted proved was that every girl had a chance, soon or late. When there were four girls in a family there was not much hope of choice; she knew that. But Meg, Jo, Beth, and Amy, all the heroines of Miss Carey and Trollope and Henry Kingsley and Florence Barclay must get married somehow. Cynthia did not care much if it was to horrible old men with titles or to impecunious curates. Just so that every girl had "Mrs." on her calling cards, Cynthia was content.

Her sympathy with these book characters seemed to her like a premonition, as time went serenely on, and still no suitors appeared at Treehaven. Bad as it was to read of the unmarried households of old England, clergymen's daughters and penniless beauties of Victoria's day, whose fathers were hunting Irish squires or, better yet, were dead in the Indian wars, it was infinitely worse to find oneself living the very plot over again in western America in the twentieth century.

If their mother had lived, or even if Aunt Leslie had lived, Cynthia would muse, they might have known how to manage love affairs. But as it was . . .

Clipping sweet peas up by Mack's cabin, Cynthia would pray for a marriage—not her own necessarily. But if Lucia —Lucia who was so bookish—should develop a correspondence with some—some poet in the East—and he should come out to California for his health, nothing seriously wrong with him, just run down . . .

They could live at Carmel; Lucia adored Carmel.

Then if Leslie would suddenly appear before her sisters

on some summer afternoon with a—a tall, stunning young man beside her; a man who would have met Les in college and never forgotten her, and who would have come down to ask Papa for her;—that would be so heartening! Especially if he would have to go to a job in New York; Les was always talking about New York.

Gray would have to have a dignified marriage, sweeping veil, downcast lashes. Gray liked everything—right. She would make someone a wonderful wife.

And if her three sisters married happily, Cynthia, although not of an especially self-sacrificing or domestic type, would be glad to stay on at the ranch and take care of Papa, and welcome the matrons and their children in the old home for vacations and Christmases.

If only they were not going to be the Trezavant old maids, living on and on in the ranch house with their cats and their roses and Papa's library . . . Cynthia felt frantically that she couldn't stand that.

"Gray, do you sometimes want—just desperately to *live?*" she burst out one day.

"Darling child," Gray said amusedly.

"I know what you mean," Leslie said.

It was a spring day; they had taken their lunch up to Booker Rock. It was only two miles from the ranch house, but two hard miles. The girls, in old shoes, old soft hats, old shirts and riding breeches, had had to follow a steep narrow trail cut carelessly through manzanita and chaparral and drenched on this hot spring day with merciless sunshine. They had divided the transportation of the simple lunch with the ease of long custom; Gray had carried the stoppered milk can of spring water; Cynthia had had on her shoulder a white sack with oranges in it; the two younger girls had had the basket on a pole between them.

Up, up, up, past the big oak they had mounted, to turn

down across a little grassy dip on the top of the hill, and
so come out again on the very crest, with the world falling
away below them in great rounded shoulders of mountain
ranges.

The old picnic ground was here; they had climbed this
hill in their very babyhood. There was a heap of dead ashes
in the cleared central circle, with an enormous oak throwing
a shadow across it; there were a crane and an old kettle,
and one or two weather-worn fruit boxes with "T. P. T.—
Treehaven Ranch" stenciled on them in fading black. And
all about were the low sprawling branches of the oaks and
the low surface levels of the brush and the far-away endless
spreading of the great world.

They could look west and see canyons and mountain
ranges going on, on, on to the far gray shimmer that was
the Pacific, twenty miles away; they could look south to
more mountains. The north was all shut away by the great
rock, but toward the east below them lay the great valley
of the Santa Clara Mission, miles and miles and miles of
fruit trees carpeting it with dull soft green, white roads
winding through it, and tiny beetles of motor cars threading
them in the thrilling and throbbing heat of the day.

Booker Rock was a great pile of granite that lay bedded
in twisted oaks and pines on the top of the hill. Its face, a
sheer drop of perhaps forty feet, rose straight from the earth
like a wall. There were small trees and bushes holding pre-
cariously to its sloping sides; sometimes the girls climbed to
the very top, catching at the roots and branches for safety
all the way. Sometimes they took their cameras up there and
photographed each other against a dizzying panorama of
mountain top and sky. But today they had been satisfied
just to reach the base of the rock and sink down in the picnic
hollow on the sparse young grass and pant in the untimely
heat. There would be much hotter days all through cloudless

June, July, and August, even into October, but this was only April, their first picnic since before the rains of March, and they had been telling one another all the way that they were out of training.

"How long since we've been up here?" Gray had asked, as they had unpacked buns, coffee, and sausages and lighted their fire. There had been no cloud on her charming fair face as she had poured the scrambled egg mixture from its well-stoppered jar into the hot sausage fat, toasted the buns, and made sandwiches of eggs and sausages and lettuce all mixed together. But her question had roused that unhappiness, that growing sense of uneasiness and apprehension, that was always so close in the background of Cynthia's mind, and immediately Cynthia had fallen into a study, moving, eating, and speaking mechanically, without any very acute sense of what she was doing. How long? There were the weeks and the months running away again.

And still thinking of it after lunch, lying in the shade, dreaming, talking idly with the sisters who were half asleep, as she was, Cynthia had asked her question, suddenly, almost challengingly:

"Gray, do you sometimes want desperately to *live?*"

"But aren't we living?" Gray had demanded, innocently, when it had been repeated.

That was like Gray. So fine, so tempered and gentle and controlled, somehow, that Cynthia often felt herself a barbarian beside Gray. The contrast in their natures was no more marked than that in their persons; Gray was fair, as her English-born mother had been; her cheekbones were high, and her nostrils finely cut; her teeth were fine and even, and her hair was a pale, brushed gold. Cynthia was dark, her brows were heavy, her forehead broad and low, her tangle of gypsy hair never in order. She had round blue eyes, black-lashed, and her lips were freshly red. When she paled with anger, as she did too often, freckles showed on the clear brown of her healthy skin. The other three girls could wear one another's clothes; Cynthia was inches taller, broader, bigger of build than they were.

"No, we're not!" she asserted boldly, in answer to Gray's last amused query.

"Oh, we are," Lucia said idly, peeling an orange. "Living? Of course we are!"

"Not really," Cynthia persisted.

"What are we—dead?" Leslie demanded, in surprise.

They laughed. It was easy to laugh, safe up there above the world among the rocks and under the oaks, with the California sky hot and still and blue above them, and the manzanita and chaparral deliciously scenting the air.

Little white butterflies were fluttering about the wild fleur-de-lis and lilac trees; quail were calling down in the woods; a buzzard hung in the motionless air above them like a painted bird against a painted sky.

"No, but I know what Cynthia means," Gray said.

"You do know, don't you, Gray?"

"Oh, yes, I know," Gray said. "You mean that we don't work, and we have very few interests outside of home, and we aren't—well, marrying. I suppose that's what you meant?"

"I mean that I could be happier slaving in a slum, and expecting a baby, and sending my husband off on a sea cruise——" Cynthia said, angrily.

"And what would you accomplish by that?" Gray asked, as Cynthia fell silent.

"I'd be alive."

"You mightn't," said Lucia seriously, "like that as much as you do this."

"I'd be alive," Cynthia said again, tears in her eyes.

"I've often thought about it," Gray began, after another

short pause, during which they all tactfully pretended not to notice Cynthia's agitation. "Not," she had to explain with her gentle laugh—"not that I'd be happy myself in a slum with a baby and a sea-going husband. And I don't believe Cynthia would! But I've often asked myself if we are doing our duty."

The younger sisters looked at her respectfully. Gray was leaning against the rock; even up here she did not relax the daintiness, the niceness, that was characteristic of her. Her fair face was a little flushed, and her clothes were old and well worn, but there was a certain grace about her; her hair was not rumpled, her hands were miraculously clean.

"Our duty?" Lucia asked anxiously.

"Yes. I wonder sometimes if we're selfish," explained Gray. "We have so much and we give so little."

"You mean—adopt orphans?" Lucia asked, sympathetically, and again the others laughed.

"We couldn't with Papa what he is. But we really don't give—anything," Gray went on. "Cynthia and her sea-going husband, now, they would be working—they would be living in that slum because they hadn't enough of the necessities of life.

"Millions do. Millions are wondering about money, worrying about it, all the time. We have none of that. We have delicious meals, trees, open fires, cherries and black-berries and apples and prunes—more than we can eat——"

"In other words," Lucia filled it out, "we have, with no effort at all, what most people in the world are trying to get."

"But we have so much more," Gray supplemented eagerly. "This hilltop of ours. Three hundred acres to range over— the garden, the creek, our books, each other——"

"All right," Cynthia persisted stubbornly, "I don't call it living."

"Then you're not reasonable, dear," Gray said. "It's ideal."

"Living—breathing——" Cynthia went on. "That's not a question of food and a place to sleep! You have to—to——"

"To get married," Leslie supplied simply.

"Well, not exactly. But to express yourself—to do something, yourself—try things, make mistakes——" Cynthia sputtered.

"Making mistakes isn't any fun, Cyn."

"Look at us!" Cynthia was rushing on, darkly. "Thirty years from now, when we're all in the fifties, we'll be doing just what we are today, bringing lunch up to Booker Rock."

"We could do worse," Gray said cheerfully.

"I won't," Leslie assured her. "I'm going to get married."

"All right. To whom?"

"Someone I meet!" Leslie said, after a second.

"Exactly!" Cynthia agreed, with a slight hint of cynicism in her laugh.

"Well, you can't just go out after husbands as if they were —game," Lucia protested.

"I know this," Cynthia began suddenly. "If I knew a reliable matrimonial agency—oh, I don't mean the stuff you think I do! But I mean some bureau that I could trust—I'd send my name in. I'd ask the men who wanted good, devoted, capable wives to come up here and talk to me. There'd be no law to make me marry them if I didn't want to!" she ended, defiantly.

"No, and there'd be no law to keep them from blackmailing you," Leslie said.

"What'd they blackmail me about?"

"Advertising for a husband."

"Well, that's no crime!"

"It may not be a crime," Gray said seriously, "but it certainly isn't a very pleasant thing to have associated with your name. After all, Cynthia," she diverged to say with faint reproach, "you did go to the Presidio dance, you know, and I had three days at the Fairmont Hotel with Emma and Gordon. We do go places and we do meet people. And two of Leslie's friends are coming up on Sunday for lunch."

"Then there was the Colonel," Cynthia added, again with faint irony.

Gray laughed suddenly, and a flush showed under her fair skin.

"My poor Colonel!" she smiled. She had been only eighteen at the time that one Colonel Bottomley, her father's friend and of her father's age, had come down to the ranch to ask for her hand. Gray had met him at a dance at the Benicia Arsenal. The Trezavants, because of General Trezavant, their uncle, who had commanded at the Monterey Presidio at that time, had had a sort of unofficial connection with the service for a few dazzling years.

General Trezavant had retired three years ago, and was now living in Plandome, Long Island, so that he was not of very much use to them, socially speaking. But at least Gray had had some exciting military dances, and even Cynthia had come in for the end of them and had made a useful friendship or two among the officers' wives—and then of course there had been Colonel Bottomley.

Gray always laughed and flushed with amused pleasure when he was mentioned. But of late Cynthia always had had an unwelcome thought in connection with him; it had not been a very real note of romance, after all, that he had brought into Gray's life, and it was getting to be two—three —five—seven years ago. And yet they still clung to his memory simply because—Cynthia at least knew why, if the others had not thought it out: because no newer, healthier, more thrilling romance had come along to displace him.

Colonel Bottomley had been small, dapper, gray, fifty-five.

Yes, because he and Papa had been in school together centuries ago, and Papa was almost forty years older than his oldest child.

Bottomley had been completely bowled over by Gray's young, fresh beauty and the eternal beauty of Gray's gentle soul shining in her gray-blue eyes. He had come down to the ranch and had been clumsily flattering to dignified little Gray, and finally he had blurted out that he felt like "a thief in a rose garden, Trezavant, but I certainly want to steal one of those California roses of yours!"

And Gray only eighteen! This had given Cynthia food for contented reflection for weeks. California roses! . . .

Immediately the poor Colonel, stricken with something very little short of apoplexy by Papa's magnificent, "Well, let's discuss that some years from now, Gates," had disappeared forever from view. But later, Cynthia had seen in the paper that Colonel Bottomley was being sent to West Point, and she had indulged in a little dream of Gray, the beautiful young wife of this old man. . . . Gray might have liked that rôle. . . .

"Then there was Ramón," Cynthia said, continuing the list of admirers.

"Oh, come, not a prune picker!" Gray protested lightly.

"He put himself through college, Gray," Leslie said.

"He *said* he did," Gray amended it lightly.

"What did he bring you, Les?"

"Jumping beans," Leslie answered, with a giggle, "and he washed my stockings——"

"I ask you!" Gray said. "He finds her old stockings, where she and Lucia were wading, and washes them for her!"

"Oh, and the hollyhocks, Gray, and a thirty-five-cent box of melted candy, and two cakes of soap!"

"Say it with laundry soap," Cynthia commented.

"He said he was a Moreno, Gray, and that his grandfather was a *conquistadore* and could have been the Alcalde in Monterey."

"He meant his mother was a moron."

"I think you're all awfully mean to laugh at him," said Lucia, who was always as gentle, and almost always as silent, as Gray, upon whom she patterned herself adoringly. "He meant it kindly—he did like Les!"

"I think we are too, and since we'll never see him again, why not give him the credit for admiring Leslie?" Gray said, sensibly.

"Well, then," Cynthia summarized it, angry again, "there's the Colonel and there's Ramón. We average half a love affair apiece."

"How about your Yale man at the Mare Island dance?"

"Oh? Oh, yes," Cynthia said, with an air of having to try to remember that fooled nobody. "Oh, yes—Paul. He said he was going to come to see me, he asked to call me Cynthia, and he cut four dances to sit out in the dark with me."

"And he kissed you," Leslie said, accusingly.

"He did not."

"Well, then he wanted to!"

"No—he seemed to like my—line," Cynthia confessed honestly. "We were sort of laughing and jollying each other. I get that—I don't know—that awful stiffness in my back when a boy wants to—well, mush," she added, thoughtfully.

"Cynthia!" In Gray's delightful English accents it was a reproach.

"Well—pet, then; get familiar."

"I should hope you would, my dear!"

"I try not to. I mean," Cynthia went on, sensing the eager sympathy of her younger sisters, who were watching her with bated breath—"I mean I'd really like to be friendly—as the other girls are. I mean, as far as kisses—and having their arms about you—— Gray!" she broke off, laughing, with flushed cheeks. "Don't look so horrified! There's no harm in that!"

"There's very great harm in that," Gray said, gravely. "And you know it. And you show that you know it when you say that you can't make yourself submit to it. Your innate decency—something that's stronger than you—shows you perfectly well that gentlewomen don't permit such—such disgusting liberties!"

"Innate decency gets you nowhere!" Cynthia muttered. Her two younger sisters laughed guiltily.

"Cyn, don't talk like that!"

"It's true, Gray."

"Oh, no," Gray said dreamily, "it's not true. Character is fate."

"But there are fates and fates, *ma petite crépuscule*," Cynthia argued, suddenly gay. Of them all she was the only moody one, the only one subject to quick changes and violent emotions. "To be fifty and wearing strong spectacles and keeping books in an undertaking establishment is a fate," she reasoned.

"And you might have the kind of nature that would keep you in gales of laughter all the time," Gray persisted.

"How your patrons would appreciate it!" Cynthia said.

"Your patrons wouldn't mind," Leslie took it up, with a giggle.

"Their relatives might. However," Cynthia began again, "dying isn't so bad, if you've ever lived! Dying's *easy*. It's living that's the deuce! If one could be an actress, or a circus rider, or a gypsy—or open a shop——"

"You'd meet men then," Lucia said in the pause, so wistfully, so innocently that nobody laughed. After all, they had all been thinking that.

"Isn't it something to be thankful for, **girls**, that we have

this wonderful home, all the flowers and fruit and sunshine
—and moonlight, too, for that matter—in the world, plenty
of money, and each other?"

"Gray, those are a background. Those aren't the play;
they're just the set!"

"But can't you wait for the curtain to go up?"

"It seems so slow starting," Leslie answered, for Cynthia.

"Papa, of course, is dead weight," Cynthia mused.

"Cynthia, how can you say that of Papa? He is one of the
best known of the world's intellectuals!" Gray protested.

"I know he is, darling. I know he writes economic treatises
and challenges reformers. I read the jackets of his books,
too. I know what—" Cynthia was never at a loss for
words, but sometimes she stumbled purposely to give her
hearers time to catch up with her—"I know what the re-
viewers say of him," she said. "He is at once fearless,
erudite, sound and stimulating, in these days of careless
thinking. He also," Cynthia went on, as even Gray smiled,
"can petrify any innocent male caller at this ranch with one
look through his double lenses. He—having married a beautiful English girl with money who never did anything but
adore him—naturally despises women and matrimony and
the English."

"I think Mother's death changed Papa," Gray said gently.

"We like to think it did," said the inextinguishable
Cynthia.

"How do you mean, we like to think it did?"

"Well, whenever a widowed old man is savage, everyone
likes to think it is for memory of his frail young dead wife."

"You would think," Leslie, immensely appreciative of
Cynthia's courage, suggested moderately, "you *would* think
that his frail young live daughters would have *some* claims."

"I guess Papa was always rather—forceful," Lucia contributed, with a sigh.

"Papa loves the idea that all the sweetness and softness of his nature was turned to ice," Cynthia persisted. "But I'll bet he was always a terror. Look at his kid pictures! He looks like a cross little floor mop stood up on its handle."

Another general giggle acknowledged the truth of this description. Then Gray said mildly:

"Well, granted that Papa is—a little difficult sometimes, and that he makes our attempts to—to live our own lives a little difficult, what's the solution? With money and youth——"

"And looks," Cynthia added, gloomily.

"And looks, and a beautiful home," Gray pursued serenely, "what can we do to get into useful and happy lives? Personally, I love every inch of Treehaven. I can't see myself taking poorly paid work in some hot city, rather than living here——"

"Doing nothing," Cynthia supplied, as her older sister hesitated.

"But we do a great deal, Cyn."

"We cook, and fix flowers, and make our own beds."

"Women have done worse, my dear."

"And we wash our hair, put up jam, study French verbs, copy Papa's manuscripts——"

"He owes me seventy-two dollars for secretary work," boasted Lucia.

"Exactly! And we read good books, drive over to San José and buy garden hats and new coffee pots, sometimes go up to town and get frocks, or stay at the Fairmont Hotel and go to a play——"

"I don't think you can force life, Cyn," Gray mused, as Cynthia paused, and the younger girls looked at her for an answer. "Everything comes to him who waits, you know."

"And what's that poem?" Leslie said. " 'It matters not by time or fate, a yumpty-yumpty-yumpty-tee, and gangle-

gangle-gangle-gate, I know my own will come to me!' "

"It must be Shakespeare, Les. Nobody else could possibly put words together like that!"

"Ah, but you know what I mean!"

"And then there's the other," Gray said; "the one I love." And in her cultured, sweet voice she quoted it:

> *"For though the sad waves, slowly breaking,*
> *Seem here no painful inch to gain,*
> *Far off, through creeks and inlets making,*
> *Silent comes flooding in the main."*

"But, Gray, there are households of nice, useless women everywhere, who never do anything with their lives!"

"Yes, I know. And at the same time you do draw your fate toward you—you rise to whatever level you can make."

Cynthia, long and slim, twisted about on the carpet of sharp little fallen oak leaves, cupped her brown chin in brown hands, and stared into space thoughtfully. She might have been a young leopard, a young panther, dreaming in the sun.

"But how do you begin, Gray?"

"Well, Guy says——" Gray was beginning interestedly, when some cross-current of thought shocked her wide awake. "Good gracious, speaking of Guy," she ejaculated, "Papa asked that some one of us go in and say good-bye to Aunt Caroline. She's going away early tomorrow."

"Let's forget it!"

"You know that will make him furious, Cyn."

"Let's go home and be very bright and jolly about it, and say we've decided to walk up there after dinner."

"But after this walk, when we've all had showers and changed to cool things, you know how we'll hate to start up that hill."

"Draw lots," Leslie said lazily; "the loser to do it for the whole crowd."

"But I have a music lesson at five," Gray protested, apologetically.

"All right, we'll let you off, Gray. You've more than done your share by Aunt Caroline, anyway. You pick a number," Cynthia directed with the ease of old custom, "and whoever comes nearest to it does the job."

"A number under twenty, Gray."

"All right. Wait a minute!" Gray scowled faintly, concentrating. Then she turned to the thick trunk of a madrone tree beside her, and pulling down one of its hanging strips of bark to expose a fresh damp space of white inner skin, she scratched it busily with the point of her heavy pocket-knife. "Can any of you see that?" she asked.

"No."

"All right—I've written my number, so you'll know it's fair. Go ahead."

"Six," Leslie guessed. "Nobody ever takes six."

Lucia looked anxious, thoughtful.

"Thir——" she began. "No! Nineteen."

"Fourteen," Cynthia said confidently and carelessly.

"Fourteen it is!" Gray exclaimed, surprised. "Look— fourteen. How did you ever happen to pick that!"

"Darn it!" Cynthia ejaculated disgustedly. "I never knew anyone to take fourteen. Well—come on, then, it's three o'clock. And I suppose I ought to go home first and change."

"I wouldn't, Cynthia," Gray said, as they began to scramble down the trail again. "Go in as you are, all hot and mussy, and explain that we've been picnicking, and then they won't try to keep you. If you dress you'll be much later, anyway, and it will be just that much harder to get away."

"I'll bring them down to dinner, if Guy will come. But

I think he's rather saving his ankle. And it's Aunt Caroline's last night."

"Tell him about the cribbage hand last night, Cyn."

"Oh, yes, and Papa said to tell him the English book catalogues had come!"

"Is it your dinner night, Cyn?"

"Oh, help, I think it is!"

"It's—what?" Gray asked.

"Asparagus, cherry pie, and the cold beef; it's easy. Have Hing start the fire."

"My night to set the table," Lucia said. "I'll keep an eye on everything for you."

"Cynthia, is your batter bread awfully hard to make? Papa sort of asked for it last night."

"No, it's easy. I'll be home by half-past five, positively— I'll have time. I'll tell Guy it's my dinner night."

CHAPTER TWO

THEY went on down the mountainside together, through the chaparral and manzanita, under the circling butterflies and the silently watching buzzards and the dome of clear blue sky. The sun was descending the western arch now and would presently plunge into the blanket of soft fog that was pouring in from the Pacific. The air was hot and clear, already summer flies were buzzing, and grasshoppers hopped in the grass ahead of the girls' sturdy boots.

All four of the young faces were flushed and moist from the heat; fine bits of oak leaf and manzanita twigs clung to the girls' temples; there were prickers in their heavy woolen stockings. The three blondes wore rough small hats well drawn down, but Cynthia's black mane was uncovered, and she carried her red hat and her big stick in her gauntleted left hand.

It was quicker going down; after a hard half-hour they reached a split in the trail. Straight ahead the home trail, a mere parting of the bushes, a narrow path that showed the marks of boots and of deer hoofs, went on down to the roofs of the ranch and the glitter of the swimming pool asleep below in the late sunlight. But to the northwest another trail wandered off, quite obviously leading to a smaller ranch house that was perched on the wooded mountain shoulder well above Treehaven. The two houses were not more than a half-mile apart by the track of the buzzards and eagles that made the journey so constantly, but by the road that came up from the village to the mountain it was a trip of nearer two miles—and even from Booker Rock trail Cynthia had to go almost that far out of her way.

However, there was no help for it—anything rather than anger Papa. Cynthia waved good-bye to her sisters from under a great oak a hundred yards along the northwest trail, and disappeared into the forest. In her shabby old riding trousers, her brown shirt, with her shock of rich dark curls and the erect joyous swiftness of her movement, she might have been Robin Hood himself, vanishing into the deep sweet shadows of Sherwood.

She took the mile at a good pace, noting various familiar landmarks along the way, and finally coming to barns, outhouses, and the overflow of a garden where prunings from periwinkle and pink and cream climbing roses had been flung out from the formal beds and paths to create a Paradise of their own under the oaks.

Then came Guy's garden itself in a clearing; it was charming, in this hot, late mountain light, with its border pinks and nasturtiums and tumbled snowball bushes, but of course it did not compare to the Trezavant gardens below. Cynthia, thinking of the superiority of their own stocks and delphinium, walked through it and up the steps of a deeply porched brown bungalow, whose windows and doors were all open, and from whose wide hallway a shepherd collie, her plumy tail in motion, lazily walked out to welcome the caller.

"Guy!" Cynthia called.

"Come in, Tondelaya!" said Guy Waring, warmly pleased. "Well, of all the good little girls!"

"I'm a scandal for filth, ticks, sunburn, poison oak——" Cynthia apologized.

But she went into the pleasant, informal living room nevertheless, and dropped into a chair near the couch where the big man was stretched with one foot propped up on a pillow.

Guy Waring was thirty-five; a brown man, with thick hair as black and curly as Cynthia's above gray eyes, and with a wide mouth shaded by a line of black mustache. He was lean, long, broad of build; he had played football in college years, and tennis and golf since; the dining room at the Little Quito ranch house was lined with trophies.

But Guy was lazy, and he was comfortable; he hated any effort that took him from home in these days. He lived as he liked to live, puttering about his mountain farm, riding a little, fussing with his motorcar, his livestock, his garden, wandering down the hill to play croquet and anagrams with the Trezavants, and sometimes painting a little.

The girls at Treehaven had loved him all their lives; loved him with the respect of young persons for a friend whose superior years and whose easy friendship with their father seemed to place him in another generation. Guy knew them all as a brother might; they told him their joys and sorrows, school worries, failures with mayonnaise or currant jelly, ambitions. They worked for weeks on presents for his birthday and made his cake with their own hands; they grumbled to him that Papa had been unreasonable about this or that.

His gray eyes would smile at them in the firelight; dear, amusing little neighbors, he loved them all. Their glowing youth and beauty, their rich mops of soft hair, their round smooth arms and legs flashing in the pool, their hands so practised in picnic-making, had all been part of his life for many years. There was no woman in his house; his wife, Rhoda, had been an inmate of an asylum for the mentally deranged for a long, long time. The Trezavant girls were the only women Guy knew, and the only ones he loved.

Cynthia sat smiling at him, panting, picking burrs from the eye-lacings of her high, oiled, dusty boots.

"What's laid you up again?"

"I twisted the doggone thing a little—nothing serious. But I've got to give it another day or two."

"Oh, Guy, how rotten! Hurt?"

"It hurt for a minute. It's all right now. Fortunately," Guy said with a grin—"fortunately my dear sister Caroline had just been taken down to the train. Otherwise I might have had her here for another week."

"Aunt Caroline gone?" Cynthia had called the man "Guy" since their friendship had begun in her eighth year. But his rather formidable older sister had always been "Aunt Caroline" to the Trezavant girls.

"Yes, went this morning. Didn't she stop in to say good-bye?"

"She may have. But we suddenly decided on a picnic at noon. So we climbed up to the Rock."

"All the way?"

"Yep. Except that we didn't go up on the Rock. Gray got a lot of columbine, and we got some wild currant. My hands!" Cynthia jumped up, hooped her hands over his face for a second, and subsided into her chair again. "Don't you love that wild-currant smell?"

"And yerba buena and fire smoke and onions and coffee!" Guy added.

"No onions."

"No onions? What did you have?"

"Eggs and sausages—and oranges——"

"You wouldn't ask me, of course!"

"Well, we—well, we——" She smiled her way out. "We thought Aunt Caroline was here. And then—your foot."

"And that was why? Five or six reasons all thought up this minute."

"That was why."

of a leather hassock beside his couch and sat there, her brown hands gripped in his.

"I never knew that!" she said, with a child's joy in being loved.

"You don't know much now," he said, in an unwilling, uneasy tone.

"But, Guy—I never knew you liked me best!"

"Not bright. Just not bright."

Cynthia laughed delightedly, triumphantly.

"Who runs might have read it, this five years," the man said, again speaking as if against his will.

"That you like *me!*" she could only echo incredulously.

"Of course I don't know that I could *get* you, Cyn. But I could probably bring some considerations and arguments to bear . . ."

A flood of totally new excitement and emotion rushed through her being. The world was a river, and Cynthia was being carried away on the wild rush of its waters. The familiar, comfortable room, with its worn books and worn rugs and worn chairs, the spring sunset sending angles and bars of glory through dangling old madras window curtains, all were inundated and transformed with glory.

Their faces were very near each other; hers and Guy's. Their eyes were riveted together. Cynthia was trembling, glowing; Guy's wide, firm mouth, under the black mustache, was touched with a half-smile.

"But, Guy, we never talked like this before!"

"And we never will again," he said simply.

There was another silence. Cynthia drew back, her bright face clouding.

"Rhoda," she said, in a changed voice.

"Rhoda."

The girl sat thinking, scowling faintly under the heavy Beethoven brows. Suddenly she smiled.

"But you do like me!" she exclaimed, in satisfaction.

"Rather."

"But Gray's so much prettier!"

"Leslie too."

"Leslie's magnetic, Papa says."

"She has something. But you," Guy said, in a lighter, more natural tone than he had used before—"you're the star!"

"Well, of course I could sit here all day and listen to that."

He laughed. The bad moment was over; they were getting back to normal again.

"You've got a personality, Cynthia. I've watched you all your life—the way you take hold of games, take hold of the kitchen, the original things you do with your clothes, the things you invent.

"Life must be a wonderful thing to a woman like you— one long thrill—one long picnic. Adventure and companionship—that's what you're going to bring to your husband, my dear—and nobody's going to understand it and wish you happiness more than I!

"And now," Guy ended, smiling, as Cynthia, her lips parted, her eyes wide, only stared at him without speaking— "now I've only said to you what I've thought a thousand times. You sit here and amuse yourself, and I'll go in and wash my hands, and we'll go down the hill!"

He hobbled across the room, Cynthia following him with bright, dazed eyes. She had been loved, been casually complimented all her life, but no man had ever held strong wine to her lips before.

When Guy came out she was in the garden; she had brought his car to the door from its usual parking place under a great oak, and was standing staring down at the panorama of valleys and hills that rolled away below her.

The mountainside descended abruptly below the cabin, in long lines of pointed redwood trees and the bushier curved tops of bays and madrones. All the little canyons were filling with clear purple shadow, but the descending sun still hung bright banners in the tops of the trees and lay warmly on the chaparral and underbrush of Deer Hill and the granite sides of Booker Rock. The air was hot and sweet and still; bees shot through the garden, and in the pools of late sunlight that fell through the big oak trees columns of tiny midges were spinning up and down in the air.

Cynthia and Guy, the commonplace phrases trembling between them, talked of the beauty of the world as they got into the shabby car and drove down the two miles of twisted, shelflike old roadway that lay between Guy's ranch and Treehaven. The girl turned her guest over to Gray and Leslie when they reached the house, and went into her own room to change her hot heavy attire for a cool cooking apron and to brush the last twigs and oak leaves from her hair.

Each of the Trezavant girls had her own room; there were six bedrooms in the house and four bathrooms. The bedrooms were ranged on either side of the big main room the family called the "Cabin." On the left, as one entered from the enormous porch, were their father's room, the guest room, and Gray's room. When there was a woman guest, she shared Gray's bathroom; a man guest shared that of Professor Trezavant. On the other side of the wide Cabin were three exactly similar bedrooms and baths, where the three younger girls were housed. Cynthia had the room matching Gray's; considered desirable because it had windows on three sides. Back of the Cabin was another porch, called the Galleria, and beyond the Galleria a dining room and kitchen in a light wooden shack of their own. Beyond again were quarters for the two men, laundry, sheds, chicken house, cow barns, garage, a jumble of shabby wooden buildings half obscured by the intervening growth of great redwoods, oaks, madrone, bay, and buckeye trees and of a score of smaller growths: hazel and blackberry bushes, roses and broom and fruit trees all mixed together.

The ranch was on the top of a hill, but the ranch house itself had been placed in a little hollow with a clearing, where there was a beautiful stretch of green lawn, strange to see in this mountain wilderness, and an exquisite acre of carefully tended garden. Lawn sprinklers were whirling over these all summer long, and the low-ceiled, informal homestead was always filled with flowers.

Tonight there was a great jar of mixed flowers in the center of the table, when Cynthia, as chief cook, and Lucia, as table-setter, called the others to dinner. Great spears of blue delphinium gave a splendor to the whole, striking out in every direction like blue rays; almost as long and stiff were the pink American Beauty roses, rising above the creamy spikes of the stock and the scarlet of crimped Shirley poppies. White Shasta daisies, stiff on crisp stems, brightened the glowing mass, and close down beside the green glass of the bowl were a few blazing stars of homely marigold.

For some reason she was still too confused to define, Cynthia could not look at Guy as they all sat down. But he was paying no attention to her; he asked who had arranged the flowers, and Lucia said, "I did."

"And did you fix those fringed daisies with the pussy willows in the other room?"

"Yes. And Gray and I got the wild fleur-de-lis," Lucia said, delighted.

"You're a wonder!" Guy said. "Spoon bread! My favorite sin, among the graver sins. Who made the spoon bread, Hing?"

Hing, an old, old Chinese, was pottering about contentedly; he could not handle the entire problem of meals and serving any more. But he was not resentful of the girls' aid, gladly taught them all he knew, and did everything they did not do.

"Hello, Mis' Werry," he greeted Guy amiably.

"Hello, Hing. You make this good spoon bread?"

"No, Missa Sinsa make him. She cook good, now."

"I'll say she cooks good!" Guy agreed. But whether he looked at her or not, Cynthia did not know, for even now she could not look up.

CHAPTER THREE

PROFESSOR THORWALD PASMORE TREZAVANT was sixty years old; a vital and vigorous sixty. His second daughter had once described him as "Beethoven taken by surprise," and in doing so had described herself, for they were as much alike in appearance as a pronouncedly masculine man of sixty may be like a glowing girl of twenty-two.

Where Cynthia's brows were merely a trifle too heavy for beauty and were somewhat startling instead, his were beetling and met above the round, short nose that was exactly like hers. Their finely cut wide mouths were alike, as was the almost violent exuberance of their black thick hair, but Cynthia's hair was silky and smoky, and her father's bushy and heavily threaded with gray. Both had clean brown skins, touched with red on the wide cheekbones, and both had low broad foreheads. Her father's eyes were a cold gray; Cynthia had blue eyes—dark blue eyes, round and heavily lashed, and sharing, once again, the look her father's had of perpetual alertness and surprise.

Their natures were alike too; forceful, impulsive, hot-tempered. None of her sisters had any temper at all; they were all like their serene, self-controlled English mother; they were three separate studies from the pencils of Burne-Jones or Rossetti—blonde, gray-eyed, fair of skin. And this made Cynthia's occasional outbursts only the more painful to them and shocking to her.

Their father's tantrums they had taken for granted since

"No, I think I'll have to work."

"Papa, you can't do microscope work at night!" Leslie, his favorite, protested lovingly.

"Notes," he said inflexibly.

"Oh, do stay down and play with us," coaxed Gray. "We'll have two tables going."

"Otherwise somebody's out, Papa," Lucia pleaded.

No one looked at Cynthia, but she knew they were all conscious of the little awkwardness between her and her father. She was the only one who was sure of her touch with him; no one else dared quarrel with him; no one else could have approached her audacity in making up the quarrels.

"He's afraid he'd hold bad hands again," she said, composedly going on with her asparagus. She looked at her father; their round eyes met.

"Oh, is that so?" the man asked, instantly engaged. "We'll see about that! Nobody could hold hands like yours last night twice."

"She's a crook, of course; that's why she gets those hands," Guy suggested.

"She's a complete and unconscionable crook!" said her father, in restored good humor.

"More asparagus, Guy?" Cynthia asked.

"Two—no more; just two, dear," Guy said.

He had never called her "dear" before in all these years. Or if he had, Cynthia had never heard it. The dinner finished with her soul and mind and heart in a queer dizzy whirl. Guy! Old Guy! It made one feel funny, like constantly giggling and as constantly scowling, like crawling into the darkest hole in the world to think, and like walking on the highest mountain tops, shouting, to have him use that tone and those glances to her.

She had been at his wedding ten years before. Guy had been twenty-five then, and his beautiful young wife twenty-two. Rhoda was an orphan; her home was in Connecticut; she had come to California to be married in the hilltop ranch house that was to be her new home.

The four little Trezavant girls had gotten a tremendous thrill out of the wedding. Their mother had dressed them all in pale blue for the occasion; they had worn pale blue organdies and broad white chip hats with a big pink rose and streamers of black velvet on each. It had been a great occasion in their lives.

Cynthia remembered her mother asking her seriously some months later if she, Cynthia, had told her sisters that Rhoda was going to have a baby. Cynthia had said yes, and that Rhoda had told her herself. And Mrs. Trezavant had sighed, and had said in that pleasant British voice that was so like Gray's, "I do wish dear Rhoda was more—more——" and had ended with the philosophical "However!" with which she dismissed, mother-fashion, the nursery mistakes she could not cure.

But Rhoda had never had her baby; she had been very ill instead, and their mother had deserted the four girls at Treehaven and had driven up the hill day after day to sit with despondent little Mrs. Waring.

After a while, with a horrible sense of shock and chill, Cynthia and Gray had heard that Rhoda's depression was not getting any better—she was going to a sanitarium for a while, to see what the doctors could do. . . .

And that had been the end of Rhoda. She had been at the "sanitarium" ever since, and Guy went over every week or two to see her. She had two nice rooms and a kind nurse, but further than that the Trezavants knew little of her. Sometimes, Cynthia gathered from what she could infer and overhear, Rhoda did not even know Guy. But sometimes she did know him, and cried, begging him to take her home.

So that Guy was married and yet unmarried; he was tied

to his wife, and yet always alone. Cynthia had never thought of him as a marriageable man any more than she thought of her father or Hing or Mack, the weazened old gardener, as marriageable men.

Tonight she considered for the first time in her life how hard it must be for a young and handsome man to give up all his hopes of love and companionship and children and home after only a year or two of happiness.

If he was anything, Guy was a painter; he had painted in Paris, he had painted in San Francisco. Now he had lived for twelve years in the mountains of the Santa Cruz range, painting trees—big trees, little trees, twisted ones and straight. He sent them to exhibitions, to dealers, and sometimes one was sold. Then there was great rejoicing.

When Guy took a pencil, and with little quick, accurate jerks of his wrist set down the gnarled limbs of some old tumbled oak, the girls stood behind him in respectful silence. It was witchcraft. He loved pencilwork, he loved the exquisite bits he called "notes," far better than the big oil studies that cost him so much time and sold so slowly. Most of his work was unfinished; for years he had had two or three big canvases going, and would drag them about the mountains in turn.

Guy had done the Trezavants' old hip-roofed barn from every angle; he had done dozens of studies of the huddled outhouses and the Chinaman's cabin; he had done the broken bridge and the old mill bridge and the deserted "cook-house" where now he kept a few sheep. He made them all look beautiful, somehow; Cynthia hoarded every discarded scrap from his easel that came her way; all the girls did, and the ranch house was filled with odds and ends of his work. He had tried to paint each one of them, at one time or another, but portraits were not his field, and in the end he returned to the usual "Guy Waring oaks," and was content.

Tonight, all the time she was busily pegging and counting, Cynthia was forming and reveling in a little side dream in which poor Rhoda very quietly and painlessly died. . . .

The spring days took on a quality that no spring days of her life had ever known before. Cynthia walked with a light step; she spoke in a new voice. Magic seemed to hover about her. Whenever she thought of Guy—and sometimes she would deliberately lead her thoughts away from him so that they might rush back to him again—it was with a new sense of possession and delight.

She saw him no more often than formerly. Even then they were rarely alone together. He made no effort to see her alone, paid her no special attention. But there was a new bond between them, a certain easy protective understanding on his side, a quivering receptiveness on her own.

Her days and nights were filled with dreams of Guy, tall, lean, wide-shouldered. Guy walking with a leisurely loose-jointedness; a fine line of black mustache on his tight upper lip; his lower lip full and protruding. Guy's eyes, keen and gray, his voice quick and deep and decisive; these haunted her. From living almost entirely out-of-doors his skin was copper colored, and his hands were as brown as an Indian's; there was red, healthy color on his high, prominent cheekbones. He was a man of bigger build than Cynthia's father, and the painter's regalia he wore, the corduroy knickers, open-collared shirts, loose ties, disreputable old caps, and short jackets of leather or belted brown wartime khaki made him look even bigger. Cynthia thought of him as a being quite apart from all the other men in the world.

In May he wanted to go into town to see an exhibition at Vickery's, and Cynthia had to go in to see a dentist, so Guy took her, as he often had taken her, or one or the other of her sisters, before, at various times.

They drove the fifty-five miles in the early morning, and Cynthia had the little filling put in and did some shopping, and then met Guy for the return trip. But Guy suggested a luncheon instead and a movie. So they had lunch at the St. Francis Hotel and saw a marvelous war picture at which Cynthia cried.

Then they came home in time for Cynthia to sit flushed and weary and bright-eyed at the dinner table and tell the girls about everything. And that night again, like the first night after their talk in the bungalow, somehow she could not look at him.

These were strange days for her. Outwardly, everything in her life went along as everything always had—arranging flowers, gossiping with the girls, cooking, tramping, playing cribbage after dinner, and all sorts of other games—buzz, and geography, and celebrities—at the table.

Inwardly she was continually quivering with excitement and bewilderment, continually shaken. Just Guy's voice, as he passed the porch in the morning, with his easel and paintbox, made her tremble; the old jokes, the old snapshots that included him, took on a new significance. And when he came down in the evenings for dinner and talk, Cynthia could neither eat nor speak nor look up in the old way.

She took to sleeping badly, or rather to lying awake in a sort of delicious dream, thinking about him, twisting whatever words he had said this way and that, to extract their full significance, staring into the moonlight and the shadows of her room as if she could see visions there.

And sometimes she got up and slipped a loose Japanese jacket over her pajamas and stepped out across the Galleria down to the great soft silver-and-black silence of the lawn. The stubbly grass would be wet and cool on her bare feet, the moon riding solemnly over the redwoods. Light would trickle through to some of the blackest leaves, a night wind would sigh wearily among the tree tops and sweep on its way. Owls were always crying in the woods at night, strange eerie notes at long intervals that floated through the dark, and the frogs at the pool shrilled together, were silent, began their insistent chorus again.

One night at midnight, so standing, she looked up the mountainside and saw a dim pink glow among the trees; the glow of Guy's study lamp. There were silence, darkness, moonlight everywhere; moonlight was dripping down through the redwoods and furring the tops of the buckeyes and the oaks down in the canyons, and moonlight was setting each fruit tree on a little island of shadow. And far up, faintly red in all the silver and black, was the square of Guy's window.

When she saw it, Cynthia's heart seemed to turn over in a slow, delicious spasm. Even afterward, when she was back in her bed again, snuggling down chilled and weary in the blankets, the thought of it made her want to laugh, excitedly, confusedly, in the dark.

The very next day a most amazing thing happened at Treehaven. Papa came down to dinner with a letter—they always had to wait until dinner time for their mail, which was eternally annoying; but this letter had come to him, so it was entirely in his right to withhold it.

He brought it down to dinner, read it aloud. Their fourth cousin, whom they had never seen, Dana Illyan, was actually coming to stay with them! Dr. Dana Illyan, unmarried, Bostonian, thirty-four years old! Gray looked him up in the family book instantly. Yes, he was thirty-four. He had had a bad lung cold, had been ordered to California, and was to stay with them for an indefinite time!

To the four brotherless girls this conveyed thrills and expectations inexpressible. Dana Illyan. What a name, to begin with! And what a fascinating age—ten years older than the oldest of them! And what a delightful profession!

Even their father seemed to share in the enthusiasm with which the girls prepared for the visitor the "measles cottage" —the two-room shack to which they had been banished for contagious nursery illnesses years ago. Long before Dana arrived, serious and handsome and very ready with this pleasant "Cousin Thorwald" and "Cousin Gray," the three younger girls were secretly planning for their bridesmaid's dresses on the occasion of his marriage to their older sister.

That was the happy, the memorable June of Cynthia's life. The days followed one another in fragrance and sweetness and heat, and the nights were cool and scented and drenched with moonshine. The girls and Dana and often Guy, too, tramped and picnicked together, joked and played games, talked and talked and talked into the magic nights.

They packed the old tin coffee pot up to Booker Rock again, and lay about idly talking and basking on the crisped fallen oak leaves; they built and rebuilt the dying fire late in the evenings, and drew their chairs about it and murmured while the clock's hands moved from eleven to twelve and twelve to one.

Dana had fallen an almost instant victim to California's charms, so that the increasing attractions of life at the ranch could only make him increasingly appreciative. He thought his four blooming cousins wonderful; his dark eyes were continually twinkling with amusement and admiration for everything they did and said.

Their comfortable home garments of loose Chinese silk, their cleverness and animation, their sharing of music, dancing, croquet, tennis, swimming, all together; the likenesses between them, the differences between them—all fascinated the visitor.

And then he had a very real respect for "Cousin Thor-

wald"; he knew, even better than the girls did, the value of
the research work that went on day after day and year after
year in the little laboratory on the hillside, and he could fall
into long discussions with his host that stimulated not only
the younger man but the older one too.

Best of all, three weeks after his arrival he appeared to
forget that there were any such menaces as congested lungs
in the world. He slept on an open porch, he scrambled up the
hot dry hillsides with only rough shoes, old trousers, and a
worn shirt for clothing, and on more than one occasion returned with the last-mentioned at least all but torn from
his body.

Every afternoon, in the burning heat of four o'clock, they
all went swimming, and afterward lay basking on the grassy
slope of the Lido, burying wet heads in dripping arms,
stretching their long young sunburned limbs on the green
expanse, talking idly and drowsily as the sun went slowly
down behind Widney's hill, and the birds hopped through
the garden on short flights from bush to bush.

The two girls who had dinner to think of would be the
first to drag themselves away from this peaceful scene; the
others would loiter on until five o'clock, until six o'clock,
prolonging the last hot sweetness of the day for every
moment they could.

"I wish everyone in the world the experience of getting
well after an illness," Dana said one day when they were all
up on the Lido together.

"You weren't so very ill, Dana."

"No—of course not. But hundreds of fellows get that
way in the Eastern winters. Colds that hang on and coughs
that hang on, and getting so deucedly tired all the time."

"You look ten years younger than when you arrived,"
Leslie said.

"I feel quite a new being. It's been—simply too miraculous," Dana mused, glancing up at the girl nearest him, who happened to be Gray, glancing down again at the little design he was drawing with a wet twig on a hot flat stone. "It's been miraculous!" he repeated. "To be bundled onto that train on a drizzling cold afternoon, to jog along for four days of alternate icy cold outside and thick heat inside, and then to get out at this place—all trees and shade and delicious smells and delicious meals—and girls—and a pool—and cherries. . . .

"I'll never forget that first night's sleep on a porch with the redwood boughs waving up and down against the stars, and Cynthia coming down with my breakfast tray, and finding me asleep, the next day!"

"But, Dana, Boston must be fascinating too."

"Ah, well, of course! But when one's a little tired and depressed and sick, it's then that this mountain heat and the redwood balm and the figs and the apricots all seem like—like getting back to childhood—and being safe and protected and little again."

Gray looked at him seriously, sympathetically. She was twisted about on her knees, sitting near him as he lay sprawled in the late sunshine, and was drying her mop of soft fair hair. Over her bathing suit she had slipped a white cotton jacket stenciled in chrysanthemums and dragons and temples and pine trees. Her fine long slender arms, burned a clear delicate brown, were bare, and where the cotton jacket stopped her smooth bare knees and bare feet emerged, sunburned to a clear tan color too. Her hair fell in a golden rain on her shoulders, and sometimes she tossed it in the sun, or spread it with her brush.

"And to find you four girls—the most amazing girls I ever knew!" Dana added.

"We don't think ourselves amazing at all," Gray told him. "We think we're probably lopsided from having lived here all our lives. And yet," Gray went on, frowning and smiling at once, "we don't quite know how to get out, how to begin living!"

"Begin living? But, good heavens, Gray, isn't this living? Books, trees, figs, cherries, and swims in the creek——"

"Well," Gray persisted, in a simple, childlike way that was characteristic of her, "we do love it. But we mean—I mean—when we talk about it," she floundered, "we mean traveling—and getting married. All that."

"Some day you ought all to travel together," Dana suggested. "Dressed as you do, in Chinese silk pajamas and things, and talking as you do of Keats and Chaucer, and as if Shakespeare were still at Avon and Robin Hood still in Sherwood Forest, you'd make the greatest sensation that ever was!"

"People would think we weren't respectable, Dana," Cynthia said as they all laughed. Guy, lying near her on the hot grass, gave her a quick side glance. "They'd know we were queer!"

"How'd you know that, Cynthia?" he asked in an undertone.

The girl looked up, a brilliant flush coming up under her sunburned olive skin.

"I don't know."

"It's a curious thing, the way you know what's what," Guy said.

"I just guessed," Cynthia added, "that four young women, three of them blonde, traveling about the world in Chinese pajamas, might be—misunderstood."

"Four red-headed girls in green came into Ciro's, in Paris, once when I was there," Guy remembered. "That was all there was to it—just four red-headed girls in green. It was the most amazing thing I ever saw! They might as well have ridden circus horses into the place!"

"Some day maybe we'll travel," Gray said thoughtfully.

"It's going to be almost a pity if some day one of you marries," Dana added, with his neat little Boston laugh. "It will—break the set."

"It's going to be a lot more of a pity if none of us marries!" Cynthia amended it with feeling.

"I don't know," Guy said suddenly; "four beautiful persons, always and eternally fresh and lovely—and girls."

"Horrors!" Leslie ejaculated so forcefully that they all laughed.

"I don't want any one of you ever to marry," Guy insisted.

He looked up, and his eyes and Cynthia's met in a long, full look. Neither spoke. The look dropped, and the conversation went on without them.

"You *would* say you never wanted me to marry!" Cynthia reproached him an hour later.

They were in the pantry now, where Cynthia was mixing a salad, and Guy was supposedly helping. Cynthia had changed her damp bathing suit for a cotton frock and a big apron, but her dark rich hair was still falling in little damp curls from the knot into which she had hastily wound it, and her brown skin and thick black eyelashes were still dewy from the recent bath.

She had scooped the luscious centers of cantaloupes and alligator pears into the bowl that was half filled with fresh lettuce; now she was measuring vinegar and oil and seasonings into the mass and meanwhile looking expectantly across the table at Guy, who sat carefully smearing little diamonds of toast with anchovy paste.

Guy neither looked up nor answered immediately, and Cynthia had a full minute in which to feel her remark both affected and silly before he raised his eyes, meeting her eyes squarely.

"No, I don't think I want you to marry, Cyn," he said.

The brown hard line of his chin, the wisp of black mustache, his keen gray eyes, and the waves of his black hair were within a few feet of her. He was not smiling; he had spoken with the utmost simplicity. An odd sweet dizziness seized Cynthia, a sort of vertigo of happiness that made it quite impossible for her to speak. Her throat thickened; she lowered her lashes to concentrate her look upon the salad again.

When Guy spoke again it was briskly, naturally:

"I'd miss you too much, my dear! We couldn't get along without our black sheep."

"You needn't worry," Cynthia said, in a voice that trembled a little. "I'll never marry!" And then, attempting to imitate his own light tone, she added, "I shall be one of those four extraordinary sisters circling the globe."

Guy caught up the cue easily.

"Well, I wouldn't count on Gray," he drawled.

"Not count on Gray?" Cynthia echoed in surprise, glad for the sake of her hammering heart and burning cheeks to grasp at the unexpected diversion.

"No. He's—" Guy jerked his head toward the sitting room where the others were awaiting the summons to dinner—"he's head over heels!"

"Dana!"

"Of course."

"Oh, Guy, you don't think so!" Cynthia had forgotten herself; her face was alight.

"Think so?" Guy, finishing the last of his canapés, gave her a significant glance. "Who runs may read," he said.

"With Gray?"

"No, darling, with Hing!"

Cynthia laughed deliciously, her face still flushed, her hair dried now into its usual fish tails and spirals over her low forehead. She held onto the big bowl to steady herself.

"Yep. She blew him to pieces before he ever got out of the cover," Guy said lazily. "Why, are you so pleased?" he asked, surprised himself at Cynthia's expression.

"Oh, yes, I'm awfully pleased," Cynthia murmured, as if she hardly heard him.

"But why? Do you like him so much?"

"We're all crazy about him. But it isn't only that. It's that —Gray's getting married would seem to—take off the curse. And then she'd be so happy; she likes him—she admires him so much! And she'd love Boston."

"You don't know that she'd love Boston, you wild black girl."

"Oh, she probably would! And she'd have children,"

"Children already—good heavens!"

"And Les could visit her."

"But, Cynthia," Guy presently asked curiously, as the girl, mechanically mixing the salad with sweeping upward movements of her round, bare young arms, fell into a happy day dream, "you surely expected that some of you would marry, and all that sort of thing would follow?"

"Well, I suppose I did," Cynthia said, with a shamed little laugh.

"Oh, come, I thought all this nonsense about being old maids was a joke!"

"Not with me."

"Cynthia!" He touched her bare arm; she had picked up the bowl of salad to carry it across the Galleria into the dining room, and the little gesture arrested her. Their eyes met —were riveted together. "You never think of yourself as not marrying?" Guy asked slowly.

Cynthia swallowed; tried to laugh. The moment had

caught them both as in a trap. They stood still, the tall square dark girl in her pink-striped apron, the dark man close beside her, looking down.

"Why—whom should I *marry,* Guy?" Cynthia whispered, not knowing what she said, and laughing nervously as she spoke.

"I don't know," he answered, as confused as she.

Cynthia, one arm circling the bowl of salad, the fingers of the free hand already pressed on the panels of the dining-room door to open it, felt as if she were in one of those dreams of helplessness, in which the dreamer's feet are bound, her muscles beyond her control. She continued to stand motionless looking at him.

The setting sun sent long streamers into the pantry and across the Galleria. Birds were vociferous in the cherry tree; Hing banged pans in the kitchen. The world was wrapped in magic at the closing of the summer day. A long, long minute passed. The girl felt her throat dry and her head bewildered. Guy was breathing audibly.

Suddenly Lucia opened the dining-room door on the opposite side of the room.

"About ready, Cynthia?" she called. "We're all starving."

"All ready," Cynthia responded, awakening. She crossed the room with her bowl, set it on the long, waiting table. Guy came after her with the canapés; Hing from the side yard, where he was scattering wheat for the chickens, called out that everything was ready.

CHAPTER FOUR

GRAY had always been pretty—"lovely" was the word that seemed to fit her more than any other. But in these days she grew absolutely radiant; her always fair skin seemed to be almost transparent now, and there was an exquisite mystic light in her eyes.

She wore a favorite, deep-flounced striped dimity to dinner one hot evening in early June, looking so ethereally lovely that not only Dana's eyes but the admiration of everyone at the table centered upon her.

Gray always sat next to her father; tonight it seemed to Cynthia that she turned to him more than usual, was more than ever in the rôle of the oldest daughter whose going away to a table of her own some day would end this relationship forever.

Was Gray really feeling this, and was Papa beginning to feel it? Cynthia could not tell. But she knew that something unusual, something happy, was in the air tonight, was hovering over the plain dining room; and that when they all went out on the porch above the lawn later, to scatter in basket chairs and sit about in the soft warm darkness, waiting for the moon, the whole world was enchanted.

Taking the last chair, as became the girl whose night it was to help clear the table and darken the dining room, she was satisfied to see with her first glance that Gray was next to Dana; indeed, their chairs were touching in the gloom. Her own chair was next to Lucia's; Papa had gone up to his cabin, but the red tip of Guy's cigarette showed in the chair opposite hers.

51

After a minute Guy got up and said to Lucia, "Mind changing? I have to get this rotten foot of mine up on something."

Then he was next to Cynthia. She had stretched herself out to an almost flat position in her chair, and was staring up at the dark sky that was blue-black above the redwoods, but she knew exactly how near he was; she could feel his glance on her as he sat down.

They fell to discussing girls—modern girls and modern men.

"Dana, you've been to Harvard, and your mother is president of welfare societies and things. Are things so different?"

"Different, Cousin Gray? What things, and from what?"

"Morals. Morals between girls and men. From what we read, and from what the companionate-marriage people say, and the social-relief people say, and from all the articles in the magazines—things are different from what they used to be."

"Different," Cynthia contributed animatedly, helping Gray out, "from the good old days of Lady Dedlock and Hetty Sorrel and Tess——"

"Different—ha!" Guy exclaimed significantly. "I'll say they're different." And Dana added more hesitatingly, "I certainly think they are."

"Now here's a woman in a magazine—this month's magazine," Cynthia said—"who questioned her own son and a lot of his college friends. The son said that it wouldn't make the slightest difference to him if his wife was—well, straight or not. That is, he said that what she had been before she married him wouldn't make any difference to him."

"And one of his friends," Leslie added, "said that he wouldn't want to marry a girl who had always gone straight. He thought she would be a fool."

"It actually said that, Guy," Gray assured him.

"I shouldn't wonder," Guy said. "With what they tell me the girls say and do, I wouldn't be surprised at anything."

Cynthia's arms were locked behind her head; she lay back, staring with bright eyes at the dark sky. Above her the white bars of the open porch roof and the close awning of fine clean rose leaves and close-set pink roses showed dimly in the light from the sitting room. Gray sat very still, with Dana in the deep shadow behind her. Lucia and Leslie were together; Leslie on a hassock at Lucia's knee, their hands locked.

"After all," Leslie said, in her proud young voice, "doesn't it only mean that girls are doing what men have been permitted to do all along?"

"But *are* girls permitted to do it?" Dana asked.

"Aren't they? Aren't they actually making their own laws, and refusing to be bound by the old ones?"

This was Guy. His voice so thrilled Cynthia that she could hardly sense what he was saying.

"No, the old laws hold," Dana asserted quietly, as if half amused by the chatter of children.

"I don't think they do!" Leslie said rebelliously.

"My dear Leslie, it doesn't really matter what you think or what we all might like to think. The fact remains that women have to uphold the purity of the race," Dana told her, decidedly but kindly.

"I don't see it!"

"Men have to be brave and honest, to defend and run their country—that's the old theory," Gray contributed in her wise way, "and women have to be pure."

"*Why* do they?" Lucia asked, in a purely speculative tone that made them all laugh at its simplicity.

"For one thing," Guy drawled, "men have always liked to feel sure that their sons are—their sons."

"Men again," Cynthia murmured to the stars.

"Well, men again," Dana conceded. "Men have been the lawmakers, of course."

"But surely—surely it isn't man's law that keeps women straight," Gray asserted, with a little warmth.

"You're quite right. Something higher than that, eh, Cousin Gray?"

"Well, of course. I don't want to talk like Miss Mitford or Miss Edgeworth," Gray went on, smiling. "But to a woman her marriage is a sacred thing. She doesn't want to go to it from half a dozen casual, coarsening affairs——"

"Gray," Cynthia interposed mildly, as Gray paused, formulating her thoughts, "is—love necessarily coarsening? Couldn't a decent girl love one man when she was eighteen and love a quite different type when she was twenty-five, and would she necessarily be coarsened if she—well, let's say, had an affair with both?"

"Absolutely! Now you take a fellow who forges——" Dana was beginning. He interrupted himself. "You were speaking, Gray?"

"I was asking Cynthia if she meant marriage and divorce?"

"Well, yes—or no," Cynthia conceded, with a youthful laugh. "What I meant," she went on more seriously, "was that marriage—mating—isn't degrading. Isn't it the natural —the—well, the irresistible thing? Why, if a girl has been affectionate—has been generous—why should she be marked for life?"

"Because she is," Lucia answered promptly. "Besides, she might have a baby!" she added, as an afterthought.

Her tone made them all laugh, after which Cynthia said dryly:

"Let's all say whatever we think, from now on!"

"Well, she *might*," Leslie persisted, a little offended.

neighbors, and regard each other as being pretty much alike. Why make so much fuss about that one thing? Women ought to be allowed to do as they like as long as they don't hurt anyone!"

"Bravo, Cynthia!" Guy laughed. But there was a little touch of the mentor, there was a tiny edge of criticism, in Dana's voice, as he said:

"Bravo, of course! But only for your theory, Cousin Cynthia. And it isn't a question of theory. We have to take the situation as we find it, don't we? And, as we find it, men persist stupidly enough in desiring to look up to their women, in desiring to have them pure and—and strong— and self-controlled, as it were."

"Dana, I'm not talking so much of you. You're Bostonian, and aristocratic, and the stun ba'n on your grandfather's fa'm dates back to Count Rumford's day——"

"Oh, come now, Cynthia, is it kind to make fun of my New England *patois?*"

They all laughed together, and then, summing up something of the wandering debate, Gray said:

"I suppose to the end of time fine women will want to hold the whole thrill and glory of their love—their desire— until marriage itself, and other women—weaker women— will give in to—to passion and regret it as long as they live."

"That's the part I hate in *'Die Walküre,'* " Cynthia said suddenly, with apparent irrelevance. "I mean when that old hypocrite Wotan, who's gotten everyone into trouble all round, and who had no business to *have* children anyway by an earth-woman, solemnly and seriously parks Brünn-hilde out on a rock for a couple of centuries just because she took a chance! Smug old brute!"

"Really," Dana Illyan said faintly. *"Really!"*

For a while there was silence on the porch. Then, as

Cynthia sat up straight and brought her feet to the floor, Gray asked suddenly:

"Cyn, would you do the 'Second Hungarian' for us?"

"I would not!" Cynthia returned tranquilly.

"Ah, Cynthia, go on!" the other voices said.

"I have to be coaxed," Cynthia submitted, flinging out her arms, standing now, under the rose vines, stretching herself, her voice heavy with sleep.

"We'll coax you," Guy told her.

"Cynthia, Dana's never seen it!"

"Well," Cynthia said, irresolutely. "Well, all right!"

"It will be too marvelous in that moonlight," Gray said.

For the moon was flooding the porch now and streaming down through the rose vines overhead in a rain of silver; the tips of the great redwoods were misty and faint in the blue light, and the plumes of the white phlox were ivory-colored. Delicious odors of honeysuckle, and clean summer fields burned and dusty, and redwood gums drifted through the warm air.

"Does Cynthia play the piano?" Dana asked interestedly, as Cynthia went into the house.

"No. Victrola," Leslie explained.

"Oh, I see," Dana murmured, thoroughly bewildered.

The strains of a magnificent orchestra playing Liszt's "Second Rhapsody" poured from the open doors of the house and mingled with the magic of night and moonshine and summer airs. There was a strip of bright moonlight halfway down the lawn, a hundred feet from the porch, and into this band of brilliance there presently stepped a slender tall woman, her body wrapped in something sinuous and white, her black mop of hair streaming free.

Moving to the very center of the light, as if it were a stage, she began to dance.

"Good heavens, is it Cynthia?" Dana whispered.

"It's Cynthia, yes," Guy answered with an odd short bark of laughter.

"We all dance, more or less," Gray explained, modestly, "but she happened to do this the other night, and we thought it was—really——"

"Swell," Leslie finished the phrase neatly.

"Were you here that night, Guy?"

"No. I've not seen this one."

The rhapsody, that had half run its course before Cynthia appeared, had now reached a stage of violent, swift motion, and the lithe body on the lawn followed the music. At one certain plunging part Cynthia lowered herself with a sort of running lunge, close to the earth, rising precipitately, as the music rose, to fling arms, mop of hair, and body itself wildly into the moonlight beauty of the night for a finale.

"She's gone crazy!" Leslie commented with relish.

Two minutes later it was over, and Cynthia had come panting, laughing, disheveled, up to the porch.

"You really are phenomenal!" Dana murmured, under his breath.

"Cynthia, what on earth have you got on?"

"The old mosquito netting. I took off my dress and just wound it round me over my undies."

"It looked beautiful out there."

"Whoo!" Cynthia gasped, collapsing into her chair.

"Extraordinarily beautiful," Guy said in an undertone. Cynthia said nothing. Her eyes caught the flash of his in the shadow.

"But truly, you know, you all are amazing!" Dana said pathetically.

"They're a worthless lot of baggages, but they're amusin'," Professor Trezavant said. "That was pretty, Cynthia."

"Papa, I didn't know you were there!"

"I've just come down. Suppose we all go in—it's getting

chilly out here. And I have to beat somebody at anagrams!"

They all went in, smiling dazedly at one another in the sudden light. The house smelled of sun-warmed wood and rugs and cloth.

"How frowzy we look!" Cynthia said, her blinking eyes finding Guy's eyes.

The others were going to play anagrams; it was not long after nine. But Guy had to go home; he must be up early tomorrow to paint a dawn picture. And Cynthia was sleepy and did not want to play.

"Come up some morning and see me doing the oak at the top of Loma Grande, gals. It would be a grand walk; you'd see the sun rise, and get home for breakfast as hungry as hunters!"

"Doing that same old oak, Guy?"

"Yes. But with the shadows lying the other way."

"Oh-h, but it's so hard to get up!" Leslie wailed.

"You start, Dana," Professor Trezavant said. Gray had returned from a short absence in her room—Gray, who was never vain! Now her fair hair was smooth again, and her skin powdered freshly after the demoralizing hour on the porch, and, yes, she had slightly reddened her lips. As she leaned forward, her bare shoulder almost touched Dana's shoulder as she drew her three letters.

Guy went away, and Cynthia watched the players for a minute and then went off to bed.

"I could get quite a disgusting one, but I won't; I'm too innately decent!" she heard Dana say—and then Gray's laugh.

Two mornings later Cynthia snatched her alarm clock and muffled its first notes at five o'clock. Her room was black and cold; she seemed only to have gone to bed a few minutes before, and her blankets were warm and inviting.

For a few minutes she snuggled back, debating in her mind. But every fiber of her being was wide awake now; there could be no more sleep.

Noiselessly she got up and reached for her clothing; her old brown riding breeches, a soft old shirt, a sweater with buttons and pockets, her high boots that had bits of grass and twig sticking to the lacing holes, and that smelled of the herbage of the hill. Cynthia splashed icy water in her face in the bathroom and ran a comb through her thick, curly hair; then she pulled an old brown felt hat without a band well down on her head and went cautiously across the Galleria, the two dogs rising silently to join her as she went.

Their feet left pearly tracks across the lawn in the strengthening light; as Cynthia crossed the highway and began to climb straight up through the forest on the slippery needles under the redwoods, the birds were beginning to call from tree to tree, and the east was ablaze.

The trail was so precipitous that she found herself catching at the slender trunks of hazelnut and wild-lilac trees to hold what she had gained as she mounted upward. The dogs, mad with dawn and the chase, foraged backward and forward, sniffing the earth, pawing and whining in excitement over some fox hole, barking at the chipmunks and jays that were safe far overhead. A great owl, with spread wings, floated down close to Cynthia's head, and as she drew back, surprised and frightened, fanned itself away into the darkest recesses of the wood. She heard baby buzzards piping, high up in a dead pine, and now and then a barking noise far, far away, that might have been coyotes in some early hunt, off in the big mountains.

A garter snake wriggled from under her feet; the world was teeming with life in this June dawn. Ants crossed the trail in orderly files; bees buzzed over Mission Bells and columbine blossoms; over blue lilac and pungent wild currant, lizards lay on the rocks, awaiting the sun; and near the spring, where cattle and other animals had trampled the wet earth into little pools and pockmarks, yellow-bellied busy little waterdogs were toiling to and fro, tumbling from microscopic cliffs, struggling out of microscopic waterways.

After a strenuous half-hour of it, Cynthia came upon Guy's sun umbrella, sweater, and camera, left in the trail. A hundred yards farther up, through the great green brakes and the detaining arms of the underbrush, she came upon him, in a clearing, with his back to the sunrise and his absorbed eyes upon the magnificent old oak.

He gave her a nod; his pencil was busy again.

"Good girl! How many of you came?"

"There wasn't anyone else dressed when I started," Cynthia chose to answer, with something less than the truth. She stood looking over his shoulder at the sketch on the easel.

"What do you think of it?"

"It's marvelous."

"I love the old boy in that light," Guy said. "I'm going to do two more from this one."

"Is it finished?"

"It will be in half an hour. Nice, the way the shadows lie there at the base?"

"Lovely."

She sat down, her back against a great tree, the dogs panting at her feet. Something was missing: somehow her adventure had gone suddenly flat.

"I brought up buns and coffee for some of you yesterday and the day before," Guy presently said, working hard, "but of course you wouldn't come those mornings. Today I brought nothing, because I knew I was going to finish the thing, and I thought I'd invite myself to your house to breakfast."

"Well, we'll go down together!" Cynthia said, apparently undisturbed.

But in her heart she was not happy; she was ashamed. She wished suddenly that she had not come up here; getting up in the middle of the night, sneaking off to the top of Loma Grande to see Guy alone! Her sisters would assure him at breakfast that they never had had the slightest idea of accompanying her; he would know that she had done it because she wanted him to flatter her—to call her "dear" again, and to say that, if he were free to marry any one of the Trezavant girls, Cynthia would be his choice.

Red-cheeked, and feeling entirely in his way and like a troublesome little girl, she sat on her tree trunk and wished the next hour over, and herself and Guy at breakfast and the day normally started. It had been a silly, impulsive thing, this early-morning adventure!

"When does Dana have to go back, Cynthia?"

"In about six weeks now. And how we're going to miss him!"

"He and Gray'll fix it up before that."

"Oh, I hope so!"

"If they haven't—" Guy said, blurring a shadow with a dexterous firm jerking of his thumb—"if they haven't already."

"It's wonderful to see old Gray so happy and pro-prietary and important!" Cynthia said.

Silence. Silence.

"Don't wait for me, Cyn. I'll be a little longer than I thought. Beat it home for your breakfast, and keep some hot for me."

It hurt her like a whip, but she was nonchalant.

"Oh, I'll wait now! I love being starving for breakfast."

At about quarter-past seven they started down through the trees; Guy, having packed his drawing carefully, carried it himself; Cynthia helped with the easel. They took a longer trail than the steep short cut she had followed, walking on the dew-soaked yellow mountain grass that was drying in the strengthening sunlight, turning down through the great solemn slope of redwood forest that the Trezavant children had named "the Cathedral" years ago.

When they had almost reached the lawn and could see the smoke of Hing's breakfast fire rising into the morning, and hear Mack and Portuguese Joe shouting at the cows, Guy said, out of a silence that to Cynthia at least had been awkward and incomprehensible:

"Remember our conversation the other day, Cynthia, about the relative merits of you Trezavant girls as wives?"

He had stopped short; he was looking at her quizzically, kindly. Cynthia stopped short, too, facing him. She swallowed with a dry throat.

"Yes."

"Did you ever think what a calamity it would be," Guy asked, "if ever I did fall in love with one of you?"

"I suppose so," Cynthia whispered, trying to smile.

"It would mean that I'd have to get out."

"Get out?" She could only repeat what he said, after him, stupidly. She was tired, and a little dizzy from fasting and from the warmth of the morning; she felt confused and ashamed.

"Surely. It would mean leaving the Little Quito forever. I'm not free, you know. While Rhoda lives—and she's only thirty-two—I never will be free. It's curable, her trouble. And she has nobody else in the world!"

He was very handsome in his disheveled painting gear, with the morning sun in his brown face. Cynthia flushed, paled; she could not speak.

"It would be worse," Guy pursued, "to have one of *you* take a fancy to me. Wouldn't it?"

No answer. She looked at him steadily, swallowed, wet her lips.

"See that?"

"I'm not in love with you, if you mean that, Guy."

"No, I don't think you are! And I think we'd be very silly to let ourselves be anything but friends, don't you, Cynthia?"

"I never thought of it at all."

Her affectation of pride, of indifference, was thin; it was all she had.

"Of course you haven't, because you are a sensible child. But it occurred to me as a speculation after our talk the other day that the fat would be in the fire if we got into any mess like that!"

Cynthia smiled, quite naturally this time, and walked on without further comment.

"It would be the deuce—my friendship with your father, and everything, considered," Guy pursued.

"I'm starving—smell that bacon!" Cynthia said for only answer.

When, brushed and fresh, but still trembling inwardly, she came out for breakfast, it was to hear Leslie telling Guy that nothing on earth would ever persuade her to get up in the middle of the night to see the sun rise, and to hear Lucia adding that she had heard Cynthia's alarm go off but had been only too thankful to turn over and go to sleep again. This, considering that Cynthia had taken pains to impress upon him that the plan had been for them all to rise early and join him on Loma Grande, and that she had further claimed that she herself had been oddly wakeful this morning and had gotten up in preference to lying awake sleepless in bed, only added straw to the burden of her misery after all.

She managed some coffee. But Gray's famous popovers

couldn't be swallowed this morning; they stuck in her throat.

And as soon as she had made a decent pretense of break-
fasting she escaped to her room.

Cynthia put everything here in order with scrupulous
care. She made the bed, straightened the dresser and the
bathroom, picked up scraps, dusted conscientiously. She
drew the shades down on the four latticed cottage windows,
put away scattered books, hung garments in the pine-
scented closet.

Once or twice, during these proceedings, she stopped short,
thinking, and once she pressed her hand tightly over her
heart with a little groan.

When everything was done she got into loose pajamas
and flung herself down on her bed, drawing a thin checked
Canadian blanket over her slippered feet. She lay there, her
hands linked under her head, her eyes on the ceiling.

The summer day grew warm outside. The birds were
silent now; the kitchen was silent. Now and then Cynthia
heard a girl's voice and a light laugh; now and then a screen
door banged lightly. She could hear the sprinkler whirling
and dripping somewhere outside her windows; the smell of
cooking peaches drifted in.

Gray cautiously put her head in the door.

"Catching up sleep?"

"Dead!" Cynthia answered, speaking with a little effort.

"Guy's sound asleep, down in the hammocks. We got
that same old netting and put it over him."

Gray noiselessly closed the door again, and Cynthia
thought of the netting and of the dance two nights before.
Then she had felt so confident, so gay, so much her own
mistress! Now . . .

Now she could only lie here in this dim, sweet, summer
bedroom, shamed and broken, and wish that she might die
before she must meet Guy Waring again.

CHAPTER FIVE

"GRAY, you look so lovely in that blue!"

"Blue for blondes," Gray said, in a voice that trembled with happiness.

Cynthia put her arm about her. The two girls were alone on the porch. They had come out, bathed, fresh and dressed for the evening, into the afternoon peace.

It had been a happy day, this hot July Saturday. Two extremely personable young men had telephoned Leslie to ask if they might come up to Treehaven, and they, with Guy and Dana and Papa, had more than balanced the sexes at a merry and noisy luncheon table. Afterward everyone except Professor Trezavant had lounged about on the Lido for a while, and then there had been a wild hour of splashing, racing, diving in the pool. The afternoon shadows had found them all basking and talking on the grass, and then the young men, warmly invited to a picnic the following Saturday, had departed, and the girls had come down to the house to dress.

Lucia was still curled up asleep, and Leslie was sleepily wandering about gathering her clothes, when the two older girls came out, to stand for a minute of leisure in the glory of the sunset.

"Gray," Cynthia ventured, "I'm awfully—glad, for you."

Gray could say nothing; she gave Cynthia a side glance, turned her shining eyes away again.

"Only I'll miss you—awfully," the younger sister added.

"I know," Gray assented quickly, in a thick voice.

"But if you had a little apartment in Boston, Gray—

imagine, of all romantic and historic places! And if you were coming out here summers——"

"I never could love any place as I love Treehaven!" Gray said.

"Well, I could," Cynthia observed dryly, with a little laugh.

The other girl said nothing, and after a minute Cynthia went on:

"You don't like me to talk about it?"

"Oh, yes, I do, I do!" Gray assured her, with a shamed smile. "I like it better—better than anything. Only—only I'm so afraid," she murmured, "that something—something will happen!"

They had wandered down across the lawn; now they were at the hammocks, and Gray sat down and, locking her hands behind her head, stared off at the cooling eastern sky over Booker Rock and Deer Hill.

"Idiot, what can happen? We all," Cynthia said, dropping on the grass, glancing up at her sister over her shoulder— "we all see it."

"It seems—too much!" Gray breathed.

"Not for anyone as lovely and as good as you are, Gray."

"He—Dana," the older girl said, "is—so wonderful. He's so wise, Cyn. He's—everything."

Cynthia thought of Dana's compactness; that trim, groomed conventional body that seemed so well matched by the trim, groomed mind. And she thought of another man, big and loosely built and eager, with tumbled black hair. . . .

"Well, whatever he is, he's crazy about you, Gray," she presently asserted stoutly.

"I wasn't sure of it——" Gray began, and stopped.

Cynthia looked up eagerly.

"But now you are?"

"I think so."

"He told you so? Ah, Gray, darling, do tell me! I'm so interested. I'm so—anxious!"

"Night before last," Gray murmured, in a half-suffocated voice—"night before last, when it was so hot, we came down here after the cribbage, you know, and we talked— oh, for about fifteen minutes. Papa was smoking his pipe on the porch——"

"Gray, you're engaged! One of us, engaged!"

"No. No, truly, Cyn. I'd tell you if we were." Gray's eyes were serious, almost troubled. She stared into space. "I wish—we were," she said hesitatingly.

There was a silence.

"But—I know he likes me, Cyn," the older sister presently added.

"Did he kiss you?"

"Well—that was it," Gray murmured, all roses.

"Gray," Cynthia said with conviction, after watching her sister's face for a moment, "then that seems to me—*settled*. Dana isn't a college kid; he's a man, and he's a very—well, conservative—cool—you know what I mean—sort of man. He means it. Anything from Dana has ten times the significance that it would have coming from most men."

They sat silent, their hands linked, both staring away into the distance, almost afraid to believe in the strangeness of it.

"We take it for granted in books, Gray, that men shall like girls. But it seems so different when it comes along."

"I know."

"For all that, we're—not bad-looking," Cynthia pursued. "I've always—sort of—thought it wouldn't come to us."

"I know," Gray murmured again.

A pause.

"He goes two weeks from today?"

"From tomorrow."

"Hasn't it raced by!"

"Terribly. It seems about two weeks ago that he came down that morning with his brown overcoat——"

"Remember how he kept laughing at everything we did?"

"He says he never imagined there was any place like this, with four sisters, all dancing and singing and cooking and swimming and playing tennis and getting up theatricals——"

"I know. He told Guy that, too."

"And of course," Gray said, "it's all mixed up for him with getting well, sleeping on the porch, and moonlight and roses and figs and manzanita——"

"It *has* been romantic, Gray!"

"Ah-h-h-h!" Gray said, on a long breath.

"Cynthia," she began again, after a pause, "do you think you've ever been in love?"

Cynthia cleared her throat.

"With whom?" she asked, with an air of dryness.

"I mean," said Gray, "it's quite different from what—one thinks."

"Not all fun," Cynthia observed, very low.

Her sister caught her up eagerly.

"Ah, that's what I mean! Not all fun! You feel so *shaky,*" Gray said soberly, sudden tears in her smiling eyes.

"Perhaps when one's actually engaged, Gray, and actually coming right up to the wedding day—perhaps then it's—not so bad."

"But to feel it, waking or sleeping," Gray began again. "To be measuring—hoping—afraid——"

"I know."

"You know there's nobody else in the world I could say this to, Cyn."

"Well," Cynthia responded gruffly, "it's something to have me to say it to!"

"I—like him so much!" Gray faltered. She touched her eyes with her handkerchief.

"Don't worry, darling. It's all going to come out marvelously."

"Since night before last I've thought so."

"I've known it all along—the girls have, too. And you can see Papa knows it. And Guy."

"Really!" Gray exclaimed rather than asked, fervently.

"Certainly."

"He's so wonderful, Cyn."

"He's marvelous," Cynthia agreed, simply.

"If I could have—just this," Gray said, "I think I could bear anything else that God sent me. I know," she went on—"I know we've had tremendous advantages, we girls. We've never worried about money, we've had Papa to guide us to good reading—all that.

"But in another way we've led an unbalanced sort of life. And if I could find myself—just a normal, happy woman, adoring my doctor husband——

"Cyn, you can't think what it would mean to have a son, if you loved his father!"

"It's ideal. And in a week or two we'll be quite accustomed to the idea of your getting married!" Cynthia said healthily.

"I know. I *think* I know it." Gray fell silent. She was so close to her Kingdom, it would be so wonderful now to find the gates open—to ride in with her Prince beside her.

"Do you ever think of them back in Boston there, Gray—his mother and his brothers? Has he five brothers? Do you ever think of yourself meeting them all and trying to make hit with them all?"

"Oh, all the time!"

"Do you suppose some of them would come on for the wedding?"

Gray was not listening. The hammock was gently moving.

Cynthia, seated on the grass, had an arm across her sister's knee. Sunset lay in burning gold on the slopes and rough wooded shoulders of Deer Hill; every flower in the Trezavant garden stood crystallized in the last shaft of light.

"Cynthia——" the older sister said, and paused.

Cynthia looked at her expectantly.

"You've never been in love, have you?"

"You asked me that."

"I know I did."

"And I said," Cynthia answered, clearing her throat, "with whom?"

"As far as that goes," Gray said, "you might easily have fallen in love with somebody at college."

"I had a case on a red-headed boy once—Dr. Henderson's son."

"You were sixteen."

"Seventeen. He gave me a purse of chipmunk skin for my birthday. Don't you remember I left the purse in Lucia's closet and bugs got into it and it smelled to high heaven?"

"Perfectly. But I don't mean that."

Cynthia looked at her sister, looked away, looked back again.

"Cyn, you wouldn't do that!"

"I don't know that I would have much to do with it."

"You're not—not beginning to like him?"

"Guy," Cynthia said, and was still.

"I've wanted to say this to you so many times—just lately. Perhaps you don't see it, Cyn, but I see it."

"I see it," Cynthia admitted, with a brief laugh.

"You know what—*wretchedness* that would mean for us all."

"If I liked Guy?" Cynthia asked, in a thoughtful tone.

"He's—*married*, Cyn."

"So I've heard," Cynthia said dryly.

She turned her head to look over her shoulder at Gray, her eyes somber.

"But, darling," Gray pleaded anxiously, "it—it couldn't work out!"

"No, I know it couldn't."

"Well, then—what?"

"Nothing," Cynthia said.

"Poor Rhoda, after all, gets better sometimes."

"Exactly."

There was a quality in Cynthia's voice that made Gray uneasy. But she could think of nothing to say.

Guy did not come down to the ranch that night, nor the next night. When he did come, they knew, who knew him so well, that he had seen his wife in the time between their meetings. He always seemed quieter, older, after one of these terrible visits; Gray thought that she had never seen him so grave and so worn.

After dinner, while she and her two younger sisters and Dana played cribbage, Professor Trezavant sat on the porch with Cynthia and Guy, talking.

But when the card players came out into the starlight, Cynthia and Guy were there alone.

"Lord, but you're restful!" Gray heard Guy say.

Cynthia was deep in a basket chair, the spreading ruffles of her pale pink organdie gown a mere glimmer in the shadow. Guy was sitting on the top step, smoking his pipe, his shoulder almost touching Cynthia's knee.

"I thought Papa was out here!" said Gray.

"He had some work he had to do."

"And so did I," said Guy, "and this is the way I do it."

"And what have you two been talking about?"

Gray was in a chair now, Dana sitting beside her on the

step. Lucia and Leslie, refusing to be drawn into the group, yawningly departed for bed.

"We were talking about George Eliot."

"George Eliot! Why George Eliot?"

"I was saying that I hadn't read her stuff since I was a small child," Cynthia said composedly, from the shadows, "and that I thought I would read *Middlemarch* again."

"She stands up surprisingly well," Dana contributed, lighting a cigarette. "My mother was quite ill last winter, and I used to hear the nurse reading *The Mill on the Floss*. How long since you've read any of them, Gray?"

Gray had not heard him. The mention of his mother's illness had set her thinking; here was a possible explanation of Dana's reticence. Perhaps he felt that he must go home first, and see his mother, and then come back—or write to ask Gray to marry him? Something was holding him— something was keeping back the one little phrase for which her very soul was starving.

Guy knocked the ashes from his pipe and put it into his pocket.

"I'm on my way," he said.

"I'm going to turn in. I'm dead," Cynthia observed immediately.

"I'll walk over to your car with you, Guy," Dana observed. "It's pretty chilly out here."

"It's after eleven," Gray added cheerfully. But in her heart the refrain of "only eight more days and seven more nights" was ringing like the sorrowful clapper in a bell.

"Good-night, cousins!" Dana said.

"Good-night, Gray. Good-night, Cynthia."

"Good-night, Guy," Cynthia said.

Gray went in to bed, but Cynthia sat on the top step for a while, where Guy had been sitting, her head resting against the pillar of the porch as his had rested. There was no moon tonight; there were millions of stars pulsing—pulsing over-head. The Milky Way was a powdering of silver dust, curved across the dark blue sky. One great star hung wink-ing, red and blue, close to the rise of black redwood ranks, on the ridge that rose opposite the house.

After a while she heard the door of her father's work-shop slam; that meant that he would be down in a moment —he might question her—he might wonder that she had not gone to bed long ago.

Gathering her pink ruffles about her, Cynthia fled noise-lessly into the stuffiness and warmth of the low-ceiled house. The place smelled of wooden walls baked in the long day's sun.

She went into her room and began automatic preparations for bed; looking keenly at the pink ruffles before she suspended them from a hanger, rinsing the flesh-colored gauzy stockings in the hand basin and stretching them in the bathroom to dry.

When she was in her pajamas and the only light in the room was the reading lamp beside her pillow, she knelt down and took from the bottom drawer of her old-fashioned desk a heavy cardboard folder filled with odd photographs of all sizes.

From this she took one special print, a snapshot taken on a sharp clear winter day six months earlier. It was the picture of a broad, dark smiling man, with a shabby old hat on his tumbled dark hair, a pipe clenched in his teeth, and for clothing corduroy golf trousers, laced boots, a soft-collared shirt open at the throat, and a short leather jacket.

Accompanied by two Airedales, he was standing under bare autumn trees, grinning at the world in general, and in particular—her heart remembered—at the girl who had com-manded him to pose for her camera.

The picture cupped in her two brown hands, Cynthia sat on the edge of her bed, staring at it for a long, long time.

CHAPTER SIX

"YOU'RE a capable wench," Guy told her.

Cynthia looked at him, smiling, over the bowl into which she was slicing great firm tomatoes.

"I am?"

"You're worse than capable. You're efficient."

She considered this.

"*You're* efficient, Guy."

"Well, in a way I am. With a pencil, maybe I am. But you're so clever with anything that takes hands!"

"I can make a good salad," Cynthia admitted.

She had seemed to grow older in these last few days; her sisters saw it, and Guy had seen it too. It was like the exquisite unfurling of a bud; the ripening of a fruit. Her dark eyes glowed and welled with light; apricot color stained her brown skin; there was a richness, a new vitality and beauty, in her supple brown body, her clever hands, her swift movements.

Cynthia was not thinking in these days; she was not reasoning. In the dim background of her mind she was still perfectly aware of Rhoda Waring's existence, and of the impropriety—worse, of the futility!—of any thought of love in connection with Guy.

But this consideration was dim and shadowy, or rather it did not seem to have anything to do with the situation. What she was feeling was so absorbing, so intoxicating, so entirely different from anything she might ever have fancied "falling in love" to be, that it was impossible to fit it into the old way of thinking and living at all.

Suddenly, quite without warning, the world had become glorious. Life was thrilling, every phase of it, every thing in it. Just to be alive was enough; walking in a garden, dreaming over a book, dressing oneself in old mountain clothes or making oneself lovely in ruffles and lace—it was all wonderful. Cynthia no longer talked restlessly; she no longer wanted to go away from Treehaven. On the contrary she was afraid of oversleeping in the morning now; she was the last reluctant person to leave the group at night.

She did not think of herself as loving Guy; she did not think at all. The world *was* Guy and herself. She knew—and discovered afresh in the evidence of every passing day—that she held over him a quite irresistible power. To exercise this, to prove it to herself over and over again, was the greatest adventure she had ever known; Cynthia could not believe it. She was exploring a fascinating country whose ways led her far, far away from the humdrum existence she had always known.

Guy, who had always been like an uncle, an oracle, an elder to the Trezavants! Guy, helpless under her eyes and her voice and her nearness! It was to Cynthia like finding herself in a small craft racing through tremendous seas. Each day saw her riding one more breath-taking billow, and each night found her, exhausted with the sense of safety once more regained, lying wide awake in her bed, stretched straight and young and fragrant between the sheets, glorying in her own beauty and youth and in this new power.

Guy came down to the house on one pretext or another every day now, unless, indeed, as was the case today, the Trezavants invited themselves and their Boston cousin up to the Little Quito ranch for luncheon or supper. He did not come expressedly to see Cynthia, but she had a thousand ways of knowing that until he caught sight of her and had a word with her he would not—simply because he could not—go away.

Cynthia might casually meet him on the porch.

"Oh, hello, Cynthia!"

"Hello, Guy." And she would bring her glowing dark beauty close to him, lifting heavy eyelashes to look seriously into his eyes, showing him her book or the puzzle she was trying to solve or the embroidery she was doing. He did not know, poor simple Guy, what was brewing between them in those magic, careless minutes on the porch, or in the big Cabin sitting room, or down on the croquet lawn—but she knew!

When she made him his favorite chicken curry, and served it with a demure look, her fingers touching his hand for a second as she passed the plate, she knew exactly why Guy lost the thread of what Papa was saying about the medicinal fungus on mouldy barley. But Guy did not know, and that was the best of it all!

She knew why he followed up any little conversational lead of hers with such complete attention: "Yes, what did you say, Cynthia? How do you mean, you were mad? How do you mean, you and Gray made a mistake?"

Today, when all the girls and Dana had come up to his house for Dana's last California lunch, she had given his complete unconsciousness one more test, and he had responded to it exactly as she had expected.

They were to lunch out-of-doors at Guy's brick grill under the oaks, and Dana and all the others had decided first to walk up to the Power Line Trail, to give Dana one more look at the distant foggy Pacific, off to the west. First, Cynthia had been enthusiastic for the three-mile walk, and then Guy had been all for it too. And then at the last minute she had said no, she would remain behind and get the salad made and set the table and light the charcoal fire, so that when they came back it would be a mere matter of broiling a few chops before they could lunch.

So the others had started off without her; Dana and Leslie and Lucia and Guy, and Gray of course, talking very charmingly to a friend of Dana's, who was to go East with him tomorrow and who had come up to Treehaven to be quite dazzled by all the Trezavants the night before. Their voices had come ringing back down the trail to Cynthia, very busy under the oaks for a few minutes, and then she had had the ranch to herself.

Ten minutes later, just as she had anticipated, Guy had reappeared. He had sent the others on without him; it had not seemed fair to him to leave everything to Cynthia, and he had come back to help.

His helping consisted only in amusing her with conversation as she busied herself with preparations for the simple meal. A great pot of *polenta* bubbled and smacked on the fire, corn was boiling, and red-and-white chops were neatly strapped into a broiler. Cynthia toasted French bread, buttered it with a little brush, put white enamel plates to heat. She felt excited, reckless, today.

"Wouldn't I make someone a good wife, Guy?"

He took his pipe out of his pocket, spoke steadily:

"You would that."

"It would be funny——" Cynthia mused.

"What would be funny?"

"To be—for instance, married to you now, Guy—to belong up here, instead of down at Treehaven. To have the others our company, and to have them go away and to be here alone."

"What would be—funny about it?" Guy asked, filling his pipe, pressing down the tobacco in the bowl with a great firm thumb.

"Funny isn't the right word."

"It would be very lovely," the man said thoughtfully, "to have you up here taking care of me."

"And you—" Cynthia added, neatly brushing the orderly grill with an old buzzard's wing and regarding her completed preparations with the cook's appraising eye—"you taking care of me."

"And I taking care of you." He was silent for a moment. "I suppose this sort of talk doesn't make it any harder," he added, after a space.

"What sort of talk?"

"This sort."

"Make what harder, Guy?"

"Nothing," he said, civilly.

Cynthia sat on the old blackwood table next to the grill. Her face was flushed from cooking and from the heat of the day; her dark hair curled on her damp forehead in little rings and wisps; her blue eyes were very blue. She wore tramping clothes; the thin old shirt and khaki breeches showed the firm rise of her young breasts and the slimness of her hips and legs.

"If Gray marries, you'll just go on here, I suppose, you other three?"

"Gray wouldn't marry until spring, anyway."

"But it wouldn't make any difference in what the rest of you did?"

Her candid, round-eyed look.

"What else should we do? Are you," Cynthia queried curiously—"are you making talk with me, Guy?"

"I thought perhaps—— You're always talking of getting into the city some winter, getting into work of some sort. This winter would seem to be the one for the break."

"Oh, I love Treehaven!" the girl said, considering. "And it may be Gray's last winter at home. And anyway, I don't

know what I could do—you can't just break in on medicine
or the arts, can you?"

"But this life doesn't seem quite fair to you or the other
girls," he said.

Again her curious, bright-eyed look.

"Why, Guy, you never used to feel that way."

To this he made no answer; he was not looking at her.
After a while he said suddenly, almost carelessly, as he
knocked his pipe against the edge of the grill:

"I saw Rhoda last week."

Instantly Cynthia's face changed, and she turned a little
pale. It was as if a cold wind had blown across her mischief
and teasing.

"I thought you had. When you didn't come down for
three days. And then I telephoned, you know, and Lung
said you weren't here, you had gone off in the 'beely.' "

"I didn't know you had telephoned," Guy said, looking up.

"For Papa," Cynthia countered, readily.

A silence. They were so still, under the tent of the great
spreading oak, that a jay hopped nearer and nearer through
the surrounding underbrush of hazel and mulberry leaves,
his blue coat shining against a background of red madrone
twigs. The waters of the Quito rustled and splashed over
Guy's little dam; hot sunshine enveloped the world of
mountain and forest in a thick soft haze.

"They're coming back. I hear their voices," Cynthia presently said, lifting the broiler to lay it on the hot grill. And
in a changed voice she asked, "How is Aunt Rhoda?"

"Pretty much the same. She knows me, almost always,
but she doesn't get things straight."

He sighed. There was another silence.

"For instance," said Guy, beginning again, "she asks for
your mother. 'Where is Mary? Why doesn't Mary come to
see me?' They say she rather frets for her. I've thought

sometimes that if it wouldn't make Leslie too nervous, she might come with me some day. She's your mother over again."

"How——" Cynthia cleared her throat. "How does Aunt Rhoda look, Guy?"

"Faded, of course. She has a wistful sort of vacant look —it's very pathetic. She usually——" his voice was resolutely unemotional, "she usually cries when I go away; she wants to come too. I have to lie to her."

Cynthia was very serious now; she drew nearer him.

"Guy, it's so terrible for you! When you thought you were going to have a real home here, and a wife in it and children!"

"It isn't me, so much," he said briefly.

"She won't get better, Guy?"

"She does get better. That's the worst of it!" he answered, with a rueful laugh. "She really is better than she was three years ago. She's stronger, for one thing. Miss Merry, her nurse, says that there are times—times when she seems to understand it all, and when she's bewildered to find herself there."

"Has she the same nurse?"

"Miss Merry, yes. And they have their own cottage—three rooms—and they have good food. The sanitarium sends over things, but Merry gets a lot of outside stuff."

"But she's sad, Guy?"

"That's the worst of it. She cries a good deal. And she'll never be well, Cynthia—that's the tragedy. She may live for forty years."

"And you may."

"And I may."

"I wish you didn't have to see her, Guy. It always breaks you up so."

"I'm all she has," he answered. "She hasn't another soul.

another friend, in the world. Here they are!" Guy added, standing up as the sound of the others' voices was suddenly quite near. "I never see you alone," he said confusedly, in a low voice; "when can I ever see you alone?"

Before she could answer, the mountain climbers returned, ravenous and noisy. Cynthia and Guy separated, to serve the dripping, crackling chops and the steaming, pearled cobs of the corn and to pour the clear, smoking amber of the coffee.

It was sweet and shady under the oaks; the scents of dry autumn grass and broiling meat and coffee drifted about in the still hot air. There had been a blanket of creamy fog over the world this morning; now there was no shred of cloud in the pale blue sky. Already the early August sun was softened, and the air thinned with the first breath of change.

The two Eastern men were enthusiastic in praise of it all. They would start eastward on their long journey home to-night, and within a few weeks be facing the long Massachusetts winter, the dull gray days, the ice and wind and snow again, and they were willing to lose no moment of this last day of dreamy sunshine and mountain sweetness. But Dana was nervous today; Cynthia at least was aware of it, and also aware that Gray was very quiet.

Her own thrilling game went on; it was always going on. She need not speak directly to Guy, nor even look at him, to realize that he saw nobody, heard nobody, was conscious of nothing but herself.

Cynthia could not eat in these days; nor sleep in these strange late summer nights. Yet she never had felt so rested, so nourished, so completely atune with life. Her spirit was floating in some ethereal element that fed body and mind as well. She needed neither food nor sleep.

Today she played with some salad, sipped coffee, listened.

The miracle of this state of affairs was that she need make no effort to hold Guy's notice; any casual monosyllable, any lazy lifting of her lashes, would accomplish it. When she suddenly turned the full battery of her interest upon Dana's friend, Frank Ainsworth, Guy was uneasy; he continually interrupted, continually attempted to get into the conversation himself.

"How do we go, this evening, Miss Trezavant? You told me, but I've forgotten."

"My sister Gray is going to drive you and Dana and one of us, maybe Leslie, over to San José. Then you take the train, and tomorrow morning you're in Los Angeles."

"You going to drive with them this evening, Cynthia?" This was Guy.

"I'm making the chocolate." Cynthia turned to the guest again. "You know, Dr. Ainsworth," she said, seriously, "we have certain old customs—they're a ritual now—at Treehaven. Whenever any guest goes off by the Los Angeles train, someone stays home and makes hot chocolate or iced coffee for those who come back. Tonight it'll be hot chocolate because it's so cold these evenings, and when Gray and Les get back we'll all sit around the fire and talk about you and Dana."

"Nicely!" Lucia, who was extremely literal, hastened to say anxiously, and they all laughed.

"They'll be back about half-past ten," Cynthia continued, "and then we'll ring two bells in Papa's workshop, which means 'chocolate!' and he'll come down, and we'll all sit about the fire until midnight."

"And how horribly homesick I shall be for you!" Dana said.

Gray's eyes, Cynthia saw, moved quickly toward him. She said nothing.

That night, when Lucia and Gray and the two doctors

were on their way to San José, and good-byes had been said
to the ranch, "until," Dana said cheerfully, "next year,"
Guy came down the hill to help Cynthia make the chocolate.

She had known that he would, had thought that he might
come to dinner. But he did not come to dinner.

All through the dreamy, unreal meal, with Gray strained
and bright, and Dana by fits and starts nervously talkative
and nervously silent, Cynthia had been listening for the
telephone bell. She had known that sooner or later it must
ring, and ring it finally did, but not until Cynthia's heart had
long been sick with suspense, and the clock had struck nine,
struck half-past nine.

Every fiber of her being had been drawing her toward
it then; every ounce of ingenuity she could command had
been occupied in the business of thinking up some half-
convincing excuse for telephoning Guy. The sound of the
bell's sharp tinkle had been like cooling waters to her parched
soul.

"Cynthia? Did they get off?" Guy's voice had come over
the wire.

"Is that you, Guy?"

"This is Guy."

"Oh, yes, they got off an hour ago."

"Les, too?"

"No, she's here but she's gone to bed. She got terribly
sunburned today, and I had to cocoa-butter her, and she felt
all greasy, and she's turned in."

"Could I have some chocolate if I came down?"

A pause. Then, "There's enough," said Cynthia.

"Then I'm coming!"

Twenty minutes later he had come in upon her alone,
with her big pot of milk and her bowl of rich mixed
chocolate, waiting beside the fire; with two long forks and
a pile of sliced bread to furnish the only other refreshments.

Guy sat in a deep armchair, his head leaning back; Cynthia was in a lower chair, with her body bent forward and her brown hands linked between her knees. They smiled at each other.

"I had to come," Guy said.

"I thought you would. I knew——" She stopped.

"You know what I've been trying not to tell you for six weeks," Guy said, simply.

Cynthia did not speak. She changed her position only enough to glance levelly, seriously, at him with half-closed eyes, before looking back at the fire again.

"I'm sorry," Guy resumed, simply. "If I had seen it coming I would have stopped it. I think I would have stopped it," he added, after a moment.

Was she still acting, still just flirting with Guy? Cynthia did not know. She could not think. Her heart beat with a wild, hard, happy hammering; she felt a little dizzy.

"Perhaps——" she began, and stopped, clearing her throat. "Perhaps we couldn't have stopped it."

"Yes," Guy said. "The feeling of a girl for an older man isn't an unusual thing," he said. "If I had seen it coming, I could have stopped it. It's my fault—you're not to blame!"

Again silence.

"Oh, it's *that* sort of thing, is it?" Cynthia asked, in a dry tone.

"What sort of thing?"

"Just—a crush."

"Well, isn't it?"

"The *jeune fille* idea, the *backfisch!*" she said bitterly.

"The 'Swan,'" Guy agreed.

"Falling in love with the gentlemanly secretary!" Cynthia said, trembling.

"Be a nice girl. Don't be cross at me."

It was his old tone to the little girl who used to go into tantrums. Cynthia flushed in the old way and assumed the old look.

"Only this time it's the uncle instead of the secretary," he said.

"Guy," the girl said, in a shaken, angry tone, not looking at him, "don't laugh at me!"

It was a full moment before he spoke again, and then in a different tone:

"I'm not laughing at you, Cynthia. God knows I wish I were!

"But if I thought," he presently began again—"if I thought that any harm—any pain—could come to you through me, I think I would never forgive myself!"

Tears were in the blue eyes through which she smiled at him.

"But, Guy, I've always liked you," she said simply, eagerly. "Why shouldn't I go on liking you, only more? Why shouldn't we just have it for our—our secret, that we like each other?"

"There wouldn't be much happiness in that, Cynthia. Not between a girl like you, and a—a man like me."

She made no answer; she sat staring into the fire without speaking. Guy, with an elbow on his chair, had dropped his face in his hand, shading his eyes.

"We oughtn't to talk like this," he muttered.

Cynthia continued to regard him with puzzled bright eyes.

"I was talking to your father," Guy presently began, in a resolutely conversational tone, "about sending you and perhaps Leslie or Gray on a long trip somewhere. Hawaii and Manila, perhaps, or—if Gray marries—on to Boston for the winter."

"Running away?" the girl asked, with a glance.

"What else can we do, Cynthia?"

"You might say," she began, after a moment's hesitation, "that you are glad that I—I like you."

"I am gladder of it, I am prouder of it, than anything else that has ever come to me," he answered promptly, honestly. "Only—we have to take care." .

"You *said* you liked me best of us all," Cynthia pursued childishly.

"I do. And that's why I'd be glad to have you go away for a while, meet other men, and come back to realize that your old friend Guy is not as interesting as you thought he was."

"I don't want to meet other men."

"They will want to meet you," he assured her. "You have grown to be a beautiful woman, Cynthia."

His praise quickened her beauty for a second; then the color died from her face, leaving it serious again.

"Some day," he said, "you will be married and have children, and you and I will remember this talk on the day Dana went away!"

"It isn't going to be like that with me, Guy," Cynthia said, after a silence.

"It can't," he answered, "be anything else."

Cynthia looked at him steadily for a moment, looked away. Once more she was silent, and this time the silence lasted for minutes.

She was wearing a favorite gown of golden brown chiffon velvet; Guy had seen it a hundred times before; Cynthia had had it for four or five years. But he realized tonight that he had never really noticed it until now, noticed how the velvet set off her smooth ivory skin and how dark her hair looked against the creamy fabric. She had stretched her body back in the low chair, and stretched her slim legs toward the fire; her eyes were closed; her thick black lashes lay in two arcs on the delicate umber shadows of her eye sockets.

"I might go away," she whispered, without opening her eyes, "I might meet other men. But it wouldn't make any difference."

To this Guy made no answer, and the silence lasted between them until Professor Trezavant came stamping across the porch from his evening's work, cold and cross, and impatient for the little feast.

Almost immediately afterward they heard the motorcar panting up the hill, and Gray and Lucia came in—the younger girl rosy and bright-eyed from the night trip, but Gray seeming wearied and subdued.

Cynthia looked at her anxiously, as she said that she thought she would go straight to bed. No, no toast—no, no chocolate. Cynthia please wasn't to wash the cups; let Hing do it in the morning.

Late that night, when Cynthia noiselessly entered Gray's room, Gray looked up from a book.

"Hello, dear—sick?"

"No, Gray, darling, why are you reading so late?"

"Just wakeful," Gray said, serenely.

Cynthia, rolled in a wrapper, perched on the foot of the bed.

"Headache?"

"No!" Gray exclaimed.

Cynthia cast about in her mind for some inspiration by which to guide the conversation.

"Les waked up and came out and had some chocolate after all when Guy had gone."

"I could hear your voices."

"Haven't you been asleep, Gray? Your light was out."

"I know. But I was lying awake."

"It's nearly three."

"I knew it was after two. I was just going to stop reading."

A pause. Gray's eyes were bright, but her face was very pale.

"He'll write you, Gray!" Cynthia said impulsively.

A sort of spasm went over her sister's countenance, but Gray only answered, composedly:

"Of course."

"Well, we'll all miss him!" Cynthia mused.

Gray laid down her armor; stretched a hand to her sister.

"Please, Cyn——"

"You don't want me to talk about him?"

"*Please*——"

Cynthia lingered, a very agony of sympathy in her look.

"Why was it, Gray? Why *didn't* he——"

"I don't know," Gray whispered.

"I was so sure," Cynthia went on, encouraged. "We all were so sure!"

Gray twisted in the bed, and Cynthia slid to her knees beside her sister, and Gray was crying bitterly, clinging tight to Cynthia, her wet face buried in Cynthia's neck.

CHAPTER SEVEN

THEY did not speak of this the next morning, nor ever. The family only knew that Dana was gone, and that he and Gray were not engaged, were not going to be married. Gray was quieter, thinner, older; she devoted herself to her father. Dana's letters came quite briskly for a week or two; everyone had a letter, everyone had messages in Gray's letters. Then the letters stopped, and autumn began to blend into winter on the Treehaven ranch.

The apples were all gathered into boxes, and the prunes fell, rich with sweet juice, and were spread on long trays to dry in the September sun. The last leaves fell from the fruit trees, and the sunsets grew red, up beyond the forest and against the mountains in the west. Dark came at six o'clock, at half past five, every morning there was a fine crystal frost over the lawn, and every night, if Cynthia peeped out, when she closed the front door upon Guy, going home at eleven o'clock, she saw the heavy dewy mist creeping up from the earth like a miasma, under the autumn stars.

Hing and Mack began to pile wood on the Galleria; the fires burned all day long. The girls drove in thin sweet sunlight over wet roads to San José, and had their hair clipped, and saw movies. All the orchards were bare, all the schools busy. They needed their motor lights to get up the dark hill at six o'clock.

Dinners were cozy somehow in dark and candlelight, and books were dragged off the shelves again. Cribbage went on briskly every night; outwardly the winter was just like every other winter they could remember. But in Gray's heart were the ashes of her first, last love, and in Cynthia's whole being there pulsed and flamed the fire of her secret.

She depended upon Guy now as a plant might on the sun. No day could go by without some glimpse of that loose-built figure and some sound of that pleasant voice. Cynthia did not ask much—just a moment of him, stopping with his dogs and his easel in the morning crispness, or coming in tired and quiet for five minutes beside their fire at night, was enough. Sometimes she had no direct word from him, sometimes hardly a glance.

There were other times. She walked up the hill once a week and went "sketching" with Guy. Papa approved of this, and Lucia and Leslie were so entirely unsuspicious of the situation that they sometimes quite innocently invited themselves to go too. When they did not go, Guy and Cynthia had the whole morning alone together.

Her father, exactly in the manner of one dealing with a shirking little girl, had warned her that she could not have this artistic advantage unless she made arrangements with her sisters about luncheon responsibilities; Cynthia very demurely agreed to this condition, and demurely brought for her father's inspection, Tuesday after Tuesday, her drawing board with the morning's tree or roadway or mountain trail sketched upon it. Professor Trezavant made it a point now and then to ask Guy if he considered Cynthia's talent sufficient to warrant this trouble, and Guy always said that she was coming along well.

It was on a December morning that their affair took a certain forward step. Cynthia had sensed, trembling between their careless, friendly words for many days, the nearness of some crisis, but she felt herself completely unprepared for it when it came.

They had started out, on this particular morning, through a frost that crackled and twinkled on the lawn, and through which their boots left wide silver traces. But now at noon on the hot hilltop the sun was shining brightly, and if the sky was pale it was cloudless, too.

Guy had been working faithfully for almost three hours; Cynthia had sketched, torn up her sketch, commenced another, wandered about gathering toyon and madrone berries, and had finally settled herself under a tree with a book. From under her thick, warm old white sweater a pleated flannel skirt, from school days, spread about her on the trunk of the oak; her woolen stockings were white and her low laced boots white. On her dark hair was a white beret, and she had pinned to one side of it a cluster of the rich beaded vermilion madrone berries.

She was on a low sprawling bough which, as thick as her own body, stretched itself close to the ground. Above her was the thinned tent of the great oak, and above them both the high winter sky. The air was sweet, tingling like champagne, but there was real warmth in the sunshine, and Cynthia's cheeks were flushed with it.

Guy, finishing his morning's work with a sort of shout of relief, turned his attention, as was customary, to Cynthia's sketch. He picked up his crayons, retouched it here and there, and Cynthia climbed down from her perch and came to stand behind him.

All through these weeks they had tacitly agreed to regard their feeling for each other as a settled thing. They had talked generalities of love; they had said all the indirect and cryptic things with which lovers approach the great moment. Cynthia had told him, simply and sensibly, that she would rather have his friendship than the love of any other man, and Guy, kissing her reverently on the forehead one night at parting on the dark porch, had assured her that she need never be afraid with him. His love was great enough even for that—great enough even to give her up.

But today, quite without warning, as he found her at his elbow anxiously scrutinizing the sketch he had so metamorphosed, he dropped his pencils and put his arms about her.

"My darling—my beautiful girl——" he stammered, his lips against her hair. And Cynthia clung to him desperately, hungrily, and lifted her mouth to his kiss.

"My sweetheart—my little sweetheart! Cynthia," he murmured, "we can't keep this up! There must be some way out —we'll find a way out——"

She could only cling to him, whispering "Guy!" before her lips were closed again.

Their hands still tightly locked, they sat down on the great oak branch and talked together as if the floodgates of their very souls were loosed.

"I've always loved you—since you were a bad little girl of nine—when I first came up here," Guy said. "'Our black sheep,' your mother used to call you, and you used to toss back your little mane and glare at me—and I loved you then!"

"When you loaned me your socks."

"When you came in as wet as a trout off the mountain and they were all hunting for you."

"I was crying, and you let me have Donny to play with."

"I fixed you up all warm on my couch, and you went to sleep."

"And you gave me soft ginger snaps, Guy! I've never eaten one without remembering that awful storm."

"You're so beautiful—you're so wonderful——" he murmured, his eyes moving over her face.

"Ah, but I'm not. I *am* the 'black sheep.' None of us is as pretty as Leslie, except perhaps Gray sometimes."

"You're the loveliest woman I ever saw!" Guy persisted.

She hardly heard him; indeed, their words were entirely unimportant. What was important was that they were together, their hands tightly clasped, her shoulder against his, and his lips brushing her hair.

"We couldn't have kept it up, Cynthia. We've got to find some way out."

"We'll find a way out."

"I didn't mean ever to let you know——"

"To let me know!" she echoed, with a laugh.

"But now you do know," Guy said, on a long sigh of complete relaxation, "and we have to start fresh from here."

"I don't care what we do," Cynthia murmured, contentedly.

"No, neither do I."

"I've found you and you've found me, and that's all that matters."

"That's all."

"Papa and Rhoda—what difference do they make? The thing is that you're you and I'm I and we're together!"

"Ah, that *is* all that matters, dear!"

"It's the greatest thing I've ever had in my life."

"And it's the greatest thing I've ever had in mine, Cynthia."

"You've been in love before, Guy."

"But not like this!"

"It probably seemed like this."

"Why, I believe you are jealous, Cynthia!" the man said, with a delightful laugh.

"I'm devoured with it."

"Oh, come now!"

"But I tell you I am," she said, in a voice whose rich happiness denied her words. "I tell you I *am*—fiendishly jealous. You'll see!"

"Is it a promise?"

"Is what a promise?"

"That you'll show me how jealous you can be, some day?"

Cynthia fell thoughtful, her head resting against his shoulder; he felt her body move in a long sigh.

" 'I have no joy in this contract today!' " she quoted Juliet somberly.

"I'm still stunned," Guy murmured in reply, and they were silent for a while.

"Where do we go from here, Cynthia?"

"Ah, that's just the question!"

But they could not talk sensibly. Instead they fell into random memories that evoked laughter, evoked moods of a seriousness that was almost reverence—almost awe.

They had their golden hour together. Cynthia was to think long afterward that this was the happiest hour of all, with Guy's arm about her and the sweet, bare, sun-washed winter world falling away below them to the thinned buckeye and madrone trees in the canyon, and the miracle of their love like some precious, new-born, delicate thing in their hands.

He loved her so—so dearly and tenderly and protectively! He made her feel it, as she sat leaning against him, turning only occasionally to look up over her own shoulder into his eyes. He told her that he had loved her from her very babyhood; that coming as a young artist to the ranch above Treehaven, just for a summer bachelor holiday, he had been instantly won by the dark-haired, blue-eyed little sister among the blonde little Trezavant girls, that he had felt nine-year-old Cynthia another reason among many for buying the ranch house on the upper Quito and establishing himself as a sort of member *de grâce* of the Trezavant family.

"And all through these years, Cynthia—realizing it and yet not appreciating for one instant all that it meant—I've been watching you—well, sort of championing you, always on your side, and more interested in what you said than in the others, and more amused by what you did!"

"It was that day last spring—before Dana came—that I first began to know it," Cynthia said.

"But oh, my darling, what have I let you into!" Guy exclaimed, when they had talked for almost an hour and Cynthia was afraid to be any later in starting for home.

"Nothing!" she said confidently, laughing.

They were standing now, and he drew back to arm's length to look at her, supple and tall, with slim hips and legs, and the lift of her young breasts showing under her white sweater; with a white beret on her black hair and the scarlet cluster of madrone berries close to the scarlet of her lips and cheeks.

"Cynthia, if it means unhappiness for you!"

"It won't! Why, this much," she argued, gayly, "is sheer gain, isn't it? It's ecstasy—it's heaven!"

"But there may be breakers ahead."

"We'll swim them!"

"You're wonderful!" he repeated, for good-bye. Cynthia stretched up on tiptoe for one more childish kiss against his hard brown cheek, and felt the breath once more squeezed from her body before she ran down the half-mile of hill between her and the reproachful luncheon table.

Her father must have been particularly outrageous, for Gray said gently to her afterward that Papa was nervous today and that Cynthia had been a darling not to blaze back at him. But of what her father had said or why she was being praised, Cynthia had not the faintest idea. She was floating far above the earth on a plane of celestial azure.

And now the magic went on, only with a new rapture. Guy, very brown and serious and handsome, came down to dinner, and he and Papa talked through the meal about disarmament. But it didn't matter. Cynthia giggled with her two

younger sisters about their sudden passion for mail catalogues, and was quite content. Leslie had one tremendous
tome and Lucia another, and they sent almost every other
day for some trifle or another and compared results with
much feeling.

Afterward they talked idly before the fire, and finally
played anagrams. Guy, paying no attention to Cynthia, took
"lung" from Lucia with an "r," lost it to Papa, took "ruling"
from Papa with a "g" and an "e." But Cynthia had no misgivings, and when Leslie said, "Grueling! You're just too
smart, Guy," she had only to look at him and to catch his
unsmiling, answering look, to be just as happy as she had
been this morning, up on the mountain, as happy as if they
two had been alone.

When the game was over, and they were all talking, Leslie
standing by the fire, too tired and cold, she herself said, to
make the effort to go to bed; when Lucia had departed
kitchenward with hot-water bottles, and Papa was smoking
benignly—then Guy and Cynthia lingered at the game table,
and Guy spelled out, "I love you," in the little yellow card-
boards, and Cynthia, laying her warm brown hand over them
for a moment, as if it were his hand she touched with a
caress, spelled in answer, "As I you, Guy."

"Anyone suspect?" he ranged the letters to ask.

She fumbled lazily in the heap; stacked them, tumbled
them over, spoke casually to Gray, who was sitting dreaming by the fire.

"Nobody," she spelled then.

Guy found the four letters for "must," and set it up under
the "nobody," and Cynthia gave him a look full of meaning
and understanding. She walked out to the porch with him
for a minute at about eleven, but it was bitterly cold out
there; she came back almost immediately and very decorously

set about straightening the room for the night, as she had done a thousand—two thousand—times before.

Pipe ashes and torn game papers and the San José evening paper to put into the fire, chairs to drag into their formal positions, the big center table to wipe with a duster, and the table runner and books and jar of flowers, which the anagrams had displaced, to set straight again. Books to go back into cases, rugs to jerk level with a quick, practised heel, and all the time Gray chattering quietly with Papa and Leslie moaning, "Oh, I'm so dead—I ought to be helping you, but I'm so dead!"

Old Mack, the garden man, always set up five small airtight stoves in the bedrooms early in November, each girl could have a fire whenever she chose to take the trouble to bring in wood and newspapers to start it. Winter nights were bitterly cold on the mountain, and toward Christmas time there was usually more than one morning when the girls awakened to find their world delicately powdered with snow. Sometimes, when he had to go down to San José for chicken wheat or rope or tools, Mack would stack the running boards of the truck with the fine, sweet, clean powder, and the children of the valley city would gather about to exclaim and delight in the sight of snow.

They always had a snow man on these occasions in the center of the lawn at Treehaven, and Cynthia would tint his cheeks with the red from an old paper lantern or Japanese napkin, and get a handful of oakum from the toolhouse to represent his flowing brown hair. There was always great screaming and running about in the snow, and little cakes of it would fall from their boots when they came panting in to the fire, and melt on the rugs and the oiled pine floor.

This year, to everyone's exultation and satisfaction, Christmas was snowy. Christmas fell upon Monday, and on the day before, when the four girls and Guy were high on the hillside gathering greens and berries, the first delicious, hesitant flakes began to fall from a low, warm, ominous sky.

"Mack *said* it was too warm for clearing and too cold for rain!" Leslie said, raising her face to catch the caress of the slowly drifting flakes.

"But can you believe that it's going to snow for Christmas!"

They came jumbling home, hot, excited, powdered by the now fast-falling miracle, stopping long enough at the work-shop to shout to their father that it was actually snowing.

"Shut that door!" Professor Trezavant shouted by way of answer, and, giggling, his daughters continued upon their way.

Christmas was a great feast with them, even though they had been raised without any religious education whatsoever. On the contrary, their father had been at great pains to keep their minds free from what he regarded as only a form of fear and superstition, and had read to them more than once as they grew up articles from his own pen entitled "The Christian Winter Saturnalia" and "The Creed of Fear," and other anti-creed articles from other pens even more force-ful in nature.

Despite all this, Gray had bravely joined the English Church in her high school days, and had been baptized and confirmed, and Lucia some years later had followed suit. But Leslie and Cynthia had remained outsiders; even while they regarded Papa as slightly maniacal on the subject and felt a certain tolerant interest in their sisters' religious experi-ences.

And at Christmas time, without any superfluous scruples about consistency, they united in enthusiasm for filling stock-ings, decorating the house with wreaths and branches of scented evergreen, seeking and felling and trimming their own tree, exchanging presents, preparing the traditional feast of turkey and pudding and pies.

Even Papa joined in these rites, invariably going into town for a whole day and a night just before Christmas and getting each girl presents exactly like her sisters'. They were fine presents too; Papa in material, tangible ways, was generosity itself. A five-dollar bottle of perfume apiece; a subscription to a favorite magazine; an order for slippers; handkerchiefs, fur scarfs.

Two of the girls always went with him into town and stayed at a hotel and saw a play, and the two remaining girls went in by themselves a day or two later or earlier.

Gray, having allowed it to be suspected that her presents for her sisters this year were to be charming new wastebaskets all around, Javanese baskets she had happened to discover in a specialty shop, was surreptitiously at work upon fascinating pajamas of Chinese silk in exquisite shades of prune blue, peacock, lemon, apple green. Cynthia was giving everyone Dedham bowls, with rabbits and turkeys strutting about them; Papa was to have one for his favorite dessert of peeled white figs, Guy an immense one for salads, and the girls others of various sizes. Leslie, with a moaning commentary upon her own poverty and lack of imagination, had made some selection unknown, and Lucia, who upon her eighteenth birthday had come in for Aunt Lucia's long-awaited four thousand, was plunging madly and secretly upon a moving-picture camera and screen and projector that should be enjoyed by everyone alike.

Then there were Guy's presents, always exciting, and presents for Hing and Mack, and for the dogs, and fascinating little boxes in the mail from old school friends and far-away cousins. Altogether, Christmas was a happy time, and whether it was because there was something of the Victorian era he so loved in this home feast, these days of garlanding and cooking and surprises, or whether some of the supernatural grace of it crept into his heart in spite of himself, Professor Trezavant was usually quite unwontedly bland and agreeable at this time too, and so did more than his share to make it a success.

This year, among the thrills, was a great box of German honey and almond cakes from Dr. Frank Ainsworth, delightful ridiculous cakes made into men and rabbits, tins full of hard little sharp *Pfefferniisse,* rich sticky cakes stuffed with nuts and raisins and wrapped wetly in silver paper, and cookies so plain that they were like shortbread. Flatly wrapped, in four small packages on the top of the cakes, were four chiffon handkerchiefs edged with lace: flesh-colored, orange, pink, black. And on Frank's card he had written "To the four sweetest sisters I ever knew. Merry Christmas! And mayn't I have a photograph?"

The photograph they had had taken in the fall; Dana had had a copy, and it must have been Dana's copy that Frank had seen. Dana had acknowledged it with a charming, impersonal letter.

They had opened the box of German cakes because it had been marked "perishable"; everything else must wait, of course, until Christmas morning. But that Frank had thought of them, and so charmingly, and that he had called them the four sweetest sisters he had ever known, was enough to add great glory to their Christmas. Cynthia wondered if it meant to Gray what it instantly had signified to her: that the two doctors who had been their guests last summer were thinking of them in far-away Boston, and that Dana's box and greeting were on their way too.

Cynthia had suggested the taking of the photograph, knowing in her secret soul, from her own experience where Guy was concerned, that Gray must be heartsick to establish some sort of contact with Dana. They had all driven into

San Francisco together to have it taken, and had lunched at a hotel and seen a movie afterward in great spirits. And when the proofs had come home the only difficulty had been to select the best from a dozen that were good.

Cynthia had seen to it that the one they finally selected was fine of Gray. Gray, in the plain little pleated chiffon with the real lace collar, had been seated in a great carved oak chair, with Leslie on the arm of it looking down at the book that was open on Gray's lap. Cynthia was on a hassock on the other side, and Lucia half kneeling beside Leslie, her fingers linked carelessly in Cynthia's on Gray's knee.

There were other proofs more flattering of the three younger sisters, and Leslie had been quite insistent upon choosing one in which Gray's face was not good at all. But Cynthia had managed to draw Leslie out to the Galleria to say urgently, "We're going to send it to Dana, you know, Les, so let's take the one where Gray has that wonderful look?" And Leslie, like the loyal sister she was, had at once agreed.

"I wish he would send us his picture!" Gray had said innocently, as they sent the finished photograph off. The others had not dared look at each other.

But now that this tribute had come from Frank Ainsworth, they were all secretly confident that Dana would send Christmas greetings and gifts too, and Cynthia knew that that was all that was needed to make the day perfect for Gray.

Their procedure was always the same. Each member of the family had a table, and upon this table his gifts were arranged by the others late in the evening of Christmas Eve, each table being finally covered with a sheet.

When this was done, the tree was trimmed. Then every shred of dropped tinsel and every scrap of tissue paper and string and cardboard was burned in the fire, and the decorated, pine-scented room, around which the grotesque forms

of the gift tables stood so strangely, was left to the last
flicker of the firelight and the steady encroachment of cold
from the bitter black night outside. The girls scattered to
their rooms to build fires, to scrub weary, stiffened hands in
hot water, and to exchange anticipatory remarks about the
morrow.

Then a few hours of silence descended upon the hill, to be
shattered by the cocks and the cows in the early morning,
the slamming of doors and rushing of faucet water as Hing
took possession of his kitchen, and finally by the whirring of
Gray's alarm clock at eight o'clock.

Before nine they had breakfasted, and then the excitement
of unwrapping presents began, and the chorus of excited and
delighted exclamations.

It had always seemed the very pinnacle of ecstasy and fun
to Cynthia; this year, to her secret concern, she felt a little
differently about it. It was just a little flat, if very sweet
and pleasant, to buy things for one another, and be mysterious and humorous about them, and then to open them up
with appreciative and amazed exclamations.

"Oh, Leslie, oh, you *darling* . . . oh, Gray, you liar!
When we thought all along it was the wastebaskets! . . .
Oh, *Papa*—what a beauty!"

It was always the same. It had been the same for all the
Christmases she had ever known. This year she felt a little
aloof from it, a little apart. The tremendous swelling and
surging of joy in her heart had nothing to do with tissue-
paper wrappers and scarlet ribbons. No present could make
her forget the joy of Guy's love even for a minute; no
present could have solaced her if it had been taken away.
Already Cynthia felt years older than her sisters—years older
even than Gray, who was wistfully hoping for any message
from Dana. Burning on Cynthia's lips now was the consciousness of Guy's kisses, and ringing in her ears were his

words—those sweet and stolen words that echoed in her heart and soul all day long and half through the night.

Guy came down at about ten o'clock in the midst of the merry scramble, and they welcomed him joyfully and displayed for his benefit all their new treasures, as they had done for all the Christmases past.

Guy in his turn had to thank them for all sorts of things. He subsided into his new Christmas chair with his pipe before the wrappers were half opened, and watched the four sisters as they circled to and fro, trying on scarfs, sampling candy, glancing into new books with eager anticipation, heaping one possession on another—perfume, slippers, delicate pink lingerie run with silver and lavender ribbons, gay pajamas all stripes and bars.

Meanwhile the scent of roasting turkey began gradually to permeate the atmosphere, for in winter the Galleria was glassed and became part of the house. At twelve o'clock Guy suddenly started up with an exclamation.

"Listen, do we walk?"

"Do we walk?" they echoed, reproachfully. Of course they would walk. They always walked after breakfast on Christmas Day to get perfectly ravenous for the five o'clock dinner. There was to be no lunch.

Lucia and Leslie had by this time set a festive table with the water glasses ready to fill and the red candles ready to light. Gray and Cynthia had made many trips to the kitchen; everything was in readiness.

So it only remained to carry their great armfuls of gifts into their rooms and scramble into heavy outdoor clothing. Then they were out in the snow under a cold gray sky, walking at a good pace along the Woodcutter's Road that lay like a shelf about the mountain.

The air was soft and pure and sweet; the snow had crusted under foot in the night, but it was softening now, and when, at the end of their tramp, they saw the sun struggling like a great muffled orange through the heavy wall of gray in the west, and saw the pink shafts of light lying across the whiteness, they knew that they were looking their last on the beauty of the snow. Tomorrow would be fair, and by noon the wet brown earth would be showing through the orchards again.

At four o'clock they reëntered the house that smelled so warmly of wood smoke and evergreen and roasting meat and violets, and dispersed for hot baths and resting and the achievement of great dressing for dinner.

Cynthia was the first to come out of her room at about ten minutes to five, the soft lines of a new lace dress falling about her. She had time to see that Guy was stretched comfortably in his new great leather chair by the fire, and to think that the room was lovely in firelight and dull lamplight, with the glimmer of red and silver ornaments on the tree in the corner, when something in her father's voice checked the dancing of her blood, and made her feel a moment's chill—a moment's fright.

"Look here, Cynthia—Mack brought this up with the mail an hour ago," Professor Trezavant said.

He handed her a stiff double sheet of paper; Cynthia took it into her hands, glanced expectantly at him, and stooped beside the lamp to let the light fall on the paper.

She straightened up. Guy was watching her.

"I don't believe it!" she said, in a frightened tone.

"What is it?" Leslie asked, coming out to join them, and impressed by their rather unnatural aspect. Crowding up against Cynthia, she read it, as Cynthia read it for a second time.

Engraved upon heavy paper were the following words:

"Mr. and Mrs. Cyrus Appleby Slocum announce the marriage of their granddaughter, Ursula, to Doctor Clement

Dana Illyan, Junior. Boston, Monday, December eighteenth."

"Oh, *gosh!*" Leslie ejaculated, in an incredulous whisper. She and Cynthia, young faces as smooth as ivory and almost as pale in the keen lamplight, exchanged horrified glances. Lucia, coming out, a vision in blue, had only time to ask confusedly what was the matter, when Cynthia caught up the announcement and with a swift "Wait a minute!" went toward Gray's door, opened it, and disappeared within.

"She's gone to tell her; isn't that like Cyn!" Leslie whispered.

"But what *is* it?" Lucia continued to demand pathetically.

CHAPTER EIGHT

GRAY, before her mirror, was putting the last touches to the soft ripples of her fair hair. In a black lace gown she was at her loveliest; she was smiling at her own reflection, happy in some serene thought. Cynthia, entering her room unceremoniously, sat down, breathing rather heavily, at the dressing table.

"Am I late?" Gray asked, surprised.

"No—it's not five, quite. Gray," Cynthia rushed on, not knowing what to say, or indeed what she was saying, "Papa had a—a card from the Illyans——"

Gray smiled into the mirror.

"Well, I rather *thought* we would have some word!"

"Listen," Cynthia said desperately, "he's married! He was married last Monday."

There was a silence. Gray's slender fine hand with the ivory brush in it fell with a little crash to the table, lay still.

"Dana?" Gray asked after a while, clearing her throat, speaking in a shadow of her own voice.

"I didn't believe it, Gray—but it's there, engraved. To some Miss Slocum——"

"Ursula Slocum," Gray said, like a woman in a dream. She moved her hands restlessly, fluttered them over her dressing table, not meeting Cynthia's eye. "He talked of her. She's Cousin Clement's ward," she said, cheerfully, tremblingly.

She was motionless for a second, while Cynthia in her

holiday finery sat watching her in the mirror. Then suddenly Gray gave a little groan and, putting both elbows on the dressing table, buried her face in her hands.

"Oh, my God, my God, he can't have done that!"

"Gray, don't!" Cynthia could only plead. "Please, Gray, they'll all know. You've got to pull yourself together; you've got to come out—they'll all know! *Please*, Gray—you can cry all night if you want to——"

"Oh, my *God!*" Gray murmured.

Cynthia sat helpless beside her, in a very panic of sympathy, frantic to find the words that would steel her for the ordeal of this Christmas dinner, but quite unable to think coherently. The moments flew by, and Gray did not stir.

"Gray, shall I tell them that you don't want any dinner?"

Gray suddenly looked up, smiled at Cynthia with a very pale face and haggard eyes, began to powder her nose.

"No, I'll come out," she said quietly, very busy.

"You're a sport!" Cynthia said, in fervent sympathy.

"A sport!" Gray echoed the word ruefully, laid her hand for one instant's pressure on Cynthia's. "*You're* the sport!" she said.

For a moment as she stood up it seemed as if she must break. She wavered a little and whispered, "Cynthia——"

But immediately she recovered control of herself, and the two sisters went out to the fire together.

The big room was still mercifully dim. The group at the fireside scattered as they came out; everyone was very casual and kindly.

"What do you *think* of Dana!" Gray asked, sitting down, her tone only normally surprised.

"'Strawdinary!" Professor Trezavant commented, in disgust.

The sisters rushed eagerly into the breach. The matter was discussed with just the right, affectionate note of criticism. He should have written them before this; he should have written them now. It was all perfectly legitimate, but it didn't seem like Dana not to confide in them.

"D'you s'pose he was engaged when he was here?" Lucia asked.

"I really think he may have been," Gray answered, with an air of casual thoughtfulness. But Cynthia saw the sick trembling of her hands. "He did talk of Ursula. She's quite delicate, if I haven't got her mixed with someone else, and the only relatives she has are a very aged grandfather and grandmother."

"May have been some old family arrangement!" Guy suggested comfortably, from his chair in the shadows.

"I think it was something like that," Gray said, gratefully.

They all went out to dinner; Cynthia felt jarred, weak, as if she were recovering from a long illness. She imagined they all felt so. Everybody did much cheerful, eager talking; even Papa, Cynthia was rather touched to note, was making a special effort to keep the conversation moving.

But it was no use. The shock of the news from Dana had ruined all the Christmas peace and plenty; their laughter was unnatural, and their talk fitful and inconsequential. Whatever they said seemed, by some fatality, to touch upon broken hearts, disappointments in love, old maids, faithless men; Cynthia was hardly conscious of what she was eating or saying, and she knew Gray was in the same state.

Gray fought on gallantly and joined in the talk and games at the fireside later. They played "Geography" with "B" for their letter, and it was Gray who quietly contributed "Boston" when her turn came. They played "Book Persons" with an "H," and somebody must needs think of Miss Havisham. "Don't you remember, Papa? The terrible old woman in

Great Expectations, whose young man had left her on their wedding day, and who sat in the ruins of the cake and the veil for the rest of her life?"

They played anagrams, and it seemed to Cynthia that such words as "jilt," "left," "bride," "wed," were the only words they could find tonight. Perhaps the others felt the strain as she did; anyway, they shortly abandoned all games and sat quietly talking, with the candles on the Christmas tree flickering, and the bulkier Christmas gifts—Leslie's china tea set, and the movie machinery, and the big hempen hammock one of Papa's old coffee associates had sent from Manila—still in their places on the gift tables.

Guy sat in his new red morocco chair; he could not say enough about it. All four girls had combined resources to buy it for him, and they were as delighted as he with his enjoyment of it. And he had had his picture too; with tremendous care they had kept the secret of the photographs from him and from Papa until today, and the two men had studied them and compared them endlessly; this one with Leslie so splendid; that one the best of Lucia and Gray.

"But I *can't* get over Dana being married!" Leslie said more than once, during the silences of the evening. The subject was always there, close below the surface.

"No, can you?" Lucia would respond, unwillingly, apologetically, with a fearful glance at Gray.

After a little while Gray said her head ached; stupidly she had lain down without a cover this afternoon, and she fancied she had gotten a little cold. She went off to bed, Lucia drifting in with her to talk during the process of undressing. Leslie, gathering new books in her arms, went off; Papa and Cynthia and Guy remained in the dim light of the fire—talking, talking, talking.

"I'm going up to my cabin," Professor Trezavant

presently said. "I hardly looked at my mail. The first thing I happened to open was Dana's announcement, and I brought it right down."

He glanced cautiously at Gray's door; it was closed.

"I confess that it amazed me," he added, in a cautious undertone.

"I never want to see Dana again," Cynthia said, evenly.

"Think——" Her father again spoke cautiously. "D'you think your sister is hard hit?"

"Terribly!" Cynthia answered briefly.

"I'm sorry," her father said, with a shake of his head and a sigh. He went away, closing the Galleria door carefully behind him. Cynthia and Guy could feel the cool breath of air that rushed in.

"Papa is very nice about this," she said to Guy in an undertone when they were alone.

"He really loves you all," Guy told her, as he had told her many times before, in moments when she had lost patience with her father.

"I suppose he does. But he's so stiff, he's so queer, he makes such difficulties. It was so unusual," Cynthia said, "to have Dana right here with us. It won't happen again—no such luck! We don't have the—the normal social contacts, like other girls. And she was so happy!"

"There'll be somebody else," Guy suggested, rather forlornly. Big and dark and troubled, with his handsome mouth very serious under its line of black mustache, he looked across at Cynthia, with the firelight shining in her eyes and the rich red leather of his big new chair making a background for her lacy gown and her gypsy beauty.

"Not for Gray." They were silent awhile. Then, "Oh, Guy," she said, suddenly recollecting, "I have another little present for you. The girls know I have—Gray has one like it. But you needn't—necessarily—mention it to Papa."

She went to the old desk that had been her mother's, drew open a deep drawer, and took from it in a large pasteboard folder a dozen proofs and photographs. Selecting one of these, she brought it across the room and put it into Guy's hand. He had gotten to his feet to take it.

He looked at it, laid it aside, covered his eyes with his brown hands.

"My God! My little sweetheart!" he whispered.

"Do you like it?" the girl asked, laughing, leaning against his shoulder as he studied it again.

"Like it! It's *you!*"

"I think it's good," she said.

"He took singles of us all, just a few," she explained, "and he got a good one of nearly all of us—Gray's weren't so good, but Lucia's was lovely. We're saving them for Papa's birthday in February. But you can have yours now if you won't let him see it for six weeks."

"There is nothing—nothing in the world that could mean to me what this means," Guy said, absorbed in the picture again.

It was Cynthia's self at twenty-two, this representation of a tall girl with firm, uplifted breasts and rounded brown arms, straight, splendid body, brushed and ordered curly dark hair, and seriously raised eyes fringed with heavy lashes. The film of hair against her low forehead, the tip of the cleft chin, the slender beauty of the locked brown fingers —these were Cynthia, and Guy, looking from the photograph to the living model and back again, might have been hard pressed at the moment to say which one he found the lovelier.

"Sit down," he said, concealing the photograph by laying it with the other, and wrapping both in the tissue paper that had wrapped his first gift. "I want to speak to you."

She sat down, again in the red leather chair in which she

could lean forward, hands linked between her knees. Guy leaned forward too; their heads were close together.

"Have you been thinking, Cynthia?"

Her quick look went about the doors of the house; all were tightly sealed. They could hear Leslie and Lucia murmuring in Leslie's room.

"Have I not!" she exclaimed, with a rueful smile.

"About our talk today in the snow?"

"Every second, since. That, and Dana's news, have made me feel as if I were dreaming—have made me feel—lightheaded," Cynthia said.

"Will you think about it, dear?"

Her beautiful blue eyes, round and young, like the eyes of a child, wandered over him wistfully.

"It isn't so much thinking as feeling, Guy. For myself," Cynthia murmured, "I would not hesitate a second. Better women than I, in this—this fix, this situation—have taken the law into their own hands!

"But what makes it impossible is the others, Guy," she went on, with a motion of her dark head that indicated the closed doors. "It would kill them. It simply wouldn't be possible. Papa would come up to the Little Quito and shoot you, for one thing. The girls would break their hearts. To them it would seem disgrace."

He looked at her gravely, looked down at his linked hands again.

"But not to you?"

"No, not to me."

"Does it matter, then, what they think?"

Cynthia considered this. At twenty-one she had been only one girl in a group of four inexperienced sisters; tonight the slow changes that the year had brought to her mind and soul seemed actually visible to Guy; it was a balanced, wise, serious-eyed woman who was facing him in the Christmas firelight.

"Yes," she said. "I think it matters what they think."

"You're quite right!" Guy muttered after a moment.

"It would be quite different, you know, if we lived in a city," Cynthia began again after a minute. "If you had a studio there and I were a detached person, writing or painting."

"You think it would be quite different?"

"Yes. It would be nobody's affair but our own."

"The—the unconventionality of it—the—what the world would call the immorality of it wouldn't bother you?"

"No," she said, and looked at the fire. "No," Cynthia added, glancing up, formulating her thought slowly, "because it wouldn't *be* immoral. It wouldn't compare—in immorality—to marriages that are taking place every day of the year in churches!"

"I agree with you," Guy said promptly.

"To the world," Cynthia resumed, speaking as if she were merely thinking aloud, her eyes on the fire, "to the world, it would be quite moral for you to divorce poor Rhoda, set her adrift, and marry me. There would be no criticism of that! I believe I could even talk Papa into countenancing *that*."

"It would be to take away the last prop she has," Guy said slowly.

"It would be to murder her, if she ever got well enough to appreciate what had happened," Cynthia admitted somberly. "It would mean that while you were married to me, you still felt it your duty, about every ten days, to go over to visit this poor woman who is your wife and to do everything you could to help her regain her sanity."

"Impossible!" he said, shaking his head.

"Impossible. And yet, it's equally impossible," Cynthia

went on—"it's equally impossible for me to call them all out
of their rooms tonight and take your hand here and say,
'We love each other. We cannot marry because of Rhoda.
But this is our marriage—now—with all of you as wit-
nesses, for better or worse——' "

Her throat thickened. She saw darts and arrows of fire
through her sudden tears.

"Why can't we, Cynthia?" Guy asked, very low. "You'd
never be sorry, dear. I'd make you the happiest, the most
loved woman in the world. After a few years of it—after a
few years in heaven, we'd be taken for granted——"

"Not yet!" she said. "Not for a hundred years."

"But after all, isn't it the spirit of the thing, Cynthia? Is
the letter so important?"

"It seems to be. I know this," Cynthia said. "Papa would
cut me off; he'd never speak to me again. Well,"—she smiled
her little-girl smile—"I could stand that! But he would forbid the girls to speak to me. My whole life would be cut in
two.

"Perhaps I could stand that too, Guy, if you and I could
have the Little Quito to ourselves. Breakfasts out under the
oak, reading by the fire, walks, picnics—and children some
day, lots of them.

"But after a while you'd be sorry—you'd be sorry for me
and for yourself. After a while you'd resent the fact that I
wasn't—wasn't like other wives——"

"Bosh!" he interpolated as she hesitated. "Mid-Victorian
rubbish! This isn't a story by Trollope!"

"After a while," Cynthia pursued steadily, "you'd be sorry
for our little girls. The minute anyone heard the name
'Waring' there'd be questions—eyebrows up. 'Wasn't there
something irregular—something all wrong . . . ? Wasn't
his first wife Rhoda Wilcox, and didn't she lose her mind or
something?'

"George Eliot tried to get away with it and couldn't," Cynthia summarized it, "and she was a genius. It's the one thing people won't forget. We wouldn't ever have friends— ever have a circle——"

"We wouldn't need one!"

"We think we wouldn't now. But if Les married, or Lucia married, there'd have to be explanations—and even if their young men didn't mind, their young men's families might. 'Her sister is the woman who lives with Guy Waring, the artist'——"

"Oh, shut up!" Guy said.

"It would be true."

He ground his big palms together, scowling at the fire.

"I could never think of you like that, Cynthia."

"I know you wouldn't. I'm not speaking of *you*."

"I think of you as the most wonderful, the loveliest——" Guy made a gesture of despair with both his hands. "I think of the happiness we have to throw away—with youth and love and the years," he said. "One day of it—you up there — my wife——"

"I *would* be your wife," Cynthia said, in a voice that trembled. "I would feel myself so. With Rhoda as she is—as she has been, for eight years and more—I wouldn't be taking anyone's place. And with you and me bound to each other by promises, by love and faith—by children—I wouldn't be afraid."

There was a long silence.

"Only," Cynthia began again, presently, "as things are now, it would be impossible. I couldn't go up to the Little Quito in cold blood; I couldn't just say cheerfully to the girls, 'Come up and see us in a day or two!' Papa would begin to rant, like some old Scotch minister, about dastards and the unwritten law and his daughter's honor.

"Honor!" She repeated the word with a little scornful

laugh. "What's honor in your actual body compared to the honor in your soul? And in my soul and mind I'm yours, Guy, as much as I can ever be. I'm bound to you as much tonight, when you've never done more than kiss me, as truly as if we had been man and wife a dozen years!"

She stood up; the splendid figure of a woman, aureoled by the firelight.

"And time will go by," she said steadily, "and we'll grow older—you lonely up there and I lonely down here, and Rhoda wandering happily about among her flowers over at Livermore—and that'll be the end of it all!"

Guy, standing too, looked down at her and said nothing.

"And all because, for business reasons—for the protection of property, men have made laws that say that a justice of the peace—a sea captain—anybody!—must give men and women permission to love each other.

"Oh, it's different, Guy," she went on impatiently, "when religion comes in, when people think marriage is a holy thing —a Sacrament. I can see that! I can understand that. But when it's just a legal public contract——

"I wish," she whispered, close to him for a second, clinging to him for a second—"I wish I had some religion. I wish I believed that God had anything to do with what you and I do—that He cared!

"I wish my mother were here!"

He kissed her forehead, where the fine black hair was loosened into a silky film, and felt her breast rise in one quick sob. Then she was gone, and he had the familiar sitting room and the long-extinguished tree and the firelight to himself.

Much later, when Guy had gone home, and Professor Trezavant, after seeing the guest out into the cold Christmas night, had himself gone to bed, and when Leslie and Lucia

were long asleep, Gray crossed the dark, scented sitting room,
and entered Cynthia's door.

"Cyn, awake?"

"Oh—— Oh, yes. What is it? Is that you, Gray? Someone sick?" Cynthia started up, alarmed, in the cold winter
moonlight.

"Cyn, I feel so rotten," faltered Gray, trying not to cry,
trying to smile, "what with this cold—and my eyes hurting—— I wondered if you'd come across and sleep in my
room?"

"Why, Gray, of course I will, darling." Cynthia, her eyes
blinking in the light, put her feet to the floor and reached
for slippers. "Goodness, it's cold!" she murmured, not meeting her sister's eyes.

Gray sat forlornly on the foot of the bed. Her soft hair
hung loosely on her neck, and her eyes were infinitely weary.

"You'd be such an angel if you would!"

"You ought to have waked me before. Haven't you been
asleep?"

"Maybe I have," Gray admitted meekly, as they trailed
their way across the house again. The younger sister carried
her bedding with her, and Gray helped smooth it and make
it into a comfortable bed on the couch in her room.

Then Cynthia stuffed newspapers into the little stove, piled
in kindling, and placed one or two stocky, dry madrone logs
on top. Within two minutes there was a heartening crackle
from the stove, and the atmosphere of the room began instantly to soften.

"It's freezing in here, you idiot! No wonder you couldn't
sleep."

"I had to have someone to talk to," Gray said, with a
long sigh.

Cynthia squared the couch about, so that her feet would
be toward Gray's head, and they could face each other. She

lighted a low bedside lamp, established herself snugly in comforters and pillows.

"The more I think of it," she said, in a low but casually conversational tone, "the more sure I am that something happened."

"To Dana?" Gray asked.

"Yes. I'm convinced—is your hot-water bottle really warm?—I'm convinced," Cynthia pursued, "that either this was an impulse—he just let himself in for an elopement or something——"

"But that isn't like Dana."

Gray was trembling visibly, and her color had faded to an almost alarming pallor, but Cynthia knew from her voice that it was a relief to her heart to talk about it.

"Exactly! Perhaps she rushed him. Or perhaps, being an orphan, and his father's ward, she's been in love with him all her life," Cynthia offered.

"But not to write—*me*," Gray murmured.

"I know. That's the very thing. Gray, Dana was crazy about you—we all saw that. Whatever he's done, or whatever he feels now, he was *crazy* about you."

Gray's thoughtful eyes were fixed on space.

"That's what I want to think," she whispered. "I—I like him so much!"

"I'd like to give him a good kick!" Cynthia, from her luxuriously warm nest, said with spirit, and she was rewarded by seeing Gray laugh forlornly.

The room was comfortable now and getting warmer steadily; outside they could hear branches snap in the frosty night, and once an owl called drearily, and was still, and called again.

"This time last year I hadn't met him," Gray said, staunchly.

Cynthia was reading; she glanced up.

"It's a shock," she said. "But we're always theorizing, we four, about how smart we'd be in crises—we'd meet misfortune bravely, we'd 'welcome each rebuff that turns earth's smoothness rough.' "

"I know," Gray murmured meekly, rebuked.

"And this is a case of just having to take it on the chin, Gray," the younger sister went on. She half closed her book, looked seriously across at Gray. "I'm taking it on the chin," she said, soberly.

There was an electric silence; they looked at each other.

"I know you are, Cyn."

"No out," Cynthia said, simply.

Gray considered this.

"I suppose not."

"Rhoda'll live forever."

"They always do," Gray conceded.

"He can't throw her down, and I," Cynthia recommenced, cynically—"I, having no code whatsoever, will have to be true to my code—and there you have it!"

"I hate to hear you say you have no code, Cyn."

"Well, have I?"

"Of course you have! You wouldn't steal, you wouldn't lie——"

"I can see the sense in all that," Cynthia said, shifting in her pillows.

"But you can't see the sense in a girl going straight?"

"No, not when she loves a man. Look, Gray," Cynthia argued, "a girl in my position only meets so many men. Lots of girls don't have much chance to meet men. Out of the few a girl like me *does* meet, she's lucky enough to find one she loves. Yes, *loves*—and for some types of women that doesn't happen very often! Technically he's not free— actually he's the loneliest man in the world. Technically he's

married, but really—really there is no one who could be
hurt by anything he did!

"To push away the woman who loves him, force her to be
lonely, break his own heart and do nobody any good—that's
going straight. What's the *sense* of it?"

"That may seem to be the sense of it in this particular case,
Cyn, but I think there are robberies—forgeries—murders
—for which you could find excuses as good as that!"

"I envy people now," Cynthia said, in a voice of pain,
"who have a code to hang on to. Just to say 'This is what
I ought to do, and this is what I can do, and must do!' would
help so much."

"Papa would never forgive you."

"That," the younger girl said wearily, "wouldn't matter."

"But what do you think of, Cyn? What would you do if
you could?" Gray asked anxiously. "Would Guy get a
divorce?"

"How could he? Rhoda might get well, and she hasn't
another friend or relative in the world. What could she do?"

"She won't get well."

"Ah, but she might."

Gray considered this a minute.

"Then what will happen, Cyn?"

"Nothing," Cynthia answered, steadily.

"But can you stand it?"

To this the younger sister countered, "Can you?"

"Well, I haven't been seeing him every day or two," Gray
said. "And then, he doesn't—care about me."

The gentleness, the forlornness of it, made Cynthia's
throat thicken.

"Delightful to be grown women and falling in love!" she
observed ironically.

"Oh, isn't it different from what we always thought!"
Gray exclaimed desperately.

"It seems to me so unfair, Gray. If we were men we could go out into the world, forget all this in work. We could make friends and perhaps find other girls we liked— and if we did find them, ask them to marry us. Being girls, we have to sit back and wait—it's all chance, all luck, with us. We have no more to say about our own destinies than Turkish women in harems!"

It was an old argument; it had been a familiar one for many years among the sisters. But for the first time tonight Gray could seem to find no counter contention; she lay silent for a while, thinking. Then, Cynthia noted gratefully, her lids began to flicker, and she turned drowsily on one side and jerked her pillow under her cheek in a way that had meant sleepiness in Gray as long as Cynthia could remember anything.

The younger sister dared not rustle a page of her book for a long space. But after a few minutes Gray's regular breathing showed that she really was asleep, and then Cynthia could turn out her light stealthily, and snuggle down in her blankets herself for sleeping and waking dreams.

CHAPTER NINE

AND suddenly it was a cold, dark Tuesday morning, and all the warmth and emotion and glory seemed to have departed from the world, with the holiday.

The tree still stood, to be sure, when Cynthia, carrying her bedding, limped across the Cabin at half-past seven, to regain her own room before her sisters should awaken, but the big place looked disorderly and deserted in spite of their efforts to clean it last night. Scraps of tinsel and ribbons, corners of dust and wood chips, the frilled brown cases of chocolates and the wrappers of caramels were here and there, and the closed doors had kept in air that was heavy and close. The windows had sweated, and their casement panes were crossed with runnels; the stale air was cold; the violets were dead.

Cynthia felt chilled and weary. The world was all awry this morning. Her room, with its demolished bed, was cold and disorderly, and the tardy sun, just beginning to send its rays across the fringes of patchy snow and the beaded frosts of the shabby winter garden, seemed to make the outdoor world look colder rather than warmer.

She splashed icy water into her flushed face, wishing savagely that she could resist the temptation to eat candy at night; she ran a comb through her smoky waves of hair and slipped into a sensible warm jersey dress that demanded but the tying of silk cords and the buckling of a belt to be secure. Yawning wearily, she attacked the room, presently to hear Lucia's voice from the bath that connected their rooms:

"Cynthia, take a bath?"

"I did not!"

"Talk about the circumpolar regions, however you pronounce it!" Lucia moaned. They had been discussing the word a day or two before.

"It's awful!"

"Do you suppose Gray slept at all?" Lucia asked, introducing herself and her quilted wrapper into the room by a series of writhing twists of her body, and curling down in the disordered heap of blankets for a few more moments of half comfort.

"I was in there with her."

"You *were?*"

"We talked until about one. Yes, she slept after that."

Lucia's eyes were bright with concern.

"She's taking it awfully hard, isn't she, Cyn?"

"Well, you know Gray." Cynthia was struggling with the airtight stove; she did not look at her sister. "It isn't only—Dana," she said. And to the fire she added savagely, "Oh, go *out,* then! —It's that she has always been—sort of thinking," Cynthia continued, "that things would happen like that. That handsome young Boston doctors would come out of the woods like bears, and want to marry us. She believed in Dana, she knew he liked her, and she couldn't see anything else to it. I don't think—I don't *think,*" Cynthia pursued, "that Dana had—waked Gray up, if you know what I mean."

"Petting, and soul kisses, and all that!" Lucia supplied intelligently, as Cynthia paused.

"Well—something like that. But they were—— This wood is wet," said Cynthia.

"All that wood Mack brought in from the upper shed seems to be wet. But that's burning, Cyn—it's caught. Hear it crackle!"

"That's the feeblest, sickest crackle I ever heard!" Cynthia said drearily. She straightened up, sighed, and looked at
her cold and sooty hands. "Dana and Gray were congenial,"
she went on. "They're of one cut. Dignified, honorable, intelligent, and all for home and code and family silver and
taking the children to England for the summer—see what I
mean? I think Gray saw herself in a brown traveling suit,
you know, kissing Papa good-bye, writing us all train letters . . ."

Curled at the foot of the bed, as Lucia was curled at its
head, with a blanket about her, Cynthia looked at her sister
seriously, and Lucia with an equally grave face could only
shake her head for reply.

The day dragged on; the weeks dragged on. Mornings and
evenings were bitterly cold; indeed, an all-day struggle with
the cold was continually in progress. The little stoves roared
as they devoured log after log of madrone and oak and bay;
the chill crept insidiously in at the windows and doors the
instant the stoves grew cool.

Nobody really thawed until after the hearty breakfast, the
steaming rolls and eggs and oatmeal, the smoking coffee.
Then for an hour or two the girls were fully occupied; they
were good housekeepers, they liked their work. And by ten
o'clock the sunshine was usually streaming in everywhere,
redwoods dripping, steam rising cheerfully from the lawn,
stables and farmyard all activity and life, and the whole
world bright.

Gray, Cynthia, Leslie, and Lucia cooked desserts, washed
their hair, their fountain pens, and their silk underwear and
stockings, pasted photographs in their books, took wet sunshiny walks and rainy walks, picnicked, heated great pots of
fat and made doughnuts, read books, memorized poems,
wrote letters. In February they all went into San Francisco
for a night of the unwonted excitement and luxury of opera,

steam-heated rooms, and breakfast upstairs. And on Washington's Birthday two officers came over from Benecia: Captain Hunter and Captain Ingraham. Captain Hunter was fat, jolly, and fifty; Captain Ingraham, who was young and handsome, liked the Trezavant girls so much that he told them a secret: he was going to marry a young widow, a girl he had loved all her life long, in June. He felt very happy about it, and the sisters congratulated him charmingly upon his future bliss.

In March they took a fancy to learn to knit, and each one got an outfit of needles and yarn and a big chintz bag. Gray worked purling out entirely by herself, and there was some excitement over learning to purl. And in early April the forlorn old dog who had been hanging about the place for months quite unexpectedly produced a small male puppy and died.

Cynthia, tramping about in the mud, trying to get tired —trying to stop thinking—trying to work off some of the restlessness that was like a madness upon her, chanced to be puttering in the stable when this event took place. She was a little frightened when the lean, shabby, suffering creature she had bedded in straw and was trying to soothe was seen to be feebly licking a struggling little wet body beside her. It was only an animal's birth after all, a thing commonplace and unimportant, but somehow it thrilled her to see the blind little mouthing creature where none had been a minute earlier, and she redoubled her praises and patting of poor derelict "Nelly," and drew the mother dog's attention afresh to a plate of bones and gravy.

But Nelly, instead, gave a long sigh and stretched herself at her full length. Cynthia, alarmed beyond all reason, lifted the limp, scarred head.

"Here, Nelly, doggy—here, eat something!"

It was no use. Nelly opened filmed eyes, stirred her torn

flag of a tail, gave Cynthia one look of confidence, and straightened herself again. And this time she moved no more.

Cynthia gathered the puppy, a small black curly puppy, to her heart.

"Oh, you poor little thing, you poor little darling! Oh, puppy, how shall I feed you?"

She dipped a finger in the congealed gravy. But the new puppy was not interested; he continued to whimper and to mouth about forlornly, sprawling out his little flippers of feet in every direction, nuzzling his mother's cooling body.

Cynthia carried him into the kitchen. He became the moment's great adventure. That he would lick milk from her fingertip, that within a week he would wriggle his whole warm little body ecstatically at the mere sight of her, that he was drowsy and content held against her cheek, her murmured baby talk in his ears, was a constant delight to her.

There were other dogs on the ranch. He was her dog. She named him Dobbin, observing to her scandalized sisters that it was a nice, original name for a dog. They called him "Dobbs."

It was impossible to be quite unhappy, to be quite pessimistic, with spring flooding the mountains and rioting in the garden, and Dobbs tumbling after her wherever she went.

If the March nights were still frosty and black, the March days were hot, up on the ranch. Skies were flawless now, and bees buzzed in the blossoming fruit trees. Grass was suddenly up, deep and sweet, in all the sheltered places; columbine and brown lilies and delicate cream iris speckled the hills. The wild lilac smoked against the dark foliage of the wood; the redwoods wore clean new fans of green on every spray; and buckeye bloom scented the still hot air, in which far-away cocks, crowing up at the Little Quito, could be heard down at Treehaven. On all sides, when the girls waded out into fields of poppies and buttercups, blue-eyed grasses and dark purple onion-flower, the larks rose with their sweet haunting cry. Dobbs, rolling in clock-grass, got himself so burred that his mistress had to spend an hour untangling the contented little fat body that was so pleased with these attentions.

In these days they could not find enough bowls and jars for the flowers. The tennis court was royally curtained in white and gold banksia roses; salmon-pink roses draped the porches. The Galleria was opened again, and sweet peas and honeysuckle roofed and walled it. Stock and nasturtiums, snowballs and bridal-wreath and lilac bordered the lawn; Gray's border pinks were fringed and spicy again; Lucia lovingly tended her little plot of red-tipped daisies. And the delphinium's blue and darker blue spikes, and the plumes of the phlox, and sweet-william and petunias and peonies and Shasta daisies and verbena were all on their way; the girls put on old linen coveralls and broad hats, and toiled away, hot and happy and busy, along the paths and down at the foot of the lawn.

Then they had croquet matches, with Papa and Leslie furious at each other over the middle wicket; and they had guests. Professor and Mrs. Wilkes brought a Princeton scientist and his wife up for a most successful luncheon, and Aunt Olivette, coming majestically through California on a trip around the world, with young Olive and Rachel and Rachel's new husband and Olive's governess, paid them a delightful visit.

Aunt Olivette was Boston personified, plain but impressive, as were her expensive garments and her calm talk of summers down at Buzzard's Bay; Pomfret schools for the boys; Europe for Olive next year. Contract bridge and the winter Symphony Society were Aunt Olivette's main interests; she eyed Gray keenly through strong glasses.

"Where's the 'Gray' come in, Cousin Thorwald?"

"My wife was Mary Gray, an English girl, Cousin Olivette."

"Of course! Well, which one was it that Cousin Sarah Baldwin's Dana wrote so much about?"

Not a quiver among the four white-frilled girls who were hostesses; who had served asparagus and sand-dabs and cherry pie so daintily.

"It was Gray, Aunt Olivette."

"I did all I could to land him!" Cynthia said, and there was a flutter of nervous laughter.

"He's married. I got the cards—where were we, Olive?"

"In Yokohama," said the governess in an undertone.

"In Yokohama, M'ma."

"Yes. I got the cards in Yokohama," stated Cousin Olivette. "Surprised me. We left Boston in September last year, but I certainly thought then that the boy had lost his heart to one of you out here! His mother would read me his letters. Wonderful boy, Dana. He had"—she eyed them all in turn—"he had a lung congestion; he got run down."

"I know," Gray said mildly.

When Aunt Olivette had gone away with the firm observation to Cousin Thorwald that he had the loveliest group of daughters she had ever seen anywhere—real old-fashioned gentlewomen, that was what they were—the three younger girls could talk it over. But guardedly, for Gray did not like to talk about Dana, and always looked tired and white when the conversation included any mention of him. They decided that his marriage certainly had been unpremeditated; Aunt Olivette knew his mother well, and she had not known about it!

Gray was twenty-five on May third; Cynthia had passed her twenty-third anniversary on Christmas Eve, but she always celebrated with Gray. Leslie was twenty-one on the tenth. Birthday celebrations caused a little ripple in May. And it was decided that they should all study German, Fräulein Zimmer came up from Stanford three times a week to get them started.

Fräulein Zimmer, twenty-eight and pimpled and strongly spectacled, was greasily radiant over her engagement to a young instructor in mathematics.

"End ve are hengagit, vis all singo!" exclaimed Fräulein Zimmer, beaming, "end ve don't hef doo hunnert amongst us that ve lif by! *Haben Sie je etwas so unsinniges gehört!*"

The Trezavants looked at her respectfully. She was engaged.

Guy had gone away in late April, to paint, in the Hopi country. He did not come back until early June. He sent them all postcards from various hot, desert-looking places, but there were no letters for the family, and addresses were vague.

The day he came back was hot and still. Cynthia had taken little Dobbs down to the center of the lawn to dry him after a bath, and was sitting on the grass when she saw the big figure in tweeds come out between the dark rich leaves of the laurels. Dobbs, already affronted and enraged, rolled unceremoniously from his towel as Cynthia got to her feet; she paid no attention to his whimpers.

She walked toward Guy, and they linked hands, looking steadily at each other, not speaking.

And for them both the beauty of the summer day, the scent and the dazzling colors of the flowers, the rich sweetness of the shadow against the wood, were all part of an almost unbearably beautiful hour.

There was a stone bench at the foot of the lawn; they sat down upon it, their hands still clasped.

"Guy, you're so brown. You look like an Indian!"

"I feel like an Indian. I've been living like one."

"Over six weeks, you know."

"I know. I've kept track!"

"I've kept track, too," the girl repeated, with a rueful smile.

"Lord, it's good to be home!" Guy said.

"It's so good to have you home!"

"Everything all right?"

"Fine. They're all," Cynthia said, with a vague gesture toward the house and the garden—"they're all around here somewhere. I didn't know you were coming, Guy," she said tamely, in a bad moment of silence.

"I know you didn't."

"Did Papa?" Cynthia heard her own words; they seemed devoid of meaning.

"Nobody did. I didn't myself. I suddenly—had to come."

The glorious midday heat of the garden pulsed and glowed about them; there was no scent now, there were no birds. The puppy had tumbled and circled his way to Cynthia's feet; now he stood still, braced and barking furiously before her.

"Who's that cross little beggar?"

"That's Dobbs. Shut up, Dobbsie! I wrote you about him," Cynthia said.

Her hands were free; she caught up the dog and presented him, held erect with his little paws dangling over her brown fingers.

"What letters!" Guy said.

"Did you like them?"

"Did you have any trouble with your post-office box?"

"No. Except that now and then I had to wait a chance to

get over to Santa Clara. I'd go when the girls were having their hair washed in San José—twice I went alone. Once I pretended to discover the post office, and said to Lucia, 'Oh, wait, I want an air-mail stamp!'"

"I wish you knew what those letters meant to me."

"I know what yours did to me. But every time I wrote you," Cynthia said, color suddenly showing under her transparent brown skin, "it was a compromise."

"With what?"

"With my resolution not to write at all."

Guy glanced at her thoughtfully.

"Why did we resolve that?" he asked. "I remember our being tremendously heroic about it—but why?"

Cynthia laughed.

"I don't know. I've sometimes wondered. Anyway, we did resolve it."

Guy had lighted his pipe.

"I've not come back in an especially heroic mood," he confessed.

"Then I'll have to be heroic for both," Cynthia said.

She wore an old white tennis frock; her round brown arms, her rounded brown throat, were bare; her slender legs were bare, her feet hidden by old tennis shoes. In the heat of the summer day her eyes were very blue.

"I'm a disgrace when I wash this dog," she said, as Guy looked at her.

"Listen," he said suddenly. "Hansen—the old Swede I was painting with—his wife—she's magnificent, and—well, she isn't his wife. They're old; they're past sixty, and they're not married. They've got a boy of thirty, and they love each other; they're crazy about each other!"

Cynthia looked at him gravely.

"Don't tell me about people like that, Guy. We're not that sort. They may get away with it. We couldn't."

"We're free, white, and twenty-one," he said. "We could throw a few things into the back of a car——"

The world began to shimmer and tremble with beauty and romance again, and with joy and fear too. Cynthia sat still on her bench, looking at him with expectant, frightened, happy eyes. He was big and brown and assured, and dictatorial—but it wasn't that. It was that when Guy was about she seemed to lose the use of her senses, she became completely fluttered and bewildered and light-headed. The ground floated away from under her feet, the usual realities were far away and vague; the only real thing in her life was this man and his voice and the touch of his hands.

She was frightened; she was in heaven.

"Guy!" Leslie screamed, running across the lawn.

"Hello!" he called. He got up and kissed Leslie; he had not kissed Cynthia.

"Couldn't stay away any longer!" Leslie exulted.

"Couldn't stay away any longer," Guy repeated.

Cynthia walked toward the house. Quite suddenly she knew that the fight that she had been waging against herself for weeks—for hard and lonely weeks—was lost. Resistance and self-control and morality were only words. Love was, as always, the reality. She loved Guy, and he loved her—that was the significant thing. Why must they throw that away, starve it, ignore it? What a silly waste that would be!

Happily, excitedly, she sensed that he had come home knowing, as surely as she knew it, that they belonged to each other. Just when, just how they would seal their love, just what would be the terms of her surrender, her compromise, she did not know or care. It was enough that her whole soul and mind had melted into this ecstasy of conscious capitulation. It was enough that she loved, and knew herself loved in return.

CHAPTER TEN

"GUY, I am very sorry I got so angry," Cynthia said abruptly.

Guy glanced at her mildly, over his pipe.

"That was all right," he said. "I know how you feel. That wasn't anything!"

There followed a long silence. The two were alone in the grape arbor that followed one side of the Trezavant garden; in the warm, clear July stillness they might have been alone in the world. For ten minutes previous to Cynthia's sudden apology neither had spoken; for a full ten minutes after it neither spoke.

Then the girl said in a morose, bored tone:

"My father wants me to go to San Francisco for the autumn—you knew that."

"No, I didn't!" Guy exclaimed, surprised.

"Lucia wants to take some interior-decoration course, and he thought I might be with her. He told me I was getting thin and nervous, and had gone off in looks."

Her tone was dry, indifferent; her mouth was twisted by an ironic smile.

"You don't think—for one instant—that he suspects?"

Cynthia laughed, rather mirthlessly.

"I love the language of intrigue!" she said.

"Don't be bitter, dear."

"No—I try not to be," she told him, in a slightly gentler tone. "But it's—funny to hear one's own voice on those immortal sentences: 'Does anyone suspect? Is anyone watching?'"

Guy was silent, the expression on his handsome, kindly face one of infinite distress.

"Not that anybody suspects anything," Cynthia presently added, tonelessly. "But somehow—we're all restless, this summer!"

"The city, hey? That doesn't sound like your father, somehow."

"No, does it? It would only be for two or three months. Lucia would go to a studio five mornings a week, and I'd—supposedly—take a secretarial course—something like that."

"He never suggested anything like that before."

"Well, he might have. For years we all went away every day to school, you know. It isn't," the girl analyzed it, feeling for words—"it isn't that Papa actually stops us—prevents anything we want to do. It's that—having everything we need here, food and clothes and books and all the rest of it, it seems a little forced to go out into the world and try to earn all these things for ourselves!"

"Well, I don't suppose it would actually be for that," Guy mused.

"No, of course not! It would be to meet men, to find husbands," Cynthia agreed, cynically.

"Well, not that, either."

"Not—*admittedly* that." Cynthia was silent, musing. "You know this Mrs. Reynolds—this Mrs. Petrie Reynolds who came down to lunch with us two or three weeks ago?" she presently asked.

"Money," Guy responded briefly.

"Nothing but! Well, she has these two girls, Vera and Blanche, and when Vera gets married next week she wants one of us—wants me, as a matter of fact—to be one of the bridesmaids. And then they're going on some sort of camping trip, and she wants me for *that*."

Her voice died into silence; she sat staring into the hot, soft shimmer of the July afternoon.

"They all fall for you."

"Apparently."

"That prospect would have driven you out of your senses a few months ago."

"I know it would, a few months ago," she agreed very simply.

They did not speak again immediately. The descending slant of the sun sent a hot pattern of sunshine and shade into the arbor; even the shadows quivered gently with heat in this warmest hour of the day.

Cynthia wore a thin white gown that had seen many washings, and it was almost transparent in its delicate age. The brown skin of her arms and breast was shadowed through the frail fabric; the starched thin ruffles were spread about her on the old bench on which she sat, like the petals of some great fringed flower. Her face was flushed with the heat, her blue eyes were puzzled, cynical between the thick sooty rays of her lashes.

Behind her head was a pattern of great star-shaped leaves, out with bunches of unripe grapes; the small green beads were already dragging down the hairy arms of the vine. Between them the blue sky showed, barred by the white-washed beams of the arbor. White butterflies had found their way into the sweet green gloom and were wavering to and fro; Cynthia's dog lay stretched on the bench sound asleep, with his nose against her fine sunburned hand. From far off the dim noises of the ranch came to them faintly: the bleating of a calf, the sudden crow of a cock, the sleepy murmuration of doves, wheeling on the barn roof. And always, in the silence, they could hear the splash of the dam by the pool.

"Shall you go?" Guy asked, out of the long pause.

Cynthia looked up, bewildered, from a daydream.

"To the city—to the Reynolds'?"

"I don't know. I would like to go and never come back!"

To this Guy seemed able to make no reply. After a while he said:

"I love you so, and I'm so damn' helpless when it comes to making you happy!"

Cynthia merely looked at him, returned to her musing.

"Just this chance afternoon together would have seemed heaven to us both a few months ago," he said.

"I know," Cynthia responded, in the lifeless tone and words she had used before. "A few months ago."

A few months ago, she thought, just his saying, "I love you so," would have turned this whole day to magic.

"The truth is," she began suddenly, "I need something to *do*. I seem to have infinite capacity for work, Guy—service, self-expression. Gray is different; Leslie's different. They love leisure. I hate leisure! I want to be planning something all the time—working, buttering bread or raising children or running big conventions—I can't wait for life!

"God knows," she went on in a lower voice, as he silently watched her, with the same sympathetic and distressed expression on his face—"God knows I couldn't wait for life.

"But now—now I need work more than ever! It must be that there's some place for me, some work for me—out there in the world. It must be that a woman as strong as I am, as frantic as I am to be useful, and tired and busy, can find something to do! If it were caring for sick babies —running a fish market——"

"If we could go together," he said, as she stopped.

"If we could go together!" Cynthia was silent, thinking, for a space, then she said, "How happy we would be— together."

It was said so simply that Guy, trying to smile at her, found his eyes dazzled by tears.

"It seems impossible that any two persons ever could be that happy," he answered, with equal simplicity.

"If Rhoda——" Cynthia began, and stopped.

"I know," he said.

The girl, a blur of white in the green dazzle of the shadows, stared for a while into space.

"I wonder if many girls are as—as *out* of things as we are," she mused, after a moment.

"It's the old fashioned way."

"The old-fashioned way in a new-fashioned world. We're out of date," Cynthia said, half aloud, as if speaking to herself.

"I would wait for you," Guy said, "five years, ten years—all the years—if I only knew how many they would be! What is killing me is to love you as I do—to think of what our lives might be, up above here at the Little Quito—and still never to know from day to day when I may be able to come to your father and say, 'Give me my wife!'

"Or if I may ever come!" he added bitterly, and was still.

"All that matters," she said, in a low voice, "is that you love me."

Guy merely looked at her, and although Cynthia did not look up, she felt his eyes on her.

"As long as you love me, Guy."

"No woman in the world was ever as much loved as you are—or as beautiful, or as wonderful!"

"No ceremony—no priests and organ and bridesmaids and law—could make me feel myself more your wife, Guy."

"Or make me love you, or respect you, more than I do," he said.

The word respect stung her. She felt her cheeks grow warm and her throat thicken. Her heart began to hammer again, and she felt the strange faint confusion in her brain that was familiar now.

There was silence in the grape arbor until the noise of a returning motor cut through the afternoon stillness. Guy went out, presently to be heard talking to Lucia and Gray on the porch. Their voices lessened, a door slammed, there was silence again.

Cynthia sat on, alone, her brown fingers mechanically rubbing the dog's ears, her absent eyes fixed on the ground, where the pattern of grape leaves and tendrils lay like a rich, dim lace in the level last rays of the sun. The whole world of Treehaven, the great shafts of the redwoods and the encircling shoulders of the hills, was set in hot, crystal light now; every rose and dahlia stood forth aureoled with glory. In the sunshine, just beyond the arbor opening, a column of insects wove up and down; Cynthia sat so still that a lizard began to zigzag nearer and nearer to her on the dry earth of the arbor floor under the trellis; only a few feet away there could be heard the warning "c'ck—c'ck—cr'r'r!" of the sentinel quail. The still air was sweet with heavy flower scents: fragrance of stock and honeysuckle and the wet grass where the lawn sprinkler was whirling fans of diamonds into the glowing afternoon.

After a while the girl got to her feet; she walked slowly the hot mile of the Woodcutter's Road, grasshoppers leaping before her through the dry yellow grass. Once she stopped, and said, "Fool! Fool!" to the unanswering silence of the mountains and the canyons.

Violet twilight was beginning to fill the valleys with gauze when she left a great rock, upon which she had been sitting, staring absently into space, and began to walk home again. And again she stopped and said, "Fool!"

And so, every few minutes while she was dressing, and setting the table, the same excoriating thought arrested her hands, arrested her thoughts, seemed to stop her very soul, and the same word came to her lips.

"You fool. You complete *fool.*"

The word haunted all her days now, came between her and everything she tried to do, with a sense of complete and irrevocable folly, of irretrievable mistake.

But the nights were worse. Cynthia learned what it was to lie awake, hour after hour, her hands clutched over her breast as if she would like to tear away the heart that had betrayed her, her mouth dry and feverish, her eyes staring into space. And ringing through her moon-lighted summer bedroom as if it had been the clapper in a bell was the one word:

"Fool!"

The next day, when she was up at Guy's ranch house and they were sitting on the porch steps after luncheon, the man said suddenly:

"Cynthia. It's all over. Finished."

His tone made her heart turn over and her mouth fill with salt water. Cynthia echoed "Finished?" and sat looking at him. Guy was stuffing his pipe.

"Done," he said briefly. His glance showed that the color had faded from her cheeks; she was staring at him blankly, her lips parted, her lashes wide.

"Done?"

"Until I can bring you here as my wife," Guy said, plainly.

Mortally struck, the girl narrowed her eyes, looked away into space, her underlip bitten. Her breath came quickly; she did not speak.

"Until I can make the dearest woman I ever knew, my wife," Guy persisted steadily, "you and I must not see each other—except when we must, again."

A silence.

"You can't *do* that," Cynthia presently said, not looking at him. Her tone was dogged, sullen.

"I love you," Guy said, "as no woman in this world ever was loved before. I'm possessed—it's consuming me. But we must wait."

"Wait!" she echoed thickly, scornfully, still not turning. For a long time neither spoke. Then Cynthia said:

"Aren't you just a little—late?"

"I never knew," he said, by way of answer, "how much a man could love a woman. I never knew how he would want to—to save her from anything that could hurt her—from himself, too."

"I don't want to be saved from you, Guy," the girl said, very low.

Guy made no reply.

"I knew you had changed, lately," Cynthia went on, after a pause. "I knew you—didn't care, as you had cared."

"I haven't changed," he answered briefly.

"But then why—if we love each other——" She faltered. "Why not take what happiness we can—since there's so much wretchedness——"

"Is it wretchedness, Cynthia?" he asked, in the silence.

"Oh, my God!" she said. And she put her hands over her face.

After a while she took her hands away and moved over next to him on the top step. Her shoulder was against his, her hand on his arm, as she twisted herself about almost to face him.

"Kiss me, Guy!" she said.

Guy looked at her. Then he put his pipe into his pocket and got up and went into the house.

Cynthia sat on the step a long time. After a while she got to her feet and walked over to the gate and opened it and started down the half-mile trail for home.

She did not think. She merely moved, a being tortured with emotion and pain, through the silent forest. Her mind was a blank; her soul sick. A few weeks of laughter and triumph; a thousand kisses from the hard hungry mouth—the heaven of those firm, encircling arms——

And now this. Now, having known the heights, the valley of humiliation and despair, darker and lonelier than ever.

CHAPTER ELEVEN

A WEEK later she was bridesmaid at the Reynolds wedding. It took place in the largest church and the largest hotel in San Francisco. The presents were estimated at half a million dollars, and the bride's veil had been worn by her mother and grandmother and was of real Cluny.

Vera and her bridesmaids dressed at the Reynolds' apartment; Cynthia, their general pretensions to wealth and position considered, was surprised to see that it was quite an ordinary apartment, throughout which the voice of Mrs. Reynolds, in high altercation with the cook, echoed unmistakably, and in which majolica, plush, onyx, brass Turkish lamps pierced with crescents and stars, and modern chairs of bent pipe and copper were all cheerfully mingled. Life-size statues of Nubians and Neapolitan girls were lamps, and a Bacchante held aloft a bunch of grapes that were really small light bulbs.

The apartment, however, was only what its mistress called a "peedateer," for the Reynolds were constantly off at full speed for some other place: Del Monte, Coronado, Tahoe, Hawaii all knew well the handsome big noisy widow and her pretty daughters.

On the day after the wedding, with a party of seven, the bride's mother and sister were to start off into the High Sierras for a camping trip of two weeks' duration, Mrs. Reynolds explaining frankly that she could not otherwise face the agony of parting from Baybsie. Cynthia Trezavant was to accompany them on their trip.

Vera's groom was Justin Severn, and Cynthia's first impression of Justin was as surprising to her as her first of the Reynolds' apartment. Justin was forty-one, his hair was thin on top, his mouth had a queer looseness at the corners, and he seemed most at home with a cocktail glass in his hand. Justin had been married twice before, and had a daughter of seventeen and a son of four by his two earlier wives respectively.

This in a bridegroom was all frankly disgusting and incomprehensible to Cynthia, but even more puzzling, in the four days she spent with the Reynolds before the wedding, was the fact that neither Vera nor Justin seemed to be acting in exactly the conventional manner. Vera was doing all the love-making, all the flattering and praising; it was Vera who fluttered attentively about the rather sodden and sophisticated man, and Justin who accepted everything blandly. Vera seemed excited and triumphant, but not happy, and Justin had just one joke, which he exercised constantly: the exquisitely funny assumption that he didn't love Vera, and that she had "hooked" him.

"Never you mind, you landed me!" Justin would say to his promised wife hilariously, when Vera fretted because of the delays and hitches in the wedding plans. "You lan'ed me, and you're gonna *get* me!" he told her darkly, at dinner on the night before the wedding, when after some drinking he became sentimentally tearful, and thought it necessary to tell all of them that he had always played fair with Mary and Ida, his other wives. He had never thrown a woman down in his life, unless she was a—a something-or-other that meant nothing to Cynthia, for she had not heard this term before.

When he was like this, Vera and Mrs. Reynolds and Blanche doubled their attentions to him; they were tender, understanding, sympathetic.

"It was that bachelor party last night," Mrs. Reynolds said leniently to Cynthia on the wedding eve. "He has a hold-over, poor kid."

Blanche was her sister's maid of honor, and Cynthia the last of the six bridesmaids. Their gowns were of crisp full-ruffled taffeta; flesh, palest pink, salmon, carnation pink, and rose color deepening to Cynthia's lovely hollyhock robe, just as the coloring of the six girls darkened from Margaret Unger's albino fairness to Cynthia's brown gypsy glow.

Indeed, though Cynthia had not been told so, she shrewdly suspected that her coloring had been the chief reason for Vera's affectionate invitation down at the ranch a few weeks ago: "Be my sixth bridesmaid, Cynthia! Even if we don't know each other so well, we did when we were little, and our families have always been friends!"

The great church was breathless, packed with guests, glorious with flowers and palms, and filled with the solemn throbbing of organ music when the bridal party came down the aisle. There was a bishop to officiate; there were robed assistants, rows of little acolytes.

Cynthia looked on with bitter and disillusioned eyes. This was a great marriage, a wholly felicitous and fortunate event.

Everything here but love; all this without love was quite proper. And love without all this was a disgrace; this was admirable, this was acceptable. The other—the passion that brought a woman to a man's arms, under the pure high summer moon, that turned the world to trembling magic and made the least little straggling buttercup beside a rambling roadway a miracle—that was forbidden.

This diseased little drinking, dissipated man, boasting of his love affairs, twice a husband and father, yet never truly either, could take Vera's beauty and fragrance and youth to his rich hotel suite tonight, could buy her with jewels and talk of yachts and Europe and a chinchilla coat—even though his skin was like saffron putty and his breath stale, even though, even before her wedding night, his scornful careless words and looks had warned her that he knew her price and was ready in his contemptuous way to pay it, and willing to pay no more.

And the bishop and the organ and the church all made it right, all made it possible to go up to the big hotel afterward, where there were more flowers and champagne, kissing and laughing, and even a little tenderly emotional crying on the part of Baybsie's mother, because "weddings are so sweet, somehow!"

It was good to get away the next day for the mountain trip. The party was composed of Mrs. Reynolds, a married couple who were her friends, and who took this outing every year, an odd man of fifty or so, who seemed to be a college professor, two young boys, Blanche and Cynthia.

They went in big cars to Huntington Lake, and there the young persons shopped for knives and Indian gauntlets in the general store, and chugged about the lake in a row-boat with an outboard motor. The next day, in boots, breeches, shirts and sweaters, with small felt hats pulled down to cover their hair, they had another motor ride, and at noon met Dan Younger and the horses—and Jim Fowler.

These were their guides, and reaching their first camp, sore and hot and weary, at five, they found the rest of the outfit: a cook, three or four cowboys, pack animals, extra horses.

They camped on the edge of a glorious river that ran shallow here on sun-baked rocks across wide mountain meadows and sang an accompaniment to the rushing noise of tree branches high overhead. The stock ranged at large in the meadows, the campfire roared up into the chilly dusk, and the little kitchen unit was abustle; smells of coffee and of baking came hearteningly toward the tents.

Mrs. Reynolds and the Barkers had tents, but Cynthia and Blanche, and Dr. Wharrel and Joe Rich and Fred Whittell much preferred camping in the open under the bright stars. The girls occupied the twilight in selecting a comfortable sleeping site, unrolled their sleeping bags, hung their shelf of cold creams and brushes to a low tree branch, creamed their sore, burned faces, and, crouched on rocks beside the river, brushed their hair and washed their hands.

In comparatively clean clothes and low, comfortable shoes, it was wonderful to wander over to the fire and to find soup and biscuits and corned beef hash and canned peaches. Only Cynthia and the boy called Freddy were strange to the proceedings; their noviceship drew them together, and they confided to each other on the next day's ride that they were making it a matter of pride not to balk at anything or be the first to quit or complain.

Freddy was simply one of those nice boys who do not count; he was a senior at the State College; college and sport matters interested him, and nothing else. The other boy proved to be rather a failure as a traveling companion; he was sick, headachy, or chafed or sunburned or poisoned by oak all the time; he could not sleep, and he hated riding. He did a great deal of smoking and of lying in the shade sleeping.

So that, as possible material for flirtation, both boys were to be counted out. But Cynthia liked the old professor, who was anecdotal and friendly and very good at games about the fire at night, and she liked Blanche. The girls rode together and fished together, and lay awake at night talking together. They washed their clothes in Granite Basin and the North Fork of the King River, and gloried in cold mountain baths, when the soapsuds that smelled so fragrant and clean drifted downstream under the trees, and when they could plunge their bare sun-browned bodies deeper and deeper into the swirling emerald of the splendid pools.

Knowing that the men were a safe half-mile away, to stand bare upon a hot rock, with a tapestry of ferns, underbrush, great rising pines for a background, with pebbles and butterflies on the shingle at her feet, and the river tumbling and eddying and basking in its chiseled bed below her, was for Cynthia the very cream of the trip. Her brown slimness would cleave the hot air, and herself rise gasping and laughing to the shattered surface of the water, to swim to the shore and begin the process all over again.

Ten matchless days, of burning heat, of icy cold, of satisfying dirtiness, enchanting cleanliness, ten days of hunger and the satisfying of hunger, and ten nights of dreamless sleep seemed to insulate her from what had gone before: from the ranch and Papa with his Beethoven frown, and the girls setting tables and mixing mayonnaise; seemed to put Guy, with his flashing smile and his heart-stirring voice, into some far space where she, Cynthia, had been a different woman and all the world different.

They told her that she was the life of the party; Cynthia shook her head, but she knew it was true. The games she introduced, her vitality and enthusiasm, her voice in the singing, her zest for every new experience lent a new color to the familiar trip. Dan Younger, most lean and laconic and experienced of mountain guides and packers, voiced his approval of her with one or two monosyllabic comments in the very beginning; he told her frankly that she reminded him of a girl at Miller's Basin who had gypsy blood in her veins, and was a "card." The other cowboys, who a dozen times a day lent friendly assistance to the tenderfeet whenever it

was possible, and, bashful and slick-headed, joined the circle
for games and conversation at night, also betrayed by their
manner that they liked the "tall one" better than the "white-
headed one." And Cynthia liked them all in return, and
speedily came to feel more than mere liking for one of them:
Jim Fowler.

Jim was twenty-five; he looked, but for his height, ten
years younger. He had a great shock of fair hair, kind, wistful blue eyes, and a clear sunburned skin; his beauty was
that of a young mountain animal. He was quiet, but not shy;
friendly, but never in the way. He had been a packer, with
his uncle Dan Younger, for all the summers since he had
been seventeen; he knew every road and every stream, and
where the trout rose and what flies they liked. Jim could
bring a full string when everyone else caught only one or
two fish.

During the winters he had worked in various ways; he
knew San Francisco, had been to Los Angeles—he was no
country bumpkin, although he spoke with the mountaineer's
drawl and hated cities with a deadly hatred. His ambition
was to have a milk ranch at Miller's Basin, and still be free
during the hot months for packing parties like this one
through the Sierras.

Cynthia had never known anyone at once so simple, so
wise, so experienced, and so unsophisticated. Jim's big clever
fingers were completely at home with fishing tackle, camp
gear, stable tools, harness. He liked history; and loved to
pit his random knowledge of great events and great characters against that of the others in some game.

But above all he loved and knew horses, and Cynthia,
watching him, thought that not since the days of the centaurs
had boy and horse seemed so completely one.

Jim could lasso them, hobble them, cure their cuts and
sores, mix them curative messes when they got sick; he

seemed to understand what they were experiencing, and certainly they trusted and understood him.

In the mornings he spread salt for them, and before he slung on the heavy saddles he sloshed bucket after bucket of water over their backs, scrubbing them vigorously as the dirty streams ran down through the matted greasy hair. Their bits must be right; their straps neither too tight nor too loose; their feet comfortable. All the men worked with the horses, but Cynthia noticed that when Dan was at all concerned about any one of them, it was to Jim that he turned.

When he was mounted, Jim was nothing short of magnificent. He rode every horse and mule in the string indifferently, and the wildest animals seemed to enjoy their frenzied efforts to get away from the bit and the quirt as much as Jim enjoyed reining them in. Cynthia saw him ride a dozen animals, sometimes with only a bridle, sometimes with not even that, up rocky steeps, across creeks, over fallen trees; the horse at a gallop, the low branches of the trees sweeping close to his back, water splashing and rocks rolling beneath the big clinking feet.

It was always the same; Jim never seemed conscious of the fact that his mount was not part of himself. He never glanced about for any possible audience, or smiled, or gave the slightest indication of showing off. Sweating, dirty, his fair hair tumbled and his shirt open at the throat, he would come whooping and shouting into camp, at the back of a dozen loose and flustered ponies, guiding them with his waved hat, and his own horse with the pressure of his knees.

When the party stopped for lunch or to fish, it was usual to have the pack train thunder by; the lunch camp would be pitched on the river bank only a few hundred feet from the trail.

Cynthia would look up from her bacon and roll to see Jim gallop along, the laden mules floundering ahead of him, dust rising among the rocks, shouts and the clatter of hoofs breaking the eternal silence of noontime in the high mountains. Sometimes the animals got off the trail entirely—it was never more than a narrow shelf along the steep face of the rock—and then it was astounding to see the long-legged boy on the pinto charge up or down the apparently impassable cliff, hanging to the saddle with one careless foot as he caught small rocks from the ground to hurl at the unruly beasts.

One night Dan scolded him: Cynthia, resting exhausted with her back against a fallen pine after sixteen miles in the saddle, was not in their sight, but she could hear their voices.

"Lissen, you're all wet, Dan——"

"Lissen, you've got to cut it out! You've got a swell chance with a girl like that."

"Lissen——" Jim's voice was a growl. "Who said I had?"

They went away; the voices died into silence. Cynthia sat perfectly still, with her face reddened and shame and pain in her heart. She hadn't been quite fair with Jim. She knew it.

A few more strenuous days finished the trip; they emerged at Miller's Basin; their suitcases were there. It seemed odd to see one another in white tennis silks; it seemed extraordinary to be sliding over smooth roads in a big car. Lunch at Merced was hot and weary, but Cynthia carried in her heart all day long the memory of tall, silent Jim's good-bye, the touch of his hand. He had given her a little nugget and ten fine soft flexible chipmunk skins, "for a coat collar."

At six she was at home; her sisters had met her in the sweltering village, for the Reynolds had to hurry on, they

could not come up the hill; they were due in Santa Barbara
the next day, and they had to wash, pack, read mail, and
telephone Vera, "and everything."

Cynthia, sitting beside Leslie on the front seat, with
Lucia and Gray perched on the jump seats behind her, could
talk freely, happily, to her interested companions; she could
tell them about Dan, and her horse "Macdougal," and
Blanche's horse "Dave," and assure them that Blanche was
sweet when you knew her, and that Mrs. Reynolds was
awfully nice—they all were awfully nice. . . .

Delicious shady lawn, delicious orderly rooms, Papa welcoming, Hing delighted, Guy there.

He got up and transferred his pipe to his left hand, and
her fingers were tight in his again—her heart remembered
how . . .

Everything began to go around in slow, sickening circles;
her head ached sharply . . . she wasn't cured . . . she
wasn't cured . . .

"We thought we'd lost you for keeps!"

"Tell Papa about the deer, Cynthia!"

Cynthia sat in her own chair on the porch; twilight was
cool in the garden at five o'clock, and in the turquoise of
the sky one star trembled. The air was sharp and pungent
and smelled of loam and of the sweetness of dew on dusty
leaves.

She smiled at them all; she must be unusually kind and
helpful and sympathetic now, when she had had the wedding excitement and the outing besides. But in her heart
she felt utter exhaustion and a sort of dry despair; nothing
had changed in three weeks; Guy was the same, life the
same. Winter was coming; Mack would soon set up the
stoves and bring in the wood—they would have fig pudding
and chicken pie, instead of salads and strawberries. Fear

of the long quiet season seemed to sweep over her spirit; sharp clear sunlight on packed wet leaves, spider webs diamonded with great drops of rain—Guy up at his house, working on tree sketches, Cynthia down here explaining to Papa why Martin, the carpenter, hadn't come up from San José to fix the door. . . .

Nothing new; nothing changed. And yet there was a change, too, so subtle, so painfully unwelcome to her thoughts that she would not recognize it for a while. There was a change in Guy.

He loved her less. Or he loved her differently. The quality that had made their mutual discovery of love so thrilling, so absorbing only a few months ago, was gone. Guy was dark, troubled. He no longer tried to find opportunities to see Cynthia alone; he avoided her.

From holding the control of the situation, from knowing that it all lay in her hands, Cynthia was reduced to an agony of helpless longing—like all the wretched crying women of the books she knew so well, she would remind herself in bitter self-contempt—like Tess and Hetty and Anna, and the miserable woman in *The Gadsbys,* and the great army of other weak, pitiable beings who voluntarily changed their own status from queen to slave.

Cynthia found Patmore's lines, and read them with anger and shame in her heart.

"*O lovely woman, you who may on your sweet self set such a price,*
Knowing man cannot choose but pay, how have you cheapened Paradise!
How given for naught the priceless gift, how spoilt the bread and spilt the wine
That, spent with due respective thrift, had made brutes men, and men divine!"

A week, ten days of madness had cost her this. She was not remorseful, not repentant; her heart was too hot with pride and resentment for that. But to know oneself to have been a fool, to have held the winning cards and to have thrown them away, to be unable to conquer these days of strange, shamed, feverish thoughts, and these nights of futile tossing and fretting and remembering this was a sort of insanity.

It was Guy who held the whip hand now. Guy had been restless and helpless and suffering in the spring; now he was cool and controlled and somehow remote—he was sorry for Cynthia, whose right it had been to be sorry for him only a few months ago!

There were times when she hated him, smoking the eternal pipe, looking into space with thoughtful, narrowed eyes, nodding his head. She was the agitated one now, and despised herself for it, despised herself for the tantrums, the trembling, the tears that were so easily roused nowadays.

"I feel that I'm failing you, my dear, and I don't know what to do about it!" he said on one of the few occasions when they were alone.

The "my dear" touched her like a whip. Men didn't say "my dear" to women they loved.

"No—no, it's not that!" she managed, thickly.

"I'm to blame for everything, horribly to blame," Guy said, simply. "I know that. But there doesn't seem to be any possible way out, except just to put it behind us, and go on, and be good sports, and keep our mouths shut."

He had formulated it slowly. He gave her an expectant glance at the finish. Cynthia's level look in return was hostile.

"Simple," she commented, dryly.

"No, it's not simple," the man observed with a sigh, after a pause.

He was being patient with her; men always were that when a woman was unreasonable.

"I think it would be—easier, if I could go away——" Cynthia began, and stopped.

Treacherously, her voice was quivering, her eyes were full. She despised herself, despised the weak words that seemed to be flowing from her with no volition of her own.

"You don't—like me the way you did. You never say so any more!"

"No," he agreed grimly, "I don't like you. I wish to God I did!"

There was a silence.

"The moment I can," Guy said, after a while, "I am going to come to you and ask you to be my wife. I never will love any other woman; I never have.

"But I can't throw Rhoda down."

"You—you throw me down."

"No. No, I don't throw you down."

He was smoking. Cynthia was silent.

"You see, Rhoda isn't like most—cases, Cynthia. She knows me; she misses me. Thursday, when I was there, she came out to meet me—the nurse wasn't anywhere in sight —she was gentle, reasonable——"

"Oh, don't tell me how rational and affectionate she was!" Cynthia interrupted. "I'm *sick* of it!"

She got up abruptly from the log upon which they both had been sitting in the course of a winter Sunday walk, and rejoined the other girls just on ahead making preparations for a picnic lunch.

CHAPTER TWELVE

BUT Cynthia had no appetite today for ham rolls and dried-apple cake, and Gray, uneasy about her, made her go to bed when they reached home just as the November sun was setting and the day was getting chill. Cynthia had a fire in her room and all the new books; Gray left the door open, so that Cynthia would not feel shut out of the family group, and the various members of the family, Papa, Lucia, Leslie, paid her regular visits. Her dog lay on her feet; late in the evening, taking a wet walk, Guy came in, cold and rosy, and sat beside the bed for a few minutes.

"Thought you might all be in bed, but I saw the lights."

"No—they've been doing a jig-saw puzzle."

"Feeling rotten, eh?"

"Not really. But I've been cold and grippy and cross all day, and Gray made me come to bed. It's comfortable—snug."

"It's blowing up for another rain. Bed's a good place to be."

Gray had left them a moment. Cynthia advanced a hand, touched his wrist.

"I'm so sorry I'm so disagreeable, Guy."

"You're—wonderful," he said briefly, clearing his throat.

"My strength," she said, smiling, "is so weak. And my weakness is—so strong."

"I know what you mean."

"Guy, come out here and help us with the sky!" Lucia called.

Cynthia's fingers stirred in his; she was very lovely, lying back against white pillows, her smoky hair loose, her eyes dark blue with weariness and sadness.

"Stay where you are for a day or two," Guy said, departing.

"Oh, I shall be up tomorrow!"

But in the morning she did not get up, nor for many mornings. Gray heard her muttering, tossing in the night, and although the doctor, arriving in a mud-spattered Ford at breakfast, was not alarmed, there was fever, and he thought it best to be careful.

Then there was suddenly a throat complication, and after that pain in all her bones; pains in stiffened fingers, backache, heaviness and soreness.

The doctor from San Francisco said a form of arthritis; curable but troublesome; Miss Trezavant must resign herself to a long fight.

Miss Trezavant cared not at all. She lay placidly in her comfortable room, listening to the falling and dripping of rain, or the snapping of frost, hearing the crackle of fires and the shouts over cribbage or anagrams. Papa paid her visits twice daily, and seemed to like to find his wild bird here, placid and occupied; Cynthia embroidered, worked crossword puzzles and cryptograms, read Shakespeare and Milton, was always interested in her simple trays, and was strangely beaten and at peace. Sometimes she fancied that she felt her soul growing just as the Chinese bulbs grew on their rocks in her sunniest window.

Guy came to see her every day and was never empty-handed. A book or flowers, or three of Lung's matchless sponge cakes, or a sketch, a puzzle, or a glowing orange persimmon; Cynthia must have her gift.

"It shows what a *friend* he is," Lucia observed warmly.

"When we don't need him he doesn't pay any attention to us, but when we *do*——!"

"Cynthia, you've grown to be the loveliest woman in the world!" Guy told her.

Salt tears filled her smiling eyes.

"It's worth it—then."

"Ah, no, it's not worth it—it's not worth one hour of pain!"

"Not much pain, now."

"I have been thinking," Guy told her one day. "And I know now that we must take the law into our own hands, when you are well. You are my whole life. We can't go on this way!"

Cynthia, languid against her pillows, looked at him in silence.

"I love you so dearly," Guy said simply.

"I am not well yet," Cynthia reminded him. That fact deferred all plans for the time being.

"You see," Guy presently explained to her, "all Rhoda's affairs are in my hands. If I—let us suppose, got a divorce, it would mean—or rather," he amended it, "it *will* mean finding an administrator, getting all that sort of thing straightened out."

"They wouldn't let you go on, anyway?"

"No. I think not. The others are old Cotter, of the bank, and Dr. Watts—they'd feel, probably, that, married to another woman, I wouldn't be the person to manage Rhoda's affairs."

"Is it much money, Guy?"

"Quite a lot."

"Then it would make a difference in your affairs too, Guy? It would mean living differently?"

"That, of course. But it isn't that," Guy said. "It's—if Rhoda ever got better. She can't get well, I suppose, after all these lost years. But—you see she isn't a 'case'—she's a person. She's——"

He made a hopeless gesture with his hands, rumpled his hair.

"She has her own cottage, you know."

"I knew that."

"I'm the only one to see that she's not neglected. It took me months to find her the right nurse—she's a big bruiser about forty—Miss Merry. She's quite a character. She cooks, and Rhoda helps her, and they have a radio and a Victrola and books—Rhoda won't read much, but she likes to look at the movie magazines; Merry reads to her."

"Does she have any more of those violent times, Guy?"

"No. Always very gentle—pitiful, really. She trails me about—Merry says she has some way of keeping track. She'll say, 'Guy hasn't come for nine days,' or whatever it is."

Cynthia lay silent, reflecting on this without any particular emotion. For the moment, while she was chained to this bed and this room, it was enough to have her big gentle friend from the studio up the mountain come in daily to see her, sit here beside her, talking, smiling, as absorbed in every detail of her life as she herself was. They were still strangely bound together, and yet pain and helplessness had seemed to remove her to a world of her own where she was strangely free.

He went away, came again. It was night, and Cynthia was reading Kipling, stopping sometimes to look out through the open door into the living room, where Papa was scowling over the backgammon board, and Leslie writing one of her long letters to Lieutenant Ross. Or it was morning, just that faint gray beginning of a winter morning in a sick room that only an invalid knows; chairs and bureau emerging from darkness, window brightening, sudden streaks of sunshine mingling with the sound of an awakening kitchen and barnyard, and the sparkling of melting frost on glass and the scent of wood fires and of coffee.

It was pleasant to lie lazily warm in her blankets, and have Gray or Lucia creep cautiously in, to smile encouragement, to light Cynthia's fire, to bring hot towels and scented soap to her bedside. Leslie would tenderly brush the black silky curls: "You're getting so *pretty*, Cynthia!" and Gray would beam hearteningly over the dainty tray that she presently carried in. Just enough to tempt her appetite: a wineglass of orange juice, two prunes in a tiny crystal saucer, two thin slices of dark brown toast. Gray made each tray a work of art and love, and Cynthia would reward her with a special smile three times a day.

Then fussing, the making of a fresh bed, the donning of fresh daytime pajamas, Cynthia rolled in a blanket, and cool air streaming in over a wet sunshiny windowsill, and then back to smooth sheets, and a heartening hot-water bottle and the pleasantness of writing equipment or playing cards or drawing board, or some puzzle or new magazine. The whole house circled about Cynthia now, and everything that came into it was hers first.

Presently everything would settle down into late morning quiet—a composite of peace and felicity that was underscored rather than broken by the sound of the hissing, sleepy fires, the drip of wet branches on the porch, the deep breathing of Dobbs, curled on the rug. Leslie's scales at the piano, or the scratching pen with which Lucia recorded German verbs.

They were all working vigorously at their German again, and Herr Ricker, coming up twice a week from Stanford to guide them, was quite obviously and ridiculously in love with dignified, lovely Gray. Gray, of course, never appeared and never would appear to know it, but, as the younger girls agreed, it all helped.

Leslie had an admirer, too; he was in Guam now with his ship, but young naval Lieutenant Elmer Ross wrote to Leslie regularly, and his distant attentions heightened the general sense of romance among the sisters.

And then at Christmas Cynthia had a long letter from Jim Fowler. Jim Fowler, mountain packer, twenty-five years old, and living with his married sister in Miller's Basin, had inherited twenty-two hundred dollars from his Aunt Kate's husband, Clyde Bowdish, and had bought his little milk ranch, with a man named Stocker for partner. And he loved Miss Cynthia Trezavant, and wanted to know if there was any hope for him.

Cynthia wrote him a simple answer in her crippled handwriting. She was ill; she had not walked since October. But she thanked him for remembering her.

She was past twenty-three; two men had loved her: Guy, married to Rhoda; and Jim Fowler, a big, rough, gentle guide and packer and trapper, from Miller's Basin.

Placidly she played cards, read, dreamed, worked on the wool embroidery pattern that Leslie had brought her from San José, puzzled over words and squares and tiny bits of jig-saw patterns.

In late March, when the plum trees were popcorn balls and the grass was wild with larks and quail, she walked out to the porch.

The day was hot; the sky high and blue. Cocks were crowing, and calves bleating up toward the farm buildings; bluejays looped the lawn with bright color. The warmth of the heavenly, scented day fell like a blessing on Cynthia's exhausted body; she was thin, awkward, stiff—but she was free. Her fingers obeyed her now when she spread them; she could stretch her long body luxuriously under the blankets at night, she could turn at her ease.

The world was new; she had never lived before. Her sisters fluttered about her in ecstasies; she was brushing her hair again, she was out in the kitchen making her own special salad dressing again.

"Don't tire yourself, darling!"

"Tire myself? If you only knew how good it is to get tired again!"

One afternoon, in a still, sunless peace that lay warm and soft over the ranch and the mountains and the great shafts of the redwoods, she and Guy walked slowly about the place, Dobbs at her heels.

"I am thinking of going down to Arizona next month to paint deserts and cactus and pueblos," Guy said, when they were sitting down on the orchard wall.

"I knew you were."

"I tried it last year."

"I know."

"It didn't work."

"No," Cynthia agreed, with a desperate little shred of laughter. "I know it didn't."

"I wish," he said, "you could get into your old brown outfit and come along."

Her heart twisted. No prospect that life could have offered her would have seemed so wonderful as this one: to be dressed in the old mountain climbing outfit that she loved, comfortable boots, untrimmed felt hat, open-throated shirt, soft old corduroy and suède coat, and to have her dog on her lap, and to be seated beside Guy in the car, rambling through the spring softness of the world.

"What a mess it is that you can't!"

Cynthia sat staring into space, her brows drawn together in a faint, puzzled frown. The hard year had chastened her beauty into something finer, more delicate and transparent than it had been; the brown skin was bleached to a clear, soft tan, the blue eyes had new expression, new depth.

"I'm so tired," she said, after a while, with a sigh. "I'm so tired of being—half alive. It seems to me that no matter what I was doing—no matter how hard it was—it would be better for me, I'd be happier, than this eternal doing what other persons think I ought to do, what other persons have decided, centuries before I was born, was the right thing for me to do."

Guy was looking at her steadily, with a serious expression on his handsome brown face, the faint black line of his mustache lifted in a half-smile.

"There doesn't seem to be any happiness for women any other way."

"And that's one reason I despise women—or despise being a woman, anyway!"

"Women seem to be completely happy when they have too many kids, too much fruit to put up, too many hands to cook for, and the folks coming over for Sunday dinner," Guy said.

"Ah, I could do that! I could manage the kids and the fruit and the folks!" Cynthia said eagerly.

She was in lilac silk Chinese brocade, with the tips of her purple kid slippers showing under the wide trouser legs, and the coat of silver and purple tied with purple tassels. Guy looked at her and laughed.

"I know," she said defensively. "But just the same, I could do anything I had to do. I wouldn't necessarily dress this way on a milk ranch."

Milk ranch. Jim Fowler had bought a milk ranch. . . .

"I wonder if you could do this——" Guy began, and fell silent, and was silent for a long time.

"Hang it!" he presently exclaimed, interrupting his reflections with a rueful laugh, "I don't know what to do. I don't know what to say! I don't know what girls think about these things—how much they matter!

"You haven't got any mother, after all!" he added, as Cynthia, watching him expectantly, did not speak.

"No. But I'm not quite a fool!"

"Here's the situation," Guy said. "I'll pack up my stuff this week. I'll go over to Livermore and tell Rhoda and Miss Merry that I'm off for a long painting tour. Rhoda——" He scowled. "Rhoda may cry," he said, "or she may not care at all. Anyway, she likes my illustrated letters, with pictures of Indians in them, almost as much as she does me.

"Well! Then I turn the Little Quito over to Lung Gow, and put a lot of painting stuff and my suitcase into the back seat. Then I come down here and say good-bye to the Trezavants for six months or so——"

The girl caught a quick breath.

"Six months?"

"Or years."

"Suppose," Cynthia asked, swallowing with a dry throat—"suppose you——let's just suppose——you found some woman you loved—down there in Arizona, then—then could they take away your guardianship of Rhoda?"

"No; that's just the point. They couldn't. You see," Guy explained, "it isn't a question of my private life. Old Cotter and the doctor—Dr. Watts—they're my friends. They know what my life has been for ten years; I believe both of them would be glad to know that I was happy, that something had given me a break at last.

"But if I divorce poor Rhoda—she being quite helpless and not really knowing what it's all about—then that gives her damn' relatives—distant relatives, but they're watching Rhoda's money like cats—a chance to rush in. They'd say I've kicked her out, I've got a beautiful young wife—children perhaps—and how am I spending Rhoda's money?

"They'd get some lawyer—there'd be a fight.

"As it is, if I came up to see her every few weeks, and if she went on in her own cottage with her own nurse, there'd be no change.

"We signed our wills a few weeks after we were married —it'll all be mine. But I suppose they could prove that she wasn't in her right mind even then; you see what a mess it might make, and that it might kill her? If any dim idea of it really penetrated," Guy added, scowling into space, and biting on his pipe stem, "it *would* kill her!"

"The—amusing thing about it is," Cynthia said slowly, searching for the word she wanted, "that it seems to me so natural—so *right* to go off with you. What would we do, you and I—find a bungalow somewhere down there?"

"We wouldn't go to Arizona; we'd go to Mexico—to Mexico City, the most fascinating city in the world. We'd have a hacienda."

"A hacienda!" The very word was enough; her eyes glowed.

"With a high wall, a grilled gate, and a bell in the gate to go 'dangle-dangle' when we had visitors."

"And Mexican servants?"

"Two. Three. And I'd paint, and you'd wear your Chinese clothes, and we'd walk before breakfast when the sun was rising, and lie about in our shady garden in the afternoons.

"Then some day," he went on, as she did not speak, "we'd get a wire that poor little Rhoda was gone, and then we could go up to the Consulate and be married——"

"And not feel one whit different——"

"No. For we are married now," Guy said seriously. "You are my beloved wife. All these months, when you've been so ill, I've felt—every hour—that my place was beside you, that it was partly because we couldn't be together that you had gotten into all this."

"I know. But suppose the worst came to the worst, and you fell in love with some ravishing grass widow and left me."

"I should think we could count out that possibility."

"Yes," Cynthia said gayly, "and so has every other girl who ever took the leap."

"In your case it wouldn't be taking a leap. You've known me almost all your life; the circumstances are unique. But no," Guy interrupted himself suddenly. "I'll not argue it; I've got no right to argue it. You're here, and you're safe. It's my business to get out, and this time I'm going to *stay* out.

"We talk of only the good side," he burst out again, suddenly. "But there's the other side, too. There's catty women cutting you, people whispering and goggling when we walk by. Then there are your sisters——"

"Papa would of course forbid them ever to see or mention me again."

"I suppose so."

"And cut me off with a shilling."

"He couldn't do that," Guy said. "Not after his lifetime anyway." The girl looked at him in surprise.

"How do you mean he couldn't?"

"Your mother's fortune was left to you four. He merely gets the income for life. But each one of you upon marrying is to have some allowance—if he approves, some hundreds a month, I think it is. It's an odd will—perhaps all wills are odd. He could keep it from you while he lived. But he can't touch it any more than I can. I'm a trustee too, you know, or executor, or whatever it is."

"You mean that if Gray had married last year, Papa would have paid her a regular income?"

"Gray, or any of you, if he doesn't forbid the marriage. Only—with us, it wouldn't be marriage."

Cynthia sat silent, assimilating this thought.

"It's quite extraordinary that he shouldn't have told you so."

"It's entirely characteristic of my father. It would make us more important in our own eyes, and he hates women to be that."

"It may have something to do," Guy said, "or at least I've sometimes wondered if it had something to do, with the fact that he doesn't exactly welcome suitors on this ranch."

"Only obscurely, I think," the girl said absently, after a moment's thought. "It might affect him, for he so loves power—loves to run everything. But I don't believe he'd think it out that way."

"Perhaps not."

"Then—if we went off together, and if later you died or if I went to New York and got into some sort of work, then I'd have an income?"

"As soon as your father died."

"Papa's sixty-one. But it isn't that," Cynthia said, with a little laugh. "Let him live as long as he will. It's only to feel that when *I'm* sixty-one——"

She fell silent. The spring day glowed and shone about them; bees clouded the banksia roses that were sending long shadows over the tennis court.

"Take me with you, Guy," Cynthia said, very low.

He did not look at her.

"It means your whole life, Cynthia. There's no going back."

"My life here has nothing in it," she said, tears in her eyes. "We—we love each other. Isn't that—what matters?"

"It ought to be," Guy said, in the low, husky voice he had used before.

"We'll prove that it is," Cynthia said.

"If I could look forward," the man mused, restlessly. "If I could be sure that I'm not a skunk!"

"We'll have a few years anyway, won't we, if we go to Mexico?" Cynthia said. "What will we have if we don't go?"

"I don't know. I'll be down there alone, I suppose."

"And I'll be here alone. And we'll go on with our German, and Gray'll be twenty-six, and Leslie's young lieutenant will come and tell her all about his being engaged to a general's daughter in Manila."

"I don't know what to do," Guy said.

"I do. I believe," Cynthia said, thinking aloud—"I believe, with my painter, and my hacienda, and my Chinese clothes, I will be more than equal to the situation. I think I can convince my sisters—everyone that it can be done!"

They left the fence and walked down through the orchard in the unbearable beauty of the spring afternoon.

"It's settled. I'm going with you, Guy."

"Lord—Lord——" the man said, slowly.

"What is marriage, if that isn't?" he presently added.

"It would be marriage. It *will* be marriage."

"We'd feel it so."

"I will feel it so," Cynthia said, resolutely. "I am already writing the letter I shall leave for my father. I shall tell him that everything he has ever taught me has made me feel that human beings must live their own lives, and by their own codes."

"He might see it our way," Guy observed, thoughtfully.

"He might."

"Guy, when do you go?"

"I don't know. I thought toward the end of next week. I

hadn't any definite plans. This will take a little longer. I'll have to see Dr. Watts—see Rhoda. We'll talk of it to-morrow."

The girl, suddenly excited and confident, could laugh at his confused and troubled manner, his uncertain tone.

"I'm going with you; that's settled, anyway," she said.

Neither spoke again.

CHAPTER THIRTEEN

AFTER that there were days of delightful security and steady going forward. Cynthia had never felt more sure of herself in her life. She felt all a woman; her character developed and strengthened by illness and helplessness, her soul uplifted by a great love.

This big, gentle, brown man, who made so many excuses to come down the hill in these days to see his neighbors, was hers and she was his. Her life might be strange, twisted— this step of theirs might be a great mistake. But somehow Cynthia did not think it would be; courage and time overcame all obstacles, and in a few years there would be some fresh shifting of the situation. Some women went under, no matter what the circumstances of their lives, and other women fought their way through to completeness and success, whatever their handicaps. She would acknowledge this great love of hers bravely, gloriously, before the world —and let what would follow!

Her whole being was fed with secret springs of joy. She went about the everyday duties of the house with a dancing step. There seemed to herself to be a perfection, a completeness, in her every movement; she could not be gracious, gentle, helpful enough in these days that glowed and pulsed with the heartache and beauty of last times.

"Guy, are you really going Thursday?" Gray asked, over anagrams.

"Positively."

"I don't know what we'll all do without you, or what we

would have done without you this winter!" Gray spoke for them all, but her glance went to Cynthia, who was placidly ranging her letters before her.

"I don't know why you go!" Lucia protested, resentfully.

"Will it be Mexico, eventually, Guy?"

"Probably."

"I wish we could all come down there!" Leslie said, disconsolately.

"Why don't you?"

"Four fair young women wandering forth to seek knights," Professor Trezavant said, not quite kindly.

"One dark one." Guy put his pipe back into his mouth.

"Cynthia," her father asked, "what are you going to do when our one squire deserts us?"

The beautiful, happy, downcast face flushed; she did not look up. Her brown fingers continued to shift the letters about, and the corners of her mouth lifted to a faint smile.

"I shall sing willow, like poor Barbara!" Cynthia said. Her uplifted eyes sent a brief smile to Guy, were lowered again.

Sometimes, on these hot spring nights, she had a fancy to wander in slippers, pajamas, and cotton robe down to the hammocks, to sleep there under the moon. Leslie had a bed on her porch outside her window; Gray and Lucia liked to sleep indoors, hating the blast of awakening morning sunshine. But Cynthia, from her very childhood, had loved the swinging beds out under the redwoods, at the edge of the lawn, on moonlight nights.

She would sleep there on Wednesday night, with her alarm clock set for five o'clock. Near her, in the grove, when she went to bed, would be her big suitcase packed with her lace gown and her slippers, some white thin frocks and oriental silk trousers and coats, and her little suitcase filled with creams and brushes and combs.

At half-past five—just dawn—Guy would stop his big car outside the gate at the foot of the lawn, and Cynthia would join him there and they would go down, down, down the hill, and out into the big world of adventure and love and beauty.

They would lunch at King City—or Santa Barbara if all went well—it didn't matter where. Papa would hardly follow them hotfoot with a gun, Cynthia assured Guy amusedly. No, it would be more his nature to shut his runaway daughter out of his life completely and hush up her story.

But after a few months—a few years—when Cynthia's letters to her sisters had brought him, in spite of himself, to a realization that what his second child had done was an exception to prove a rule, then perhaps he would soften. Or Rhoda might die. Or Cynthia might write a great book. He might see a picture of his brilliant daughter "with her two young children."

The other three Trezavant girls might go on here indefinitely, with their quiet, model days, their evenings of decorous laughter over games, their duties for spring, summer, autumn, winter, their restricted town trips for music and dinners.

But Cynthia Trezavant was going to live!

On Wednesday, however, resolution and courage alike deserted her. Cynthia was almost sick with excitement. She could not settle to anything; she could not eat, and at the most casual word or look from her sisters she felt a sort of convulsion at her heart.

It was a quiet, sunless May day; there was a hush over the world, a brooding warmth and shadow. There seemed to be no birds in the orchard today; fog beaded the new bluish green tips of the redwood sprays and lay in a white rime on the lawn. Sounds from the farmyard came muffled and distant; the drip, drip, drip of the dam and the dreamy humming of bees only made the smothering silence more strange.

In Cynthia's closet, closed and standing against the wall, was her big suitcase. Arranged near it on the top of her closet shelves were the flat smooth piles of underwear; the little tan and cream and flesh-colored rolls of stockings, the folded frocks that were to go inside it. She would wear her dark blue belted coat, her white fox skin, her small white hat, but there were a silk coat and two other small hats that must be packed.

Her shaken thoughts ran upon these things all day long. Not to betray herself, not to make any mistake! Her sun glasses, her gauntlets, her camera. . . .

"Cynthia, what's the matter with you? There simply isn't any knot in your thread today!" Leslie protested.

Gray smiled at Cynthia, tenderly, sorrowfully, wise. Gray knew—or thought she knew; it was Guy's going, of course. Cynthia had come to depend on him; they all had. Gray told herself that she knew why their neighbor was running away from the spring, running away from them all, so inexplicably. She had known, years ago, that his feeling for Cynthia was different from what he felt for all the rest of them. And Cynthia, if she had been fascinating in her childhood, had touched new depths of charm in this invalided winter, had shown the promise of a lovely woman, waiting to develop from the wild gypsy girl they all loved.

"Anyone going to San José this afternoon?" their father said, at breakfast. He never lunched; they would not see him again until late afternoon.

"We thought we'd go and see what we could get that was superlatively flossy, Papa, for Guy's last night."

"Ah, so it is! We lose our one last swain. I shall expect to see one or two of you languishing, needing sal volatile."

He was in his cruelest mood, when he considered that a sort of bitter teasing, a biting satire, was funny. "Well,"

Cynthia thought, "you won't feel so funny tomorrow, my dear father. . . ."

"The foolish virgins with their empty lamps—is that it?" Professor Trezavant went on, amiably, absently, his eyes on his paper. "In some way I have seemed to be unable to supply the women of my house with oil. The bridegroom departs and leaves them mourning."

"Guy is hardly a bridegroom, Papa," Gray reminded him composedly. "Not while poor Rhoda lives."

"You're quite right—our one suitor is hardly a suitor," her father agreed, with an air of good nature. "And yet," he added, "it has sometimes seemed to me that certain members of my family more or less overlooked that interesting fact! It has sometimes seemed so to me—I don't know, I'm only a man after all—I admit inferiority of intellect——"

"Oh, shut up!" Leslie and Lucia said in their souls, as they had said so many hundreds of times before. But Cynthia could afford to smile cryptically, as she went on with her breakfast, and Gray, as always the peacemaker, said reproachfully:

"We'd all be very strange not to love Guy, Papa. I always thought you liked him too, and were sorry he was going away!"

This shifted the values of the conversation a trifle; Professor Trezavant, an expert at teasing and irritating his family, never could endure the slightest hint of retaliation.

"I am not aware that I have indicated anything else!" he said, stiffly.

"We shall miss him, of course," Gray continued, sensibly. "And then other things will come in, and summer will be here, and he will be back.—Look at the weather forecast in your paper, and see if it's going to be foggy all day, will you, Papa?"

"Extraordinary," the Professor muttered in disgust.

"The least little joke, and you're all at me like a pack of wildcats. Where's your sense of humor, my dear Gray?"

"When you talk like that," Cynthia thought, in her soul, "you just make it a little easier for me to do what I'm going to do, that's all."

The dreamy unreality of the mist-shrouded morning went on; the three other girls went off to San José for strawberries and avocados, and Cynthia could settle down to letter-writing: a letter for Gray, with messages to the other girls—a letter to Papa. . . .

These would be mailed far down the long roadway that led to Mexico City, some time tomorrow—they would bear the postmark of San Juan or Salinas or Monterey. . . .

At one o'clock Cynthia went into the pantry and cut herself a rye bread sandwich bulging with cold duck filling. With a basket of cherries she carried it down to the lawn, settled herself in a hammock with a book, and began to read and to crunch together.

Guy found her there. He threw himself, brown and big and serious and handsome, on the lawn and looked up at her as they talked.

"Bite?"

"Well—— But I've just finished a late breakfast." She gave him half of her sandwich none the less.

"Clearing," Cynthia said. For the fog had been lifting itself in great visible blankets from the tops of the trees, and sunshine, mercilessly hot in the windless peace, was struggling down through the layers of the redwood branches.

"It'll be wonderful tomorrow," said Guy.

"Wonderful."

"I wonder if you and I will ever see these two ranches again, and Deer Hill and Booker Rock?"

"Of course we will. Yours belongs to you, and my sisters are here."

"You're quite sure of yourself, Cynthia?"

"Absolutely. This isn't," the girl said steadily—"this isn't an intrigue, a running away. This is a decision that you and I make with our eyes wide open, to forego the—the letter of marriage, for the spirit. It's better than sneaking and lying. It's honest and in the open, even if it's wrong."

"If it's wrong, I'm to blame," the man said.

"But it isn't," Cynthia persisted; "it isn't. Unless," she added, "we're to take the standards of Mrs. Reynolds, who sold Vera just as much as if she'd put her up on a slave block! Vera loathed Justin—it used to give her the creeps to have him kiss her! Blanche told me that Vera went into regular spasms about a week before the wedding and screamed at her mother to take her away, to get her out of it—and Mrs. Reynolds calmed her down, and soothed her, and talked about Paris and a place at Monte Carlo, and fur coats and boxes at the opera, and after a while Vera quieted down and said she'd go on with it.

"He was forty-one, Guy, and Vera was twenty-two—and he was bald and sick and silly and drunk most of the time. But that was holy matrimony, with a bishop marrying them, and organ music and prayers!"

"That made a horrible impression on you, didn't it, Cynthia?"

"It made me feel that it's safer to go on your own instinct than to take the code the world follows."

"I've been staggering around like a chicken with its head cut off, all day," Guy said. "I haven't known what I was doing."

"Neither have I. But my things are all ready, piled in my closet, with the suitcase right next to them. And when I come down here to sleep tonight I shall quietly carry it along and put it in that clump of hazel bushes there. Then tomorrow I'll go up to the house at five, as I often do, when the sun wakes me too early, and dress in the house and take my little case and come down here."

"I'll be parked right outside here. I'll be at the gate waiting for you."

"Don't oversleep, Guy!"

"Oversleep! I'll not sleep at all."

"If anything should go wrong now——" Cynthia said, and stopped.

"I know," he said, briefly, shaking his head.

"It would only mean," she began again, after a while, "that we waited our chance or faced the music, or whatever was necessary, and started all over again. But it would be so much easier to run away from the hullabaloo!"

"We'll get away all right. But when you come right up against it," Guy said, "it seems so—so different, somehow."

"Not too late for you to get out of it, Mr. Waring."

"I suppose not," he agreed, with a look.

"There was something I wanted to ask you," Cynthia said seriously, after a moment. "How was Rhoda on Tuesday?"

"Not well at all. At least, I couldn't see her. She was asleep, and from Merry's manner, which is always mysterious, I gathered that she had been under some strain— almost a breakdown, Merry said."

"What's the explanation of that, Guy?"

"I don't know. Anyway, it was nothing serious. I telephoned this morning and talked to Rhoda herself, which is unusual—and she was very cheerful. She said that Merry had told her that I was going away, and she wanted me to have a nice time—all that. She asked when I was going, and I said soon, I didn't know. Then she said, 'Not today?' and I said, 'Oh, no, not today,' and that was about all. I'll write her from the first place we stop."

"And where'll that be, Guy?"

"Santa Barbara, I hope. We ought to make it easily."

"Three hundred and fifty miles."

"Nearer four hundred. But the road is marvelous, and starting at half-past five, we ought to be down King City way for breakfast. Not that it matters."

"Not that it matters."

"We can stay there two or three days, if we want to. Or we can go on. Or we could go by Monterey."

"Will Mexico City be hot, Guy?"

"Mountains. No, not too hot.

"I was thinking," he said, after a silence, "that next fall we'll go to New York."

"New York!"

"We'll come back here in—say, October. If your people will see you, we'll come here to the ranch; if they won't, you stay in Santa Barbara, or somewhere near, and I'll come up and straighten everything out with Rhoda. Then we'll take the Car Beautiful and start East. I've always wanted to try it; I've always been looking for the right companion."

"We'll do everything!" she said.

"We'll do everything."

"Guy, do you suppose when persons get married—I don't mean like Vera and Justin, nor everybody—but do you suppose there *are* regular marriages with ring and book with as much happiness—as much security—as you and I feel now?"

"Not many," he said.

After a while he said:

"Is there anything you'd like to have me say about fidelity and protecting you and considering myself as much married as any man in the world?"

"No," Cynthia said.

Her sisters reappeared, hot and weary, a few minutes later. They had had their lunch, an "ikky, cafeteria lunch," Lucia described it, in San José; now they wanted to swim.

"The water'll be like ice!" Cynthia warned them, preparing, nevertheless, to join the party.

"San José was sticky and mussy and hot!" Leslie panted, sitting beside Cynthia on the hammock, putting back wet hair.

"I'm going," Guy said. "I know how casual you dear girls are about bathing suits when no gents are about. Gray, I got your books from London. I'll bring 'em down tonight."

"You angel," Gray said. "What time are you coming down?"

"Five. Half-past five."

"Maybe Cyn and I'll walk up and come down with you," Gray said. "We were going to take a walk somewhere late this afternoon."

"Come on! I'll give you tea."

"We won't want tea. It's too hot for tea."

"I'll give you grape juice."

"Maybe we will and maybe we won't!" Gray called after him, as he went away.

But after they had bathed and dressed coolly, and rested on the lawn for a while, she and Cynthia did start up the hill toward the spring sunset that was laying shafts of yellow gold under the shadowy redwoods. The afternoon was hot and still on the blazing hills, but there was delicious foggy coolness still lingering under the avenues of the lofty trees; the two girls in thin white with shade hats walked along slowly; the trail they followed was crossed now and then by a swift plumed gray squirrel, by a chipmunk or rabbit, or by the iridescent blueness of a jay.

"Cynthia, you're going to miss Guy terribly!"

"He'll be back."

"I know. But hasn't this winter, when he's been so wonderful, brought it all back?"

A silence.

"Brought what all back?"

"Your liking him. Your—caring. Wasn't it better for a while? I mean when you went away with the Reynolds—wasn't it better then?"

"I'll never love anyone else ever, if you mean that," Cynthia said, slowly.

"Cyn, if it wasn't for Rhoda, you two would be married?"

"Ah!" Cynthia ejaculated, and paused.

"Is he going away on that account, Cyn?" Gray asked timidly.

Cynthia walked along in silence for a dozen steps. Then she said:

"Partly, I suppose.

"Gray," she presently began, "isn't it funny that he and I can't marry, on account of a woman who wouldn't know whether we were married or not?"

"It's not that. It's that—well, there must be laws. And for a man to have two wives would—well, complicate, to say the least," Gray said.

"Fine women have taken the law into their own hands, Gray; better women than I have just said, 'I take you and you take me, in God's sight——' "

"You mean George Eliot?"

"And lots of others."

"I don't believe they ever feel—quite straight," Gray mused. "Do you mean, Cyn," she added, "that you think Guy would ever suggest an arrangement like that—when he comes back in October, say?"

"He never said so," Cynthia answered, walking along.

"Papa'd kill him," Gray exclaimed.

"Papa," Cynthia predicted, scornfully, "would do no such thing. He'd be as mad as a snake, and then he'd shut up, for the honor of the family. Papa could rush around breathing Victorian—Victorian? Georgian!—threats, as long as he liked, but he wouldn't *do* anything. And you know it!"

"Well, let's not discuss what couldn't possibly happen," Gray suggested, displeased.

"Anything could happen!" Cynthia observed recklessly.

"Not between persons of honor."

Ruffled, they went on up the deliciously scented shady trail, through the pulsing rich green shadows and shafts of apricot sun, and within a few hundred yards they were crossing the forest garden outside of Guy's ranch house, and had found Guy himself on the steps, smoking, and staring absently at the sunset light across the flowers.

He greeted them; they all sat down on the steps together.

"What are you going to do with these dogs, Guy?"

"Oh, leave 'em here. One dog's enough on a motor trip."

Cynthia's heart stood still, but Gray had noticed nothing amiss. The one dog was to be Dobbs, of course.

"You do take one of them?"

"Wolf, maybe," Guy said, after an almost imperceptible second of hesitation. "Cynthia, you look cool."

"I feel boiling. But it's lovely here."

"It's too lovely to leave," Gray lamented in her gentle voice.

They sat still, as if tranced by the exquisite beauty of the dying day on the garden. In the silence they could hear the throbbing of a motor engine, far away.

"Someone coming up the hill."

"Not likely, at this hour."

"Maybe it's the Frenchman, going up to the summit."

"Maybe it's the Ranger, looking over the fire trails."

They were all idly silent again, and again they could hear a car struggling on the grade.

"Maybe they've detoured them from the Big Basin Road again."

"Maybe it's some late delivery to our house."

Gr-r-r-r! the motor engine grunted, nearer and nearer. It was of no importance to any one of them, and especially was it unimportant to Cynthia and Guy, who came up the hill. But it was so unusual an occurrence on this lonely road that curiosity kept them all still for a space while the car, unseen down the road among the trees, chugged stoutly nearer and nearer.

"It's passed Treehaven," Cynthia said.

Amazingly, it turned in, a moment later, at Guy's gate. More amazingly it proved to be a yellow taxi—a yellow taxi here where no taxi in the world had ever come before. A taxi, threading the prune trees and disappearing behind the redwoods, only to appear again on the drive now—close to the porch——

A horrible presentiment of evil seized Cynthia, and she felt her throat thicken and her hands grow chill.

It stopped; a big woman in white—a big woman in a nurse's uniform got out and helped out a small, sick-looking, draggled little figure in a mussy blue silk gown, with her hat riding at a strange angle on her disordered hair.

"Well, here we are!" the nurse said, with a great hearty laugh.

"Guy——" the other woman faltered, holding out her hands.

Cynthia had not seen Rhoda Waring for almost twelve years; years that had changed her from a glowing young wife, radiant with hope and happiness, to this gray, trembling thing in the tumbled blue gown and dreadful hat. But she knew her. The world went black.

"Guy, I'm home again," Rhoda said, beginning to cry. "The doctor says I'm much, much better! It was to be a surprise—for you——"

He went to her, the tall brown man in homespun, put his arm about her.

"Rhoda, my dear—I didn't know you were coming!"

"We didn't know it ourselves," the nurse, having paid and dismissed the taxi, said in her jolly big voice. "But we've been planning all this for months! When you telephoned this morning, Mr. Waring, we were dreadfully afraid we'd let the cat out of the bag!"

She shoved her hat back; her broad, shining forehead was wet with perspiration; she was beaming with pride and joy.

"Dr. Watts and Dr. Leonard managed all this," she exulted. "But I'll tell you all about it later—radium treatments at the top of the spine! *That's* where the trouble was. Pressing on her—poor darling!"

She was fussing over Rhoda, whose eyes were fixed upon her appealingly, helplessly.

"We want to lie down," said Miss Merry. "Oh, come with us, Mr. Waring; she won't move without you. She's splendid, really splendid, but of course it's an emotional strain. I'm sure these young ladies—you're the Trezavants, of course—we know every one of you! I'm sure they'll excuse you——"

"Guy, where's the blue spruce?"

"The—the——? Good heavens, fancy your remembering that spruce!"

The poor sick little face broke into a tearful smile.

"I remember our buying it down at Morgan's Hill, the day we got the fig trees."

"We need rest—and quiet——" the nurse continued her joyous recitative. "But we're *home*——!"

"I owe it—I owe it all to Merry, Guy!" Rhoda stammered, crying again.

"Never you mind whom you owe it to—you've got to lie down now and take it easy. It was a hot day to start up this hill!" Guy was managing to say, eyes upon the forlorn little wreck that was his wife. But his voice was thick, and under his country brown a sick pallor had spread across his face. His big hands were shaking.

"But—but you're glad I'm home, Guy? We planned it—when I began to get better—for a surprise for you! I've been much better than I let you know."

The weak, plaintive little voice hesitated, stopped.

"But I've always been easily tired," Rhoda said.

"Tell me, had you the slightest suspicion of it?" boomed the nurse.

"Not the —not the slightest," the tense mouth under Guy's line of black mustache said briefly. He was half supporting, half guiding his wife toward the house.

Cynthia stood motionless, her apricot cheeks paling under their sunburn, her smoke-black curls rich against her brown throat, her blue eyes blazing darkly. The curved, slender body moved with the violence of her breath; her breasts, their splendid fullness visible under the thin old white gown, rose and fell; the shadow of her broad hat fell upon her face. Youth and love incarnate, she had nothing to say, she could make no gesture, as Guy and the nurse helped the woman who had once been Rhoda Waring into the house.

The Trezavant girls turned toward the gate for the downhill mile home. Gray grasped her sister's hand; it was cold and shaking.

"Cyn——"

"Just—if you please—not to talk to me, Gray——"

"I'll not!"

Footsteps came running behind them; Guy, very pale, had caught up with them and stopped them; he arrested Gray, with a hand on her shoulder. He looked only at Gray, his voice quick and light.

"Gray—for God's sake, look out for her—for Cynthia! We—we love each other so much——"

He went to Cynthia, put his arms about her. Her two

hands were pressed against his shoulders; their lips were together.

"Good-bye!" Guy said.

He went back again. Cynthia stood, in the last rays of the sunset, her bared, dark waves of hair disordered, her eyes following him.

CHAPTER FOURTEEN

AFTER a while Gray touched her arm.

"Come on, Cynthia."

"Yes—of course," Cynthia said, in a whisper.

She and her sister went down the hill together.

After dinner, when she was alone in her room, she put away all the clothes that had been selected and piled neatly for her flight. She put them away in their old places; pajamas, frail silky underthings, stockings. Her white hat into its old box; shoes on their racks again.

She felt bruised and feeble, somehow, and her head ached faintly. Cynthia wondered if she had not eaten any dinner; that might account for her sense of vagueness and weakness. They had all known at the table what was the matter with her, of course; they had all been kind; even Papa had refrained from more than a casual, optimistic comment upon Rhoda's return, a mere, "Well, now we will see how permanent this new spine treatment is!"

Not that it mattered; Cynthia had been too completely immersed in her own thoughts to hear what Papa or anyone else said.

After dinner Papa had walked up the hill in good-neighborly fashion for a word of encouragement to Guy. Lucia and Gray had walked with him, planning to wait outside, not let Guy know that they were there. Leslie had just had a letter from Lieutenant Ross, and with her usual lack of coquetry had seriously set herself about answering it at once.

Cynthia, complaining of headache, had said she was going to bed.

But first she had to unpack everything; unplan everything. Her heart was bleeding away, and there was a dreamy unreality to what she thought and did—but no matter, girls didn't die of this sort of thing.

Oh, Guy—so tall and broad and brown and sweet, so kindly and protective and big—— Oh, roadways south—Santa Barbara—San Diego—and a girl in white, on the front seat of Guy's old car. . . .

But no, she wouldn't think of Guy.

The ranch house was hot and unaired, after the warm day; the wooden walls seemed to hold in the heat. Cynthia thought that she would go down to the hammocks—no need to take her alarm clock now, no need to be afraid that she would oversleep.

But she mustn't think—she mustn't think. . . .

If she took a flashlight down by which to read, Papa and Gray would see it when they came down the hill. If she stayed in her hot room reading, then Gray would creep in, with motherly little croonings and pattings. . . .

She went across the dark lawn to the hammocks, settled herself in pillows, her dog lying on the grass below her. It was much cooler out here, dark and sweet. All the stars were out.

Presently Papa and Lucia and Gray came walking down through the trees, talking very cheerfully. Evidently the girls had gone in, and had seen Rhoda after all, for there was comment upon nice Miss Merry, and Cynthia heard Papa say, "Weak—but she's quite normal. Very delicate! But otherwise quite normal, I should say."

They all went in, lowering their voices, hushing their footsteps; "Cyn has a bad head," Cynthia heard Gray remind them.

She lay staring, breathing hard, trying not to think. The hammock swayed gently. Sleep was nowhere. Ahead of her were endless days—wakeful nights. . ... .

She, who was to have been wandering south with Guy early tomorrow through the heavy summer dews and the wakening morning world . . .

The moon rose over Deer Hill; first a paleness in the quivering peacock of the sky, then a rim of blazing silver, splitting crystal rays into the night, and then the full serene glory of the rounded circle, swimming placidly above the furry pompons of the oaks and the gothic spires of the dark redwoods.

Cynthia heard a clock in the house strike ten—strike eleven.

It was two o'clock when she waked Gray.

"Oh, Gray, I'm so sorry to bother you—but I'm dying, I think. Gray—he's—he's with her—he's being k-k-kind to her—I can't bear it! Poor broken little thing—she looks fifty —and think what her life's been—and what mine has been —you and the girls and health and friends—but I c-c-can't help it!"

"You're freezing, you poor idiot! Haven't you been asleep yet?" Gray mumbled, blundering awake in the cold dark room, getting out of her bed, crowding Cynthia back into its warm blankets.

"Oh, this is so delicious!" Cynthia whimpered, crouching in gratefully, crying, catching at Gray's hand. "Don't leave me, Gray. I'm going mad, I think! I couldn't eat any lunch— Guy had half my sandwich—and I didn't eat any dinner, and my head feels so light. I couldn't sleep—hours—and that horrible cuckoo clock at Papa's laboratory striking and striking . . ."

Her eyes blazed brightly in a colorless face; her eyelashes were stuck in wet points; her dark hair fell in a rich tumble on her shoulder. Gray, hearing Cynthia's teeth chatter, went for hot milk.

Presently Cynthia sat up in bed, drinking it gratefully, her feet gingerly approaching a hot-water bag.

"You're so good to me, Gray!"

"I'm so sorry for you."

"We love each other," Cynthia said simply.

"It's too bad."

"And, Gay, when a man like Guy loves you——"

"I can imagine it," Gray said faintly.

"We were going away together tomorrow."

"Cynthia!"

"We were."

"Were you crazy!"

"I guess so."

"You wouldn't do that, Cyn!"

"I tell you I was going to."

Gray watched her, with a paling face and rounded eyes.

"You *couldn't* do a thing like that!"

"I had packed. And he had packed. We had it all arranged, for weeks."

"Cynthia Trezavant!" Gray said weakly.

"So you can imagine——" Cynthia jerked her head faintly in the direction of the Little Quito ranch, and Gray nodded, her memory supplying the whole scene of Rhoda's arrival a few hours ago.

"But, Cynthia," the older sister presently asked earnestly, "what will you do now? You'll have to see him; it'll be as bad as ever."

"I know."

After a long silence Cynthia said suddenly:

"I'm warm and I'm comfortable, and I'm full of delicious hot milk, and you're an angel. I can really sleep now, Gray. I'll go to my own room."

"Take the hot-water bottle then," Gray said. "And I'll read for a while, and look in on you in half an hour."

"I'll be asleep in five seconds—really."

"I believe you will." Gray caught her sister's supple form with an embracing arm as Cynthia passed her, and looked lovingly into her eyes. "You'll have to go away, Cyn, that's all there is to it!"

"Yes. But where?" Cynthia demanded, in sudden anger and despair.

Jim Fowler answered her. He came to the ranch to see her a few days later, and he and Cynthia walked about, in commonplace friendly fashion, talking and laughing. But all the time Jim was trembling with desire for her and she knew it.

She must have been less than woman not to thrill at it. The girls might tease her about her conquest after he was gone, but they had to admit that Jim was physically glorious, and personally a nice and simple and gentle fellow.

"He's the handsomest thing I ever saw," Leslie said.

"I don't think you ought to encourage him, since you don't like him, Cyn." This was Gray.

"But I'm not encouraging him, Gray, and I do like him."

"Is he mad about you, Cyn?" Lucia asked, a little wistfully.

"Well——" It was heart-warming to admit it, even about a boy like Jim Fowler. Her mouth twitched in a smile.

"Is Miller's Basin much of a place, do you suppose?"

"A mountain town. Gorgeous views, of course. We just drove through it, and I didn't see much."

"You'd run the whole place!" Leslie said, with a chuckle.

"Imagine Cynthia landing like a machine gun in a place like that."

"Imagine the fun of riding through the Sierras every summer—living that sort of a life!"

"Imagine what his children would look like. They'd be super-children."

It was idle talk for three of them. But it began to stir Cynthia unexpectedly. Cynthia running Miller's Basin. Cynthia learning to ride as Jim rode. Cynthia with fair little girls with sculptured chins and straight Grecian noses. . . .

Jim came up to the ranch again. And this time they walked up to the Little Quito, and afterward the girls kept him for dinner.

On the road, walking down, suddenly his big arms were about Cynthia, and her head was tipped back for his kiss. They sat down on a fallen log beside the road, and Jim kept his arm tight about her, and kissed her temples and her hair and her red, full mouth, and the bunched tips of her fingers, again and again. They spoke hardly at all.

After that, when he came, they always wandered away together. And the force and beauty and cleanness of his passion sang in Cynthia's veins like wine. There was no reasoning about it; there was no argument. Simply, she came to know that when Jim appeared sooner or later he would kiss her, crush her in his big arms, and every fiber of her being learned to respond to this splendid, simple, ineloquent lover.

One day, when he had made perhaps five or six calls, her father told her that he didn't wish to see that "cow-puncher" on the place again. If his girls couldn't find men friends among gentlemen, they could remain old maids. Cynthia would please remember that her money was in his hands until his death. She would please not count on a cent of it if she had any intention of encouraging this yokel. . . .

Cynthia listened in bright-eyed silence. She said nothing. But when Papa had slammed off to his laboratory, she laughed.

Gray looked at her fearfully. This sort of laughter boded no particular happiness to anyone.

"Isn't Papa exactly the sort of man whose wife *would* leave her children's money in his care!" she commented.

The other sisters exchanged anxious glances.

"Cyn, think before you marry anyone without Papa's consent," Gray said. "He really can hold out on your money, you know."

"I'll have to think fast, then," Cynthia answered, unalarmed. "It's nine o'clock now. Jim's coming for me at half-past nine, and we're going to San José to be married this morning! You can tell Papa or not tell him. But if you take my advice you'll not know anything about it! I'm eloping, and you don't have to miss me until lunch."

She stood up.

"I'm going in now to write a note for Papa's pin cushion if I can find a pin cushion," she said. And then, behind Gray's chair, suddenly stooping her dark head to Gray's fair one, she added in a changed tone, "Wish me happiness, Sis!"

Gray spoke seriously, her fine face a little pale.

"I'll not know anything about it," she said, "because it's the easiest way out, Papa considered. I'll be as amazed and shocked as he is. But I *do* wish you happiness, Cyn darling —and may God bless you and your husband!"

And suddenly they were all together, the four sisters; crying and laughing, their arms laced.

"God bless you, Cyn, and your husband too!" the three loving young voices said together.

CHAPTER FIFTEEN

THE day that Margaret Thornhill Barry came to talk at the Women's Club of Miller's Basin was one of the hottest the place had ever known.

It should not have been by the calendar; it was still June. But the season was advanced this year; already the encircling hills were burned tawny brown, and the gardens up and down Lincoln Street were dry. The far-away shoulders of the Sierras, where Jim Fowler was taking a party of Eastern men through the Gap, were as faint as gray-blue gauze in the heat; orchards simmered; each tree had its hot ring of shallow shadow; fields were quivering and pulsing under the sun.

The women of Miller's Basin, however, abated no whit of their welcome to the town's most distinguished daughter. Margaret had been raised in Miller's Basin, her father had been Ben Thornhill, the doctor there. Everyone knew Margaret, had been in school with her, or had had children in school with her, or had taught her, or had known her folks.

That a Miller's Basin girl should go East and make good writing stories for the magazines, and marry Kane Barry the playwright, had seemed to tie the little California mountain town in with the great Eastern city with Eastern culture and Eastern letters.

Now, for the first time in eleven years, at thirty-two Margaret was coming back. Oh, her folks had seen her in all that time; Doc and Mrs. Thornhill did not live at the Basin any more; they were down in San Francisco, and Margaret had been there half a dozen times.

This year she and her father and mother were coming back to the old place for a day and a night. Margaret's husband was in England, getting a play ready for autumn production, so Margaret could stay with her old chum, Tibby Rhodehouse, and Doc and Mrs. Thornhill would occupy the spare room at the Hamiltons'. And Margaret would talk to the Women's Club in the afternoon, and talk in the high school auditorium to the Parents-Teachers Association at night.

The local paper went wild with enthusiasm. Cynthia Fowler felt that she could not pick up a paper without being bored by the story of this lucky girl. Her husband in London, and she to go over there in August and join him; oh, well, it was nothing to Cynthia—Margaret wasn't much to look at, and she had no children. She did not have a Jimmy and a Peter.

Cynthia would go to the club; she was chairman of the dramatic section; she would have to go. But she did not propose to get down to the high school that night; it was a Union High School, two miles from town, and the car was not working very well. It was natural enough for Miller's Basin to make a fuss about this girl, but she meant nothing to Cynthia, after all. Cynthia tried not to think about her.

The day started hot at half-past four in the morning, when Peter awakened fretful; he was teething, poor little heavy, bothered baby.

"You poor little soul, you're so hot!"

Cynthia carried him out into the kitchen, which was the coolest room in the house at this hour, and dipping her finger into a pail of cold water, rubbed it on his gums. He bit at the wetness eagerly.

"Let me rub 'em for you, precious!"

"No, mummy, no, mummy, no, mummy!" Peter mumbled.

"Baby said, 'No, Mummy!'" Jim, who had followed them, trailing out from bed in a draggle-tailed old nightgown, said enthusiastically.

"It did sound like that. Today," Cynthia said to the thirty-months-old child, "is going to be a scorcher!"

"Beckfuss?" Jimmy inquired, hopefully.

"Not yet." Cynthia laughed forlornly. The day was one long problem of wondering what to do with the children when they awakened so early; they would all be tired today; she was tired already. It was not yet five o'clock. If once— once—once they would sleep until seven or eight . . .

But they never did, and one had to get through it somehow. One had to go on. Through seven—and eleven—and blazing four o'clock, and so on into the unearthly quiet of evening in Miller's Basin, and into tomorrow. It would get hotter and hotter and hotter until sundown, and then it would get slightly cooler; one could sit on the steps in the dark, and that was restful.

Merciless burning dawn was streaking the backyard with light; long shadows lay from the fence and the shed. Roosters were crowing.

Sometimes on such a day she took lunch and the car and the children and went up the mountain road for fifty miles, where it was always cooler and where there was sometimes a breeze. But one could not do that every day. Anyway, mid-July was only a few weeks off, and then they would go with Jim up to Rangers Valley, and while he took his mid-summer parties to and fro through the mountains, she and the babies, and other small-town women and children, would camp under the cool, high redwoods.

Cynthia had done that last year, and but for the discomfort of caring for one lively baby and expecting another, the experience had been a success.

Her thoughts went ahead to the smoking long hours of the day, as she settled Jimmy off in the crib with a cold bran muffin to crumble, and lay down again on her tumbled bed, the baby in her arm. Neither one would go to sleep, of course, and if he did his brother would immediately awaken him, but it was just possible she might doze. She ached with fatigue.

If poor little Peter would stop fretting, the weather would not be so important. But to a teething baby every rising degree of temperature was a separate trial. Prickly heat, chafing wet garments, swollen gums, Peter knew them all; his days were long stretches of fretful restless shifting from his crib to his mother's arms, to his high chair, to his pen out under the oak; his nights were times of torture for both Cynthia and himself.

This morning she did not sleep again. But she came so close to sleep several times that it was misery to feel his hot little wet importunate hands rubbing her eyes open.

After a while she got up and carried him into the kitchen Jimmy was asleep, quite nude, and dangling at a racking angle over the open side of the crib, head down, tawny little mop hanging, and brown foot on his pillow. But Cynthia knew better than to attempt to straighten him. Anything rather than wake him!

The kitchen was getting hotter as the rays from the east smote upon the cracked green window shade. The world was filled with warm smells: the smell of paint from the Rockeys' shed, the smells of yellow soap and washed tinware, souring milk and sweet, rotting tomatoes.

Peter plumped into his dilapidated high chair, Cynthia sat down in a chair beside him and stared about her and sighed. Her thin old pajamas felt so hot and heavy that she hated the idea of warmer clothes. Most of the housewives of Miller's Basin wore their bed gear about the kitchen and the yard during the morning hours, saving stockings, underwear, and voile or lawn frocks for the afternoon. Nobody would see her, and nobody would care anyway.

She gathered up the tail of her black curly hair and pinned it firmly away from her face. Then, at the sink, she splashed her face with cold water.

"Wa-wa!" Peter wept, holding out fat little hands.

"Wa-wa for you too, darling!"

She carried a cold wet towel to him and splashed his little head generously. She could feel the feverish little gums gripping eagerly on the dripping cloth as it passed them. Poor little chap, he would want the performance repeated a score of times during the hours ahead.

Milk had to be smelled cautiously this morning. It still seemed sweet in the bottle, but there was but a dwindling cake of ice in the cracked box Jimmy had made two years ago, and Cynthia was not surprised, upon heating the milk for Jimmy junior's bottle, to see it forming delicate filmy curds in the saucepan.

She stepped out of the kitchen and went past the dry, yellow weeds on the shady north side of the cottage, and set the ice card conspicuously on the shallow porch. The ice card had numbers in its corners: twenty-five, fifty, seventy-five, one hundred. Cynthia, turning the second number up in a moment of extravagance, thought that there would be few houses in the Basin that did not show this red card today.

It was pitiful to see how Peter was suffering with his big hard teeth. Jimmy's had come in without trouble, but the baby was a perfect martyr to his little red-glass gums. When Cynthia returned to the kitchen, Peter had evidently given up hope for the moment; his shabby little nightgown elbows were on the tray of his chair; his baby face was hidden in his hands.

She drank a glass of water, mixed Peter a few spoonfuls

of a crumbled, sweet brown breakfast food, with a little cream and ice, and fed it to him. He liked it; he was hungry and hot, and it was food, and cold. Between his bites, Cynthia ate some of it; she poured some cold coffee into a glass, cracked ice into it, sugared it, and drank it, and felt better.

Joe Black came with the milk. At eight o'clock the blessed ice wagon creaked dripping through the town, a great wave of coolness and gratitude following it. Now Peter fell asleep, and Jimmy and his mother must be elaborate with whisperings and cautions in the kitchen for fear of waking him.

Cynthia wiped dishes, wiped her sink board, combed her hair, put on some clothes. The kitchen and sitting room— they adjoined by a plain wooden door—were made orderly and shady. Cynthia, beginning to feel languid and tired, sponged Peter when he awakened, powdered him, and buttoned upon him a single, faded, thin blue garment that had been Jimmy's. He sat on the bed while she made the crib afresh, and sat on the crib while she made the bed.

The clocks of Miller's Basin were only striking nine when she carried Peter out to the sandbox and established herself there beside him in the shade.

"Want me to water down your sandbox for the boys, Mis' Fowler?" said Aunt Lou Bates, at the fence.

"I wish you would!" Cynthia scooped her sons aside with an experienced arm, and the kindly neighbor turned the hose sprinkler upon the dry sand and soused it well.

This was glorious. Both boys could have all their clothes off now and scramble rapturously into the wet mountains and puddles. They had old spoons and strainers and cups with which to dig and build; brown and happy and sandy and wet, they fell to work.

"Goin' down to the club this afternoon, to see Mar'grit?"

"I'm going to try to. A good deal depends on Peter's teeth. He had an awful night."

"You think they'll never git a-past them tooth and colic days," the older woman said reminiscently.

"Awfully tiring. And you feel so badly for the poor little things!"

"She's real sweet after all. She han't been quite so cocky sence that second young one come!" Mrs. Bates thought. She did not know Cynthia ~~~~ well, but she had learned from her married daughters that Jim Fowler's wife wan't any too popular in the Basin. Mis' Fowler had come there with considerable notions about Miller's Basin folks, and had tried to show 'em her ways; getting up theatricals and eatin' out in her dooryard. It seemed to Aunt Lou Bates a silly way to act, and when Cynthia Fowler had taken the Morris cottage next door to her just before the second baby's birth, Aunt Lou had regarded her over the fence with none too friendly an eye.

But shucks, Aunt Lou had generously conceded, after a few weeks' observation, there wan't no harm to the poor little thing; she'd just b'en flighty and young when Jim brought her to Miller's Basin. She was a smart manager and a good wife to Jim, and she certainly done her best by that baby. What if she had traipsed about considerable, taking her family up to the Ridge one night for supper, and eatin' on the roof the next? She'd settle down all right when the next baby come along.

And settle down she had into the pale, draggled, heat-wearied mother of small babies that was the accepted Miller's Basin type. Not only Aunt Lou, but the other women of the town, had begun to like her and understand her better.

Cynthia's first night as a wife and as a resident of Miller's Basin had been spent in the house of Jim's sister, Lily Poteet. A square, porched, unshaded wooden house of eight uncompromising rooms, it had already been well filled by Lily's husband, Otis, his old mother, three children, and a boarder. Jimmy had always had a single room, but on this occasion Lily had moved Lillian and Gracie into Uncle Jim's room, and had given the bride and groom the girls' room.

Cynthia had been stout of heart, and she had never thought of weakening or escape. But this had been a terrible experience.

Lily's house, that Jim had accepted as indeed he did everything with good-natured indifference, had been all flies, noise, light, heat, smells. The Poteets were fighters; they lived upon recriminations and rackets, and seemed none the worse for them. This atmosphere had been home to Jim for years; he did not notice anything peculiar about it.

Cynthia had thought at first that she would die of it. It had seemed physically impossible to walk down Lily's creaking, uncarpeted stairs to the kitchen, on the morning after her runaway marriage, to sit at the end of the table, drinking coffee, eating greasy fresh bakery snails, smiling at Lily's sandy, lean, shy, barefooted little girls who were peeping in at the doorway.

But even when her heart and her courage had failed her, her manners and her pride had remained. She could not make affectionate, simple Jim ridiculous before his own people. She could not quite so quickly brand herself as a fool. She would stick it out.

She had let them chaff her; eye her surreptitiously; misjudge her. Lily had never liked her. In Miller's Basin, Cynthia wrote Gray, the women of a family never liked the newest importation. As soon as Lily's brothers, Milton and Sonny, married, then Lily would take Cynthia to her heart as a member of the real family and turn her criticism upon the younger brides.

But Ote had liked Cynthia, and the children had liked her. And they had not stayed long with Lily. She and Jim had found a cottage; five rooms next to a garage, at 67-A Lincoln Street. The letter meant that the place was behind another—behind the Atlantic & Pacific Grocery, as it happened, but facing on a lane.

Cynthia had tried at first to make it picturesque with burlaps and hollyhocks; but immediately the weather had fallen like a smothering blanket upon the town, and this, and the dawning of motherhood, had completely floored her. She had abandoned her scheme of decoration as a hopeless mess, and while-Jim was in the mountains she had lived principally on fruit and ice, lying languid in her shaded bedroom, sometimes coming out to the steps at night to watch the crowds streaming by to the movies, and the lights going up and down on the garage, and the dark blue arch of sky, and the stars.

When Jim was home it was better; Jim was always kind and good-natured, and he enjoyed his meals and the movies, and loved Cynthia in his Miller's Basin way. Men took their wives for granted in the Basin. They quarreled with them at breakfast, and they got "mad" when they first knew a baby was coming, but that did not prevent them from wanting hot meals, affectionate treatment, smooth beds, and from loving and spoiling children when they came.

Cynthia, with deep misgivings, discovered in the first refreshing autumn that Jim was unambitious and lazy. He was a pleasant companion, always good-natured and often amusing, but he did not care much about anything. His Uncle Dan paid him five dollars a day for the ten weeks' summer work, and this, to Cynthia's dawning and rapidly growing consternation, appeared to be about all the income of which Jim was sure.

Romantically, impulsively marrying him, driving with him up into the hot central valleys of the big state, she had imagined herself as mistress of a milk ranch; imagined gentle Jersey cattle like the cows at Treehaven, imagined shady great oaks and crisp cold mornings; like those camping mornings in the Sierras last summer, when they had fished for Lock Haven trout in granite lakes.

One look at Miller's Basin baking in untimely June heat had dispelled half of this illusion at once; it had not taken Cynthia many days to lose the rest.

The dairy ranch—suggestive of shade, coolness, pans of creamy milk, ice house—had somehow turned into a chicken farm out on a hot, bare hill. Jim had explained this casually with the phrase, "Stocker wouldn't sell, so I went in with Silva."

Silva was the Portuguese who lived out on the chicken ranch with his family. Cynthia had only seen the place once; once was enough. It had smelled of chickens; hot little feathers had blown over the dooryard where the dark Silva children, regular in steps of exact years, had sat torpidly staring. There were three rooms in the stark little cabin; apparently they all lived in one. That one had a stove, beds, an oiled dark floor, an odorous sink, pails of water; it smelled darkly of garlic and cheese, baby's beddings and carbolic acid.

There were washtubs under the scant foliage of an apple tree outside, dogs drowsing about like flies, a wire safe hung to a tree. Marigolds languished; chickens drank from the blue stream of soapy water that oozed across the dry ground from the tub. Everywhere were chickens and the round soft droppings of chickens; chickens pecking, chickens watching with round, suspiciously turned eyes, chickens fluffing in dust.

"Do you own it, Jim?"

"Half own it."

"Maybe we could camp sometimes—up there where the trees are by the spring?"

"Nope. I'll be off with Uncle Dan all summer."

Of course. He would be off in the High Sierras all summer, and she would be in Miller's Basin waiting for the baby. She had forgotten that.

Well, it was all like a funny dream. The main thing was not to show the white feather, not to weaken.

When winter came, things had been much better. Winter was one long struggle with mud and cold and fires, to be sure, but Cynthia had had a taste of this at the ranch, and she could cope with it.

Why she had married him, what strange impulse had brought her here to this unknown alien world, she never could quite decide to her satisfaction. It did not matter. Jim was her husband, and as good a husband as his own particular code and his own sweet temper could make him. Jimmy junior's arrival clinched matters; not that she would have jumped the traces anyway.

She had married in one mood; she must work out the results of that marriage in another, in all the moods there were. No getting tired, no running away now, with a husband, a new name, a hot little dry house, a son. Of life ahead of her, of years of this, Cynthia could not think. But she could look back and see all her days with all their lessons and mistakes falling into a pattern. She could feel that she was beginning to understand.

Long before Jimmy junior came she began to wonder what problems she had had or imagined she had had, what trials, in those old days when there were always leisure and coolness at Treehaven, always ice and the pool, redwood shade, books, and the companionship of her sisters. She mused on the scholarly, handsome neighbor of thirty-five, up the hill, who had come into the picture; upon a girl's recklessness and despair in first love. . . .

It all seemed unimportant and unreal from the viewpoint

of Miller's Basin; the simple realities of her new life, its immediate pressures and duties, completely engrossed her physically, and her mind seemed to retire to a distance and study the situation dispassionately from the side lines.

Often she found herself picturing it all, the old easy life, as her eyes might have followed a story on the screen. It was an ended dream. Once or twice a year she wrote to Gray; that was all that was left.

Gray answered cautiously. Papa was still infuriated at any mention of his second daughter; Guy's wife, Rhoda Waring, was placidly established up at the Little Quito ranch house, and was "completely cured, but very frail. She depends on Guy for everything. Her nurse, Merry, is still with them, and such a dear!"

A dream, that old world. Miller's Basin was her world now.

When he was at home, Jim slept late. He hated anything like a regular job for several reasons; one of them was that when he had a job he had to get up in the morning. His summers in the Sierras were demoralizing in that way at least, for when he was with Dan Younger, Jim lived royally, dashed about all day on horseback, could work in dramatic fits and starts, and was usually much featured by the camping party because of his winning smile and the youthful browned body that was so beautiful when it was up on a big horse, or stretched on the face of a great warm rock, or diving into emerald pools.

Waking late in the autumn mornings when the summer trips were over, Jimmy wanted a lazy breakfast with his wife and baby. Food was important to him; he liked to make a real feast of the occasional wild turkey or delicious salmon trout he brought home. In duck season he went off regularly, twice a month, bringing home much more than the bag, and disposing of his surplus in Fresno; Cynthia suspected that this was quite illicit, but Jimmy did it so naturally and easily that she never had the heart to say so.

He loved the occasional opportunity to move cattle. If a herd of milk cows had to be sent down to the valleys, when the mountains put on their winter covers of snow, Jimmy was the boy to do it. He rode down to Merced Fair, and came back with the big black stallion; he took steers to the railway shipping point. Anything that was riding, camping, hunting was the breath of life to Jimmy; any other sort of work was slavery.

His talk with his friends was all of hunting, fishing, adventures in the mountains and by the lakes. Since his seventh year he had hunted deer; he knew where to find them, high up in the mighty folds of the mountains; he loved the excitement of the chase. His gun—young Hudson Fottrell, son of the richest man in the state, had given it to him after an adventurous trip through the Sierras—was dearer to him than anything else in the world. He oiled it, cleaned it, dissected it tirelessly.

Any sort of puttering out in the shed or on the end of the kitchen table satisfied him. In a moment of prosperity just before their marriage he had bought an old car; his care of it kept it usable month after month; he would take the baby, when there was a baby, out to the side yard, and sit the little fellow down on the grass to watch Dad work.

But offices were abhorrent to Jim, and he despised the men who worked in them.

Just before Peter's first hot summer Jim had had a serious quarrel with Dan Younger and had drifted about town for some days telling sympathizing listeners about it and threatening to get up a "string of cayuses" of his own and become an independent guide with a head guide's pay of ten dollars a day. Cynthia had watched the progress of this affair anxiously; it would be a grave thing to have Jim out of a job all summer. In the end Dan had rather surlily approached his independent nephew with conciliatory offers, and they had made the peace. But Cynthia had known that on some occasion of weariness and heat and misunderstanding up in the mountains as the summer wore along the trouble would break forth again.

She herself never quarreled with Jim any more; it had been one of the first bitter lessons of her marriage: that there was never anything accomplished by quarreling with Jim. He merely became aggrieved and sulky like a child; left the house with great slamming of doors, or deliberately avoided doing some small customary task that helped her: did not bring in her stove wood, or left her to pick and clean the ducks unaided.

Then suddenly he would laugh good-naturedly and say, "Well, come on, let's forget this, and stop acting like fools!" and the next step was a succession of adoring kisses and perhaps a contented reflection upon the happiness of their marriage and the confidence and sense of their relationship. Cynthia would then have to decide between patiently returning to the cause of the dispute, patiently reminding him that even now he had not said that he would not gamble, would not drink too much with the boys down at the Lodge again. If she was to be kissed and praised, might she not force him to make some promise, some suggestion of reform?

This course, on the few distressing occasions when she had the painful courage to pursue it, only led to fresh and worse trouble. Jim would express himself as disgusted with her; she was nagging and brooding; she couldn't forget and forgive, and let bygones be bygones. Gosh, women were queer! They loved grievances; they never could let anything go. Here he had wanted to be friends with her, and had kissed her, and she was holding off—had to consider her

pride—couldn't let go—it was the damnedest thing he'd ever
seen. . . .

Volleys of this sort usually exhausted her. He was not
going to change anyway, he had not learned any lesson; she
might just as well hold her peace.

She learned to hold her peace. She learned to be alone and
not lonely; penniless and not afraid. She learned to handle
the heart-breaking and back-breaking responsibilities of
motherhood single-handed, and to carry the burden that is
that of the small-town woman—the burden of neighbors'
eyes and neighbors' voices, of hard living conditions, of
burning, merciless summer heat, and cruel winter cold and
mud and darkness, and not to complain.

Hardest of all was the sense of loneliness, of isolation.
Cynthia had lived all her life in an atmosphere of good
books, of good talk. The books the women of Miller's Basin
liked, their comments upon them, set her teeth on edge. She
much preferred their discussion of upside-down cakes and
green tomato pickle.

These native women loved Miller's Basin. They went away
from it only to rediscover its superiorities. They kept their
hot, boxlike houses spotless with no apparent effort; Cynthia
was mystified at the cleanness of the kitchens, the darkened
peace of the bedrooms, the leisure that enabled almost every
housewife in the village to sit on her shady porch all afternoon long, playing cards, or watching the world go by.
Mrs. Bates, for instance, washed her kitchen floor about once
a month; her blue-and-white-squared linoleum was always
immaculate.

But Cynthia could not go into the kitchen to get Peter a
glass of milk and a Graham cracker without leaving spots of
water by the ice box, drops of milk on the sink board, crumbs
on the floor. Of course Mrs. Bates's children were grown,
but Clara Rockey, who lived on the other side of the hot,

grassy lot that held Cynthia's shabby five-room cottage, was about Cynthia's age, and had five small girls, and Clara's house was the town's boast and model. Clara had married at seventeen; "more fool me," she usually added smilingly to the statement. She was a pale, strained, waxy-looking woman, with colorless hair pulled tight off a lumpy forehead. Clara did her own washing, her own baking, her own sewing, because Hen Rockey thought that being busy kept women out of mischief. When Maxine, Denise, Claire, Rose Marie, and Olive had been born, Clara had wrestled with the Angel of Life in her own dark little bedroom, unaided by doctor, nurse, or merciful anæsthetic, because Hen's mother, a highly religious old woman who lived with Hen and Clara, had persuaded Hen that any mitigation of the pains of childbirth was against the divine decree that the woman should bear her children as her punishment. Clara's mother in law was her nurse when she was ill.

Old Mrs. Rockey had borne but one child, and that forty years earlier. Clara bore her five gallantly and knew there might be five more. Yet she was always clean and cheerful, and her house was always in order; her children played amiably under the three trees that graced her backyard, and Hen was faithful to her even if she could bear nothing more than girls.

"He never looks at another woman," she would tell Cynthia. Jimmy made a rather dry comment upon this statement that made him and Cynthia laugh guiltily whenever they thought of it.

CHAPTER SIXTEEN

CLARA was going to the Women's Club to hear Margaret Thornhill Barry, and Aunt Lou Bates was going. Clara would have to take Olive along because Olive was nursing, and Cynthia would take Peter, sit far in the back of the hall, and slip out if the teething baby became troublesome. All the other children would be left with Clara's mother, Mrs. Utter. Grandma Utter took this responsibility lightly enough; she was an enormously fat woman who sat in a littered backyard, among milk bottles, ropes, broken machinery, chickens, barrel hoops, tin cans, and scores of other objects fascinating to childhood, and threatened her charges with being "tarred real good on their bottoms" if they so much as looked at the gate. "Ef anything kills 'em, I didn't go fur to do it!" Grandma Utter told the young mothers genially; Clara and Cynthia, accepting her generous help with a laugh, never worried about the children when they were in her care.

Clara came over to the fence with her baby to talk to Cynthia, who was soothing hers after a tumble in the sandbox.

"He feels the heat, don't he?"

"He's still cutting those two big teeth."

"Ain't it a shame that the poor little things have to do it?"

Clara sat down, panting, and wiped the sweat from her waxen forehead.

"Shall we go to hear Mar'gret Barry this afternoon?"

"I meant to."

"I know. But it's so hot."

"It'll be cool in the clubhouse."

"I know." Clara fell silent, and the heat pulsed and throbbed about them, as shrill whistles and one clang of a great bell from the village said noon. "Gramma's in a terrible mood this morning," Clara presently added, in a mild, speculative voice.

"What about?"

"It always makes her kind of mad to have me take the children to Ma's."

"Well, then, why on earth doesn't she take them off your hands herself?"

"Oh, you know Gramma," Clara said, with her resigned smile. "She wouldn't speak to nobody at breakfast, and she told Hen afterward that it was just half a year to the day his father died."

"I thought she always shut herself into her room all Christmas Eve because of that?"

"Yes, but half a year—half."

"I see. But isn't it a long time?" Cynthia asked lazily, after a pause.

"Hen was four."

Clara had spoken quite simply, but after a moment both women laughed, rather guiltily, and with a glance toward the back windows of the shuttered neat Rockey cottage next door.

"Where's Jim now?" Clara presently asked idly.

"I imagine he's gone back with Dan. There was a party going up from Rangers Camp last week. I didn't get any note from Jim. But Bud came down, and he told me that Jimmy and Dan were scrapping all the way through, last trip."

"Ain't that a shame?" Clara said.

"Men don't seem to have much sense." Cynthia was anxiously watching Peter's bottle, which remained almost full of its blue-white mixture of milk and barley water. He was not hungry. Instead he was falling asleep, wet and hot against her breast, sending heat through her whole body. Clear beads of sweat dotted his forehead and dampened his soft fuzz of hair.

"Well, you'll git up to Rangers Camp yourself next month, won't you?"

"I will," Cynthia admitted with a laugh, "if Jimmy sends me some money. But if he's going into the mountains again it'll be six weeks before he gets back to Rangers. I told him about it, and I wrote him about it—but you know how men are."

"I'm goin' to git up there for a coupla weeks. But it seems such a shame with Hen working so hard to have him eating round. He hates the Cafeteria."

"Why doesn't his mother stay and cook for him?"

"I think she's going over to her sister in Pacific Grove next week."

Cynthia made no comment. She presently carried the baby into the house and lowered him into his smooth crib; it was cooler in there than outside; he did not waken. She made herself iced tea and ate a cold baking-powder biscuit; she gave Jimmy junior cool sliced peaches and more Graham crackers, and milk with a lump of ice in it.

At three o'clock she and Clara and their babies were at the club. Cynthia wore a disgraceful old thin linen, a relic of long-ago days of leisure and comfort; its lines were still smart, but she had washed it so often and so unsuccessfully in the tubs under the oak tree that it had become discolored and twisted and tight, and she loathed it. Her hat was the hat she had snatched from the closet before that runaway from Treehaven more than three years ago.

Margaret Barry was a few years older than Cynthia; she

was slight and pale and plain with bright eyes and a joyous manner. She wore a thin crisp frock of handkerchief linen and a broad white hat.

The women were crowding about her; they wanted her signature on club programmes for little girls. She looked up interestedly at Cynthia and said, "Oh, I don't know you! You're new to the Basin? Jim Fowler's wife—and this is your darling brown baby?"

She had great applause when she finally was introduced by proud old Mrs. Binney, who was perspiring gallantly in her dainty violet voile and black lace hat. "She needs no introduction; she's our own girl of the Golden West," said Mrs. Binney. "I'm not going to say 'the famous Margaret Barry'; I'm just going to say 'Peggy Thornhill!'"

Everyone laughed at the daring of this, but Margaret did not mind it a bit; she said prettily in the darkened clubroom that was so hot and where the fans were throbbing like butterflies' wings in the gloom, that sometimes, when her husband was not around to get hurt, she just loved to be called Peggy Thornhill again, and she wanted all her old friends of the Basin always to think of her that way.

And now, what did they want to hear? About her work today when she'd been so—so "lucky"—and about Mr. Barry's work, and about their going to London together in a few weeks? Or about the discouraging days in the beginning when the manuscripts came back and back?

At this all the women began to applaud, so Margaret began with that, and made the story of her early discouragements and adversities so merry that they were more delighted with her than ever.

Cynthia had to slip out before the talk was half done, because of little Peter's discomfort. She carried him three blazing blocks to the disorder and shabbiness of the Utter backyard, and sat there for a while talking with the wheezing,

cool old mistress of the place, and letting Peter suck rapturously on a silver spoon, dipped and redipped into a cup
of ice water. Grandma Utter had out a big watermelon,
frosted with icy beads from her spring house; the children
were wolfing the cold, sweet pink pulp, and Cynthia was glad
to relinquish Peter to a pen in which Clara's fourth daughter
was crawling and chattering, and enjoy her own great ring
of the cold fruit.

Grandma Utter's iron-gray hair dripped water; the collar
of her thin, clean percale showed a dark column of stringy
stout neck; no other garment showed, except sandals. She
said she had recently given herself a "real good wash"; evidently the children had shared these ablutions, or had been
allowed to play with the hose, for their heads were dripping
too.

Cynthia hardly heard what she said. She was thinking of
that other woman, Margaret Barry—that happy, cool, successful woman who could spare broiling Miller's Basin a
day in which to be praised and adored, before she went
down to cool San Francisco to trips and the packing of
trunks, travel, more praise, and the sight of strange cities
and seas. Oh, it was not fair, it was not fair!

In the twilight she herded her little boys home; her house
was baked dry, odorous from the heat; the four walls seemed
to hold in the throbbing, smothering air.

More crackers and fruit and milk; then all three moved
to the doorstep and sat looking into the burning dusk and
watching the long day die and the hot moon rise up over old
Cap Poteet's eighty acres that his father had plowed first in
1850.

Dry red-brown pigs were rooting in it now, but it would
be sown again next year. It had two oaks in its center,
towers of darkness and cool against the blaze of meadow.
There were big signs advertising gas and cigarettes along

the highway side of it, but Cynthia was on the opposite side, some six blocks away from the lights and noise of the town. Sometimes, when there was a circus or a carnival, she could hear echoes of the band, but usually only a dim mingled murmur of sound came up to her. She could see the garage sign, high up against the glowing blue night, and the fanning up and down of lights at the movie-house doorway. Motor-cars chugged and backfired, sounded their horns and were silent again in the night.

The thought of Margaret Barry burned in her heart like a burning coal. Margaret owned the town tonight. After cooking, serving, and clearing away supper for seven, Clara Rockey came over, still fluttered with enthusiasm over the distinguished visitor. Clara had gotten Hen, who hated to take the car out in the evening, to say that he would go down with her to the high school to hear Margaret Barry talk tonight.

"Then Joe Rhodehouse drives her down to the midnight train, and she gets to San Francisco tomorrow morning," Clara reported. "They say it's real cool and foggy down there."

"I'll go over every half hour and look at the girls, Clara."

"I knew you would. It ain't keepin' you home?"

"No. I wasn't going anywhere."

Jimmy junior, sprawled restlessly asleep in the dilapidated porch hammock, awakened suddenly—perspiring, bewildered, very sick. He and Rose Marie Rockey had eaten some "green beads" from a dusty bush in Grandma Utter's side garden just by the bay window.

Rose Marie was not sick until the morning. But as soon as she was better, Clara gave her a good whipping just the same for eating anything without asking Mamma. Cynthia, an unwilling witness to poor three-year-old Rose Marie's punishment and shame, suspected that the baby did not in the

least realize what it was all about, but there was no use inter-
fering. The mothers of Miller's Basin did things their own
way and were not to be turned aside by any new-fangled
ideas of child psychology.

She brooded on Margaret Barry; the thought became a
bitter obsession with her, making life seem harder and duller
even than it was.

CHAPTER SEVENTEEN

POVERTY gnawed at Cynthia's spirit; she went to the bank and saw old Colonel Lennox, and he very graciously advanced her twenty-five dollars, so that she could move with the babies up to Rangers Camp, where sooner or later Jim must arrive, and where they could get their financial affairs straightened out. In the years of her marriage Cynthia had done this over and over again; the Fowlers' affairs did not seem destined ever to attain a settled condition.

Their rent was three months overdue; thirty-six dollars in all. But that was always to be expected in July, for Jim did not go out with Dan until late June at earliest, and Dan never paid in advance. Jim must be with him at least six weeks before he would advance that precious first hundred that Cynthia was awaiting now—the hundred that refreshed her arid financial desert like a running stream of clear water.

Red Francis was taking a truck up to Rangers Camp.

"Sure," said Red, spitting thoughtfully on the floor of the big, sweet, dim livery stable where Cynthia interrogated him, "sure I'll take you and the kids up. But it's kinder slow, with the truck. I don't make more'n twelve an hour on the grade."

"It'd cost me three dollars on the bus."

"Well, if it's worth it, you come with me. But my wife won't travel that way. Says she feels every bone in her body broken, bumpin' along."

Red was going on the ninth, and Clara and Hen Rockey

coffee for herself and Red, and brown bread sandwiches with cold scrambled eggs and sliced tomatoes in them. She wrapped them carefully in paper napkins. She and Red would buy fruit—figs or plums or peaches—along the way, to complete the meal.

All this meant work; she was perspiring, she was tired already, and the clock had not struck the half-hour. She drank milk, took casual bites of bread, as she went to and fro. And as she did so, she remembered delicious picnics, expedition mornings, down at Treehaven. The big cold ice boxes filled with chicken and cream and berries and green-black avocados; the cellar where watermelons and peaches and golden apricots waited, cool and damp. She remembered her cool bedroom and her closet with its fresh organdies and batistes; she remembered her slim little pink checkbook that always had a balance. . . .

And the great redwoods shadowing the croquet lawn, and meals on the Galleria, scented with honeysuckle, and the pool dripping forever over the dam with a cool sound infinitely restful and refreshing. . . .

At four she and her trunk were out by the road. It was not a particularly heavy trunk; she had dragged it down easily enough. Peter, in a thin cool romper with his tight white sweater over it, was on her arm; her free hand held tightly the small palm of the excited Jimmy.

Red was pleased not to be kept waiting. He swung her trunk into the truck with one mighty movement of his big arms, and afterward held the baby expertly while she climbed up into the high, teetering seat. Jimmy was placed beside her, between Red and herself; she stretched down to take the baby, and a minute later they were off.

It was a high seat. For a few minutes Cynthia had a delightful sensation of being tremendously up in the world with the cool dawn wind in her tired face.

Presently she discovered that it was a hard seat too, although there was a flat carpet cushion on it. It joggled, and the light back of the seat was too far back to be of much use to her. She had Peter on her right arm, and with her left she had to steady Jimmy, who was almost shaken from his place as they bumped along.

But the air was cool, and the novelty of the experience gave them all a sense of great adventure. All the world was dark now, and the villages through which they went were asleep; it was nearly five o'clock before the shoulders of the mountains showed gray and soft in the sunrise and the tops of the oaks were netted in fine shafts of red-gold. Dew was rising, and larks circled giddily up toward the moving banks of the land fog; cocks crowed and cows called loudly; smoke was beginning to rise from the roofs of the farmhouses and roadside inns. Cynthia had not felt so cool, so happy, so excited for weeks. She sang songs to the children, and she knew Red listened as appreciatively as they.

"What's the matter with your old car, Mis' Fowler?"

"Only one thing, Red. It won't run."

He chuckled over this for the better part of an hour. "Only one thing, hey? It won't go, hey?"

They got down at a gas station; Cynthia made cramped little Jimmy totter about, peeled him a warm peach, and gave him a tin cupful of water. The baby had a drink too, and had his soft little hot temples sponged. It was broad hot day now, and there were more than a hundred and fifty miles still to go. Cynthia's back was on fire, and a faint heat headache pressed behind her eyes.

"You ain't got your bedding in that trunk?"

"Bedding! It seems to me I'll want to sleep in the creek with just my head out!"

Red laughed also at this, ruminatively and savoringly. The truck rumbled on and on; they were traveling at a rate of about twenty miles an hour. Cynthia dragged Jimmy, who was asleep, upon her left knee. Peter, also heavy in slumber, was breaking her right arm. She began to watch the signposts. Sierra Meadows; seventy-two miles. And Rangers Camp was fifty miles beyond Sierra Meadows. Well, they would get there somehow.

It was half-past nine o'clock of a hot, clear summer morning. There was no shred of merciful cloud in the sky. The sun poured down in a steady, flawless stream; the road was open, although as they mounted steadily toward the northeast they began to rise past wooded canyons over which buzzards hung motionless and from which quail called with a quick, fluty drumming. The motionless dry air was scented with pine and juniper; clouds of stifling dust rose whenever the truck, meeting a lumber wagon or a hay cart or some slim luxurious pleasure car with white-clad tourists inside, floundered clumsily off the pavement into the gullies.

Presently Cynthia heard the ripple of water; they had reached a wandering fork of the glorious King River.

"Red, could we stop a minute?"

"Sure!"

But she was almost too cramped to get down, burdened as she was, and when she found herself by a deep cold pool, fifty feet from the roadside and well into the sweet green woods, with the baby seated flushed and tearful and just awakened against a pine trunk, she began to cry with sheer weariness and nervousness. Cynthia splashed her face, she drank deep of the swift icy water, but she could not stop crying. However, she proceeded none the less swiftly with the processes refreshing to small boys—washing their faces, loosening their hot little garments, combing Jimmy's tawny mop and Peter's black curls, wet and smooth. The baby's dear little troubled brown face was bursting with color; his Beethoven eyebrows were drawn together in anxious amazement at the treatment to which he was being subjected. Cynthia laughed forlornly at him as she gallantly started back to the truck.

"It's only ten o'clock, Red. But this would be a lovely place to lunch. You didn't have any breakfast except a cup of coffee and a snail."

"Well, I dunno. Maybe we'd better be gettin' on. I have to git loaded and start back at nine. We can eat whiles we're goin'."

This time she established herself and the children on the flat floor of the empty truck. There were some terrible old oily quilts there, used for packing, and Cynthia made a sort of odorous nest of them; the jolting was already shattering back here, and there were rougher roads ahead. The boys stood on their unsteady legs, were bumped down, rolled and wept, and were quieted again. After a while Cynthia passed a sandwich up to Red, and after pouring herself a cup of warm, sweetened coffee from the milk bottle, surrendered him the remaining pint. The children were fed; there was a stop for a drink.

"Oh, keep quiet!" she told them wearily, back on the quilts again. For the heat of the day was insufferable now, and she began to worry about half-remembered tales of sunstroke or prostration, of infants "succumbing" to hot weather.

They all went to sleep, a perspiring nightmare of a sleep for Cynthia, rasped by her uncomfortable clothes, pressed upon by the hot small bodies of the boys, her face and hands burned by the furnace breath of the relentless day.

At four they were at Rangers Camp, having slept through the stop at Sierra Meadows. Rangers Camp: a great shady space under mighty trees whose velvet shafts were mahogany-brown in the afternoon sunshine. They stopped at a porched general store with fishing poles and leather jackets at its wide-open doors; there were tents here and there off in the forest vistas, and campers wandering about, coolly superior, by virtue of earlier arrival, and comfortable in khaki and faded linens. Eyeglassed school teachers were there with cameras; an eager group surrounded a great cart of green watermelons. There were a post-office shed; an emergency hospital; notice of a movie show and a dance at Sierra Meadows.

Cynthia was too wretched with stickiness, weariness, stiffness to move. But she must move. She must lift her babies down, straighten her hair, pull on her shabby old white hat, thank Red, and stand guard over her trunk and her children until someone came to her aid.

Mrs. Moss came out of the store and recognized her. Well, she was glad to see the Fowlers! She'd seen Jim a week back goin' up again into Muir Pass with Dan and some Chicago folks. Mrs. Moss held Peter, and Cynthia tottered somehow to the post office and the agent's office, and got the key to her locker, and got Willie Moss to break out her mattresses and bedding and move them to Camp 3, Site 22, North Madrone.

"Want your tent up, Mis' Fowler? Me and Bud'll do it."

"Willie, if you will, I'll buy you a watermelon!"

"Oh, whoopee!" Willie said eloquently. Cynthia walked the long mile to her camp slowly. She was broken. Her legs were trembling; her whole body bathed in perspiration. Her face burned dryly and her eyes were on fire. No matter, they were here.

Mrs. Moss had blessedly taken possession of Peter. Many times a mother and grandmother, the older woman was a saint as well. She knew what Cynthia was feeling, and what it would mean to have experienced hands care for the prickly, weary, hot, teething baby for this one night.

While Cynthia was doing only what must be done, laying the stained old mattress flat, smoothing blankets on it, getting out frying pan and oatmeal, six buttered hot biscuits with jelly and bacon in them came from Betty Howden, Mrs. Moss's daughter, and four peaches from "Peter and Gramma, and Gramma says Peter's fine, an' he's asleep, and you're to git a good sleep!" said Sonia Howden, aged eleven, the messenger.

"They're so kind!" Cynthia said, in tears. Dusk, cool and sweet, had come down upon the Sierras now, and the camp-fires were sending fountains of sparks up toward the clear soft sky; the river was singing, and young persons, strolling through the woods, sang too. Night would be cold, with owls hooting and small persons sneezing in their camp beds.

The blessedness—the miracle of cool night in the forest —wrapped Cynthia and Jimmy in dreamless deep sleep before the first star came out in a blue, moony sky over Sentinel Rock.

The next day, a cool, sunless day, when the waters of the river looked rough and unfriendly, she set her one small platform and its adjacent cooking site in order. Her grill was about two feet square; it was blackened by years of use, and had cold caked ashes at its base, but it burned splendidly; the woods all about were carpeted with fuel— she had only to walk to the nearest skeleton of a fallen forest giant and strip it of white dead twigs, to lay in a week's supply.

Some of the campers near by had four or five platforms in one group; some had awnings, built-in tables, cupboards against trees, folding chairs, individual campfires. Others were plain and poor; none plainer or poorer perhaps than Cynthia's little camp, her few blackened utensils, her shabby comforters, her tin cups and the single grocery box she used as a storeroom.

She swept the drifted pine needles away from her grill;

turned her box on end to serve as a seat as well as a closet; set up a washroom in the tent, with a tin basin, an old saucer, and a cake of soap. The mattress would be laid just back of the tent, in the protection of the trees, and Cynthia and the children would sleep under the waving redwood branches and the dark blue sky and the stars.

Getting her little world to rights in the pleasant days that followed, greeting old friends and neighbors in the big forest, she reflected upon her affairs. She had exactly eighteen dollars and ten cents in the world. If Jim had gone up to Muir Pass again, he might not be out for another four or five weeks. The money must last that time.

Well, it could be done. Milk was ten cents a quart in the camp; the children used three pints a day. For the rest it was bread and fruit and corn and cookies. . . .

It could be done. But it was a straitened and humiliating way to live, with every stamp and every lump of sugar important. No intelligent woman ought to have to do it. Cynthia's brain ached with thinking; somehow she must get out.

"Next winter," she told Clara, "I shall have to get a job."

"Jim mind?"

"Mind?"

"Well, a man ain't going to set home with children."

"No—but I'll have to pay someone. Old Mrs. Crowley."

"You said that before Peter was born," Clara reminded her. "Look at me with five of them, and Maxine only eight. Maybe you'll get started again."

Cynthia, working busily on under her neighbor's dreary monologue, would feel her heart sink. Life was a little too much for her on these terms. She really did not know how to face it. If Gray might be with her for a while, or even Lucia; if Papa would send her some money, or let her come home for a rest, she felt that she could go on. But as it was, heat and poverty and fatigue and bewilderment were beginning to tell heavily on nerves and strength.

"Father still mad at you?" Clara would ask, sympathetically.

"I imagine so."

"Answer your letter?"

"Not a word. I wrote him," Cynthia told her one day, "that I was sorry; I begged him to forgive me. Awfully hard to do that."

"I'll say."

"At first I thought I never could. But you can do anything," Cynthia said, with a glance at her boys, "for your children."

"That's right, too."

"Once he—forgave me, I know he'd be proud of them."

"Men are queer," Clara would muse. "And some women are too—mothers, I mean. Hen's Aunt May hasn't spoken to her daughter Min Veely for seventeen years."

"What for?"

"Well, Aunt May had a sister who married a feller named Bob Veely, see?—and she died. Well, it musta been five years after that that Min met him—he'd been livin' in Walla Walla. But Hen's Aunt May told her he was her uncle, and if she married him she'd never forgive her!"

"Idiot!"

"Min's cried herself sick about it, but Aunt May won't give in. When Min's baby died she tried to see her mother, but Aunt May told her it was a judgment on her."

"Delightful family, the Rockeys."

Clara would laugh, guiltily.

"What's your father got against Jim Fowler?" she might ask.

"Nothing."

"Just didn't want you to marry?"

"If Papa would let us visit the ranch," Cynthia would muse aloud, "and send me my old allowance, Clara, I wouldn't have a care in the world. My mother left us money, but he has the say about it, all his life long. Isn't it queer— isn't it queer that having been responsible for my existence in the first place, he can *know* that I'm unhappy—know that we need money——"

"You'll never get men to feel responsible for their children," Clara would observe. "Look at Joe Munseer beating his kids—he's got that little one half-witted, Ma says . . .

"What'd happen," she asked one day, "if you just took the kids and drove over to see your folks? Would your father turn you out?"

"I don't know." Cynthia thought about it. "I don't believe so," she said.

"Do your sisters feel like he does?"

"Gray and Lucia?—gracious, no! I *know* how they feel!"

"But the other one?"

"Leslie. She's married and lives in Manila now. She has a little boy."

Her heart would twist a little. It was a sweet, far-away dream, that place of sister love and home security.

"All you done was marry a man you liked."

"That was all. And I was twenty-three."

"You know sometimes," Clara told her, "a real good scene kinder clears the air. If you went home, and they got cryin' and talkin', and your father said his say——

"The night Nell Clute come over and bawled my brother out to Ma, and Ken said he'd brain her, and Pop ordered Ken out of the house—well—it all turned out real good. My uncle—he was sheriff then—come over and married them, and Ma kissed Nell, and we fixed up a sorta party . . ."

Literal little Clara, with her waxy face and tired body, could not understand why Cynthia would laugh so delightedly at narratives like this.

It was not until the fourth day at Rangers Camp that Cynthia began to feel really rested. Maxine and Denise Rockey had caught a string of fat, juicy trout, and Clara had hospitably asked Cynthia over for the feast. Cynthia had slept well the night before; Peter's teeth were through the hot little glassy gum at last, and she had taken the children far up the river in the early morning and had washed her clothing and their own in a pool, given them soapy baths and had a thorough bath herself, and had treated her silky mop to more than one soaping and soaking.

In the late afternoon, cool and clean and in fresh linen, it was a joy to saunter over to Clara's platform, Jimmy frisking beside her, and Peter at peace at last, kissing her cheek, murmuring the few fragments of words he knew into her ear as she carried him along.

Hen had had to go back to Miller's Basin that morning; the two women were alone with their children. Clara had baked potatoes in ashes; the fresh sweet fish were fried in bacon fat and corn meal; there was a basket of figs.

The odor of wood smoke and pine balsam was sweet through the great aisles of the forest; sleepy sounds of birds came from the underbrush; happy human voices, all about, mingled with the voice of the river and the rushing sweet music of the pine branches, and were dulled into a sort of organ note of peace and content and coolness. The last sunshine lay in burnished red-gold here and there on the layers of the redwoods; a hundred little grills were scenting the woods with coffee and with good odors of toasting and frying.

Cynthia, with her baby in her lap, sat on the steps of the platform and watched the supper preparations contentedly.

Jimmy trotted about, carrying spoons and wooden plates; Peter was completely entertained by the activities of the others. Suddenly there was an interruption.

"Mis' Fowler," one of the children from the lower camp announced, arriving breathlessly, "Jim's here, and he's got his foot 'most cut off where a rock hit him!"

Cynthia stood up. Wild cosmic noises seemed thundering in her ears; the sunlight in the forest turned brassy, and she felt her mouth dry and bitter. She handed Peter to Clara, and ran.

CHAPTER EIGHTEEN

THE next day the Fowlers had to go back to Miller's Basin. They came down on an omnibus, rolling the hot long miles through the smothering white dust and over the hard white highways in six hard hours.

Part of the way Cynthia had to hold Jim's bandaged foot on her lap, to ease him. At the noon rest she dressed it, soaking the wrappings in which the doctor had swathed it with some strong-smelling stuff.

She had to hold Peter most of the way, although Jim could hold him when he was asleep. Jimmy was angelic; Cynthia's whole heart went out in love and gratitude to her good little first-born son, so patient and obedient and sympathetic in this nightmare of a day. Jim junior's fair little face was flushed with the heat; he got tired and cramped on the big leather seat, but he kept gently patting his father's injured foot with brown little tender hands.

Big Jim's horse had slipped on a boulder and rolled and struggled and slipped down the face of a precipice of loosely broken rocks. Anyone else but Jim would have been killed; he had managed to control the animal somehow, and they had landed, apparently whole, in the creek bed some forty feet below, with rocks and earth showering down after them from the trail.

Not until some hours later had Jim shown Dan his bruised and swollen shin; the two men had treated it after a fashion. But two days later there had been pain, and Dan

had sent Jim and Bill Texas back for medical advice. The
party had been seven days out then, but it had taken Jim
and Bill but three to get back to Rangers Camp, even with
the incapacitated foot. No question now that the matter
was serious; the camp doctor had sent them on at once,
sick husband, wife, small babies, to the outside world of
hospitals and sanitation.

Cynthia could act, heroically, swiftly, capably. But she
felt confused and stunned; life was more like a troubled
dream than ever. Dan had sent no money back with Jim;
he had probably not thought of it in the concern he felt
for Jim's condition and the inconvenience that losing his best
cowboy caused him. It was with only twelve dollars in the
world—and those borrowed!—that she arrived at home in
blazing mid-afternoon after the long trip back from Rangers
Camp. Jim had been duly established at the Basin Valley
County Hospital.

The hospital had supplied everything; nightgowns, nurse,
meals, dressings, everything was free. But there would be a
charge of ten dollars for X-rays, and somehow Cynthia
must get this money and get out there tomorrow—it was
four miles out of Miller's Basin—to find out what the
doctors thought of Jim.

Her little house looked deserted and dusty; the broken-
down motorcar stood in the backyard, useless. The rooms
were simmering in the afternoon sunshine that came through
cracks in the window shades. Ants radiated away from a
forgotten jam jar when she opened the pantry door.

She remembered Gray's phrase when a too full or trying
day had daunted her in those old idle happy days when
nothing really had been trying and nothing daunting.

"I am about to dig down to a new level of endurance
and steadfastness," Gray would say, dusting, arranging
flowers, pressing a frock, packing a luncheon, or making

mayonnaise. "I shall shortly be drawing new drafts of energy and efficiency from the depths of my being."

Alone, half sick, frightened, despairing, Cynthia desperately tried to achieve this too. She went about her unpacking, cleaning, cooking, with resolute, steady calm. This phase of her life would pass; Jim would not lose his leg, the boys would grow older, and perhaps—well, perhaps Papa would die. Papa was sixty-five, after all.

"You'll be telling other women about today," Cynthia said aloud. "You'll tell them of Jim's accident, and Peter's teething, and coming down from Rangers Camp, and the hospital, and having no money, and everything. . . ."

The Cutter boys came over after dinner. They wanted to know if she would let them fix her car; they were eager to do it; it would be as easy as pie. And then would she "loaned" it to them for three days' fishing? Cynthia thankfully agreed, and saw them eagerly begin preliminary tinkerings and investigations. If she had the car next week she could go up and see Jim every day.

"We have fallen upon evil days," she said aloud to the airless, starry night.

"You talkin'?" little Jim asked drowsily.

He was lying on a spread comforter on the porch floor behind her. The younger child was in her arms, fretting, dozing, awakening to fret again. There was a dance in the village tonight; she could hear the throb of the bass notes, identify some of the steadily jazzed tunes.

The moon rose over Cap Poteet's eighty acres; the sky was soft clear blue, the Milky Way flung a scarf of dimly throbbing stardust. A warm soft breeze went over the world, and Cynthia felt her clothing wet and clammy against her arms, her breast. She could hear the Rockeys' windmill creak, hear a spatter of water; she could smell dust and gleaned fields, and apples ripening.

The voices of two women came to her from the street.

They were walking down from up Larkins' Hill way, for the nine o'clock movie.

"That's Fowlers'."

"I know."

"Ain't it terrible? They say they got to. Imagine cuttin' off the leg of a big, strappin' feller like that! Lizzie phoned at dinner."

Cynthia sat perfectly still. Cold sweat was on her palms, and beads of water stood on her forehead. Lizzie Larkins was the operating-room nurse out at the "County."

They were going to cut off Jim's leg! Jim, who loved his horse and the trails of the big mountains and the dewy mornings when sunrise found him high up in the Sierras with his gun. . . .

She saw him the next day; sat dumb and stunned, in the big, orderly ward beside him, with Peter in her lap.

Most of the beds were empty. A nurse far down near the door was talking to two undergraduate nurses at a table. They were all rolling bandages. The day was burning hot; all the shades on the southwest side of the big building were drawn down tight. A green glimmering radiance danced over the white beds and clean painted floor.

Jim liked to have her there. He did not talk much; he seemed weak and subdued. Like all sick men, he looked younger than he was; he looked meek and boyish and helpless in the thick hospital nightgown.

"Hurt you, Jim?"

"No-o-o. I was asleep. It hurt like hell for a while in the night. But they gave me some dope."

"Who told you they had to operate, Jim?"

"Doc."

"Can you eat?"

"Sure. Milk toast and soup, and ice cream for lunch. She says she's got a piece of watermelon stowed away somewheres."

"Watermelon!"

"She said so."

"You're being wonderful about it, Jim."

"It's hardest for you."

She could smile at him gallantly: "I'm all right!" But she cried forlornly, unmindful of watching eyes, when she and the boys were bumping home in the hot white dust the omnibus raised, an hour later. And to enter the dry hot cottage, where there was so little comfort, so little food, where flies buzzed, and softening tomatoes and souring milk scented the little square rooms, required almost more courage than Cynthia could command.

And again the maddening thought of Margaret Barry came to her—the thought of that pretty, happy, fortunate woman who was traveling now, buying frocks, signing checks. . . .

Jim came home three weeks later, jerking, lurching on his crutch, and was established in the shady front room, Cynthia propping open the door that connected it with the kitchen, so that he might not miss anything that went on in the house. All Miller's Basin came to see him; the women brought soup and jelly, cream and roasted chickens, fruit and iced puddings, so that the Fowlers had no immediate commissary problems, and ice, wherewith to keep all these unwonted luxuries fresh, became Cynthia's chief concern.

But that phase passed too with the end of the hot weather, and Cynthia found herself faced with the most desperate situation she had ever known in her life. Dan Younger and the other men came back from the high mountains; night came early and cold, dawn was late and soaked with dew; all the leaves fell from the fruit trees, and Cynthia could look from her kitchen door straight across the Mockbees' orchard to the Licketts' house and see the

pumpkins heaped everywhere, big and orange and bright
against the dark earth. There were frosts in October, and
Jim was moved into the kitchen, so that every bit of the
cottage's warmth might be concentrated there.

It was then that Cynthia began to appreciate the full
force of the stunning blow that had fallen upon them.

She had seen Jim twist over on his face in the hospital
bed and cry brokenly over the loss of everything that made
life sweet to him; she had comforted him then. She had
seen him force himself to sound bluff and brave with his
friends later when they came in to sympathize and console.
His gallantry, his laughter, his wit had been the admiration
of Miller's Basin.

Now came a third phase, a phase that Cynthia perceived,
with a sinking heart, might become permanent. Jim, always
rather indolent, always opposed to anything like an effort,
settled down into his chair in the kitchen with a dull, good-
natured acceptance of the whole situation that to Cynthia's
active, high-keyed nature was completely incomprehensible.

He liked his meals; he played countless games of solitaire
with an old slippery pack of cards; he adored Peter. But
with Jim junior's noise and demands he was less sympathetic, and he often fretted at Cynthia—wanted his
scrambled eggs less dry, wondered what was the matter
with his coffee.

He could limp about on a crutch and cane, but in the
cold and frost of early winter he seemed to feel no particular interest in doing so; he liked the kitchen best, and
would ask Cynthia, when she went downtown to market, to
tell Lew or Bill to come up in the afternoon and sit with
him.

Almost every afternoon some of the men came; they would
sit smoking in the kitchen, great clods of mud dropping
from their big shoes. And in the evening neighbors often

came in, charitably concerned for poor young Mrs. Fowler in this bad time.

Mrs. Gerhard, the doctor's wife, leaving a bunch of cosmos on the table, left a folded ten-dollar bill there too. Clara Rockey, wife of the most penurious man in town, slipped over three or four times a week with pans of biscuit or bowls of stew. Other good women reminded Cynthia that their pumpkins were just "a-rottin' " on the fields, or brought her a delicious fat quarter from the shoat "Pa swung the gate on." She could have all the milk she wanted from Chess Mockbee's place a mile away if she would go there for it; Silva came in from the languishing chicken ranch once or twice a month with the gift of a big soup chicken.

Even so, she hardly knew how they all managed to live from day to day. She wrote desperately to her father; to Gray. There was no answer. She went to the Miller's Basin General Store and down the road to the glove factory, looking for jobs; she applied at the hotel. No use, this season. The canneries were closed; the Golden West Annex was closed; Miller's Basin was hibernating. At Christmas time, writing telegrams in the telegraph office, she earned a few dollars; a week later the hospital sent for her. Fourteen men had been injured in a slide up beyond Rangers Camp, and emergency practical nursing was in demand. But Peter was whooping in bronchitis on this particular dark, clouded, cold New Year's Eve, and Cynthia dared not open her kitchen door, much less desert her three helpless men for even a day.

She grew thin; there was a new expression, a new fine chiseled beauty in her dark, mobile face. Cynthia kept her poverty-stricken little domain spotless; she would not allow a word of fear or discouragement to escape her. But sometimes she lay wakeful in the long nights, wondering, wondering. . . .

It made it no easier for her when Jim began gradually to evince still another change of attitude. From despair, from bravado, from the exacting petulance of the invalid he passed into another stage, a stage of wistful gentleness and apology that, to Cynthia, was infinitely harder to bear than any of the others. She was so spunky—and so kind—gosh, she was so brave, with all of this on her—and he couldn't help her. . . . But if she'd just wait until he could hop about . . .

"One-legged fellers can do lots of things. We'll get through this!" he would say. Sometimes, seeing the big tumbled fair head bent over Peter's tiny problems, and hearing the eager, anxious note in Jim's voice, Cynthia would have to turn away to hide from him her tears.

"Gee, I love you so, Cynth," Jim, the undemonstrative, would tell her, catching at her shabby apron like a child, as she went by him on one of her thousand errands. She might kneel down, warm, dark, glowing, and put her arms about him, and lay her brown face against his bleached and thinner one. "Don't ever leave me, will you?"

"My poor old Jimmy!"

"You love me, don't you, Cynth? I'm getting an awful crush on you!" he would say. And once, as she stood at her dishpan, she heard him add, dreamily: "There was only one feller I ever was jealous of—and that was that uncle or cousin, or whatever he was, of yours, who lived up the hill. The painter—'member?"

Her throat contracted, her knees weak, she said evenly, "You mean Guy?"

"Yep. Him." Jim said no more. She dared not ask him any further question.

One day old Dr. Gerhard came to her with a suggestion. He had been trying to persuade Jim to go into San Francisco for special treatment of the leg wound, which had never quite healed, and also for proper diagnosis of another injury received at the time of his accident. Now Cynthia's generous old friend had not only made the arrangements for Jim to enter the City and County Hospital if he would, but had secured the promise of a job for Mrs. Fowler in that same hospital's linen room as mender, laundry checker—"something."

"But the boys, Doctor?" she asked. Her tone was doubtful, but her heart was singing. Work—change—money—self-respect were all dancing like visions before her tired brain.

"You'd have to board them for a while. There's a place right on Potrero Avenue there that would take them," he said.

Cynthia's bright, eager face hardly clouded. All the women who boarded babies were not necessarily murderers; she could see her children daily; she would achieve the impossible, be up early in the mornings, work tirelessly into the nights —they would say that there had never been anyone on this job as efficient, as willing as Mrs. Fowler. . . .

She was smiling; the old doctor saw the bright tears in her eyes, and saw them shining wet on her brown cheeks.

Jim was as eager as she when she went home and told him. He would be glad to have the bothersome "tickle" taken away from his wound; he would be glad to get away from horses and all the talk of packing and hunting and fishing that was Miller's Basin. Cynthia laughed joyously for the first time in weeks as she caught up little bewildered, sticky, cooky-smeared Peter, and announced to him that he was shortly to be a young man about town.

New vitality ran in her veins. She flashed about the five poor, winter-bound rooms singing. They would store some few things in Grandma Baker's basement; they would pack clothing, immediate necessities in the back of the old car.

Clara, a tried and true friend through these last nightmare months, should have the kitchen cabinet and the clock, despite her bewildered protests. "Clara's accustomed to them shelves, and you could of sold that cabinet, if one door *is* off," even Hen protested. But Cynthia was so glad to see the last of these possessions that had been a part of her prison that she would not be denied the luxury of making the gifts.

She signed a note for seven months' overdue rent; neighbors deluged her with gifts for the trip; there were preserves, sleeping socks, towels from the five-and-ten, and one splendid soft Canadian blanket from the town's richest old woman. "There, I've twenty of 'em, and I've hung onto 'em for thirty years!" said Aunty Dwight.

The last night came; Cynthia could hardly sleep for joy. The cottage was stripped now; the car stood outside, loaded, roped, waiting. The children's shabby best clothing was laid out on kitchen chairs; the very last of the coffee was in the pot.

They started at dawn. San Francisco was just three hundred miles away; they must move along steadily to make that on February roads. Cynthia felt rain in the dark wind before morning; looked anxiously at the sky when the light reluctantly began to spread. Clouds from the south, but it was not raining now. Clara ran across the frosty yard to the lighted kitchen; the two young women cried as they kissed each other good-bye.

Jim, rolled like a mummy, was on the front seat, with Peter, alert and conversational and enchanted with this unprecedented proceeding, in his arms. Jim junior, a smaller sausage, was wedged in between his parents. Cynthia took the wheel. She had on her old sweater, her old thick coat, mittens; her hat was tied down with a bandana; an old blanket was over her knees.

"If you folks don't look like the original covered wagon!"
Clara said.

Cynthia turned to Jim in a moment of panic. It was a
scary thing, this burning of bridges after all.

"Jim, ought we wait for a better day?"

"We wait for nothing, do we, Pete?" Jim shouted.

Three minutes later they rolled out of Miller's Basin—
forever, as it happened, although Cynthia little suspected
it then—and took the wide dark road to the northwest.

A cold steady wind blew straight into her face. Clouds
gathered in the dawn; rolled apart; there were watery patches
of blue sky toward the south. The broken old top of the car
had been set up, but it did not afford much protection from
the wind, nor from the soft, swift rain that presently began
to fall. Cynthia worked her windshield scraper with her left
hand; drove with her right.

They breakfasted luxuriously in a small town on the price
of the car. The Mockbees had bought the car for twenty-
two dollars; Chess would take it from Cynthia tonight and
drive it down from the city tomorrow; he had gone in by
train on business yesterday.

Breakfast cost eighty cents; but, oh, it was delicious. At
ten minutes past eight, an hour on her way again, Cynthia
knew that they had achieved the first hundred miles. But
the next hundred miles, along flat, wet, monotonous country
roads between fields, were slow. She was afraid of slipping,
skidding; the rain delayed her. It was raining only at
intervals; she made the best of the clear times, when the
road flashed in bright sunshine and the larks whirled up
from new grass at the fence posts.

At two o'clock they were still twelve miles short of their
second hundred; it was discouraging. Cynthia steadied her
wearied hands at the wheel; she felt cramped and stiff. Presently she stopped in a town and lifted the babies down and

partially unrolled them, and let them run. She went into the station rest room, a dismal place of leaks and smells and cold, and got Peter into dry clothing. But for Jim's sake she dared not delay long. He and his crutch could not be gotten out of the wet and muddy car; they must go on.

Early in the afternoon the weather settled down to steady, saturating rain, with wild gusts that brought the cold water in upon their faces and shoulders. Jim admitted that trickles were running down his back, and the baby stopped Cynthia's heartbeats for a few minutes by an attack of asthmatic wheezing and sneezing. It was simple madness to drive on through these endless curtains of rain, rain, rain, but what else could she do? The villages through which they occasionally passed were shut up, empty, lifeless; chickens were huddled against shed walls, and an occasional housewife running across a backyard, with her apron over her head, or an aggrieved cow lowing at a fence, were the only living things to be seen.

Perhaps they would have to find a roadside hotel for tonight; a waste of precious time and money, but Cynthia began to feel that this adventure might be actively dangerous to Jim and Peter, and that even if she finally reached San Francisco, she herself would be too thoroughly exhausted to get him to the hospital, make herself presentable, investigate homes for the boys, and finally apply for her job. Weary, wet, cold, acutely anxious, she drove on past the endless fields, and the endless crossroads, and the obdurate signs that said, "San Francisco, eighty miles . . . San Francisco, sixty-nine miles."

"Is he asleep?" She glanced at the baby.

"No. He seems to be dopy," Jim said, his own anxious eyes meeting hers. "He's shivering."

Cynthia, her heart rising on one wild flight of prayer, stopped the car and took the child into her wet arms. His little face was burning; he shuddered violently and opened his heavy eyes.

"We'll have to stop somewhere now, Jim—the nearest farmhouse, anywhere! He's sick. My darling—my baby—my own little patient boy!"

One second lost while she took the comparatively dry blanket from her own knees and wrapped it about him, then she was driving again with rain running down the windshield and mud spattering under the soft old tires.

Suddenly a wet signboard was before her. "San Francisco, sixty-two miles. Los Gatos, twelve miles."

Her heart plunged, raced, stood still again. A sort of sickness—a vertigo—came over her, and Cynthia rested weak and broken against the wheel. She was just twenty minutes from Treehaven; from fires and clean beds, from Hing's hot meals and Gray's gentle voice. Her lonely, homesick heart cried out for them; tears rained down on her soaked gloves as she bent her wet face over her hands.

But her tired, colorless, rain-spattered face was bright with a smile as she turned to Jim.

"I will arise and go unto my father," she said, laughing and crying.

CHAPTER NINETEEN

IT WAS Gray who turned from the fire when Cynthia opened the door of her home; the same dear old Gray, in a silver gown with Gray's own fastidious frills at wrist and throat. It was Gray who gave a great cry of love and joy and welcome, and who came running to Cynthia, catching Peter, kneeling, still holding him and Cynthia, to kiss Jim, laughing, sobbing, washing away all the pain of the hard years with that one moment of ecstasy and reunion.

Then there was uproar, doors opening, voices; Lucia, grown beautiful and womanly, was helping Jim in, kissing him in good sisterly fashion; Jim was settled in a big chair; Hing beaming in the doorway, Jim junior bright and chattering and winning, as Aunt Gray stripped off his soaked apparel A nurse Rhoda's old nurse, Miss Merry—was mysteriously here, helping Jim into a warm dressing gown. . . .

Cynthia sat dazed, in a chair opposite Jim. Her sisters drew off her clothes; she was presently warm, dry, drinking hot tea. The fire burned, and in the winter afternoon that had already closed to dusk, glints of light flashed on the beloved old books, the old rugs, the old heavenly walls of home.

She felt as if she were dying; she could never move again. Every bone ached; every kind word and touch made her cry feebly. She held Peter, warm and dry in a blanket, and Gray took his temperature, and—yes, it was Dr. Illyan, Cousin Dana Illyan from Boston, who was quite inexplicably holding Peter's little hot wrist and listening at his chest.

"Dana, how long have you been here?"

His bright smile through fine lenses; his crisp, Bostonian voice.

"Only since yesterday, Cynthia. But it seems to be exactly where I belong! Already one invalid in the house, and now you bring me two more!"

Her languid eyes moved to Gray in interrogation.

"Papa," Gray answered the look gravely. "I wired you last Sunday night. He's had a—a stroke."

"Papa!"

"I was coming home from Arizona," Dana said, in the silence. "I lost my dear wife there three months ago, Cynthia. I telephoned Gray from San Francisco, and she told me about your father. So I came right down."

"I'm so sorry, Dana!" Cynthia looked at Gray again. "Is Papa——? Will he get well?"

"We don't know, dear. He knows us all, and he doesn't suffer. He keeps asking for you. I didn't want to frighten you in my wire, so I said, 'Papa not very well.' But he's—he's——" Gray's voice thickened: she could not go on.

"In your wire?"

"I sent you a long night-letter yesterday, Cynthia." Gray burst into tears, stooping to kiss her sister. "Lucia and I couldn't wait to have you come h-h-home!" she sobbed.

Cynthia looked down at her sick child, looked across at Jim, gaunt and broken-looking among these prosperous, groomed folk. She tried to smile, but she was crying too.

The exquisite peace of it soaked into her being slowly. It was days before she could sense it fully, but they were marvelous days. Broken, weary, content to rest and sleep, to eat her meals and care for the little boys, she drifted about the familiar old rooms like a shadow of the girl who had run away from them four years earlier.

Someone telephoned San Francisco for her, on the wet cold night of her arrival. Mr. Fowler would not be brought into the hospital; Mrs. Fowler's plans had changed, and she was at home with her family. Cynthia heard Gray's pleasant, intelligent voice at the telephone; "Mrs. Fowler" sounded like a stranger. Mrs. Fowler was at home with her family.

"Gray, if I *had* managed to shove that horrible old car as far as the city, I wouldn't have had energy enough to get out of it!"

"Oh," said Gray wisely, "we always have energy enough to do what we *must* do. . . . And when Mr. Meckbee came for the car he seemed quite pleased with it."

Early in the wet, wintry spring morning after her arrival Cynthia went in to see her father. The invalid's room smelled just as Papa's room always had smelled; something reminiscent of the laboratory still hung about it. It was dim in the stormy morning light, but a fire crackled in the airtight stove, and the place was agreeably warm.

She approached him timidly, sat on the edge of his wide bed, touching his hand. The twisted face, the graying Beethoven brows drew into a wry smile.

"Well, Cynthia, you've come home?"

"Yes, sir. Last night. I would have come in then, but Miss Merry said you were asleep."

"I'm better."

"They said you were."

"I sleep too much," muttered the thick, deformed mouth resentfully.

"Sleep is good for you, Papa."

"I have to have a nurse, Cynthia." He began to cry.

"Only for a while."

"Dana say so?"

"This morning. I've my little boys with me, Papa."

"You have little boys?"

"Two little boys."

"Ah, well——" he said, indifferently. It was only his own affair that interested him. "Come back soon, Cynthia," he pleaded. Cynthia stooped and kissed the bushy grizzled hair above his sallow forehead before she went away.

There was an odd hush about the house, with Papa ill, and a nurse installed, and Jim rather awed and quiet in a great chair by the fire, but it was all deeply satisfying, all deeply soul-filling to Cynthia. The old lamps, the old fires, the familiar delicious meals were all infinitely enhanced in value by the years between her last days here and today. Just to look out through a twilight window at the tossing redwood branches and the wet lawn strewn with great syca-more leaves pleased her deeply, mysteriously; to carry trays, to spoon spinach and apple sauce into the children's small mouths, move to and fro as the married daughter of the house, home again, was strangely felicitous.

Guy and Rhoda were in Mexico. Dana must leave for Boston in a few days. Gray clung to Cynthia; she mustn't go away again—ever, ever, ever.

"You'll have to help me with the business, Cynthia. Just yesterday Papa made me bring out a big box of papers; he's kept everything so secret, you know—it's horribly con-fusing to me. But now I'll have to—or one of us will have to—help him. I told him yesterday that you needed clothes, and he said we must go over to San José and get every-thing——"

A long-numbed nerve started into sudden life in Cynthia's heart.

"Imagine clothes again!" she said.

"He said he would sign the check. He's trying to hold on to everything—poor Papa."

The boys were left for a whole afternoon with Aunt

Lucia and Merry. Cynthia and Gray shopped, and Cynthia came home in that state of joy in living that only a great boxful of new clothes brings to a shabby woman. A sapphire velvet with a lace collar; a brown jersey house dress; a new coat furred and warm and soft; new shining shoes. And small suits, too, in linen and sturdy ticking, and little reefer jackets to match little navy caps.

Jim had a heavy soft dressing gown in dark blue and tobacco brown.

"Means I have to keep this up?" he asked shrewdly, upon receiving it.

"Keep what up?"

"This loafing."

"Well—in weather as wet as this——"

"Go on kidding me!" he said dryly. From the beginning, true to his simple country type, he had taken a completely hopeless view of his case.

Cynthia had been five days at home when the Warings returned from a long stay in Mexico. Gray had exultantly announced, by telephone, that Cynthia had come back, and Guy and Rhoda came down at once, late in a cold spring afternoon, to find the Cabin at Treehaven lighted and warm, and the family group about the open fire.

Cynthia got up from the rug, where she had been sitting with Peter. Her brown cheeks were flushed as she greeted Guy; under the filmy bang of her black hair her blue eyes looked big and frightened. Guy saw that the brown splendid body was thinner than it had been, but there was the same squaring of her shoulders, the same lift to her breast. She kissed Rhoda; kissed him very simply. They all sat down.

Guy was changed; it confused Cynthia, for some minutes after their meeting, to see how much he had changed. He had always been lean and big and shaggy; he seemed much bigger and shaggier than he had been, but he was broader now; his once dark hair was thinner, and quite gray, and there were lines, deeply cut lines, about his mouth. The smile was the same, and his drawling voice; the grip of his big hand was the same.

After a while the new Guy settled into the lines of the old, and Cynthia could look at him squarely, studying him, remembering him.

"Guy's gotten so gray, Rhoda."

"What did you say?" Rhoda stammered. She had been nervously concentrating her attention on Gray, to whom she clung childishly.

"I'm as gray as a badger!" Guy admitted.

"Well—look at my gray hair!" Cynthia challenged them all, tipping her dark, brushed mop sidewise. Across its blackness ran a smooth band of pure silver.

"She knows it's perfectly stunning!" Gray observed affectionately.

"Seem good to be home, Cynthia?"

"A miracle. Since Jim's accident——" She had taken a hassock at Jim's knee; she turned now to smile at him over her shoulder. Her manner was quiet, but she was a little pale, and she could feel her heart hammering. "Since Jim's accident we've had such an upset sort of time," she said.

"How—how long will you be here?" Rhoda asked, her teeth showing suddenly against her lower lip.

Cynthia, whose eyes were on the fire, looked up, surprised at the excitement that Rhoda's tone seemed trying to suppress.

"Oh—for a while," she answered, with the kind smile they all had for Rhoda.

"Until I can get up on a horse again," Jim added. He reached a big, thin, clumsy hand for her fingers. Everything he said nowadays was referred to her. "Didn't we, Cynth?

Don't I, honey? You tell 'em!" It was as if, coming helpless into this strange atmosphere, he clung to her, needing
her more than ever.

Gray was radiant tonight. Her Cynthia was home again,
vitalizing the fireside group, vitalizing every moment of the
waking day, in her old way. Cynthia, more beautiful, more
warmly magnetic than ever, with new wisdom and sympathy
in her glowing brown face, and with the new lock of silver
making her black mop look blacker than ever. Cynthia
tender and quick in response to husband and sons; Cynthia,
as always, alert and eager with words, with help, with affectionate coöperation, but best of all, Cynthia happy—so glad
to be here, so appreciative of the plenty, the comfort, the
love, the beauty of home.

After a while, rousing herself from the memories of old
times that Guy's presence brought back from the idle happy
conversation she had shared but absently, Cynthia observed
that she must carry Peter in to bed.

"He's been asleep here for half an hour!"

"He's gorgeous," Guy said. She looked full at him,
steadily.

"Isn't he beautiful? I'm going to say good-night to some
of you," Cynthia went on, moving her eyes with a little
conscious effort, and bending over the unconscious head of
the baby in her arms, "because it takes me half an hour
to settle off these young gentlemen. Jimmy, you come
straight in when Mummy calls, won't you?"

"I'll see he does," big Jim promised.

Cynthia went away, tall and splendid, her body bent
slightly as she carried the child. She turned at the bedroom
doorway for a farewell smile; the Warings were all ready
to start for home.

But when she had gently lowered the sleeping little boy
into his crib and turned to light a low light in the dark

nursery, she saw that Rhoda had followed her, and was close beside her, smiling, in the dusk of the twilit room. And suddenly Cynthia felt that she had known all her life long that this moment of dusk and terror must come to her.

The door behind her closed. The two women were alone. Rhoda, toothed like an animal, trembling, was watching Cynthia closely.

Cynthia lighted a light; they could see each other.

"So you've come back!" Rhoda whispered, still smiling.

"Come back?"

"What did you do that for?"

It was a little hard to speak. Cynthia swallowed:

"Why did I come back?"

"Yes."

"I don't understand you."

They were whispering, watching each other closely.

"Oh, yes, you do!" Rhoda said.

"Why—why *shouldn't* I come back?"

"Here?"

"Here. It's my home."

"Yes," Rhoda said, "and the Little Quito's mine, isn't it?"

"True," Cynthia answered, swallowing again. "Oh, Gray, come in—oh, someone, come in! This is a dream!" she thought. "This is only a dream!"

"You and Guy——" Rhoda began, and stopped. Cynthia, breathing through her nose, her lips shut, looked at her.

"It didn't matter that that was *my* home, did it?"

"That—what?"

"You know what I mean," Rhoda said.

"I *don't* know what you mean." But Cynthia could hardly say the words.

"I found the letter—the letter he wrote to your father—

that night Merry and I got home. It was on his desk. I read it. So you see I know."

"Guy and I—cared for each other," Cynthia said.

"And you were going away together."

"Well—we were going away together."

"Leaving me alone?"

"He would have seen you." Cynthia gulped, with a dry throat.

"And that was all?"

"That was all. We never dreamed you could come back. You *did* come back, and I—I got out."

"Yes—and now you're here again."

A silence.

"This is my home," Cynthia said then, with an effort.

"And my home is *my* home. And you see—I know." Cynthia looked at her.

"I know about you and Guy!" Rhoda's voice rose to a sort of triumph.

"There is—there is nothing to know."

Cynthia gathered small nightwear from a rack; moved about automatically. Rhoda stood still.

"Lucia's going to be married," Rhoda said. "Dana's in love with Gray. They'd feel—horribly—having Guy come in and out of the house, if they knew what I know. Wouldn't they, Cynthia? Wouldn't Gray feel terribly? She loves you so—they all do. They love you much more than they do me —and yet, if they knew——"

A small blanket in her hands, Cynthia stood rooted, looking at her.

"You go away again, Cynthia," Rhoda said. "Get out, and take your children with you. And this time don't come back."

CHAPTER TWENTY

THEY talked interminably, inexhaustibly, Gray and Lucia
and Cynthia. There was no hope of catching up with the
lost conversations of the long four years.

The sisters stood arrested in the process of bed-making,
talking; they lingered over the breakfast table murmuring;
they were all together, chattering once more in the kitchen.
When Cynthia gave the boys their baths at night, Lucia and
Gray hung in the doorway, fascinated, watching, com-
menting.

Once again the old ranch house rang with voices, doors
slammed, and laughter broke out everywhere. The little
nephews were a constant source of ecstasy to Cynthia's
sisters. They adored Jimmy and Peter, and Cynthia knew
that it was for the small boys' sake as well as hers that Gray
and Lucia were so affectionate and simple with the older
Jim, that they made him feel so instantly welcome—so
entirely one of the family.

There was news of all sorts. Leslie and her young lieutenant far off in Manila had a small son; "not half as cute
as Peter, and nothing like as cute as Jimmy!" said the aunts.
But there were very winning little snapshots to be displayed,
and Cynthia studied them gravely—yes, he was cute. In
this one, in the carriage, he certainly had a dear little face.

"Les is happy?"

"Oh, *happy*."

Lucia was soon to be married, too; that was another

thrilling item. She had won the heart of one Bruce McBain, whose neat business card bore the words, "Realtor. Redwood City."

"And is he dar-r-rling!" Lucia crooned, in mentioning him.

"She is going to be one of those wives who tell you that Bruce can eat carrots when he doesn't know what they are, but *beets*—never say beets to *him*," Cynthia told Gray, in a moment of confidence.

Gray laughed guiltily.

"I'm afraid she is. And Cyn, his mother—and she's quite dreadful—is telling Lucia all about Bruce's childhood, and what he can wear and what hours he ought to keep, and Lucia just drinks it in."

"I don't care," Cynthia said, affectionately. "I think it's kind of nice!"

Lucia had towels, engagement cups, sheets. She knelt beside the big chest in the spare room and took them out and laid them in fragrant heaps on the floor. Lunch sets of damask, shiny and pale brown; Italian cut work.

"Vera sent me this."

"Oh, what's the news from Vera?"

"You knew she was divorced?"

"I suppose so."

They had lived so intimately, these three Trezavants, that there was no conversational opening that did not lead them into infinite ramifications. Cynthia, carrying Jim's lunch tray to him, might find Gray and Lucia sewing or idling while they kept him company.

"Gray, where'd we get the new book sets—Fielding and the poets, and all that leather stuff?"

"Aunt Olivette. They were Papa's grandfather's, it seems."

"Did she die?"

"No, but she came out here to the wedding, and decided to spend the entire remainder of her life in Pasadena."

"Whose wedding?"

"My dear—the murderer's."

"The *murderer's*, did you say?"

"Well, we always called him that. He was tried for murder, anyway. Olive married him."

"Olive is married?"

"Oh, yes, on her twenty-five thousand."

"They gave her that—her mother did?"

"Cynthia, you read in the papers how she won it!"

"Won it?"

"Certainly—flying. You saw that?"

"Olive has been flying?"

"Across the ocean. It was the day Leslie broke her ankle, and we were all too busy and too much excited even to look at the evening paper, and we heard it over the radio."

"I didn't even know Les broke her ankle."

"Oh, yes, on the roof, the day of our fire."

"Gray, what burned?"

And at Cynthia's stupefied tone they would all burst out laughing in the old fashion.

Eventually—for they spoke of the Warings only casually during the first confused days—Cynthia and Gray came to talk of Guy.

It was on an afternoon only a few days after Cynthia's shocking encounter with Rhoda in the nursery. It was still in her mind when Gray asked her, out of a silence:

"Cyn, do you find Guy much changed?"

"Terribly," Cynthia answered. She carefully laid away small clean garments in the children's bureau that had been her own bureau at their ages, faced Gray soberly. "Terribly," she said again.

"I'm sorry!" Gray murmured. "Poor Guy!"

They could hear Jim talking to the little boys in the living room a few feet away. It was late afternoon, and there was twilight outside in the garden; the nursery was filled with shadows.

"Has it been so hard for him?" Cynthia asked, reluctantly.

"Horribly hard. She's just—nothing, you know—Rhoda. Oh," Gray said, considering it, "I don't mean that she has always been as bad as she is *now*, exactly——"

Cynthia, sitting on the foot of the bed in the old way, her chin resting against the wooden pineapple on the bedpost, took her up quickly.

"Why should she be worse now?"

"We all think she is," Gray offered, somewhat hesitantly.

"You mean on my account?"

"Well, she's nervous—suspicious. Of course she's dreadfully jealous of Guy."

"I know," Cynthia agreed musingly, and was still

"Gray," she began again suddenly, "does she contribute. *anything*, do you suppose? Anything, I mean, to Guy's happiness to making him comfortable?"

Gray slowly shook her head without answering.

"But then, Gray, what *does* go on, up there at the Little Quito?"

"Oh, well——" Gray began with a sigh, and fell thoughtful.

"Can they ever *talk* of anything?"

"She talks a lot," Gray admitted. "She's really—opinionated, and anything you're interested in, anything he's interested in, she's quite apt to talk to death. They go to movies in San José sometimes, and he has a glorious new Victrola, with symphonies on it—German operas—everything—and they—keep going."

"Then she makes quite a fuss about housekeeping; she's always buying him shirts and neckties, and she's so pleased if he likes them. She thinks he can't get along without her."

"My God!" Cynthia whispered, under her breath.

"I know," Gray said, as if it had been more than an involuntary ejaculation. "I know. . . . He has to consider every word he says to her."

"Well, I suppose so."

Cynthia sat on in the now densely shadowed room, thinking.

"Is it nearly fifteen years, Gray?"

"Lucia and I were saying so the other day."

"Isn't that *incredibly* sad, for a man who loves things to be simple and right—and free as Guy does?"

Gray's heart was sick with anxiety. There was a question she must ask—she *must* ask. She dared not ask it.

"Cynthia, do you ever remember—do you ever think——"

Cynthia bent her lithe body sidewise to snap up a low, cribside light. Both women looked pale and bright-eyed as their glances found each other's face.

"They're all right; they've a fire out there," Cynthia said, as she heard Jim laugh out in the big lamp-lighted room that was just beyond the bedroom door.

"Do you mean," she began, very low, "I remember how I cared for Guy—what it meant to me to have Rhoda come home that day?"

"I've so hoped," Gray faltered, "that it had come to mean—nothing but a sort of memory——"

Cynthia had an armful of small gear: pale brown woolly nightgowns, small wrappers with Navajo patterns on them, little slippers battered and flat. She would undress the boys by the fire tonight, in the next room. She indicated, with a smile, their sleeping clothes.

"These are real, Gray. That was a dream."

"Of course they are!" Gray agreed thankfully. "Of course it was!"

"Living with a man, cooking his breakfast for him, worrying about the bills for your first baby, all that changes everything, Gray. Not," Cynthia said—"not that it keeps me from putting Guy in a special place—always.

"I know he's too easy-going," she went on, with a little nervous laugh, as if she were talking to herself. "I know he's only a rather unsuccessful, rather fat——" She paused. "He *has* gotten fat, Gray, and he looks so much older and so much grayer. I know all that! I know he's not always right, nor always reasonable.

"But there's something about the way Guy stuffs a pipe that isn't like anyone else stuffing a pipe. There's something about the baggy old coats he wears—the way he nails up a grapevine or sweeps leaves out of the arbor—the sound of his voice.

"'*Il est tellement dans la peau*,' I guess," she quoted, smiling with serious eyes. "'*Et j'n'suis qu'une femme!*'

"You see, he's always been in my life, Gray, in our old winters here, and in our games; he knows what I cook well and what I can't cook; he speaks my language."

"I understand," Gray murmured, in a reluctant, fearful voice.

"He was the first man I ever loved, Gray."

"I know."

"It's terrific—when you think of it—the feeling that wakes a girl up, that teaches her what it's all about!"

"But then you—you loved Jim, too?" Gray supplied timidly.

"Oh, yes. And we had our life together—Miller's Basin, and the children——"

Cynthia fell silent, without moving, her brow faintly knitted and her lip lightly caught by her teeth.

"Which must make—which surely must make that old feeling seem like a dream?" the older sister questioned.

"I suppose I hoped it would, Gray."

"You mean," Gray asked in quick fear, "it *doesn't?*"

"I don't know. I wish Guy—weren't here."

"You—Cynthia! You still like him so much?"

"I'm not sure," Cynthia said slowly, "that I like him at all."

After a troubled minute of silence Gray said:

"There's Rhoda, you know."

"Exactly. And Jim."

"And Jim, of course!"

"And you think Guy still—you think he hasn't changed——"

Cynthia considered this; bright eyes on Gray's face. And suddenly she was normal, wide awake again. She laughed reassuringly, and as she and Gray went out to the warm lights of the living room a few seconds later, she linked her arm about Gray's erect slender body.

"How about *your* affair of the heart, darling?"

"Oh, please, Cynthia," Gray whispered, in a panic, "please don't tease me about it—please don't say anything about it! I—I'm so happy here—I've not thought of marriage, for myself—and there's Papa——"

Cynthia let it go for the moment. But a day or two later she seized the opportunity to say:

"Gray, I like Dana so much!"

"Isn't he—isn't he nice?" Gray breathed, in a fluttered, gratified voice.

"Well, of course, he's a very important person—is Dr. Illyan."

"Oh, I suppose so," the older sister conceded faintly.

"Gray, if he asks you, either to go back to Boston with him, or to promise to——"

"Please, Cynthia! Honestly——" Gray was in agony.

"Listen, darling, don't be a fool. He's always liked you, tremendously. I always thought, and so did Les and Lucia, that there was something queer—something *extremely* queer —about his marriage. Either——" She paused.

"Well, you know what happened? You knew he had said —sort of joking——" Gray commenced eagerly. She could not look at Cynthia, but she would not let this misunderstanding go by. "Years ago, he had said, sort of jokingly," she explained, "that if Ursula didn't get better, and drink her milk, and all that, he'd have to take her to Arizona. And then when he went home from here five years ago, her grandfather sent for him and said she had been talking about it—living for it—she must have been a very simple, childish little thing."

"Ah, *well!*" Cynthia said, in the pause.

"That was it."

"I knew there was some explanation."

"Not that he didn't love her, Cyn. He *did.*"

"I know."

"But I had—I had—grown so fond of him——"

"Don't let him go again, Gray!" Cynthia said, as Gray's voice quivered into silence.

"Oh, now——" Gray murmured, suffocating. She devoted herself to the feeding of Peter, who sat upon her lap opening his red mouth wide, like a baby robin, at every approach of the spoon. Cynthia, now and then lending a hand to Jimmy, who was supposedly eating his luncheon unassisted, in the high chair, went on cutting out cookies. The noontime kitchen was hot, and scented with baking cake; the old Chinese pottered at the sink beside a sun-flooded window.

"It's heavenly out. I've a good mind to get them out for an hour and let them skip their naps."

"They get so tired and cross, Cyn."

"I know they do. But by the time they wake up . . ."

Presently Gray said shyly, reopening the subject of her own accord, and thereby betraying herself for the hundredth time to her sister:

"There's Papa, you know. He depends on me more than ever. The only daughter at home, when Lucia marries."

"You idiot. What am I?"

"But Cyn, you have so much to do, with the boys and Jim."

"Jim'll be about on a crutch as soon as the mud is gone. And as for the boys, they're better off here than anywhere. Now, Gray," Cynthia went on, "if you are fool enough to let your happiness go, just because of the imaginary claim of Papa and me——"

"I don't know that it *is* my happiness, Cynthia!" Gray said, bashfully, proudly, uncomfortably.

"You know it is!"

"I'm twenty-nine, Cynthia."

"Yes, and he's forty. It's perfect."

"Well," Gray said faintly, "we'll see when he comes back."

"When does he come back?"

"Oh, I don't know."

"He goes Saturday?"

"Well, he said something about it."

"There isn't much doubt as to how he feels," Cynthia, tumbling her cookies into a hot collander, said definitely. To this Gray, glancing cautiously about, returned only her usual faint, "Oh, *don't!*"

After a while she began: "If Jim wanted to go away, Cynthia, then Papa'd be alone."

"But why should Jim want to go away?"

Gray was looking straight at Cynthia; their eyes met.

"You mean on account of Guy?" Cynthia asked slowly.

"Guy—sort of—carries everything before him. He acts as if he had—had the right of way with you, Cyn."

Cynthia frowned, biting her lip.

"More than with you—or Lucia—do you think?"

"Oh, much more!"

"Well, even so," Cynthia offered, after thought. "As long as it doesn't mean anything to me——"

"Might it suddenly begin to?" Gray asked, in the pause.

"I truly don't believe so," Cynthia said.

"Jim," she began, after a while, "is getting adjusted to this life here. It's hard for him, he hasn't got his bearings yet. He was always so active, Gray; always galloping somebody's horse up and down Centre Street, always tinkering with harness or kyacks.

"We're all so tremendously intimate here—he doesn't quite feel in it. And Guy's *always* taken the lead in the conversation—always has made so much of me——"

"It's too bad!" Gray said inadequately, in the silence.

Tears were in Cynthia's eyes; she laughed them away shamefacedly.

"Yes, it's too bad," she echoed. "Because—Guy has so little, without us; we can't snub Guy," she added. "And Jim—Jim tries so hard to be 'good'—not impatient, and not selfish! It makes my heart ache to see Jim trying to—to *count*—in the group."

Her throat thickened; she stopped short, still smiling, but with wet lashes.

"I think Jim would be perfectly happy here the rest of his life, Gray, with me and the boys, and what he could do, around the farm, and with a horse to ride. He's country-bred, you know; he's a country type; they're not high-keyed at Miller's Basin as we are. But Guy—Guy seems to put him in his worst mood—he gets silent—he gets blue."

"You see, you're so vivid and lovely and—and so important, Cynthia," Gray explained it shyly. "I've seen it, and Merry's seen it, that Jim and Guy both want to make you laugh, to seem smart to *you.*"

"Oh, Gray, shut up!" Cynthia stammered, her cheeks scarlet under their brown, her eyes confused, even though she was laughing.

"It's true."

"But Jim," the other woman began—"Jim's my husband —and what I think of Guy—it's all silly—it's all mixed up."

With a jerk of the dark head that wore a silver stripe, she turned and went to the oven for more cookies, and when she came back it was to say, very simply, and more seriously than she had spoken before:

"I'm glad we had this little talk, Gray. I see what you mean, and I'll be careful from now on not to worry Jim about Guy, not to make him think I specially like Guy. Guy's so different—I feel toward them both so differently; Jim's still a care, and of course Guy always amuses me—helps me, in a way. But Gray, dearest," Cynthia finished, resting her head affectionately against Gray's shoulder, as the oldest sister stood up to take Peter in for his nap, "you take your happiness if it comes—don't worry about me! I'll be all right. I'm not a crazy idiot of a girl any more. I've had real troubles, Gray; I can take care of this one!"

Peter, sleepy and heavy with food, was standing on the table among the cut cookies. His mother laughed joyously as she selected for him one cut like a heart.

"Would you yike this?"

"Jare," said Peter, in solemn affirmative.

"I may have two, mayn't I, Mom?" Jimmy asked.

"Wait until he's gone," Cynthia breathed.

"Cyn, you lift such a load from my heart!" Gray said.

"I'm too happy—I'm too grateful for the way everything

has come out," Cynthia answered seriously, "not to do my best now. Why, Gray, after all I've been through, Treehaven is simply heaven. Darling, I'll be good!"

"I know you will!" Gray told her.

She carried Peter away, and Cynthia went on with her baking, while Jimmy devoured broken cookies and scraps voraciously.

"We like Aunt Gray's house, don't we, Jim?" she asked. "Mom's never been so happy anywhere else."

It was true. It was a miracle to her merely to awaken now, in the peace and beauty of her old room, to start the wood fires in the crisp mornings, to look from the familiar windows at the frosted lawn and fog-shrouded redwoods, to wander to the kitchen and talk with old Hing over the breakfast preparations.

To have her boys happy and adored here, racing up to the barns, thrilled over the new, damp, panting calf, carrying the kittens with firm little brown hands locked about their writhing little furry stomachs, was ecstasy to Cynthia. Just fresh lace collars, on a new velvet frock, and the simplest new hat from "Babette's" five dollar window in San José, were delights to her now. The plentiful meals that had been commonplaces to her for the first twenty-three years of her life were an unending marvel—the silver pitcher of cream, the oranges and the hot biscuit, the big English joints of beef bedded in Yorkshire pudding, these were luxury to which she thought she never could be quite accustomed again.

Then the beauty of the place, after bare little weather-bound Miller's Basin, was a constant surprise. Great oaks, lawn, banksia roses and lilac bursting into February bloom, hills whitened with manzanita blossoms and smoked with blue lilac, canyons filled with solemn twilight shadows, or humming with springtime murmurs at noon; Cynthia would catch at Gray's arm a dozen times a day: "Gray, isn't it heart-breaking? Isn't it beautiful?"

The jays, the chipmunks, the larks, all enthralled her; her dog was her children's dog now, and trailed the little fellows wherever their sturdy blue overalls led.

CHAPTER TWENTY-ONE

ON THE day before Dana left, they all went up to Guy's, just
as they had gone there for a picnic Cynthia long remembered
on the day before Dana's departure, years ago.

But this late February day was too wet for a picnic, although the hot sun was flashing down on new leaves everywhere, and the sky was high and blue. They had tea instead
indoors, Cynthia's baby in her lap, and Jimmy leaning
against her knee. Rhoda, who was easily tired, lay on a fireside couch in pillows, watching the company with her keen,
suspicious eyes, her big teeth resting on her lower lip. Guy
and Lucia took charge of the tea table, Bruce McBain
watching his wife-to-be in a very trance of adoration, and
young Aunt Lucia very capable in loving advice to little Jim.

"No, sweet, you must have the brown cooky—the white
ones aren't nice at all. . . ."

Cynthia was happy. She knew from Gray's manner that
something had been settled between her sister and Dana,
that Dana would not go away tomorrow, as he had gone
away before, leaving Gray lonely and puzzled. Gray would
marry her Boston doctor, and everything would be—at last!
—as it should have been years ago. Lucia would marry,
too, and drive up in bridal importance from Redwood City
to tell Cynthia of card parties and of week-end trips with
"Brucie."

And Cynthia would live on at Treehaven, making the
world smooth for her old father, never so dear to her as now
in his helplessness and unhappiness, if indeed he had ever

before been dear to her at all, and for Jim, and for her boys. A life of service, and sacrifice, and love—what woman ever wanted more than that? And under it all would run the un-admitted current—the strong, sustaining consciousness that Guy still found her fine and sweet, that her neighbor up the hill was bearing his burden, too—and the more easily because she was near.

She and Rhoda had never spoken again of the latter's strange outburst in the nursery on the night of the Warings' return. Did she even remember it, Cynthia would wonder, or had it been merely a moment's insanity, a desperate burst of jealousy and fear of which Rhoda herself had only a confused and imperfect memory?

Even quite rational persons said things in anger that were incredible to their cooler recollection. Perhaps, after the fatigue of her trip, and in the first strain of meeting Cynthia after years, Rhoda had been carried even more than ordinarily out of her senses.

She knew Cynthia had cared for Guy; but they all knew that. And she had found Guy's letter to Cynthia's father; what could he have said in it that would be really in-criminating? Suppose Cynthia, after some betrayal by Rhoda, did feel herself obliged to go to Gray or Jim, and admit frankly that she had been very unhappy over her affection for Guy those long years ago, that she had gone so far as to plan an elopement with him—what of it? They would discount much because of the poor twisted brain through which the information came.

She must not let herself be afraid. Fear was worse than anything one might ever fear.

She tried to be simply and naturally kind to Rhoda, to assume those little airs of confidence and seriousness that pleased the unfortunate woman so deeply. Once daringly she said of Lucia and Gray, "Perhaps they don't understand,

Rhoda, for after all, neither one has ever been through the performance of having a baby!" and that Rhoda liked it she had immediate proof, for Rhoda echoed eagerly, "No, they don't understand as—as *we* do," and later told Guy the circumstance, and quoted what Cynthia had said.

This afternoon, saying good-bye after the successful tea party, Cynthia lingered by Rhoda's couch. The two women were alone.

"I think there's going to be some pleasant news down our way tonight or tomorrow."

"Oh, what?"

"Gray and Dana."

A shocked— an unhappy—look flashed into Rhoda's sick, colorless face.

"Not—engaged!"

"Lucia and I think so."

"Oh, no," Rhoda said, immediately in tears. She hid her twisted face in her hands. "I can't let Gray go," she said. "I won't let Gray go. She's mine; there's nobody like Gray!"

"Ah, well," Cynthia said, sorry to see her so stirred, "she won't go for a while. But she's so happy, Rhoda."

She sat patting Rhoda's hands, soothing her.

"You want Gray to be happy, dear."

"No, I don't," Rhoda said stubbornly.

"Oh, come! You love Gray."

Rhoda wiped her eyes and blew her nose.

"She wouldn't leave your father!"

"I'm afraid she thinks she shouldn't, Rhoda, and that's— that's just where I need your help," Cynthia said, artfully. "I want you to help me persuade her that she *can* leave Papa."

"Oh, but I can't—not Gray!" Rhoda almost wailed. But she was thinking; Cynthia saw that she was impressed.

"You knew she liked him, Rhoda?"

"Guy thought so, years ago, I know. But since we've been

home, so many things have been funny," Rhoda explained. "Your father being ill, and your being home, and Dana being here at all——"

"We're conspiring against Gray!" Cynthia said to Guy, as he came in.

"Well, they're conspiring against you, out in the car.— No," Guy interrupted himself to ask, struck. "Is that a go at last?"

"We think so."

"Well, that's fine!" Guy exclaimed in great satisfaction. "Old Gray, eh? She gets a splendid man."

"He *is* a splendid man."

"Announced?"

"We think, when we're all at dinner tonight, that the great news will be—well, sprung," Cynthia said, the old mischievous light of her girlhood dancing in her blue eyes. "So be early. Lucia and I say that if Gray wears her new dress—you know, the goldy lace, Rhoda—we'll know it."

"We'll be there. Hurry, Cynthia," Guy said; "they're all waiting for you, out in the car."

"Good-night!" Cynthia's buoyant voice said. She was gone, and Guy bent over his wife, straightening rugs. Rhoda clutched at his wrist.

"She's beautiful, isn't she, Guy?"

"Cynthia? Most people think the other girls are prettier. But yes, I think she's beautiful," Guy answered, with an air of considering it.

"How—how can she possibly be in love with Jim?"

"Jim? Oh, he's a nice enough fellow."

"He's a *boor*, Guy."

"Oh, no. He's always good-natured and polite enough."

"Enough!" Rhoda echoed triumphantly. Guy laughed.

"Well, he's her husband."

"But she's no more in love with him than I am."

"I think she's very fond of him. And she adores the boys, and they're his. Poor Cynthia," Guy said, "she's been through such a hard time that I don't imagine there's much —romance, you know what I mean—left in her."

"They'll have to stay here, if Gray marries," Rhoda said, half aloud, a moment later. Guy, jerking a chair to its usual place on the other side of the room, gathering up cups and napkins, stopped in his efforts to restore the place to order.

"Who?"

"Cynthia and Jim."

"I should think they would, anyway. That's—that's the real trouble, as far as he's concerned, that he can't very well go anywhere else," Guy said. "It's hard to think of just the right thing for him to do. And it puts any man at a terrible disadvantage to sit beside a fire and have women wait on him."

"He doesn't seem to mind it."

"Well, that's part of the trouble, too—his not minding it. I think Cynthia carries it off mighty well," Guy added. "She's fine with him."

"Oh, you would think she was fine if she cut his throat!" was the nature of Rhoda's angry and jealous thought. But aloud she said nothing.

Gray came into her kingdom timidly, frightened at her own joy. Dana was gone, but only for three short months; early in June he would return for the last of the Trezavant brides. Leslie cabled delightedly, in answer to Cynthia's cable of four words only, "Gray Dana June love" and Lucia, with her characteristic generosity, took second place in all the new rush of happy plans. Lucia was to be married very quietly at Easter; she and Bruce would be home from their

honeymoon in time to lend a hand with all Gray's arrangements.

"Cynthia, you scare me!" Gray said over and over again,
laughing and frightened, as Cynthia boldly carried out one
detail after another of the miracle that was to turn woman
into wife. "Suppose something went wrong? And we have
so much time!"

"We have exactly nine out of the original twelve weeks,
my dear girl. We have no time!" Cynthia went steadily on
through the happy acquisition of trousseau and linen, engagement gifts and wedding presents. Gray must have a fur
coat; this was the time to buy fur. Gray must have her share
of Mother's silver; the fine old tablecloths were spread out
and studied.

With every letter from Dana, Gray's hold upon happiness
grew stronger. Dana had taken Aunt Sarah Appleby's house,
"until you can look the field over." Dana had to go—or,
rather, "we" had to go to Munich next spring, but tell the
girls "we" would be out for a few weeks in midsummer.
Dana was receiving presents already. "What does a lone lorn
man do with china and rugs when he is living in a doctors'
club?" The thing was announced, and enclosed were clippings. Gray showed the clippings and carefully folded por-
tions of the letters to Cynthia; she clung to Cynthia, dizzy
with a vertigo of excitement and joy.

There were cards for both sisters. Lucia rejoiced over her
modest Scotch name, "Mrs. Bruce McBain." Gray sat staring like a woman tranced at the little pasteboards that said
"Mrs. Clement Dana Illyan." Cynthia shared the confidences,
the fears, and the ecstasies of both.

"Oh, isn't all this thrilling! Isn't this what we always
thought it would be!" they said sometimes to each other.

"Only we thought it would all come so much younger—
five, eight years ago," Cynthia said. "We used to long for it,

pray for it, engagements and presents and trousseaus! And how much we had to live through, first! Those winters when I was in Miller's Basin, and you two were alone here——"

"I used to get so blue and lonely I cried," Lucia said. "I cried all day on my twenty-third birthday."

"It doesn't matter when life finds you, if it finds you," Gray said dreamily. She herself was growing younger every hour. Not at twenty had Gray looked as dewily radiant as now, when the weeks went by, and Lucia was safely married and away, and it was time to expect Dana.

"Only, Cynthia, it doesn't seem right," she protested, "to leave everything to you!"

"What else could I possibly do, Gray? Papa's no trouble, and I know he turns to me, he trusts me."

"Oh, as for that," Gray agreed, "you've twice the business head I have. But somehow, I've always felt it was my duty—— I simply couldn't go away if you weren't here, Cyn; I know that."

"Come now, Gray, you wouldn't send Dana away now, just because Papa needed you."

"Oh, but Cyn, indeed I would!"

"But my darling, you've given Papa the best years of your girlhood. You've managed his house, and taken his orders, and put up with his crankiness since you were sixteen."

"I love his crankiness!" Gray cried loyally, tears in her eyes.

"I know you do. But it's your turn now, Gray. You want your own life, your children, your home and husband."

"It seems too much. It seems like a dream, and as if Papa could put out a cord and draw me back again."

"That's just what you mustn't feel," Cynthia told her, anxious with a persistent fear that at the last moment Gray's delicate sense of duty really would draw her back to her obligations at the old ranch.

"If you and Jim weren't going to stay——" Gray would begin, over and over.

"But we *are*."

"But when the rains begin, and Rhoda listens to every word Guy says to you, and Jim watches every look you give to Guy——"

"Rains! We won't have rains until November—this is May. I'll run them all!" Cynthia would say confidently.

"Jim has his radio—and his solitaire—of course——"

"And his sons and his wife, my dear—and he loves his meals. Besides, I'm going to have a mounting block built, so he can get up on his horse," Cynthia summarized it. "Besides, he's going to try experiments with vegetables—he's always reading those farm magazines. Don't worry, Gray."

"You don't think Rhoda'd make trouble?" Gray asked once.

A sick little plunge of fear at Cynthia's heart.

"What trouble could she make?"

"I don't know."

"Rhoda and I are getting quite chummy," Cynthia observed, mildly. "But never," she went on, "never did a matchmaking mamma feel as keen as I do to get you off my hands!"

"But why?" Gray demanded, for the pleasure of having Dana praised; for the thrill of having that rosy future of hers sketched by Cynthia's glowing imagination.

"Because you're going to be so happy, Gray," the younger sister duly told her. "I see you, in furs, trotting about Boston—Boston, imagine it! I see you and Dana making plans—buying tickets for Europe . . ."

Gray could listen to these predictions for half-hours together, even though she never attempted to put them into words herself. Happiness frightened her as solitude and loneliness never had done; every hour of the long waiting years seemed to make today's fulfillment more of a miracle.

When a mid-May evening brought Dana back, Gray suddenly left the waiting group at the fire; Cynthia followed her across the Galleria into the dining room; Gray was behind the door, shrinking up against the wall.

"Here she is, Dana, the goose!" Cynthia left them there, in each other's arms, and went back to the living room, where Guy, who had brought the guest in a spring rain from San José, and Rhoda and the little boys and Jim and Merry were laughing together.

"She's scared to death! She was in the dining room, behind the door!"

"How happy they are!" Rhoda said, with a touch of pain in her voice.

"Oh, happy! It's so wonderful—when it comes to a man and a woman like that!"

"It was like that with us, wasn't it, Guy?" Rhoda reminded him, and Cynthia felt a pang of pain at her heart. What a mess—what a mess it all was! Rhoda twisted and jealous, Jim wistful and uncertain, herself the cause of their uneasiness, sound and young and looking from one to the other, as she crouched in her blue velvet gown on the hearth rug and took the small sodden shoes and socks from Jimmy's feet, which he stuck by turns straight up in the air.

Dana brought Gray back, flushed and laughing and lovely, and they were all together.

"She was trying to run away from me," Dana said.

"Maybe she wants to stay with us?" Rhoda suggested.

"Not she!" Guy smiled.

Much later he said to Cynthia, in an undertone:

"Didn't you have a blue dress like that years ago?"

She looked up to nod, and was confused to see Jim watching her, his eyes narrowed. Rhoda was in Gray's bedroom with Gray; she was alone with the two men.

"Very much like this," she answered tranquilly. But she knew Jim was not appeased by her careless manner and tone. When she next made an excuse to speak to him he answered absently, almost roughly.

The next day, when she was beside him down on the lawn with her sewing, and they had only the two small boys for company, he said suddenly:

"Guy—was he in love with you?"

"Years ago?" Cynthia asked, looking placidly up, looking down again. Her tone was completely unalarmed.

"Yes. He was, wasn't he?"

"Oh, yes," she said, smiling.

"He still likes you!" Jim stated, unwillingly.

"I think he does in a way," Cynthia agreed, with careful indifference. "He was bound to fall in love with one of us, I suppose."

She matched a small brown sock to another brown sock, ran her hand into them, speculatively.

"We all knew one another so well. But the strange thing," she went on, conversationally, "is that it wasn't Gray."

Jim was silent for a moment.

"If he hadn't been married," he presently burst forth again, "you would have married him, wouldn't you?"

"Well," Cynthia answered, considering it composedly, "if it hadn't been for Rhoda, Guy would probably have married years before, while we were all young."

"Ever tell you he liked you?" Jim shot at her abruptly.

"I knew it. You're not jealous of Guy *now*, Jim? Poor old fellow! What has he in his life!" Cynthia reasoned, busy with her big basket of freshly washed clothes.

"That's right, too," Jim agreed, after a pause.

"He's had a bitter, lonely, frustrated sort of life," Cynthia
went on. "I feel terribly sorry for him."

The boys and the dogs came careening against her knee,
and she busied herself with Peter's little rigging, which had
slipped and twisted. When she was free again, Jim laughed.

"That's right, too!" he said.

"What's right?"

"Guy—Guy Waring," Jim explained; "he acts as if he
had so—so much. But he hasn't."

"He's had very little, poor Guy."

"But he always thinks he knows it all."

"Well, he *does* know a lot, Jim. He reads a lot."

"He's stuck on himself," Jim muttered. After a while he
said, "They never had a kid?"

"No—that was the beginning of her—trouble. She was ill
all the time the baby was coming—melancholy, I think, and
nervous. My mother used to go up the hill to sit with her.
And then it died, and she went completely to pieces."

"Kids make up for a lot."

"Ah, don't they!"

"If you'd married him, you mightn't have had any."

"Might not."

"It seems to me, to women," Jim asked tentatively, "kids
make up for everything, don't they?"

Cynthia, sitting beside him, running tapes through little
much-washed pajamas, looked up with a swift nod and smile
for answer. But her heart was sick. How he feared Guy!
How he would hate him if he knew the truth!

"Sitting round doing nothing," Jim went on, "I think of
that morning last summer when I was behind the pack train
and hurrying to catch up. I'd been chasing Barney, the mule
that was always getting loose.

"But Dan, mind you, knew damn' well that Barney was
up ahead of the train making for Johnson's Meadows. If

Dan had chosen to yell to me—or tie the mule up where we had to pass it at Somers——

"I remember giving Hank a kick; he went right up the side of the rock, but we got up to the trail; we made it. But his forefoot loosened a rock——"

She had heard it all a hundred times; the men had discussed it in her kitchen all winter. She said:

"Life seems to be that, Jim. Looking back and wishing that you had been able to see the outcome of things beforehand."

"What would you do different, Cyn, if you could? I know damn' well," Jim added, his musing voice seeming to rob the words of any bitterness, "what I'd do. I'd take the long trail past the creek and catch up with the pack train when they were in camp. There wasn't any need for me to hurry. But what have you ever done that you were sorry for? Had Peter, hey? 'Member how you cried when you knew he was coming?"

"I was so sick, all that time, and it was so hot. And we had no money. But imagine us without Peter!"

With the tenderest expression it ever knew in her brown face, under its frame of dark silky hair, she glanced at the boys again. Peter's little Beethoven forehead was scowling portentously; he was spading a sand castle to a height beyond his wildest dreams.

"Would you marry me again if you had a chance not to, Cyn?"

Her flashing affectionate smile.

"It was the smartest thing I ever did."

"Yes, it was," Jim drawled, ironically. But his eyes were happy. "Look what you gave up," he said. "It was only luck —I don't mean luck—that your father—you know what I mean—that he was sick and couldn't kick us out when we showed up here unexpected."

"Well, calling that luck—hadn't we had our share of bad luck too?"

"I'll say we had!"

"Marrying you was my way out, Jim. No one knows," Cynthia said, "I suppose, except a girl—a girl tied at home, waiting for lovers, marriage, waiting for life, with no real work to do, no self-expression, and knowing that the years are racing by—no one knows how bewildering it is, how stupid one is, how horribly afraid that nothing's ever going to happen.

"Any troubles, Jim, with husband and babies and money, are *real* compared to that! It's the difference between being awake and being in a dream. No one wants to live in a dream."

"Maybe my accident kind of waked me from a dream too, Cyn. I used to be such a—kid. I never knew what you were going through, making fires and keeping the kids clean— gosh," Jim added with a gruff laugh, "it seems to me I'd do it all better if I got another break!"

"You'll get another break."

"I won't get my foot back."

"No, but there are lots of things you can do; you'll get used to your crutches one of these days. We can picnic where the horse trails go, and you can go everywhere else in the car. It's just a question—— This isn't worth mending," Cynthia interrupted herself to murmur, tearing a small romper into strips. "It's just a question of your getting yourself adjusted, Jim," she went on. "When Dana and Gray come back next year, or when Lucia comes up, they'll think *you're* the one who's in on all the secrets!"

"I'll bet he likes me as much as I like him!" Jim presently growled.

"Guy?" Very much in the rôle of wife and mother, she looked up, looked down at her sewing again. She had had a moment of feeling that it was restful, secure, sitting out here on the lawn with Jim in the spring afternoon, but his voice disturbed her, made her vaguely uneasy. "I'm sorry you feel that way," she continued after a moment. It was unfortunate, certainly, that Jim should take it into his head to dislike Guy, of all men.

It was tiresome to have even a small secret always on one's mind, to know that there was something eternally unexplained. It would have been so comparatively simple to tell Jim everything years ago when he had come, big and shy and adoring, to the ranch to walk about with her, and when she had known that before the afternoon was over he would kiss her. . . .

"Jim, I wasn't listening!" she apologized, arousing herself from revery.

"How far'd it go? I'm just curious," he said. "How well did you and he—you and Guy—like each other?"

Cynthia suppressed an exclamation of impatience.

"Oh, we liked each other—just as persons always do," she answered, almost on the note of a yawn.

"Your father know it?"

"No." She held up a small, dark blue garment, studied it affectionately, her head tipped to one side. "But his knowing it wouldn't have had anything to do with it, would it?"

It frightened her to be talking like this, and she cast about for some natural way to change the topic of conversation.

"He'd have had a good right to punch him in the jaw!" Jim said.

"Papa?"

"Sure. What right had Guy coming round here making love to one of you girls?"

Her mending completed, Cynthia wrapped a faded pink crib blanket trimly about the score or more of little garments on the top of her big basket.

"Well, if *we* didn't——" she said, unsympathetically.

"You didn't what?"

"Mind. If we didn't mind Guy's—liking us."

"Aw, shucks, you were only girls!" Jim said.

Cynthia stood up; it was time to take the boys and Jim and the sewing indoors, time to shut windows, pile up fires, light lamps, make the ranch house comfortable for the night. Jimmy and Peter had to have their suppers—Jim must be established beside the fire, in his new dressing gown, with his card table and the radio within reach.

She moved through it all, and he watched her, and the small boys watched her, and when Guy presently came down there was another to watch her; the gracious woman, with her brushed dark hair showing a silver wing, and her rounded tall figure and sweeping draperies moving with the quick, eager movement of her body.

At the dinner table they were watching her still; Jim with his boyish big country features, his boyish big hands, his raw country voice, and Guy leisurely and gray-headed and sure of himself, with his easy, pleasant accents, and the slow smile of his wide mouth under the little black line of mustache.

"Tired tonight, Jim?" Gray asked him kindly, noting something amiss.

He roused himself.

"No, I feel fine!"

Gray was unsatisfied. After a while she asked Guy curiously:

"What are you smiling at?"

And Guy shook himself from a dream, as Jim had, and answered innocently, "Was I smiling?"

Rhoda looked from one to the other, sharply, in dissatisfaction, in suspicion. Cynthia caught more than one of her glances, and dim uneasiness grew clearer in her soul. She was on the brink of the volcano, now—but if Gray were but once safely married—if Gray were but married . . .

It was too bad to spoil all this heavenly time with fear, to be really so much less than she seemed—so much less secure and gracious and good. But there was no help for it; the past *was* the present for women, and women had just to go on.

When the fireside group broke up she walked out into the cold starry night to say good-bye to the Warings, went back to the sitting room to help Jim to bed; stepped into the dark warm nursery to pin the boys snug and dry into their cribs; moved about with hot-water bottles. And fear gripped her steadily tighter and tighter.

This time last winter, she thought, her problem had been the heart-breaking one of poverty, loneliness, hard work. She remembered the bare, foursquare kitchen at Miller's Basin, the smell of dish towels boiling, the smell of ashes, the smell of small crib beddings aired and dried in a close room.

If she might have come through all that with clean hands —if she might really be the woman they thought her today!

Sometimes in the mornings her spirit would awaken to confidence and common sense. Her mistake had been the mistake of a too generous girl deeply in love; she had seen the folly of it, and paid for it a thousand times.

Oh, but those were all words—words—words. The truth was that there was a secret she did not share with her husband, her sisters, a secret that would have affected every member of this home group if it were known, and Cynthia must keep it a secret, however little she wanted to do so, however humiliating it was to have that cloud always between her and the sun.

CHAPTER TWENTY-TWO

A FEW days before the wedding she and the boys went up the hill to borrow Uncle Guy's silver for the great occasion. Guy was alone, working on a sketch in the big studio off the dining room. Gray-headed, smiling, his old blue smock daubed with paint, he came out to meet the callers.

"We're gold diggers—or rather silver diggers," Cynthia announced.

"Oh, Rhoda was going to lay out that stuff for you, and I think she forgot!"

Guy led the way into the dining room, and the small boys and Dobbs scrambled after. The flawless blue heat of a May day blanketed the mountains, but the rooms inside Guy's low brown cabin, under enormous redwood boughs, were cool. Window shades were drawn against the battering sunshine, and into the shimmering gloom great bowls of sweet peas sent banners of sweetness. Guy opened the sideboard drawer, and Cynthia gathered up spoons and forks. And as she did so the electrical—the magical—quality with which he seemed to invest the very air he breathed made her feel weak and confused.

"I want to leave some silver for you and Rhoda to eat your lunch with. By the way, where is Rhoda?"

"Wasn't she down at your house?"

"No, nor Lucia either. Lucia was coming up from Redwood City to help decorate. Gray and Dana were making lists of something, and nobody else was there."

"We'll be down tonight." They were out in the garden

now, and Guy jumped both small boys to the front seat of the car, and lifted the dog in, as Cynthia put the rolled silver carefully in the back.

"Well, I'll thank Rhoda then."

"You don't have to thank Rhoda!" Guy said, laughing.

Cynthia, her foot already on the starter, was struck by a sudden thought.

"Guy, she couldn't conceivably mind our taking it without asking—our going over her head this way? There's no hurry——"

He had been ready to laugh again, but the same thought had come to him, too.

"Well—I can't imagine——" he said, smiling, narrowing his eyes.

"She *might!*" Cynthia persisted urgently, suddenly sure that she *would*.

"Such funny things distress her," Guy admitted, slowly.

"This easily might!" Cynthia was crowding the wrapped silver into his hands again. "Put it back into the sideboard, Guy, and don't say that I came up."

"It might be wiser."

"She's all wrought up about Gray's going, anyway," Cynthia reminded him. "It's upsetting her frightfully. And if anything keeps Gray from marrying *now,*" she added, with a shred of uneasy laughter, "I shall go right out of my mind. They're so marvelously suited, Gray and Dana, and they're so happy! But Gray's just fool enough—just *old maid* enough—to pull some heroic last-minute renunciation, if Papa takes a turn for the worse, or Rhoda collapses."

"What you've done for them all, Cynthia, coming home just when you did!—Isn't it a strange thing?"

Cynthia's brown hand was moving the gas lever idly to and fro on the wheel; she moved her eyes suddenly to Guy's, looked down again.

"Oh, I hope so. It's like a miracle to have Lucia and Papa and Gray—and Jim, too—the happier for anything I can do."

"Gray never would have left your father."

"No, I suppose not, after all these years."

They were both silent, held in the spell of this rare moment of being alone.

"It's lovely up here this morning, Guy."

"It looks like heavenly weather for Gray."

"The strange, wasted years, Guy," Cynthia said suddenly. "What does it all mean? Who's happier—what's righter or straighter, for Rhoda being as she has been, all these years, and our breaking our hearts? I might have been living up here, I might never have met Jim—these might have been our boys. Why *wasn't* it that way?"

"I wonder," Guy said steadily.

Cynthia jerked her dark head up as if to speak again, met his level look. For a long minute they stared at each other. Then Cynthia touched the starter, and the engine sprang into life, and she drove the boys down the hill for lunch and naps.

That night Rhoda said to her suddenly,

"You were up at my house today, weren't you, Cynthia?" There was a second's pause.

"Yes, and where were you?" Cynthia demanded then, naturally. "We looked over the silver, decided that you were the one who knew about it, and the children and I came home."

"I was on the hill with Tony, getting huckleberry. I saw the car come up."

"It didn't matter. But Gray rather hoped you'd come down for lunch."

"Did you telephone?"

"Did I what?" Cynthia was being very friendly and

casual, for Rhoda was working herself into the state of nervous excitement they all knew and feared for her.

"You—you didn't telephone, did you?" Rhoda stammered.

"Never thought of it."

"And for half an hour you and Guy were deciding that you didn't know which spoons and forks to bring down!"

"Come now," Cynthia said, with the little bravado of affection that so often worked successfully with Rhoda, "you're not jealous of *me*, are you?"

"Yes, I *am* jealous of you; yes, I *am* jealous of you," Rhoda said, in a sudden passion, "and I think it's about time that all these others, who think Cynthia's so marvelous, and Cynthia's so wonderful, know *why* I'm jealous of you!"

Cynthia, watching her, in a vertigo of fear and horror, felt cold despair fingering her spine. With a sane woman in this mood, she would stand small chance; this woman was not sane.

They were in Cynthia's room; they two had come in after a family dinner, to freshen up with powder and hairbrushes, leaving the others in a circle at the fire. Dana, Gray, Lucia, Merry, Bruce, Jim were waiting for them, a few feet away.

"Rhoda!" Cynthia whispered.

"Oh, and 'Rhoda!'" the other echoed, with a sneer. Cynthia put an arm about her.

"Don't be so angry at me, dear!"

"Don't call me 'dear!'" Rhoda muttered jerking her shoulder away. But she was touched by the little overture and began to cry.

"Rhoda—don't cry, *please*. They'll all see your eyes. I'm as sorry—I'm as sorry," Cynthia pleaded, at her wit's end, "as you can possibly be, about anything—everything—that happened so long ago. I've Jim now, my own husband, and the boys. Everything's different——"

"Everything's not different," Rhoda said stubbornly, "when you sneak up to see Guy alone—— And you're *always* trying to see him alone," she broke off to say petulantly. "You know you both hate me, you *know* you both wish I was dead——"

"Rhoda, dear! You mustn't talk like that!" Cynthia drew her down, firm fingers on Rhoda's weak wrists, to a seat beside her on the bed, looked into the sulky, evasive eyes. "For Gray's sake—just for five more days," she went on, in an urgent whisper. "You don't want to make Gray unhappy, do you?"

"I don't want Gray to go away!" Rhoda said wilfully.

"But darling, to be so happy!"

"That's just it. *I'm* not happy."

"But it certainly isn't going to make you happy to say anything that will distress Gray?"

"And Jim," Rhoda added, with her elfin laugh. "You never told Jim about you and Guy, Cynthia, and I know it. I know it because Jim told me the other day that he had always been jealous of Guy! He never would have said that —he never would have said that——" Her exultant soaring tone broke off into a somber, bewildered whisper. "I don't know what I'm talking about!" she finished, with a child's petulance.

"Rhoda, you know me," Cynthia, hardly aware of what she said, murmured persuasively, "you trust me. Why, when Gray's gone you and I are going to see each other every day —we're going to get letters from Lucia and Leslie and Gray——"

"*You* are, maybe. I'm not!"

"They'll be for both of us. Why, Rhoda, I don't know you in this mood; I think you're tired. You don't talk like this!"

"I *do* talk like this. And I know that Gray never would go

away if she knew you and Guy were in love with each other, and going to see each other"—the tone was rising ominously again—"going to see each other all the time, and laugh at me, and have secrets from me——

"And Jim wouldn't stay here either, if he knew!" she interrupted herself to add, in a shrill, thin tone hardly deeper than a whisper.

"Rhoda—if you'll listen——"

"I won't listen! And *you're* the one that'll have to go away," Rhoda rushed on. "I told you so when you first came back! I won't live here if you're here! I'll tell Gray why! I *will!* I'll tell her tomorrow. You can't come up to my house and talk to Guy and laugh at me! Dana can stay here; he can practise here! Or they don't have to get married——"

"Ah, Rhoda, for Gray's sake, won't you be generous? Any upset now would mean that she wouldn't marry Dana. How could you tell them all something that might make Papa dangerously ill, might give him another stroke, and that would make Jim feel so badly, and make Guy feel so badly——"

"Ah, you and Guy should have thought of that before!" Rhoda exclaimed, with an air of scoring.

"Can't you see, Rhoda, how sorry one might be for a thing like that, how far away into the past it seems to have gone? Guy and I *did* love each other dearly, but we're older now; he has his wife and I have my husband——"

"His letter—I found it the very night I came home, when I was so happy to surprise him!" Rhoda said bitterly.

"But we couldn't know that!"

"It said, 'We know we are doing a thing that will distress you and the girls infinitely. But we have loved each other —have belonged to each other for many weeks——' "

"Sh-h-h!" Cynthia whispered, with a glance toward the closed door.

"That's what I'll show Gray, and you can't 'sh-h-h!' me," Rhoda whispered back, shaking. "I will, Cynthia, tomorrow, unless you go away! That's what you have to do, go away. You and Jim and the boys," Rhoda went on feverishly, gripping Cynthia's wrist as she spoke. "Tell them, tell them that you're going away! Then I'll keep still. But if you don't—if you don't tell them tonight, right now, at the fire, that you and the boys are going away—a long way, too; not just to San Francisco or Oakland, but far away—then tomorrow I'll bring a copy—I have it!—of that letter down, and I'll tell them all!"

Cynthia was looking at her steadily.

"Rhoda, how can I go away now?"

"I don't know. But you must."

"After Gray marries——"

"Ah, you say that, but you wouldn't go!"

"If I *promised*—next week——"

"I wouldn't believe you!"

"My father is so ill, Jim's not able to take care of himself, the boys need watching every minute——" Cynthia pleaded.

"You can't stay here, fooling me about Guy!" Rhoda persisted, inflexibly.

"I'm *not* fooling you about Guy."

"He still thinks there is nobody like you. I see it!"

"We like each other; we are old friends, Rhoda," Cynthia argued; "it isn't an easy situation. Gray's half convinced she oughtn't to leave us, as it is. It's going to take all the engineering we can do——"

"Don't say 'we,' for *I'm* not trying to get Gray to go. I want her to stay here!"

"Not really, you don't."

"I do," Rhoda said, crying. "She's my only friend. She understands me. I want *you* to go away. Guy loves Peter and Jimmy; he's always making them boats and cutting them fishing poles. He wishes we had children!

"If I tell Jim and Gray that you and Guy used to love each other, then you'll *have* to go away."

"Rhoda, I have no money of my own. Papa has given all the other girls their money, but he never approved of my marriage; he never sent us any money. I can't put that to him now——"

"Especially as he's quite smart enough to be furious! He'll never want to see Guy again!" Rhoda exulted. "No, Cynthia," she said, getting to her feet, and moving toward the door, "you think you can have everything your own way; you can't. They all believe you're such an angel; they all love you so. But you've got to go, and if that means that Gray stays, so much the better for me. And unless you tell them, tonight, that you and Jim are going away, I'll tell them tomorrow, and you get out of it the best way you can!"

She opened the door into the big room, and Cynthia heard a welcoming murmur of voices from the fire.

"Cynthia!" Lucia called.

"Coming!" Cynthia called back. But she did not move. She sat perfectly still, at the foot of the bed, staring, staring, staring into space with darkened eyes.

CHAPTER TWENTY-THREE

PRESENTLY she went out to take her usual seat, a low red leather hassock on the floor beside Jim's wheeled chair. Rhoda, looking pale and ill, and unwontedly silent, even for Rhoda, was stretched on the deep divan, Guy seated at its head, with her gray hair resting near his shoulder. Lucia and Bruce were in one big seat together, their arms laced; now and then they quite openly kissed each other, and laughed. In the center of the half-circle were two high-backed chairs with arms, and in these Dana and Gray were sitting, "like two portraits of themselves," Cynthia immediately said. Dana obviously was too happy to do much talking; Gray's deep eyes were alight with the new mystical beauty that had bloomed in her in the last few happy weeks.

"This might almost be old days!" Gray said contentedly, when Cynthia was in her place

"With additions," Lucia added.

"With nice additions."

Wood snapped on the hearth in the old way; outside the ranch house spring cold and darkness shut down like a cover over the world. The lamps burned softly and struck glints of light from Gray's fair head and from Cynthia's wedding ring. Everyone was rather thoughtful tonight; tomorrow Leslie would be here—Cynthia had never seen Leslie's boy, or Leslie herself for almost five years—and the day after that would be Gray's last day at Treehaven as Gray Trezavant. A sense of solemnity, of approaching change, was over them all; Cynthia linked her fingers in Jim's long, cool fingers; Lucia snuggled close against her husband in the fireside seat.

"Cyn, can you remember our ever living in any other place than this?"

"Not very well. I was six when we came here, I think. I had my sixth birthday here."

"Hurling the cake firmly into the fire, when your mother wouldn't let you cut it," Guy contributed.

"Oh, I remember that, you poor darling!" Gray said, in rich appreciation.

"Lucia here was just about able to toddle."

"Lucia," said her husband, "I'll bet you were adorable."

"I'll bet I was a nasty baby."

"I remember Les and I started a camp in the spare room and lighted a good brush fire in there."

"I remember that! Lord, what an uproar!" Guy said.

Cynthia glanced up at him, smiling, and caught Rhoda's glittering look instead of his. The woman had a strange, half-sane look on her face; immediately she spoke, and Cynthia could tell from her tone that she was half mad with jealousy, that she had been listening to these memories in which she had no part, watching the affectionate, happy look on Guy's face, writhing at the fond, amused, proprietary tone he always used to the Trezavant girls.

"Shall you and Jim and the boys be here all summer, Cynthia?"

"Oh, Rhoda," Gray exclaimed, "don't suggest anything else! I couldn't turn Papa over to anyone else."

"Won't Les be here?"

"Well, only a few weeks. Then she has to go see the Rosses in Pasadena. I'd be lost," Gray finished, in genuine alarm, "if I didn't think Cynthia was going to take on my job."

"You've had it long enough," Cynthia said. "I've got to

help Jim get used to hobbling about on his crutches, and take care of Papa. I'll love it! I have a secret passion for adequacy; nothing delights me like running about with trays and bandages," she said.

"You're easily pleased," Lucia said, drowsily. Her little head was snug on Bruce's shoulder.

"You mean you'll stay here, Cynthia?" Rhoda persisted, with a nervous and excited laugh.

"You and I'll have to hold down the place, Rhoda."

"All right!" Rhoda said, trembling. "All right!"

"You sound anything but all right," Guy told her, gently: "you're tired, and I ought to take you home."

Inexplicably, Rhoda was suddenly crying, and trying to twist about to hide her tears. Gray said quickly:

"Finish what you were reading, Dana, before the girls came out?"

"Oh, yes—I came upon something in *Julius Cæsar*. But Guy—Guy had Kipling there."

"Read the thing you did read," Guy said, turning pages close under the lamp. "Mine'll wait."

Rhoda's subsiding sniffle could be heard as Dana found a place.

"This is too wonderful!" he said, beginning.

So many nights they had done this through all the years, Cynthia thought, as Dana's fine voice followed line after line.

Guy read "The Song of the Cities," and "The Young Queen."

". . . *beautiful, bold, and browned,*
Bright-eyed out of the battle, the Young Queen rode to be crowned."

"That's Cynthia!" Gray said.

"It always makes me think of Cynthia, too," Guy agreed.

"Oh, I love these evenings when we read," Cynthia moaned sleepily, her head against Jim's knee. The firelight shone on her warm tints, her cloud of rich dark hair, her Beethoven brows drawn over the shining blue lights in her eyes. About her, on the mixed colors of the rug, spread the delicate transparent skirts of her white gown, scallops of batiste, bordered in blue. About her brown throat was a chain of stones as blue as her eyes, and against her low forehead fell a film of silky hair.

"Say Hodgson's 'Eve' for us, Cynthia," Gray demanded suddenly.

"Oh, yes, 'Eve'!" Lucia begged.

"I think I've forgotten it," Cynthia protested drowsily.

"No, you haven't. Sit up now, and begin. Go on, Cynthia!"

Cynthia sat erect, straightening her tumbled hair, and as she did so she met Rhoda's steady look and remembered all that they had said to each other in the bedroom an hour ago. Rhoda had threatened before, but that didn't entirely reassure one—she had been like a woman possessed tonight. Cynthia had forgotten her fears for a while; now they rushed back at her again.

"Honestly, I don't believe I can remember it!" she said.

"Ah, go ahead!" This was Gray. "Dana's never heard it!" she said.

Cynthia repeated the Hodgson poem slowly.

> *"Eve, with her basket, was*
> *Down in the bells and grass . . ."*

Somehow Rhoda's look was choking her, making it almost impossible.

> *"Picture that orchard sprite,*
> *Eve, with her body white,*

Supple and smooth to her
Slim fingertips,
Wondering, listening,
Listening, wondering,
Eve, with a berry
Halfway to her lips!"

Eve—and all the other spring-mad, youth-mad girls since Eve—girls drunk with moonshine and the scent of the honeysuckle flowers and the miracle of first love. . . . Cynthia could not look up; Guy, with his pipe, with his dark eyes and the black line of mustache above his hard, fine mouth, was but a few feet away from her.

"Oh, what a chatter when
Titmouse and Jenny Wren
Saw him successful and
Taking his leave!
How the birds rated him,
How they all hated him!
How they all pitied
Poor motherless Eve!"

Poor motherless little Eve, and poor motherless Cynthia! . . . Somehow she finished the poem.

"Picture her crying
Outside in the lane,
Eve, with no dish of sweet
Berries and plums to eat,
Haunting the gate of the
Orchard in vain. . . .
Picture the lewd delight
Under the hill tonight—
'Eva!' the toast goes round,
'Eva!' again."

"My God, what a horrible poem!" Dana said, under his breath.

"Isn't it?" Gray said. "The whole tragedy of women right there in a few lines."

"Is it such a tragedy?" Rhoda's wavering, mischievous voice asked innocently.

"It was for Eve," Dana reminded her.

"But nowadays," Rhoda persisted, in that nervous high voice of hers that was so oddly also a whine, "if nobody knows——

"I thought girls were—getting away with that sort of thing nowadays," she added, after a pause, as nobody spoke.

There was something faintly disagreeable, something vaguely disquieting, in her tone. She was laughing nervously, but no one else laughed.

"No matter who else knows, the girl knows," Gray offered, seriously.

"And someone else may always find out!" Rhoda added. Again she laughed, with an air of triumph and significance. "Isn't that so, Cynthia?"

Cynthia managed to smile. Glancing up over her shoulder at Jim, she found his eyes moving from Rhoda to her with a somewhat puzzled and resentful expression.

"For Eve there wasn't anyone else to know," she observed.

"No, for her there wasn't!" Rhoda admitted, with a faint stress on the personal pronoun.

"What gives me the creeps about that poem," Lucia suddenly put in, animatedly, "is the feeling it gives you of— of the man triumphing, the man—or the snake, rather —getting what he wanted and going off perfectly satisfied; Eve was weak, and he knew she would be, and his wrecking her life, turning her out of the garden, didn't mean anything to him!"

"Perhaps he was sorry," Rhoda suggested. "Don't you think he might have been, Guy?"

"Not listening, dear!" Guy apologized promptly. His undisturbed voice seemed to break the nightmare spell that enveloped Cynthia, and she breathed easier.

"Rhoda, you'd heard that poem before?" Gray, also unconsciously helping to restore the atmosphere to the normal, asked unsuspiciously.

"Oh, yes," Rhoda admitted. "Only I was wondering——"

"Wondering what?" Gray asked, in the encouraging tone she often used to Rhoda.

"Nothing," Rhoda answered, with her brief mirthless laugh. Immediately her face grew dark and sullen again, and she lapsed into her usual condition of apathy, only half listening, speaking rarely, nervously.

"Personalities being always in the worst possible taste," Dana said brightly, "may I be permitted to observe that any poem is fortunate in being recited in Cynthia's delightful voice!"

Cynthia sent him a smiling glance of acknowledgment, and Lucia said, "Moved and seconded."

"It seems to be the fashion to fall in love with Cynthia," Rhoda observed, drawlingly.

"As long as Bruce doesn't!" Lucia laughed.

She and her Bruce had been married at Easter, and had set up their new home in a charming six-room Spanish bungalow in Redwood City. Lucia was now an authority on gas stoves and dining-room rugs, and had assumed a loyal, deferential, daughterly attitude with Bruce's rather trying parents.

"Don't fall in love with Cynthia!" she commanded him now.

"Not a chance!" Bruce said promptly, and Lucia laughed sleepily, in the curve of his arm.

A little later there was a flurry of scattering. Bruce and Lucia had the cottage; Dana, his old quarters in the room off the Galleria; and Cynthia explained with all her own animation and enthusiasm that she was moving one boy into her own room tomorrow, and another in among the wedding presents in Aunt Lucia's old room, to make space for Leslie and the baby.

"Full house," Jim observed.

"But I love it!" Cynthia said.

"Certainly nothing was ever more fortunate than you and Jim being able to come here just at this time," Guy contributed. "You're the whole show."

Cynthia, in her white scallops, was standing; Gray was beside her, with an arm about Cynthia's waist. Now Gray laid her head on the taller woman's shoulder, and said lovingly:

"She's giving me my happiness."

"Nonsense!" Cynthia protested, kissing the top of Gray's head.

"You are, Cyn."

Guy was helping Rhoda with scarf and coat for the cold drive up the hill. And again Cynthia caught Rhoda's watchful look.

"I'll be down in the morning, Cynthia," Rhoda said. It was a threat. Cynthia's heart stood still for a moment, and she felt a little sick. It would all have been so simple—it would all have been so happy—but for this cloud.

She set about the familiar process of straightening the room. Jim was helped to their own room, helped to bed. A fire was burning warmly in there; Jim was tired. He had his hot milk with the bitter crystals in it; he had magazines, and was settled off comfortably in pillows. Cynthia went back to see the Warings off, closing the door on the blast of night air. In a high green sky a moon was riding among clouds, dew rimed the lawn, leaves moved restlessly on the orchard trees, and bushes stirred and were still.

"B'r'r'r!" she shuddered, coming back to warm herself at the fire. Lucia and Bruce had stumbled off among the dark laurel leaves to the "measles cottage." Gray had disappeared. She almost always crept in to take a glance at her father at night, as Cynthia usually did, too. Professor Trezavant would be sound asleep; Miss Merry, either comfortably settled on the cot in his dressing room, or moving stealthily about with extra blankets and hot-water bottles, her short hair in a plain braid, her plain large face freshly cleaned with cream, the silk cord belt of gray wrapper firmly tied.

Cynthia found Dana alone at the fire; he had put up the screen. The logs had perversely blazed up; there was quite a bright glow. One lamp was lighted, and between lamp and firelight the room was at its loveliest.

"It's wild out."

"I know. The air came in like a knife."

"We're going to have a late summer."

"But the days are marvelous," Dana said. Then, concernedly, "Cynthia, are you tired?"

"I'm always tired at night, dead. I simply ache from head to foot, but I love it."

"I believe," he agreed approvingly, "that you do."

"Oh, yes—I beg ten million pardons!" Cynthia moaned, laying her dark head on the low mantel in a devastating yawn. "I beg ten thousand—ah-h-h-h! pardons!"

"You ought to be in bed," Dana observed.

"I'm going." But as she straightened up, there was suddenly no sleepiness in her blue eyes. "Dana, I may not have another chance at you alone. I wanted to ask you—first, about Papa."

Dana looked at her attentively without speaking.

"He could go on, as he is, indefinitely?"

"He might, for years. He probably will for some time. Then there will be another stroke."

"And that will be the end?"

"Not necessarily. It might be the beginning of the end. Nobody knows about these cases."

Cynthia was silent, looking from her cousin's face to the fire, looking back again.

"You mean that the prospect rather appalls you, Cynthia?"

"No," she said hesitantly, "not that." How far he was from suspecting her real thought, from reading the wretchedness of her mind at this moment! "If Papa is to go on indefinitely," ran her fear, "and Gray discovers between now and Thursday at four o'clock that Rhoda is either going to force me to go away or tell what she knows—then Gray and Dana won't be married——"

Her sister joined them at this moment. She had been in to have a look at the two boys, she reported; both were fast asleep but completely uncovered, of course. She was off to bed, she announced—"deliciously tired." Dana too said good-night.

Cynthia murmured vaguely, abstractedly, that she would put out the lights. She was going to bed immediately herself. . . .

She sat on, staring blindly into the fire, listening to the subsiding noises in the Cabin, listening finally only to the thrilling harp of the winter-spring night outside, the rushing of boughs, the clatter of a branch across the roof, the liquid rasping of frogs.

This shabby old Cabin was home; she loved every inch of the room. She knew what flowers looked best in the vases she and her sisters had filled, emptied, washed, and filled again for twenty years; she knew where the old books belonged, in the low bookcases that ran about the walls, and

how the spring sunlight slanted in when the door was opened
in sunshiny March, and how the winter sunsets burned
against the western windows. She and Leslie had made
candy at this blackened brick fireplace years ago on wet
Saturday afternoons; there was no game in the world that
the Trezavants had not played here, under these same lamps:
authors, anagrams, murder, backgammon, lotto, parchesi—
the games seemed to march past Cynthia in a long procession
tonight. And the years of homework! Laughing girls flushed
and jaded after the long school day and the cold drive,
sleepy from dinner, sprawled on the rug wrestling with the
French subjunctive, with the classic myths. . . .

"Cyn, how d'you pronounce Persephone?" a young voice
from the past seemed asking again. And Cynthia could hear
herself answering firmly "I—religiously—refrain from pro-
nouncing it!" and hear her sisters' long-ago laughter.

Those had been happy, innocent days, with so much talk of
possible lovers and possible marriage, up in the shade of
Booker Rock . . . here by the fire. . . .

The clock struck twelve, struck one, struck two. Now and
then Cynthia leaned forward, and with a firm brown hand
caught twigs and light wood together from the big wood
basket and threw them in the fire. She crouched a little lower
—and lower—as the time went by, listening to the grinding
of boughs out in the spring dark, and the dance of a branch
on the roof.

Peter started up in his crib with a bewildered little cry,
and she went in to him, and lifted his soft little limp sleepy
figure to her shoulder and her kisses. When he was settled
down again, warm and dry, she covered Jim snugly, pinned
the big blanket pins, murmured against his unconscious little
ear. Then she went back to the fire.

She caught up a blanket as she went, rolled her blue-piped
white ruffles in it, sat down again, leaning back in her big

chair, one fine hand holding the blanket closely about her, the other lying idle on the arm of the chair.

"I mustn't let myself get frightened," she said, half aloud. "It will do no good to get frightened. By this time tomorrow Rhoda will either have told them or she won't. . . .

"In three days ·Gray will either be safely off to Boston, or she won't. . . .

"Getting frightened won't help."

For a few excited and satisfied moments she thought she must get hold of Guy—Guy would take Rhoda, early in the morning, and go away. . . .

Or Guy could stop her, tomorrow morning, and forcefully take the incriminating letter out of her hand—after that she might rave and scold as she liked. . . .

That wouldn't do. Rhoda wouldn't go away, and to use force with a weak, forlorn little creature who could not fight back, who could not retaliate, would be unthinkable, unforgivable.

"I'll be as mad as Rhoda, sitting here thinking, thinking in the night!"

The dim room about her was full of strange little creaks and rustles. A mouse came out, flickered like a shadow against the baseboard, was gone again. The wings of the night went over the house like a great sigh; Cynthia sat on, immovable.

One desperate thought after another went through her mind. Rhoda, overcome with excitement, and never strong, might die in the night. She might drive off the road, coming down tomorrow—only nobody ever did, under such circumstances. The persons killed by accident were always the needed ones. . . .

Leslie would be here tomorrow; dear old Les, with the nice-looking little boy, with his silky straight hair parted so neatly. What would he think of his two little brown bears of cousins, galloping over the ranch in sun suits that left most of their small bodies bare? And what would Leslie think of Jim, Jim in a wheeled chair? Would Gray be crying over Rhoda's revelations, when Leslie came? Would Cynthia have exhausted her arguments to Gray, *please* to be married, *please* to let things go on as they were. . . .

Something scratched at a window, and Cynthia half rose in her chair, her heart thundering. The noise stopped, and she went back to her revery.

Her mind felt confused and heavy now, and the wheeling monotony of her thoughts had exhausted her. She lay back in her chair, passive, not thinking any more, not trying to plan, merely quiet.

"I can't think any more; I'm not getting anywhere with this. There must be something entirely right and simple to do, and I suppose, when I've had my coffee and my bath tomorrow morning, it'll occur to me. . . ."

Dreamily, wearily, she was talking to Rhoda.

"Be generous, Rhoda. Not to me, but to Gray. She's always been so generous to you!"

No use, if Rhoda was in her spiteful mood. And Cynthia fell into her apathetic waking dream again: "There is a way out, if only I'm smart enough to let it just pour into me—without effort. . . ."

The solemn years began their march about her; the dark girl among the fair-headed Trezavants, the ambitious, restless, discontented girl. Cynthia's blanket loosened; she rested her elbow on the chair arm, her chin on her hand, and she felt at once a great wakefulness, and a drooping, aching need for her warm bed, for sleep.

It was long after three, and dawn was turning the garden from moonless blackness to a dull, strange gray, when suddenly she knew what she must do—so simple, so easy, so obvious. Cynthia, stiff and cold and weary, got to her feet, extinguished the one dim light, crept to her bedroom door.

It was dark, silent in here; gray had not yet reached these western windows. Swiftly, trembling a little, she undressed, knelt beside Jim's bed. Without waking, but with a murmur of affection and satisfaction, he jerked his head over to her shoulder, and Cynthia put her lips against his temple and kissed him softly.

Then, with a great sigh, she crawled in between her own sheets. The hot-water bottle, placed there by Gray hours ago, was tepid; no matter, Cynthia was too completely worn out to know or to care. She snuggled down against her pillow, shut her eyes. No need for any more worry or thought—everything was thought out now, and she could sink deeply, exquisitely, warmly into sleep.

CHAPTER TWENTY-FOUR

THE morning was heavy with fog; there was no garden, and the trees near the house dripped with the milky whiteness that was fuming softly about the barns and fences and pressing noiselessly against the windows of the lighted farmhouse. Cynthia, awakened as usual by the boys at six o'clock, felt that it was still the middle of the night, felt heavy and unrefreshed and possessed with sleep, even while she stumbled about lighting fires and getting the children and Jim and herself started for the day.

Cold water splashed in her flushed face, a rush of cool sweet air when she crossed the Galleria, and the heartening morning stir in the kitchen, scent of baking cornbread, warmth of fire, and strengthening daylight coming through the fog at the low ceiled old windows, all helped to restore her to herself; she was smooth-headed and crisply blue-aproned when Gray came out at eight o'clock, and they talked weather, and about Leslie's boat being delayed by fog; but no—nothing really delayed those big liners.

"Are you going to come to Aunt Gray's wedding, you darling?" Gray asked, kissing the warm soft curve of Peter's neck, as he busily spattered and splashed his oatmeal.

"Am I married, Aunt Gray?" Jimmy asked interestedly.

"Are you going in with Dana to meet Leslie, Gray?"

"And Lucia, too. You think you won't, Cyn?"

"I think one of us ought to be here. Merry's wonderful, but after all there's a lot of running about to do, and she has her hands full with Papa in the mornings. I hate to ask her to keep her eye on the boys as well. And there's Jim. It's a long ride for him, and it makes the car dreadfully crowded if both of us go. . . ."

She was arranging Jim's breakfast tray; he usually stayed in bed in the mornings. Cynthia folded a newspaper against the shining thermos coffee bottle, tipped her dark head while she studied the last detail. With a final warning to the boys to be "nice to Aunt Gray," she carried it away.

The daily routine had fallen into comfortable lines. Jim was customarily asleep when Cynthia rose and crept noiselessly from the room to dress the boys, but at some time during the breakfast stir he awakened, and when she brought his tray in he was looking for her eagerly.

In the dark winter mornings she had had to light lamps, but this was early summer, and by eight o'clock the fog was gone, and the room bright. Cynthia set her tray on a chair, brought Jim a hot towel and a comb, shook up three big pillows and propped him comfortably. While he attacked his breakfast, she went about the room straightening it, putting everything into order, chatting with him about such articles in the paper as drew his comments. And all the time her heart beat with slow, steady hammer strokes, and her breath came short.

When he was half finished she sat down beside him and looked at him with an odd, serious attentiveness that instantly arrested his notice. She wore a dark blue-and-white checked gown, with a crisp fold of organdie about the open collar; her face was a trifle pale, but very earnest and lovely, as her blue eyes met his.

"What's up?" Jim asked, uneasily.

"There was something I wanted to talk to you about."

"Fire away."

She struggled to compose herself, trying to think of the right words with which to begin. His look narrowed.

"Anything wrong?" he demanded.

"No—it's just that—that—— It's about myself, Jim. Something I want to tell you."

He watched her with growing interest. Cynthia took the plunge.

"You know that Guy and I liked each other very much, years ago?"

His face reddened uncomfortably; he cleared his throat. "Sure."

"Rhoda came back in the midst of it. We were going to run away. She found a letter Guy had written to leave for my father."

It was said. But there was no easing yet of the strain upon her; his eyes, vaguely uneasy, were as yet uncomprehending.

"You and he were going to run away?"

Cynthia nodded.

"The hell—— " Jim mused, half scowling, half smiling.

"We had it all planned for the very day she came back from the sanitarium,"

"Zat right?" Jim asked, watching her attentively now.

"Rhoda's got a crazy idea that if she told you—and told Gray—that Guy and I had—cared so much, all those years ago, you'd not want to stay here, and Gray wouldn't marry."

"What business is it of hers?"

"Rhoda's? It isn't her business at all, of course. And that's why I'm talking to you—that's why I'm going to talk to Gray."

"She'd like us to get out?"

"I suppose so."

"And she'd like Gray to send Dana off?"

"She's demented, of course. She can't reason clearly, poor thing. I suppose she's jealous of Gray's liking Dana, but more particularly she's jealous of me. She wants me to go away, to leave here with you and the boys and not come back."

"Well," Jim muttered, "she can roll her hoop."

Cynthia was silent a moment, wondering if he knew the truth, even now. She must cut down to the very quick, now or never.

"Guy know all this?"

"About the way Rhoda feels now? No—she spoke only to me."

"She thinks Guy is still in love with you?"

"Not that so much."

"Is he, Cyn?" Jim asked suddenly.

Cynthia put her chin proudly in the air; her face flushed.

"I don't know. Does it matter? That isn't the point after all. The point is that Rhoda has a letter—Guy's letter—and she threatens to show it to you and to Gray if we don't clear out."

Jim stared stonily into space. When he spoke again, there was a slight change in his tone.

"What's the letter say?"

Cynthia did not answer, nor meet his questioning eye, and there was a long silence. Jim shifted his position in the pillows.

"I get you," he said finally. And for another interval neither husband nor wife spoke.

"I'm terribly sorry——" Cynthia began presently. She stopped.

"Gee, I see it all now," Jim muttered in the pause.

"I ought to have told you before we were married, I suppose. But it seemed my own affair."

He brought his attention to her with an effort, rousing himself from somber brooding.

"That's right—it *was* your affair."

"I was very unhappy; I was very young. We had lost our

mother, you know, and Guy was the only friend we knew."

"He certainly proved himself to be *that*, all right!"

Flame was burning in her dark face. In a rather thickened voice she said:

"There was that side to it, of course. He was older than we were; he was my father's friend. But we cared for each other—and Rhoda was away in a sanitarium——"

"And if I remember correctly, she had all the money, and he was living off the interest!" Jim said bitterly. Cynthia could find nothing to answer him.

"No wonder he's so stuck on himself," Jim added after a while.

"I don't think he is," Cynthia presently offered, wearily and coldly. She felt suddenly bored. It was all so unnecessary. "I think you're wrong about that, Jim. He did love me very much, and I cared for him. I had never been in love before! Rhoda was out of it, and I hadn't met you. We—went mad, for a little while, and then we seemed to come to our senses, and we talked it over, and the only reasonable thing to do seemed to be to go away, start alone somewhere together."

Jim was not listening; his eyes were narrowed on space.

"I think he's as sorry about it all as I am," Cynthia finished.

For a long time he lay considering this.

"I suppose she thinks she can frighten you."

"Rhoda? She threatens to—what she calls—expose me."

"Blackmail, hey?"

"I suppose it's that."

"Well, she's got another guess coming," he growled. "We won't move a step."

"Oh, I'm so glad you feel that way!" Cynthia exclaimed, in the first beginnings of relief. "We couldn't go away now," she went on, eager to take the conversation into new channels. "Gray has handed all of Papa's affairs over to me —I'm managing everything—it would be impossible for her to marry and go away if I weren't here!"

Again Jim's thoughts were not with her.

"You and him, huh?" he murmured, as if he were thinking aloud.

Cynthia had gotten to her feet; she stood troubled and uncertain, looking down at him. Suddenly she knelt down beside him, and put both her strong hands over one of his.

"Jim, I'm so sorry to tell you this now after we've lived so many years together and have been through so much and have been so happy. I should have told you before we married, but believe me, my dear, I *didn't* think it was important then. You probably consider I wasn't square with you, but it was all so different from what it sounds now— I was young, and a fool.

"Be generous about it, Jim. The things we do when we're young and ignorant aren't so terribly important. I'd give my right hand—now that I have you and Jimmy and Peter— to have it different. I'd give years off my life not to have to tell you, and tell Gray, all this. If Rhoda hadn't found that letter you never need have known—and it would have been just the same!"

She stopped, and he looked at her gravely, apathetically.

"That's right," he said.

"Don't let it worry you!"

Jim cleared his throat, spoke gruffly.

"It isn't *worrying* me!"

"Can't you just—forget it?"

"It makes a man feel like a fool, Cyn."

Her heart was sick with shame.

"A crazy woman making trouble?"

"Oh, it isn't her," Jim said. "Can't you see—it's *him*. I don't want him hanging round here having the laugh on me."

Color burned high in Cynthia's face.

"He *isn't.*"

"I guess women don't see it like men do," Jim said simply.

"The laugh on you!" Cynthia protested. "Look at him, Jim—what has he, compared to what you have? You have me, you have your boys, you have everything! And he's been tied to a crazy woman for all these years."

"I never said he had any snap," Jim conceded. "I never said he'd had an easy time of it." He was silent, thinking, and Cynthia remained as she was, kneeling, her hands over his hand. "Rhoda's going to Gray?" Jim asked.

"She said so. I'm going to talk to Gray first."

For the first time there was sympathy in his voice; it brought tears to Cynthia's eyes.

"Rotten for you!"

"Oh—that——" she said thickly.

"She'll be mad," Jim mused.

"Gray? She'll forgive me."

"Oh, you!" Jim dismissed Cynthia easily. "She'll be mad at him," he predicted. "She'll know what a rotter he was!"

"I was as much to blame as he was," Cynthia said thickly.

"Oh, no, you weren't," Jim told her confidently. "Girls —they always give in!"

Cynthia looked at him steadily, with no change of expression. But in that bitter moment the weakness of the long-gone years took its full toll, and her heart burned with anger and humiliation.

"Sure they do—sure they do," he added, in his country voice. The woman who knelt beside him felt a sudden hatred for all men: for Guy, for Jim, for her father—even for Dana, upon whose freedom Gray had waited in such meek virtue, for so many years. "No," Jim mused, "if he wanted you, you didn't have a chance!"

Again she got to her feet; her voice was cold.

"Well, now you know. And if Rhoda tries to make any trouble, you'll be ready for her."

"Sure."

"And—as a last word, for we needn't discuss this again— I am terribly sorry. Not that—I don't mean that——" She floundered, went back simply to the original phrase. "I am terribly sorry."

"I'll tell you what," Jim began abruptly, bringing his full attention to her suddenly, "we'll stay here, and we'll get Gray safely married. We can do that, anyway. And then I'll get out."

"*You'll* get out!"

"Yep. I'll go off somewheres—get myself a job——"

"You mean without me—without the boys? You mean for us to follow you?"

"Well," he said deliberately, "you can do as you like about that."

"But Jim——" She was silent, baffled. "What good would that do?"

"I'd feel better!" he said.

"You don't think——" She was suddenly softened by his forlorn yet determined aspect; by the effort he was making to appear self-reliant and strong; she knelt down at his bedside again. "You don't think I could let you go away alone, Jimmy?" she asked.

It was the wife's tone, low and tender; her arm was about his shoulders; her blue eyes were close to his.

"You wouldn't go away from us, Jim?"

He stirred restlessly.

"I'd feel better—for a while."

"Ah, Jimmy, can't you forgive me? It was so long ago——"

Jimmy averted his eyes, jerked his shoulder away from her.

"I don't want to talk about it!"

"Well, all right," Cynthia said, in a hurt tone. She got to her feet, shrugging her shoulders philosophically. "I'm sorry you feel that way!" she said.

"I'm sorry for the whole damn' thing!" Jim muttered. He did not look at her; there was a rattling at the door knob, and Cynthia, feeling a little dazed and numb, went across the room to admit Jimmy and Peter, who had come in for strips of Daddy's toast.

She went to the kitchen, came back with a fresh buttered cube of cornbread and a smoking cup of coffee. Jim said "Thanks!" somewhat gruffly as she placed them before him, but even that monosyllable made her heart lift with hope.

There was plenty to do this morning, keeping Papa quiet, changing beds about for Leslie and her little boy. Gray decided against the long run into town, and let Lucia go off with Dana and Bruce. She and Cynthia busied themselves happily, counting plates, referring to lists, setting the lunch table for the late lunch. Hing had two Chinese boys helping him in the kitchen now, but still there was much to do; Miss Merry came out and stared at the green-and-pink Canton china, lifted down from high shelves and soaking in the pantry sinkful of hot soapsuds.

"Rhoda's all upset again," Cynthia chose a moment to say casually, when she and Gray were alone.

"Rhoda?" Gray, who had mentally been three thousand miles away, at a reception at Aunt Hannah Crabtree's in Milton, Massachusetts, said vaguely.

"Yes, she's completely off the reservation."

"What makes you think so, Cynthia?"

"Haven't you noticed it?"

"Well, I thought she looked rather badly last night," Gray admitted. "Twenty-four salads; we can leave them right here without moving them again," she murmured, her fine hand resting on the thick plates.

"Rhoda knows that Guy and I were very close to each other years ago, and she seems to have made her mind up that Jim and I shall go away."

Gray looked merely amused.

"What on earth *for?*"

"Well, I suppose to separate Guy and me." Cynthia opened a deep drawer. "There, there are fifty napkins there," she said. "That's oceans, don't you think?"

"Lucia and I counted forty-seven this morning."

"Well—I—think—I'll—put—a few—more——" Cynthia was securing the flat, shining squares of ironed damask from other drawers as she spoke.

"Cynthia, Rhoda hasn't any crazy notion like that?"

"She's coming down here this morning to tell you and to tell Jim that Guy and I loved each other. She thinks that will prevent you from getting married."

"To—what!" Gray exclaimed, with an incredulous laugh.

"She feels—— Poor thing!" Cynthia interrupted herself to say compassionately.

"Poor thing!" Gray echoed. "But Cyn," she added, "we all knew—or at least I did—that you and Guy liked each other. Remember the day Rhoda came back, and we were walking down the hill, and he came running after us——"

"We were eloping that night," Cynthia said, briefly, in the pause. "I told you."

"But what on earth does Rhoda expect to accomplish, telling on you *now?*"

"She feels that you and Jim don't understand how serious it was."

Gray looked at her sister; Cynthia returned the look steadily.

"Was it more serious than I knew—than I suspected, Cyn?"

"I'm afraid so," Cynthia said, simply.

"Cynthia!" Gray whispered, in quick protest.

Cynthia said nothing.

"I can't believe it!" Gray said.

"I never told you. It seemed to me—my own affair. It does even now," Cynthia said, shaking cubes of sugar into red and pink and green china pagodas.

"Well, of course it is," Gray conceded, in a milder tone. For a moment she watched her sister in silence, and when she spoke, it was almost timidly:

"But what does Rhoda think it has to do with *my* marrying?"

"I don't know," Cynthia responded, wondering if she had been a fool to be so fearful of Rhoda. "I suppose," she added, "she thought that if she could drive me away, you wouldn't be able to go."

"Why, I think that's ridiculous of Rhoda!" Gray exclaimed indignantly, after assimilating this.

"It is," Cynthia ranged the three Cantonware sugar bowls neatly on a shelf, placed their matching, fat bodied pitchers beside them. Her heart was quite light, and she felt happier than she had felt for years, felt almost giddy with a sudden sense of well-being. Nothing more to fear; nothing to do now but go straight ahead. She was somehow miraculously free, she was clean.

"Cyn," Gray said shyly, "I know you don't like to talk about all this——"

She paused, and Cynthia said with a little effort:

"No, truly I don't."

"It's only this—I'm going away tomorrow," Gray said with a rush. "I may not have another chance."

"As long as you *are* going away tomorrow!" Cynthia said, with a nervous little laugh.

"Rhoda," Gray diverged to say impatiently, "can't think

I wasn't going—can't think that this—*this*—would make a difference!"

"If it did," Cynthia observed, steadily washing and stacking plates, "it would mean that you broke my heart. If, because of anything I ever did, you sent Dana away again, it would kill me!"

"But I wouldn't *think* of doing such a thing!" Gray assured her, in surprise. And she put her arm, tea towel and all, about her sister.

"You don't think anything you ever did would make any difference in the way I feel for you, Cyn!" she said reproachfully.

Cynthia smiled at her, hands still in the dishwater, blue eyes close to Gray's hazel eyes.

"I seemed to have to make a fool of myself to learn anything, Gray."

"You loved him," Gray explained it promptly. Her fine clear skin was flushed with excitement and surprise, but her voice was its usual gentle self, and her eyes were kind. "I'm only so sorry that you had to go through all that alone, my poor little wild Cynthia!" she grieved.

Tears stung Cynthia's eyes again, but she smiled through them.

"We loved each other," she amended it. "There were a few weeks of heaven, Gray, when I would go up to the Little Quito, and he and I would talk, and have tea, and kiss each other. That only lasted a little while."

"Then you stopped it all?"

"Guy did. He seemed suddenly to come to his senses and realize that we were simply crazy. We had been talking love, and the hopelessness of our love—everything else seemed dim, unimportant. But he woke up."

"And felt—horribly, of course?"

"I imagine so. I know that I was actually ill—do you

remember how ill that winter? It was really a sort of heart-break."

"I never dreamed it!"

"So then, when I was better, and Guy came back from Arizona where he'd been painting, we planned to run away. It seemed so much better than hiding everything, lying about everything. But we were too late. Rhoda came home that day.

"And Rhoda's coming home made it all seem so horrible, Gray. Guy's wife—and the girl he loved—it was all so different. I was desperate then. I didn't want to talk to him about it; I couldn't talk to anyone else—it was all blackness. . . .

"What a *fool!*" she said, and was still.

"Oh, yes, what a fool," Gray's gentle voice echoed, tenderly, "but what a terrible situation, too, Cyn! Poor little Cyn!"

Cynthia, suddenly in tears, turned back to her dishpan.

"And I never knew!" Gray murmured, still marveling. "I *might* have known. I remember how excitable, how restless you were, all around that time of Vera's wedding—— Cyn," she broke off to ask sharply, "Jim knows?"

"Jim knows," Cynthia could answer simply.

"Ah-h-h!" Gray said, in relief.

"So that's all," Cynthia said, turning about, quite openly wiping her eyes. "Guy and I met here a few months ago just as old friends; we've not spoken together since—of all this, anyway; I'm Jim's wife, and he's Rhoda's husband, and we both have our work cut out. It was only yesterday, when she threatened to make you unhappy with her own mixed-up ideas, that I thought I'd better tell you."

"I love you for it!" Gray said, after a moment.

They were done with the plates and the sugar bowls and pitchers. Cynthia turned her white dishpan upside down, and rubbed lemon on her fingers. She began to make mayonnaise, while the boys had their lunch, talking to them meanwhile about their treatment of dear little Cousin Buddy, who might be afraid of waterdogs, and of Dobbs, and of the cows. Peter contributed only an occasionally hopeful monosyllable to the conversation: "Boy? Cow? Moo-moo?" but Jimmy was very garrulous, and said he would take Dad's gun and go bang at anything that frightened dear little Cousin Buddy, and illustrated it by a roar and a falling back that almost tipped him out of his high chair.

"Isn't it fun, getting the old place ready for a party again?" Cynthia asked. And Gray, making herself lovely for Leslie's arrival, echoed radiantly, "Oh, *fun.*"

Presently Cynthia carefully helped Jim to his favorite seat under the loaded rose vines of the porch. The white-painted pillars looked dazzlingly clean in the morning sunshine and shadow; the high redwoods were fresh and green, after the cooling bath of fog. One of the Chinese boys swept leaves from the steps and paths; inside, in the shaded nursery, Peter could be heard making the sound of a drowsy bee as he went off to sleep with Tubby, the brown bear, clasped to his heart.

Rhoda appeared at about one o'clock, a pale and constrained Rhoda. She came out to the dining room, where Cynthia was laying a table for ten.

"Rhoda, I thought you went with the others to meet Leslie!"

"Cynthia," Rhoda said heavily, "have you decided?"

"Decided what?"

"You know what I mean."

"I'm sure," Cynthia said soberly, as she filled glasses, "that you wouldn't do anything that would make Gray unhappy?"

"I won't talk about it," Rhoda said, in a warning, nervous tone. She did not look at Cynthia. "You—you ruined my life," she said. "Why, why shouldn't I ruin yours?"

"I didn't mean to ruin your life."

"Ah, but that doesn't matter! You should have thought of that!"

"But I didn't think. And now," Cynthia said—"now don't we all have to make the best of it, don't we all have to pull together to give Gray her chance?"

"Are you going away?" Rhoda demanded, in a sort of repressed passion.

"Rhoda, how can I go away? Think of my father, and Jim——"

"I'll go in and talk to Gray now—this instant—I *will*, Cynthia, unless you promise me that before the wedding— now—today—you'll get out, and not come back!"

"Gray knows, Rhoda. Jim knows."

Cynthia said it simply; she was more shaken than she could have dreamed herself to be by the sight of Rhoda's agony of hatred and white face. There was no triumph, no satisfaction in her tone.

"They do not!" Rhoda whispered, with a dry mouth.

"But they do, Rhoda."

"And they forgave it—they thought it was lovely because it was you, I suppose!"

"No, they didn't think it was lovely. But they knew it was long ago, and that I was sorry. After all, Rhoda, don't we have to forgive and forget, if we can——"

"Oh, forgive and forget!" Rhoda gasped, beside herself. "It's so easy for you to talk about forgiving and forgetting! You wait—you wait!"

With a dry, desperate sob she ran away, and Cynthia was left alone at the long table, where a great center bowl of pink roses and long spikes of dark blue and pale blue delphinium,

white daisies, and feathery bridal-wreath was waiting,
among the glint of silver and glass, to welcome Leslie home
for Gray's wedding. She moved napkins, forks carefully,
her heart beating a little fast. It was all so horribly sad—
and so mixed up.

After a while Gray, in her old blue gown, with her fair
hair shining and smooth, came out.

"Where's Rhoda?"

"Lying down in my room, I think! Poor little thing!"
Gray said.

"I'm so sorry for her!"

"Oh, Cyn, I'm so glad you can be sorry for her. She's got
everything all twisted. I'm going to try," Gray murmured,
leaning over to pick a fallen leaf from the white cloth—"I'm
going to try to find a minute to ask Guy to take her away."

"They're only just home, Gray. And he loves the Little
Quito so. And he's started a new picture."

"I know. But she's all upset."

"I pity her so."

"You're wonderful," Gray said.

"Wonderful! I feel horribly about it all," Cynthia confessed. "It was bad enough years ago, when I used to lie
awake nights saying 'Fool!' to myself; when it was always
a question of having done something 'wrong,' something
that was a 'sin.' But this—this coming up to complicate now
—to make Jim hate Guy, and Rhoda hate me, and me hate
myself! Well," she ended, "there's nothing for it but to live
through it, and keep her happy and Jim happy—if I can."

"And I have all the fun!" Gray mourned, kissing her.

"Ah, if you only *do!*"

There was the jubilant sound of motor horns; the sisters
ran out to see Guy opening the car door for a sophisticated,
pretty Leslie, and a sleepy, stumbling little boy; Leslie

grown up, talking of "tiffin" and "chits" and "number one boy"; Leslie maternally managing a little pre-luncheon lunch for Buddy; Leslie in tears of joy over every remembered old detail of books and lamps, doorways and lunch plates, roses and lawn.

She flashed in to see her father; came out rather white and with fresh tears on her lashes. Then they were all at the table, and Leslie was jumbling important questions and answers with descriptions of stewards and fellow passengers her sister never would see, and data about the meals and the manners of the *President Cleveland*.

The same old Leslie, and yet changed; and she found absorbing changes in Gray and Cynthia and Lucia, too, but especially in Cynthia. Cynthia seemed to fascinate her.

"Buddy," Cynthia suggested, as her small nephew all but collapsed sidewise at the table, "why don't you come and rest on the couch, and then the minute Peter and Jim wake up you'll be right there?"

"Is jore boys Peter and Jim?" Buddy asked, carefully getting down and letting Aunt Cynthia kiss his rather pale little face after she had wiped it clear of jelly and bread.

"Cyn's sweet with him," Leslie said, glad to share the responsibility she had sustained alone for a long fortnight of travel.

"Cyn's simply adorable," Lucia added. "She's marvelous. She's so gentle, and she's so unselfish—isn't she, Gray?"

"I think," suggested Gray the peacemaker, with a smile for Jim, "that as long as Jim is getting so he can hobble about comfortably now, and the boys are both well, Cynthia doesn't have to make any effort to seem happy!"

"It's so wonderful—getting home," Leslie murmured. Her talk was filled with allusions to new friends, army associates in Manila. The Randolphs were wonderful to her; Major

Randolph was a darling. But the Ungers made themselves rather ridiculous, and the Grants quarreled so much that it was quite a scandal.

"And Phil—our best friend, that I was telling you about, —and the Glovers—they got the house we wanted—and one day at the club—there's quite a gang of us who always do the same things . . ."

Leslie had to see Gray's clothes, and Gray's presents, and to hear all about Lucia's clothes and presents, but she gave these matters but an absent-minded attention, after all. A Mrs. Coates, her husband but second lieutenant, had *the* —most—gorgeous linen Leslie had ever seen, it appeared; she had been a Hamilton of Washington, so that explained that. Gray's railway ticket, with the little pale green slip that meant "Drawing Room A" clipped to it, over which Cynthia and Lucia hung excitedly, only reminded Leslie that she and Elmer hoped for Fort Greble, next; his family lived at Saunderstown, so that would make it lovely, and Colonel Roberts had asked for him.

They drifted out to the side porch and grouped themselves about Jim's chair; Rhoda took the hammock, and Guy stretched himself on the shady strip of lawn, at the bottom of the three broad steps, and went to sleep, with his hat over his eyes. Leslie, to whom Buddy represented everything desirable in childhood, spoke with kindly, tempered expectancy of meeting Cynthia's two little boys, but Cynthia felt a little prick of triumph when Jimmy and Peter, dressed and brushed by the amiable Merry, walked shyly out in dark blue linens whose wide white collars set off Jim's sturdy, sunburned fairness as well as Peter's glowing dark color.

"Oh, Cyn, they are simply darlings!" Leslie burst forth generously. "Oh, Cyn, the little one—isn't he Papa over again!"

Peter was still flushed and moist and solemn with sleep;

he retreated to Cynthia's knee, beetling his little brows at the new aunt. But Jim was all graciousness, inquiring instantly, "Where is *your* boy?"

Happy, happy hours, these, for all four sisters, hours when their old giddy laughter rang out with a new note, and when everything for which the old ranch house stood, every tie and association and memory, seemed a thousand times enhanced by all that they had experienced in the long years since last they had been here together. The low-ceiled rooms, and the way the beds and chairs stood in the rooms; the late spring afternoon with a blanket of fog creeping down over the mountains, the smell of Hing's roasting chicken and of wood fires, all enchanted Leslie. "There's no place in the world like Treehaven!" she said, over and over again.

CHAPTER TWENTY-FIVE

THE next day dawned in a glory of May sunshine, and by nine o'clock the sun was pouring warmly down on the red-woods and the green shadowy lawn, and the air was thick with flowery scents. All morning long the sisters were in a flurry of final preparations, and shortly after noon the first guests began to arrive. Cynthia got her two boys into their white jersey suits, bought especially for the occasion, and Leslie, taking her sister's cue, arrayed her own son in white, and the three small bashful cousins, moving about through the grown-up scene, were the center of one adoring ring after another.

Jim, exceptionally handsome in a dark blue coat and white flannels, limped on his crutches to a chair placed advantage-ously down at the foot of the lawn near the floral bower that Leslie and Lucia had effectively built only that morning; Merry and Papa watched from the Cabin porch as Cynthia, in palest pink, with pink hydrangeas pinned to her broad chip hat, and pale hydrangeas in her hands, walked with Gray to meet Dana as he stood beside the officiating clergy-man. Lucia, tears in her bright eyes, and Leslie, holding firmly to Buddy, flanked the bridal party.

Peter had been in Jim's lap, and Guy supposedly holding little Jim, but both boys broke loose and galloped wildly to their mother, and Cynthia had to keep her place as matron of honor with the appropriate addition of a small hand in either hand. She was laughing, as the ceremony proceeded, and that made serious Gray smile, too; they were all laughing.

"And a good omen, too, Gray darling!" Cynthia said, kissing the bride first of all, laughing and crying as the exquisite, ivory satin-clad figure that was Gray Illyan came into her arms. "Dana!" she said, accepting his kiss, too; the two score guests and the family group were all milling about on the lawn now, and the kisses and laughter and broken odds and ends of talk filled the next half-hour.

"Wasn't she lovely?" . . . "Ah, she was lovely!" . . . "She looked right up at Dr. Illyan all the time—Gray, did you know you were looking . . ." "Well, hello, Mrs. Illyan! How does that sound?" . . . "Wasn't it, really? I think it was the divinest wedding I ever saw. . . ."

"So you're all four married, Cynthia?" Vera Severn said.

"All we needed was time," Cynthia answered serenely.

She stayed close to Jim in the confusion that followed; it was as if she protected him from eyes that might be critical, from mistakes that he might make.

"Those kids made a swell hit, walking out into the wedding!" Jim growled. But Cynthia knew he secretly wanted her to tell him, and the others to tell him, that the little boys had added a delicious note to the occasion.

Gray gathered her full robe and gauzy veil about her, and she and Dana went up to the house together to see her father, and then everyone went up, and Cynthia capably superintended the delegating of duties to everyone.

"Les, be a darling, and get them seated—Gray and Dana up at the window table, where all the white flowers are, and everyone else anywhere! Guy, pass those, will you—Bruce, grab those and pass them. Yes, fill cups, Hing—fill all cups, Lung Hop. You pass sugar-cream, Kang. You go now, with Lung Hop, and pass sugar-cream.—No, sweetums, you mayn't pass the ice cream yet, because all the ladies and gentlemen have to eat their chicky first—but pretty soon you may—— Take Peter's hands out of that, Lucia. Don't put your hands into that, lovey; somebody may want to eat it. Here's what you two boys can pass, pass these nice black olives—and say, 'Will you have an olive?' . . ."

She was in the thick of it when she saw Rhoda beside her. Cynthia smiled with resolute kindness.

"You and I won't be sorry when all this excitement's over, Rhoda. We won't mind settling down for a little peace and quiet, will we?"

"You fooled me," Rhoda muttered. She was trembling.

"Ah, no, I didn't fool you. What else could I do?"

"You could have gone away!"

"That would have meant Gray didn't marry," Cynthia reiterated patiently. Leslie put her head through the swinging pantry door.

"Cynthia! Come out! They're making speeches!"

"Oh, Rhoda, come, we mustn't miss the speeches!" Cynthia exclaimed. "Bring those rye sandwiches. Lung Hop, in a few minutes you bring out all these little boxes of cake . . ."

Radiant in her pink frock, she was out among the guests again. She did not see Rhoda for some time; then Rhoda was discovered sitting in the window seat, not far from Gray, looking sick and tired. Cynthia, who happened to have Peter up in her arms, while she tried to make him talk for old Mrs. Cannon, felt a pang of sheer pity weaken her heart as she caught sight of the less fortunate woman.

There was no time to think about it; the bride had gone to her room to get into her going-away gown, the guests were only waiting for a sight of her to depart themselves. It was almost six o'clock, and the sun was setting; flowers were wilting on all sides now; Leslie looked happy and tired; Lucia was businesslike about arrangements for tomorrow.

"I'll be up early, Cyn. Don't kill yourself moving things about and cleaning up."

"Oh, we'll have lots of time now," Cynthia said contentedly.

"Cynthia." This was Guy. "They're beginning to go."

Gray had come back, in dark blue, with a white-frilled blouse and a dark blue hat. Her coat with its fur collar, her new blue bag, her white gloves were laid on a chair; the guests were disappearing fast now, and cars were turning and honking in the drive.

"Gray, would you like just a sandwich before you go?"

"I never," Gray answered, in a happy sort of flutter, "want to see a sandwich again!"

"Oh, come, it's my favorite late supper when I'm kept at the hospital," Dana protested, and while they all laughed Gray flushed exquisitely at the thought of her wifely responsibilities to a tired and busy doctor.

The family was alone now, and the house doors were shut against the deepening swift cold and dark; Cynthia took her boys off to bed, returned to find that it was really time to get started for San José, where the Illyans were to be put on the evening train.

Everything that could be said was said, over and over again. Hadn't it been perfect—and how could Gray ever thank them enough—and wasn't it lucky that Les and Buddy could be here for a few weeks anyway, to keep Cynthia and Lucia from being so lonely . . .

Guy had taken Rhoda home after she had burst into tears, and clung to Gray, kissing her good-bye furiously. Coming back, he carried the suitcases out to the cars in good brotherly fashion, reminding Gray she had better run into her father's room for a last kiss.

It then appeared that Cynthia was not going to San José.

"Don't make a fuss about it, Lucia," she pleaded, out by the lighted cars. "In the first place, Jim and the boys are tired to death——"

"But the boys are asleep!"

"I know they are. But they might easily wake, after having eaten just about their weight apiece in everything they shouldn't have touched—wedding cake, probably, and crab salad. And then Jim would have to call Merry—he's still terribly awkward with that crutch——"

"Oh, *Cynthia!*" Leslie protested.

"I know. I'd love to go and see the last of darling old Gray, but then there's another thing: Jim loves to talk things over, the first time, with me; he'd hate the idea that we'd all had two hours of it before he got in on it. I'd rather stay."

"Nonsense, get into the car!" Guy directed.

"No, really; I'd rather be here. And then besides, Merry's going," Cynthia argued. "Tomorrow's the day she always goes, and she asked me if we'd drop her at her sister's in San José early, and I said she might just as well get into the car and go over with you! *Please,* Guy. Please be nice to her!"

Guy looked down at her, glowing and softly brown in the light of the cars and the young moon. Cynthia was a little pale, but her eyes shone the darker for that.

"All right," he said. And as Merry immediately came out in a checked brown and tan coat, a blue hat, and a pale gray dress, there was time for no more. Gray and Cynthia were in each other's arms for a long minute, and the kiss they exchanged was a very tender one.

"Thank you, Cyn!"

"My darling, if it were true that I could pay you back just a little for all you've been to me!"

She waved them all good-bye; she would have hot chocolate ready for Guy and Les, when they came back. And for Bruce and Lucia, too, if they'd come.

"Oh, I've got to go home with Bruce!" Lucia exclaimed.

of blue fumed slowly, making the dim air of the nursery
pungent, curling in leisurely wreaths against the comfortable
checked curtains and the walls with their border of colored
pictures the boys had cut from magazines.

Jim was shouting: "What is it, Mother?"

"Oh, Mommy, Mommy!" Peter whimpered.

From Rhoda came painful hiccoughs.

"Oh-h, my G-god—I've hurt myself!" she groaned
through clenched teeth. With a wrench she suddenly freed
herself from the grip of Cynthia's fingers. Cynthia, feeling
those fingers sticky, looked down at them in bewilderment.

"Jim!" she cried. "Jim!"

Rushing to the window, she looked out. The porch was
empty. As she turned, Rhoda collapsed to her knees. She
moved her mouth to speak, but no sound came. Suddenly,
with a rush of red from her pale lips, she clawed forward
against Cynthia and slid flat to the floor. Once she moved
again, a plunge of thin shoulders and of the new dress
she had worn to Gray's wedding. . . .

Then there was silence in the nursery, underscored by
Jimmy's interrogative whimper and by the solemn ticking
of the clock. Cynthia stood motionless, looked sometimes
at her reddened fingers, sometimes at the empty window,
with the curtain swept aside, and the moon-washed whiteness of the night on the grape arbor outside.

"Jim!" she called. The sound of her own voice frightened
her, and it seemed to her that the night was filled with
danger, murder, and blackness. But she had started the
younger voices, and Peter broke into a heartbroken roar.

His mother went to him, lifted him against her cheek,
clung to his warm soft little body.

"Darling!" she whispered. "Oh, my God!"

Jimmy climbed busily out of his crib, and as Cynthia sat
down heavily and dazedly he scrambled into her lap. They all

sat together, while the last of the blue smoke drifted away, and the room and the world waited in silence.

Presently Jimmy got down and walked over to the crumpled figure on the floor.

"Don't go there, Jim. Don't touch that revolver; it's loaded. It might hurt you."

Jimmy, eyes wide, came slowly back to her, and Cynthia, with Peter in her arms, got to her feet.

As she did so, she heard the awkward clacking of Jim's crutches. He came clumsily in from the sitting room, and they looked with pale faces at each other.

Suddenly Cynthia was clinging to him, and he had to steady himself against her weight, against the children's hands at his knees.

"You're all safe, are you?" he asked.

She could not answer. She was breathing hard like a spent runner.

"She shot herself," he stated, staring over her shoulder at the figure on the floor.

"I think so."

"Dead, huh?"

Cynthia shuddered.

"Well, let's get out of here," he said. They all went out to the quiet, peaceful sitting room, where the fire still burned and where Gray's wedding flowers, great jars and bowls of them, wilted in the warm, softly lighted air. Cynthia sank into a great fireside chair and put her head against its high leather back and closed her eyes.

"Jim—you saved us——" she whispered.

"I heard you talking—I heard you saying to somebody for God's sake not to shoot, so I hustled."

"You saved us—you saved Jimmy and Peter—— One of them—— Oh, my God!"

"Well, gee," Jim said awkwardly, "I had to do something."

Cynthia began to cry and buried her face in her hands.

"I heard her—getting in at the window, I suppose," she said after a little. "I went in there——" Her voice thickened; she stopped short.

"If you hadn't come, Jim!"

"I saw her through the window——"

"But if you couldn't have reached her——"

"It was open. I wanted to get to you as quickly as I could."

"If you hadn't caught her wrist then, it might have been——"

"The damn' window sill was between us. I couldn't get close."

"At first I thought it was you."

"Me?"

"That she'd shot you."

"No, I slipped and fell. I saw she had plugged herself all right, so I hurried round through the front door."

"Dead—is she?"

"Oh, yes; dead as a doornail."

Cynthia bent low, her fingertips pressed tightly against her eyeballs, and a convulsive spasm shook her body.

Peter came and pulled at her dress; she lifted him to her lap and rested her weary, wet face against his soft little temple.

There was a distant rumble far off down the road.

"Hark!" Cynthia said, straightening herself. "That's Guy's car, coming up the hill. He and Leslie will be here in a minute!" And as she leaned her face against the child's cheek, her tears came again. "We're safe now," she whispered. "We're all right now."

CHAPTER TWENTY-SIX

ABOUT five weeks later she and Jim were sitting alone on the front porch, in a white summer moonlight. The complete silence that possessed the world was broken now and then by the eager shrilling of frogs from the pool, or the woodeny cry of an owl off in the dark woods.

Miss Merry was settling her invalid for the night off at the Cabin; Cynthia's boys were in bed. Lucia, who had come up, as she did almost every day, to see her father and have lunch with Cynthia, was long gone; Lesley had sailed for Manila; Gray was writing rapturously of Dana and Boston. Cynthia and Jim had the world to themselves.

Jim presently broke a long silence.

"It was good to get up on that horse again, today."

"Are you lame at all?" The white glimmer that was Cynthia, seated on the top step, with her head against the railing, stirred in the scented gloom.

"My shoulder was a little sore. It felt funny—me being sore from riding!"

"It was only the third time, Jim," her voice reminded him, from the mellow shadows under the rose vine.

"That's right, too."

"It seemed wonderful to see you galloping about again."

"You bet your life it felt wonderful."

There was a silence.

"I'll bet you're still scared when I'm driving," Jim presently challenged her.

"Well," Cynthia countered dryly, "I let you take the boys, I notice."

336

"There isn't much I can't do!"

"There isn't anything, really. Except," Cynthia added, "pack through the Sierras.

"And even that, Jim," she added, with animation, "even that doesn't mean that you and I couldn't take the boys up there if we wanted to, some day when they're older. We could take Dan, or one of the cowboys, to look out for the stock."

"I could look out for the stock!" Jim growled.

"Well, I believe you could. I could cook—the boys would catch fish——"

"My God, I'd like to sleep up above the timber line again!" Jim muttered, after a while.

"You and I ought to ride up to Booker Rock some night next week, if it's as warm as this, and sleep out. I'll have Mack get out the sleeping bags tomorrow."

Jim made no comment upon this, and there was a long interval in which neither spoke. The moon continued to pour silver upon the world; the redwoods' layers of dark foliage were frosted with it, and it dripped whitely down through the wooden bars of the porch and the tracery of the rose vine. Shadows of encircling madrones and branched oak trees fell clear on the lawn; each orchard tree stood in a blot of shadow. The sky was a clear, transparent peacock blue; there were no stars. A wash of honeysuckle scent went by on a warm breeze; the old brown earth sighed, as if she turned wearily in her sleep after the burning day.

"There are ten thousand things I ought to do in the house," Cynthia murmured. "I'm fascinated with what I'm doing, changing all the books about. I've got a box of new books, not even opened. I've so much to write Gray. I've got to put elastics into the boys' rompers. And we're missing our pet weekly programme on the radio."

"Do it all tomorrow," Jim suggested, after a moment.

"I can't, Jim. I never have a second. Going up to the barn with you and the boys, talking vegetables with Mack —and now riding, you and I, and driving into San José— and Lucia coming up—I simply haven't a minute! I've been trying to get round to that new ice cream—cantaloupes and ginger—for I don't know how long, and every day just fills itself up, and there's never a spare second! Now here we are planning to go up the hill, and I was just thinking I could get Peter and Jimmy both on old Phœbe—if she's able to move—the old pack saddle must be round here somewhere."

Jim spoke in the silence, almost as if unwillingly.

"I could take Pete up with me."

Cynthia laughed in the shadows.

"I keep forgetting that you're a past grand master of riding."

"Not any more."

"Oh, nonsense, 'not any more!' You're not a packer any more," Cynthia conceded, after a moment's thought, "but you wouldn't be, anyway, now that we're——"

"Fixed for money," Jim supplied, in the pause.

"Well——" she said.

"But I wasn't thinking of that, so much," he recommenced, as she fell silent. "I was thinking that maybe I'd go back home for a while and see what I *could* do."

"You mean Miller's Basin?"

"Or anywhere."

"Still feel that way?"

"Kinder."

"We could drive there now; there's that to consider," Cynthia offered. "You and I both driving, it'd be no trip at all."

"I thought maybe you'd stay here, until you found out how you feel."

"How do you mean until I found out how I feel?"

"Well—no use dragging you and the boys around with me."

A silence.

"No," Cynthia said steadily then, "I won't do that.

"Where you go, we go," she added, as he did not speak.

"You can't leave your father."

"I'd leave," Cynthia told him, "ten fathers!"

Jim said nothing.

"If you want to go to Miller's Basin, I can go to Miller's Basin," Cynthia presently said.

"I wasn't thinking specially of Miller's Basin."

"Where, then?"

"I wasn't thinking of anywhere—exactly." He cleared his throat. "We've been here five months now," he began. "I understand a little more than I did—before. You weren't ever the sort—to live in Miller's Basin."

A hard pain seized her heart; she remembered the hot little mountain town, Mockbees' field, and Clara, and the trip to Rangers Camp.

"You belong here," Jim concluded.

"I belong where you are," Cynthia said.

"Aw, no, you don't!" he said, and there was almost a break in his voice.

"Try to get away from me, Jim!" Cynthia challenged him steadily.

"I don't know anything about operas—books," he said, gruffly. "I don't—get—poetry!"

"Don't be silly, Jim."

"That isn't silly."

"I don't know anyone who reads as furiously as you do."

"It isn't the same."

Cynthia twisted about, and he could see the moonlight on her upturned face.

"Why, Jim, are you blue?"

He did not answer for a minute. Then he said, guardedly, in a low tone:

"You and I talked about this last week—the day Guy came back. Don't you remember?"

"But I told you that was silly," Cynthia said.

"I want you to have a chance to decide," Jim told her. Something in his steady, stubborn voice shook her to her soul. This was not the old Jim, of Miller's Basin, nor even the invalided Jim that Gray and Lucia knew.

"Things have been going on here," Jim said, "just day by day. I didn't want to rush you."

"To rush me about what?"

"Anything. But it's more than a month now."

"Since Gray's marriage; since Rhoda's funeral—yes, it was a month last Thursday."

"Well——" he said, and stopped.

"Well——" She helped him out, her eyes were round as she looked at him.

"How do you feel about it?" Jim pursued. "Is everything just—going on?"

"What else should it do?"

"I mean——" he floundered. "You liking him——"

Cynthia's face flushed a deep red.

"Oh, that!" she said.

"Well—you *do*—he does," Jim persisted unhappily. "He came up—the day after the funeral—he put his head down on your shoulder and you put your arms round him. I knew, then——"

He was silent a moment, and then added, in a darkly brooding tone, "But then I knew anyway."

"That's all over," Cynthia said. "You and the boys, and books, and fires, and the kitchen—that's my world, now."

"You could have all that, and him, too."

"I don't understand you," Cynthia said, with a long look and a faint scowl.

"If I got out. If I weren't in it. If you were free."

Cynthia spoke in a quick hurt tone:

"You aren't talking about Reno, about divorce, again, Jim?"

"It seems to me you ought to have that chance, if you want it."

"I don't want it."

"I don't want you," he said, "to say anything, to pretend anything—for fear of hurting my feelings. You—liked him first, Cynthia. He's always loved you. You might come to like him again—now that he's free."

"Guy?"

"Sure, Guy. He comes down here—this place is like home to him. Gray likes him, Lucia likes him, everyone likes him; he's always been here. I don't belong in the picture."

New notes were in his voice; she had never heard them before. They were notes of pain, of determination—it was the voice of a man. And suddenly she had a sensation of being all woman, ruffled gown, warm brown skin, fast-beating heart, firm linked hands.

"Why don't you stay and—and hold me, Jim?"

There was a pause.

"No," he said, "I can't do that.

"You're the one," he went on, as she did not speak, "who'll have to decide."

"I have a message for you," Cynthia presently said.

"You have what?"

"A message for you."

"From Gray?"

"From Guy."

"Oh," he said, in a changed tone. And then, as she said no more, he added, "What about?"

"It was simply: 'Good-bye.' "

" 'Good-bye'? Where's he going?"

"I don't know."

"Painting?"

"Eventually, I suppose he'll paint."

Jim spoke in relief; it was a respite.

"Gone, has he? For how long?"

"Forever. He's not coming back."

"What!" Jim said.

"He's gone. He's taken his dogs. The Little Quito's for sale."

She could see Jim sitting suddenly erect in the moonshine.

"What you talking about?"

"It's true. Guy's cleared out."

"Left the ranch!"

"Forever," Cynthia said.

"When was this?"

"This afternoon. He stopped at the end of the lawn for a few minutes—the boys and I were down there. It was just before you went out driving. He said Good-bye to us all."

Jim sat very still for a long minute. Then he said:

"You do that?"

"Yes—well, and no, too. He saw that he—didn't fit in. He knew he didn't belong—in our lives, with me and the children—and he had nothing else here. So he's gone away."

"Did he feel badly?"

"Yes, I think he did."

Jim spoke gruffly, after a pause:

"*You* feel badly?"

"No. I'm ashamed to say I felt relieved!" Cynthia answered, with an honest little laugh.

"You'll miss him."

"I'm thinking," she said, and he could see her sapphire

blue eyes shining in moonlight, "that Dana and Gray ought to buy that place."

"You mean his place?"

"Some day—not immediately. Gray's always adored it."

"You *mean* he isn't coming back?"

"Honestly. Never."

"What'd you tell him?"

"I didn't have to tell him anything. He knew he was superfluous, and he has taken himself out of it all. He saw it."

"Saw what?" Jim asked. "You say he saw something."

"Something I hadn't seen very clearly myself, until this week," she said. "But you—you see it," she added. And suddenly tears glittered in her eyes and spilled on her cheeks.

When Jim finally spoke it was in a humble, gentle tone. "I wish I could believe you, Cynthia!"

"I'm going to make you believe me!" Cynthia said, laughing, and wiping her eyes.

"Well, then, I guess we'll stay here at home for a while," Jim began after a long silence.

"We'll stay home now," Cynthia said.

THE END